2/13
07/15

✓ **W9-CCK-350**

DATE DUE

MISS ME
WHEN I'M GONE

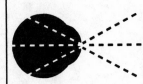

MISS ME WHEN I'M GONE

EMILY ARSENAULT

THORNDIKE PRESS
A part of Gale, Cengage Learning

GALE
CENGAGE Learning®

Detroit • New York • San Francisco • New Haven, Conn • Waterville, Maine • London

Copyright © 2012 by Emily Arsenault.
"(Since I've Got) The Pill." Words and music by Loretta Lynn, T.D. Bayless and Don McHan. Copyright © 1973 (Renewed) Coal Miners Music, Inc. (BMI) and Guaranty Music (BMI). Worldwide rights for Coal Miners Music, Inc. and Guaranty Music administered by BMG Rights Management (US) LLC. International copyright secured. All rights reserved. Reprinted by permission of Hal Leonard Corporation.
"Meet Me By the Moonlight Alone" by A. P. Carter. Used by permission of Peer International Corporation. All rights reserved.
Thorndike Press, a part of Gale, Cengage Learning.

Thorndike Press® Large Print Core.
The text of this Large Print edition is unabridged.
Other aspects of the book may vary from the original edition.
Set in 16 pt. Plantin.

LIBRARY OF CONGRESS CATALOGING-IN-PUBLICATION DATA

Arsenault, Emily.
    Miss me when I'm gone / by Emily Arsenault. — Large print ed.
        p. cm. — (Thorndike Press large print core)
    ISBN-13: 978-1-4104-5357-0 (hardcover)
    ISBN-10: 1-4104-5357-X (hardcover)
    1. Women novelists—Fiction. 2. Falls (Accidents)—Fiction. 3. Murder—Investigation—Fiction. 4. Large type books. I. Title. II. Title: Miss me when I am gone.
    PS3601.R745M57 2012
    813'.6—dc23   2012032083

Published in 2012 by arrangement with William Morrow, an imprint of HarperCollins Publishers.

Printed in the United States of America
1 2 3 4 5 6 7 16 15 14 13 12

To my parents,
Jane Rastelli and Richard Arsenault

ACKNOWLEDGMENTS

Thank you to Laura Langlie and Carrie Feron — and everyone at William Morrow — for your enthusiastic support of this book.

Thanks to Nicole Moore and Cari Strand for early readings.

And, as always, warm thanks to my husband, Ross Grant, for driving with me all the way to Red Bay, Alabama, and back, for midnight cupcakes, for buying me that Tammy Wynette CD back in 2002, and for so much more.

Plus a kiss and a smile to sweet Eliza, who kindly waited till this book was finished to arrive.

CHAPTER 1

"I Still Believe in Fairy Tales"

Franklin Road
Nashville, Tennessee

This gem might be well known among seventies tabloid readers and longtime country music fans, but perhaps not to the general reader: Tammy Wynette once saved Burt Reynolds from drowning in a bubble bath. It was post–George Jones, a swinging-single period in Tammy's life that I wish had lasted longer. She and Burt apparently had a friends-with-benefits thing going on in 1976.

And one night he came over feeling ill. She made him dinner and banana pudding and drew him a nice hot bubble bath. In the tub, he had what was later thought to be a hypoglycemic episode and lost consciousness. When Tammy knocked and he didn't answer, she opened the door to find a mountain of bubbles — and no Burt! He had started to sink into the Vitabath.

Tammy rushed into the oversize bathtub fully clothed, struggled for several minutes to keep his head above the water, reach for a nearby phone (she lived pretty extravagantly at that time, remember — thus a phone in the bathroom within reach of one's luxury bathtub), call 911, and eventually managed to pull him out and tug his jeans on to protect his modesty in case the *National Enquirer* arrived along with the ambulance. She claimed she was too panicked to think of simply yanking the stopper out to prevent Burt from drowning.

Besides, if she'd done that, she'd have robbed me of this precious mental picture: Tammy diving into the foam in a sequined gown, bouffant blond wig, false eyelashes, and full makeup — surfacing with the naked, excessively hairy-chested Burt Reynolds, his hair drenched, his thick mustache dotted with delicate bubbles.

Surely this is not what it looked like, but I like this picture of Tammy as a honky-tonk superwoman. Saving the sexy Burt not just for herself, per se, but for womankind.

Keeping in mind, of course, that taste in men, like cuisines, varies somewhat between the generations. The appeal of Burt Reynolds (even young Burt from films that predate my birth), like the appeal of a Jell-O mold, confounds me. He has nice eyebrows, I suppose, but I can't get past the walrus mustache.

I can't speak for Tammy's taste in men — that's a problem I can't solve in a few pages, or perhaps a whole book. But I love the image of her rescuing the seventies' sex cowboy from a sweetheart bathtub. She probably didn't think she had it in her, this woman whose life and music were all about the romance that was supposed to save her from herself. But there she was, pulling this gritty, hairy man out of a warm, romantic bath of bubbles, back into life, back into cold, naked reality.

If only she could have done the same for herself.

— Gretchen Waters, *Tammyland*

CHAPTER 2

BEST-SELLING AUTHOR DIES IN "SUSPICIOUS" FALL

Willingham, NH — Gretchen Waters, author of the popular memoir *Tammyland*, was found dead in the town center Tuesday night, after falling down concrete stairs near the Willingham Public Library parking lot.

Waters, 32, of Kingsley, Massachusetts, was in town giving a public reading at the library. An hour after she left the library, at around 10 P.M. according to police, her body was found at the bottom of a ten-foot-high cement stairway connecting the library parking lot to the

Greenfield Shopping Plaza.

"Looking at the steepness of these steps, it appears that Ms. Waters lost her footing and fell. An autopsy will be performed next week, but we believe that she died of blunt head trauma sustained during a fall," said Willingham police sergeant John Polaski, who is leading the investigation.

A state police detective unit has also been assisting with the investigation. They closed off the library parking lot yesterday and appeared to be taking measurements.

"This is a very unfortunate event, and we're doing our best to piece together what happened," Sergeant Polaski said. "We're looking into the possibility that a second party may have been involved. However, I can't go into further detail at this point."

Witnesses saw Waters leave the library at around 9 P.M. But instead of getting into her car in the library parking lot, she walked down the concrete stairs to the nearby 7-Eleven store. After making a purchase, she must have fallen on the way back to her car, Sergeant Polaski said.

The death of a prominent author in the center of town has put many people on edge.

"It's just devastating," said Ruth Rowan, library events coordinator who arranged for Waters's visit. "Just a terrible, terrible thing to have happened here. She was a lovely, articulate young woman and I can't imagine how this is for her family."

Waters's nonfiction book *Tammyland*, published early last year, detailed her travels through the South, learning about the female country singers. She was busy working on her second book when she died, according to Rowan.

Waters's family had been informed of her death, but

could not be reached for comment yesterday.

CHAPTER 3

Gretchen sent me an e-mail two weeks before she died. Unfortunately, I didn't answer it.

Hey Jamie,

How's it going? How have you been feeling? Better, I hope. Do you think we could talk soon?

Lately, I've been thinking of something you said once, back at Forrester. I think we were sophomores. You said you've never been able to let go of anyone, not really. That's why you had so many pen pals, etc. Do you remember that? Do you think it's still true? Because now, working on this second book, I'm wondering if it's true of me, too. I miss those talks we used to have. Remember how smart we thought we were?

Yours,
Gretchen

P.S. Also, in your days as a reporter, did you start to develop any skill for telling who is lying to you?

This was Gretchen's version of a drunk dial: a garbled e-mail full of cryptic, vaguely sentimental insights without much context. (And with a little practical bit at the end, to make it all seem casual.) I imagined her typing this up in a sleepy after-dinner haze, probably after one too many of her favorite eighties songs, and at least a couple of glasses of wine. Yes, this was the old Gretchen — who'd always make it clear she was laying her heart at your feet, but in a box so layered in wrappings and tightly knotted strings that you were never sure if opening it was worth the effort she demanded.

I'd truly missed that Gretchen. We'd lost contact for a few months. And that night, I was too tired to try to untangle Gretchen's message. I thought of calling her, but put it off. I even thought of suggesting she come visit, but I couldn't figure on when I'd feel up to scrubbing the house to overnight-guest-quality cleanliness in the future. And you know how e-mail is — if you don't answer it the day you get it, the chances you'll get to it promptly go down significantly.

17

I'm sure I would have answered it eventually — because I always do. Before I'd had a chance, I got the call from Gretchen's younger brother.

Gretchen passed away yesterday, he told me quietly. *My mother has asked me to contact her friends.*

And it seemed in the first thirty seconds that it was a wrong number — this polite young man I hadn't seen since Gretchen's wedding, calling and telling me someone had *passed away.* Did he mean some Great-Aunt Gretchen who'd slipped away in the night, or in a hospital bed? Because women in their early thirties did not simply *pass away.*

There's been an accident, he'd continued, and then I knew it was real — it was Gretchen.

That night, still in shock from the news, I'd opened her e-mail and stared at it for an hour. It hurt physically to read it, but I did so over and over again, to punish myself for not having answered it. I could remember the conversation to which she referred, but preferred not to think of it — not that night.

I thought of writing a response — just sending a note to Gretchen into the Internet ether, for what it was worth.

Then I thought about Gretchen's e-mail box receiving the message. What happens to the e-mail accounts of the deceased? I wondered. Do they sit around in the air, forever collecting spam? If an e-mail account is never closed but never opened again, does it still really exist? It was a tree-falls-in-the-forest sort of question, of the morbidly silly sort that Gretchen would have asked.

I pictured Gretchen standing with me on an early March day of our senior year at Forrester College. We were huddled together outside, taking a break from a long study session in the library because I'd wanted a cigarette. Neither of us had majors that required a senior thesis. But both of us had ambitiously taken one on in hopes of graduating with the highest possible honors. It was still freezing cold, but Gretchen was inappropriately dressed — a jersey dress, panty hose, and a plaid flannel shirt, with no coat. She shivered madly and gripped her paper coffee cup for warmth. We were huddled by the iron-gated grave of the college's founder, Anne Townsend Winthrop.

I think that guy Adam has a little crush on you, I'd said. *He was asking about you again.*

Hmm. I'm not sure about him, she'd replied. *He enunciates his swear words too much.*

I shrugged and let the subject drop. I imagine we complained for the remaining duration of my smoke, although none of the details was memorable to me later. What I do remember is that as I took my final puff, Gretchen uncapped her paper cup and tossed the remains of her cold coffee sideways into Winthrop's grave site.

She caught my look of surprise, and my immediate, self-conscious glance around us for witnesses. As jaded as I was about Forrester College, I'd never have thought of taking it out on the memorial of an illustrious nineteenth-century feminist.

In some cultures, Gretchen had informed me, *they put bottles of water or even soda on a person's grave. For the long journey ahead. It's a common thing, giving the dead something to drink.*

I'd squinted at Gretchen. *Not this culture, though.*

What is this *culture, Jamie? Anyways, if she's gotta be caged up here for eternity, listening to us all whine and deconstruct and dichotomize all day — if that's what her life's work has come to here, then pouring mochachino on her grave is about as honest a tribute as she'll ever get.*

The words were grasping and snide, but the most memorable of them now was *any-*

ways. The *s* at the end made it a word a little girl would use. Words like that slipped into her speech when we were alone together — when she wasn't in the presence of professors or the more intellectually competitive of our classmates.

Now the memory of that girlish *anyways* unfroze a tiny hole in my shock, and I sobbed till Sam came upstairs.

"What's going on?" He put his arms around me and folded his hands on my big belly. "Oh my God. It seems bigger than yesterday."

"Thanks," I mumbled, snuffling. "I had three peanut-butter-and-banana sandwiches yesterday, so you're probably right about that."

"I've been wondering about those sandwiches of yours. Isn't that what Elvis liked to eat?"

"Yeah," I said. "I figure if I eat enough of them, the kid might just come out singing 'In the Ghetto.' "

Sam was deadpan. "Do we want that, though?"

I giggled and almost answered, but then teared up again, angry at myself for forgetting Gretchen for a moment. Sam wiped my cheeks and came away with black thumbs. I'd forgotten that I hadn't washed

21

my makeup off yet.

"What've you been doing up here?" Sam asked.

"Thinking about Gretchen. What else would I be doing? Reading her old e-mails."

"Oh." Sam nodded solemnly.

"What've *you* been up to?" I mopped my eyes with the sleeve of my sweater.

"Just watching the game," Sam said. "I'm sorry. I should have been up here with you."

"It's okay. It wouldn't have made much difference."

It was kind of a mean thing to say, but I'd found it easy to say mean things to Sam lately. He hadn't shot back in months. It was starting to feel like an experiment, to see when he'd break. I was beginning to wish he would.

"I mean, just, under the circumstances," I backpedaled. "I probably needed to be by myself and just let the shock wear off."

Sam didn't reply. He took my hands in his, pulled me out of my office chair, and put me to bed.

CHAPTER 4

Gretchen and I met when we were freshmen at Forrester. Forrester is a small liberal-arts college in western Massachusetts, once a women's college, now coed with about a 35 percent male population. Gretchen lived down the dormitory hall from me. I can't remember exactly what attracted us to each other at first. She seemed a bit spacey and pretty shy, but at the first floor party, she was hilarious when she was drunk. We'd sat together on someone's couch confessing to each other what dorks we'd been in high school and our ambitious plans to be much cooler at Forrester. There was something mutually sarcastic about the exchange that no one else in the room seemed to grasp, and we ended up falling over each other with laughter, toasting each other's likely collegiate domination with swigs of Goldschläger. The evening ended with me puking my guts out in the corner bathroom, with her checking on me periodically even though she couldn't remember my name. The next morning we officially introduced ourselves over breakfast, and we were fast friends. I made friends with Jeremy while working in dining services and introduced him to Gretchen. They started dating the next year, and were an on-again, off-again couple for several years before they got really serious after college.

The three of us were pretty tight all four years. The friendship worked well because we all studied such different things. Jeremy was an economics major, Gretchen was American studies, and I was journalism. It was easier to be friends with Gretchen if you didn't have classes with her. Her classroom demeanor sometimes creeped out fellow students. She rarely spoke in class — often made a show of looking bored by doodling, yawning, stretching. And when she did speak — and this would be only once or twice during a given semester — she'd raise her twiggy arm very meekly, weak at the elbow, and say something so goddamned clever that you just knew she'd been planning it all semester and waiting for the right second to say it.

And professors loved her — probably more for her essays than for these bizarre classroom performances, but it was hard to say.

Gretchen showed off her tall, frailish figure by wearing demure dresses a size or two too small — often covered up by oversize, pilly old-man cardigan sweaters that she picked up at the Salvation Army. Her favorite was a cable-knit cream one with dirty little cuffs and a shoulder hole awkwardly repaired with pink thread.

That was in the late nineties. We graduated together in 2000, and were close friends for many of the years after college. Gretchen's and my lives followed similar trajectories for a while. We both got jobs right after college — me at a western Massachusetts newspaper, Gretchen writing for a Boston marketing company that produced viewbooks for colleges and ritzy private high schools. We both got married about five years out of college — Gretchen to Jeremy, me to Sam, whom I'd met at a party of a mutual friend. Even after that, we visited each other frequently — sometimes with husbands in tow, sometimes not. It was only in the last few years that our contact had become more infrequent.

Gretchen's life had taken an unusual turn. She got a divorce, somewhat abruptly. I never got a clear read on why — Gretchen just insisted that it wasn't working between her and Jeremy anymore, and hadn't been for a long time. The week the divorce was finalized she took a solo road trip down south, going to Nashville, Dollywood, and various other landmarks related to the legendary ladies of country music. She wrote about the trip, and those writings eventually turned into a quirky memoir about the aftermath of her divorce, reflecting on her own experiences and American womanhood generally as she traveled and contemplated the lives and lyrics of Loretta Lynn, Tammy Wynette, and Dolly Parton (and, to a lesser extent, Patsy Cline, Emmylou Harris, Dottie West, and a few others).

I had not realized up till then that Gretchen had ever listened to country music. She managed to get pieces of the manuscript published on a couple of popular blogs, then sold the whole thing to a publisher. *Tammyland* was an odd little book, but it did surprisingly well. One reviewer called it "a sort of honky-tonk *Eat, Pray, Love* on a shoestring." Book clubs liked it. A prominent reviewer complimented her wit and her appreciation for Americana. It received a considerable bump because of a popular country music biopic that came out around the same time, and then a national discount chain started advertising it as their "Book Club Pick." It sold thousands of copies after that. Gretchen quit her day job and started a second book.

Meanwhile, there were budget cuts at my newspaper and I got demoted from health reporter to part-time night copy editor. I was lucky to have any job at all at the end of it — lots of my friends didn't. It was a blow but I kept the job while I "looked for something else" — a perpetual state of affairs that lasted two years and was still going strong when Gretchen died. At that point I was six and half months pregnant and not likely to get anything soon. My husband's job with a boring but generously paying area insurance company limited our movement somewhat.

But it wasn't the job situation that kept me from Gretchen. It was mostly the pregnancy. For one thing, I had an especially miserable first twenty weeks. I had something called hyperemesis, which basically means severe morning sickness. You turn into a horrifying puke machine and you lose unhealthy amounts of weight. I had to be hospitalized for dehydration a couple of times. Even when the drama of that was over, I never felt quite well. So, while I'd always pictured myself being one of those happy, glowing little pregnant ladies, I was quite the opposite — just a miserable old crab who happened to have a distended stomach.

The really big elephant in the room in all of this, however, was not Gretchen's success or my lack thereof, or even my miserable pregnancy specifically, but the fact that Sam and I had gone ahead and chosen to have children.

Gretchen had been very congratulatory, but I knew how she felt about the matter. She found the prospect of having children terrifying. I'd always known she'd been ambivalent on the subject, but parts of *Tammyland* made me realize how strongly she felt. I understood where she was coming from. There was a time when I might've articulated very similar feelings. I simply wasn't allowed to feel the way she did anymore.

"The Pill"

I've stopped at this rest area because it has a Dairy Queen. I go all out and order a Peanut Buster Parfait. As I dig into it, a family is finishing up their ice cream at the picnic table next to mine. The skinny mom's ice cream is dripping all over her elegant hands because she can't keep up with it, as she's spending all of her time trying to help her tow-headed toddler eat his soft serve with a plastic spoon. The slightly older, equally towheaded son is standing on the bench but holding his own with his cone, although his chin is smeared with chocolate ice cream and rainbow sprinkles. "Superrrrr . . . HERO!" he keeps saying between licks of ice cream, then making exploding noises with his lips. Everyone ignores him. Nobody else says much. The dad is young and muscular with a receding hairline. He's isn't eating any ice cream. He's checking something on his iPhone.

Back when I was married, I used to witness scenes like this and try to imagine myself as the mother. Would I leave the younger one to his own devices and enjoy my own ice cream? Would I demand my husband help? Would I think those exploding mouth noises were cute?

The fact that I could never figure out the answers is a big part of why I'm sitting alone here now. Children confound me. The reasons why people choose to have them elude me. Jeremy did not feel the same way. Not at all.

Mine is one of the first few generations to grow up thinking of kids as a choice. We, of course, have not only the choice of when but if.

Which brings me to Loretta Lynn's famous song "The Pill." Truthfully, it's not among my favorite Loretta songs. I love it more as a piece of history than as a piece of music. Loretta was smack-dab in the generation of women who were of child-bearing age before the Pill was available and after.

The song is written from the perspective of a wife who's had a few kids already and declares she's not having any more — she's gonna start having a little fun because now she has the Pill. Loretta recorded it in 1972, but her record company wouldn't release it till

1975 because they were nervous about how it would be received. And indeed, there are a few racy lines in it:

> This incubator is overused because
>   you've kept it filled
> The feeling good comes easy now
>   since I've got the pill
> It's getting dark it's roosting time
>   tonight's too good to be real
> Aw but Daddy don't you worry none
>   'cause Mama's got the pill.

If anyone was ever in a position to sing a paean to the Pill, it was Loretta. She was married at thirteen and had four kids (and two miscarriages) by the time she was eighteen. "They didn't have none of them pills when I was younger, or I'd have been swallowing 'em like popcorn," she says in her autobiography. And after the birth of her twins — number five and number six — her husband "got himself clipped," as she puts it. So she never actually took the Pill herself. But she knew well the burdens of too many pregnancies, especially when combined with poverty. And she was proud that the song educated rural women about their options. She mentioned once in an interview that doctors often told her that her song reached their young rural patients better than their pamphlets ever did.

Of course, my generation takes the Pill as a given. If I were to pen a song about it, I'm not sure how it would go. As a married woman, I found the enormity of the decision mind-boggling. And at times I even wished it wasn't my decision to make. Because if kids just happened to Jeremy and me as a matter of course, I imagine we'd have gotten through it, we'd have made it okay, we'd have learned to enjoy the ups and downs of family life together. But deciding to have them was not a step I was ever willing to take.

I've been asked since Jeremy and I separated, "Didn't you two talk about it before you got married?"

Why, yes. Of course we did. We were a modern pair, and we weren't dumb. At the time, though, we both thought the answer was "probably."

He was confident of his answer. I grew less confident of it as the years went by. Because, you see, it's easy to say the answer is "probably" when you're twenty-three. When you are twenty-three, you want to believe you are the optimistic, life-embracing sort who wants to have kids. And it's okay to think that you do, because you have years to get around to it. And by the time the proper time rolls around, you'll surely have done everything else you've wanted, you'll be so much more mature and settled and eager to make your ultrasound your screen saver and sign up for Mommy & Me classes. But then you find yourself twenty-seven and feeling no closer to that. Then twenty-eight. And you realize your "probably" meant maybe and your husband's "probably" meant absolutely. Then you're twenty-nine, and he wants to start trying. And your "maybe" has now faded into a "probably not."

Babies don't make you weep, you begin to realize. They don't necessarily even make you smile. You find yourself muttering to yourself, "Someone shut that kid up!" whenever you hear a child whining or a baby screaming in the grocery store, and you're alarmed by the nastiness of your inward tone. You notice tired, vaguely angry parents at the airport. It seems to you you've never seen happy parents at the airport. You wonder if having a child means never being able to enjoy a trip again. Commercials for diapers or baby powder annoy you, with those sensual voice-over ladies talking about babies' butts like they're as delicious as a chocolate cheesecake. You start to wonder what's wrong with you, that you just can't bring yourself to think of a baby's butt that way.

You would like to stay married. But how? Only if someone changes his or her mind.

This is what the Pill has come to mean to me.

So the song I'd sing about it would be quite different from Loretta's. It would probably have some melancholy notes, even some confused and cacophonous bits as well.

But I'd still sing it.

— *Tammyland*

CHAPTER 5

Gretchen grew up in Connecticut, and her parents still lived there. On my way down 91 for the memorial service, I bought a new copy of *Tammyland* at the mall. The one Gretchen had signed for me now seemed too precious to take out of the house, but I knew I might want to read it at the hotel. I probably could have made it back home that night, but Gretchen's mother had asked me if I could come for breakfast the morning after the service. She had something she wanted to discuss with me, she said — something about reading Gretchen's new manuscript, possibly editing it.

When I checked out with *Tammyland*, the shaggy-haired cashier said, "Didn't this lady die recently? Isn't this the one who fell on some library steps, or something?"

This lady. It had been ten days since Gretchen died, and I certainly wasn't ready for small talk about it.

"I think so," I murmured as I handed him my credit card.

"Kind of ironic," the young man continued with a grim scoff. "Author dying in front of a library."

I shrugged and signed the receipt, then tore out of the store. I hadn't expected this — although Gretchen's death had made some New England papers and was picked up by the AP as a minor story. Gretchen was by no means a famous author, but the combination of the popularity of *Tammyland* and the unusual nature of her death somehow translated into media kindling.

I checked into the Best Western outside of Gretchen's hometown with a couple of hours to spare before the service. Sitting cross-legged on the bed, I took the book out of its plastic bag and examined the glossy cover. It pictured the back of a young woman — smartly dressed in a khaki miniskirt, knee-high boots with thick heels, a snug black sweater, and an olive-green messenger bag slung over her shoulder. She is on tippy toes, with her hands cupped as she peers into the window of what looks like a run-down nightclub. Against the black of the window is a pink neon sign that reads TAMMYLAND. Skillful Photoshopping, but they'd gone a bit overboard in making the

36

girl look tweedy, I'd always thought — but I guess that was the point: Northeast intellectual type finds herself in old-time country music. Still, it had always been odd for me to see Gretchen's words packaged this way. And she'd never dressed anything like that.

I looked around the hotel room. The heavy maroon curtain over the window kept all of the daylight out, the lighting was low and yellow, and the room was chilly. I went to the wall unit and turned up the heat, then switched on CNN. I usually love hotels, but I'd never had occasion to stay in one alone, or for such a tragic reason as a friend's funeral. I wondered if this would be the last time I'd be in a hotel for a very long time. Once the little guy arrived, I wouldn't be going anywhere by myself.

Sitting on the bed again, I remembered that Gretchen had written a scene or two about staying in motels by herself. I picked up the book, found the first one, and muted the TV.

The passage was about Tammy Wynette. Of all the women Gretchen wrote about, she seemed most enamored of Tammy. Even after reading the book, I hadn't quite understood the attraction. But I was still willing to try.

"Crying Steel Guitar"

Motel 6
Crossville, Tennessee

I'd hoped to get to Nashville by dark, but I'm too tired to drive the last couple of hours. One forgets, being married, what long road trips are like without someone along to share the driving. There was a construction project near Knoxville that tied me up for longer than I expected. I'm too exhausted to plow through the last hundred miles.

I've checked into a Motel 6 in a town called Crossville. The room doesn't have any obvious flaws — mouse poop or sour smell or a frayed noose hanging from the shower-curtain rod — so I toss my bags inside and drive a couple of blocks back toward the highway, where I'd seen a Popeye's on the way in. I'm too tired to eat a salad or something healthy. Too cold, too much crunching of lettuce, too much self-respect, which takes energy. Fried chicken is one of my many food vices. It was one of Jeremy's very few. So we used to eat it together, trading white pieces for dark, fingers slippery, groaning with a mutually grossed-out pleasure at the end. And when we'd share a meal, he'd always let me have the buttery biscuit.

I sit cross-legged on the bed's brown quilt and polish off a breast, a thigh, a wing, a biscuit, a tub of coleslaw, and mashed potatoes. It's more than I've ever eaten with Jeremy. I think of Tammy as I gnaw the last bits of breaded goodness off the poor chicken's ribs. Contrary to her fancy diva style and her ladylike public persona, her favorite food was anything deep-fried county-fair style. She supposedly would order her tour bus miles out of the way to get to a Cracker Barrel. "If there was a corn dog within fifty miles," one of her backup singers said of her, "the woman had to have it."

The chicken fat comforts me, and the pile of bones left in the greasy Popeye's box by my side makes me feel raw and rank, like a cave woman. I drink the last of my Coke and belch so loudly I'm certain the guy next door can hear it over the endless baseball game droning out of his TV.

I reach for my iPod and play one Tammy tune after another, repeating my favorites as the night rolls on and the television next door falls silent. "Crying Steel Guitar" and "Apartment #9" are perfect for this evening. "Apartment #9," in particular, is exactly what a newly divorced woman should listen to on a Tennessee highway, in a seedy hotel room. Tammy sings of a lonely room, a dark apartment, of the raw pain of being left, and of allowing yourself to hope that he'll come back. Loved-and-left songs are a dime a dozen in any genre, but no one embodies them better than Tammy Wynette.

Tammy was a woman who knew the dim light of a room like this. By the time she recorded "Apartment #9," she already knew it well. She was twenty-three, but she had been married and divorced by then, had three kids in a run-down shack in Alabama, had been to beauty school, and had suffered serious health problems as well as depression and electroshock treatments. She was living intermittently in a cheap motel in Nashville (with the man who would be her next husband), trying to get someone to give her a recording contract. This was the first song she ever recorded, and it was her big break after being turned down by just about every other producer in Nashville. So part of the experience of this song for me is not just the sadness in her voice, but the promise of her career. With each sob in her delivery, part of me cheers through the pathos, "Go, Wynette, go!" Because I know that when she was finished, the producer was blown away. After that song was recorded, she had a career.

So I'm torn between the sadness the song wants me to feel and the thrill of knowing what that song did for her. I know this isn't how I'm supposed to feel listening to Tammy Wynette. I know I'm generally supposed to weep and feel pathetic. Many of her later songs do that to me. But this one makes this room seem more cheerful than this icky orange light, this worn carpet, and this crusty brown quilt.

This song is an anthem of someone who felt as desperate and lonely as I've felt in recent weeks, and turned it into something she'd always wanted. There was certainly pain before and even more after it, but here is the beginning of what she was meant to do — to sing for the brokenhearted, to put a little humanity and sympathy into thousands of lonely rooms, a little bit of comfort into thousands of dim-lit worlds.

I turn out the light. I get into bed. I press repeat.

CHAPTER 6

After the church memorial service, some of the guests gathered at Gretchen's parents' house.

Mr. Waters sat on the couch, listening to a leather-tan woman wearing several strings of chunky beads. His hands were folded neatly on his skinny thigh, but his gaze was fixed somewhere beyond the woman, at the coffee table or the carpet.

"I always felt that about her," I heard the woman say. "The care she took with every word. Her thoughtfulness."

Gretchen's brother, Nathan, tended a tableful of cold cuts and salads and bread, his sandy-blond cowlick bobbing earnestly above him as he worked. I wanted to offer him my help, but knew that he'd refuse it on account of my belly. Recently I'd hit the size where my offers seemed to embarrass people.

Mrs. Waters was nowhere to be seen,

43

which didn't surprise me. She'd looked ready to collapse at the church. I didn't recognize many of the other guests.

I stood in the corner and clutched my paper plate and plastic cup. Glancing down at the windowsill, I noticed that the potted plants lined up there were all dry, one of them very wilted. As I considered whether I should dump the remains of my seltzer water into them, Jeremy approached me.

"I'm glad you're here," he said softly, nudging my elbow gently.

"Really?" I said. "I'm not. I can't think of a worse place to be."

He gave me a funny look.

"Than an old friend's funeral, I mean."

"Oh. Right."

"But it is nice to see you. It's been too long."

And it had been. Jeremy and I had exchanged e-mails briefly after the divorce to assert to ourselves that we were still friends, but I hadn't actually seen him since he and Gretchen had split. He seemed older and chunkier than when I'd last seen him — but maybe it was just the suit and tie. His innocent brown eyes seemed to have sunk a bit, and his hair was cut close to his head — a Caesar cut that wasn't entirely flattering.

"You look great, by the way," he whispered.

"I don't feel great."

"I mean, you're like the perfect little pregnant lady."

"Perfect," I scoffed, pouring my drink into one of the plants, then setting my cup down. "Absolutely."

Jeremy picked a kalamata olive off his paper plate and put it in his mouth. As he tried to chew, his eyes filled with tears.

"*Fuck*, Jamie."

I watched as he extracted the half-chewed olive from his lips, too distraught to swallow.

"The last time I talked to her, I didn't really —"

I put my hand absently on his upper arm, silently willing him not to break. If he did, I probably would, too.

"I didn't really give her . . . uh . . . the attention she deserved."

"What do you mean?"

"I was caught up in my own things. I have a girlfriend now . . . she thought it was a little weird, Gretchen calling. Gretchen wanting, suddenly, to talk to me." Jeremy sniffled and cleared his throat. "Wanting to talk to me about her new book."

I handed Jeremy a napkin. "What was

45

happening with her book?"

Jeremy blew his nose before answering.

"Uh . . . I don't know, exactly. It was complicated. She had sort of a love-hate thing going on with it, I guess. She said something kind of weird to me. She said, 'Last time, I had to make things up to keep things interesting. This time I don't need to, but I'm starting to think it's harder to write about what's real.' Whatever that meant."

"What did she make up last time?"

"Um . . ." Jeremy stepped closer to the refreshment table and flopped a couple of cold-cut rolls onto his plate. "Well, in *Tammyland*, you know the whole thing with the guy Eugene near the end?"

"Of course," I said. Gretchen met a guy at a Nashville nightclub, and they had a little romance that she wrote about in the final chapters.

"Never happened."

"*What?*"

"She made it up to make the book more chick-lit-y."

"No! She didn't tell me that!"

"Well, the guy existed. She chatted with him a little at the nightclub. But she said the music was too loud to have a real conversation, and it kind of ended there.

She made up the rest."

I didn't know what to say to this. "Was his name really Eugene?"

Jeremy shrugged. "No idea."

"That's interesting," I said. "I'll have to keep an eye out for that sort of thing if I end up helping with her manuscript."

"Helping with her manuscript?" Jeremy repeated, and I explained about my appointment with Mrs. Waters the following day.

Jeremy didn't reply.

"So you two were talking a lot these days?" I asked.

"Not a *lot*. Some. More than right after the divorce. There were, uh, some things that came up with the writing of the second book, I guess, that made her want to reconnect."

"But what did her second book have to do —"

"I could have done better," Jeremy interrupted me, his voice shaky again. "I should have done better for her. When she called, and . . ."

Jeremy's voice cracked. He couldn't talk anymore. We were both quiet for a couple of minutes.

"We all feel like that sometimes," I said, trying to think of something comforting to say. "There is no way you could have

47

known . . ."

Known what? I wondered. That Gretchen
would tumble down a flight of stairs to her
death? It seemed a dumb thing to say.
Unfortunately, no smarter or more sensitive
words were coming to mind.

Jeremy nodded vaguely and wiped one eye
with his fingertips.

"I could've been better, too. I owed her
an e-mail," I admitted. "She sent me one of
her philosophical sort of e-mails, you
know?"

"Those could be hard to answer sometimes." Jeremy nodded.

"Yeah," I said.

Jeremy gnawed down a piece of salami.

"Some other time, when I can really talk,"
Jeremy said, "I'd like to talk to you a little
more. Just about Gretchen. About Gretchen
and me."

"Okay, sure," I said.

"I mean, sometime."

"Yeah. Sometime."

I poked at the fruit salad on my plate. We
said nothing more about it.

"I'm not sure how this is going to go,"
Nathan whispered to me as he led me into
the house. "But thanks for coming. Really,
very sweet of you. It means a lot to my

mother."

The kitchen decor belied the Waterses' recent tragedy. There was plenty of sunlight glinting off the pale yellow walls and many framed photographs of lemons and lemonade stands. For breakfast, Nathan had put out a plate of leftover buns, cookies, and fruit from yesterday's gathering.

"Of *course*, Nathan," I said. "Whatever I can do . . ."

Before Nathan could say anything more, Mrs. Waters shuffled into the room. She looked slightly less terrible than she had at the memorial service. Her eyes were still red, but her gray hair was more neatly combed, parted awkwardly close to her right ear. Yesterday's wrinkled black dress was now replaced by jeans and a salmon-colored sweater.

"Hello, dear," she said. "My goodness, have a seat. Nathan, you didn't offer Jamie a seat? *Look* at her."

"I was just getting to that," Nathan mumbled.

"How far along are you, dear?"

"Six and a half months," I said, taking the chair she offered.

"Oh. Well, you look nice."

"Thank you," I said.

"I don't think Gretchen was ever going to

have kids." Mrs. Waters sighed. "The older she got, the more she talked about getting dogs."

Nathan threw me a helpless look.

"Mom, do you need anything else here?" he asked. "Or should I leave you two alone?"

"This all looks good," Mrs. Waters said, sweeping her hand over the spread on the table. "We're fine."

Nathan nodded and left the room.

"You are probably wondering why I wanted to chat with you," she said, pouring herself a cup of coffee, then raising the pot. "Nathan didn't offer you any?"

"He did." I showed her the juice in my hand. "I don't drink it lately."

"Oh. Yes, of course," she said, sitting at the table with me. "Anyway, I know Nathan filled you in that I'm hoping to find someone to help me organize Gretchen's writing. And you came to mind first, since you're such a good friend to Gretchen. And since you're a writer, too."

She was talking fast, twisting her rings, arranging and rearranging the coffee cups, sugar bowl, and creamer on the table. I was surprised at her words. It had been years since anyone had referred to me as a *writer*.

"You look surprised. Now, I know you have a lot on your plate, with the little one on the way and everything. It's not an urgent thing. It would be at your leisure."

"Oh, well . . . whatever I can do," I said.

Mrs. Waters waved at the food and said, "You go ahead and start. I'm gonna show you something."

With that, she slipped out of the kitchen. I grabbed a roll but hesitated to nibble at it. My stomach and my nerves were already pretty weak from watching Mrs. Waters try to hold it together.

She returned lugging a cardboard box.

"You want help with that?" I asked, standing up.

"You go ahead and sit down," she said sharply, putting the box next to me on the linoleum floor. "I'll be right back."

I glanced into the box. It was full of manila envelopes and paper. Stacks and stacks of paper, bundled with thick elastic bands.

Mrs. Waters returned with a purple plastic crate full of more paper, CDs, and a ton of notebooks.

"This is all Gretchen's," she said breathlessly. "It's all here but her laptop. I'll tell you about that in a minute."

"This stuff's . . . all from her apartment?"

"Yes. From her office. Gregor was very nice about helping us with it."

51

Gregor. Gretchen's twentysomething hipster boyfriend, with whom she'd been shacked up for about six months. Another reason I hadn't felt particularly close to her lately: I'd met him once and the relationship perplexed me.

"Oh . . . Gregor," I said. "Was he around yesterday? I don't remember seeing him."

"He visited with us yesterday morning. And he was at the church service." Mrs. Waters sighed heavily as she fell into her kitchen chair. "He didn't come to the house afterward. Anyway. I wanted to know if you'd take these things with you."

"Um, of course," I replied. "If that would help in some way."

Mrs. Waters dumped a teaspoon of sugar in her coffee.

"Now . . . you know Gretchen's deadline was coming up soon? And I believe she was almost finished with the book."

"Oh?" I said. "Okay."

"What I'm asking you, I suppose, is if you'll be Gretchen's . . . literary executor, I guess, is what you'd call it. I mean, we don't have to be official about it. But that would be the basic idea. Do you know what that would entail?"

"Uh . . . Sort of . . ."

"Now, Nathan talked with Gretchen's

agent a little bit, and the publisher is taking her book out of their next catalog, putting it off indefinitely. They understand the difficult circumstances here. Although I think they'd like to publish what she had at some point, if it's mostly done. And I would, too. Because I'd hate to see all of her work go to waste."

"Of course," I said.

"And it's not about money, anyway. But whether or not this is published, we will work something out that would be fair to you, where you'd be compensated —"

"Oh, I couldn't . . ."

"And to be honest, publishing or not publishing isn't my main concern at the moment. I just want these things in the right hands. I want these things to be treated with care, but I don't feel right about one of us doing it. I have to confess to you, Jamie. Part of the reason I picked you is because you're *not* family. I don't know how objective I can be — how objective any of us can be — with some of this material."

I stared at all of the manuscripts. "You've read all of this?"

"Oh . . . no. But I've glanced through some of the notebooks. I've seen enough to know *I* can't be objective about it."

Mrs. Waters paused and bit into one of

yesterday's tea cookies. Light green crumbs fell onto her pink sweater. She sighed, put down her cookie, brushed them off.

"Tell me, Jamie. Did Gretchen ever talk to you about Shelly? Do you know who that is?"

It was a name that had come up in conversation several times in college, during late-night talks between Gretchen, Jeremy, and me. But it startled me to realize how long it had been since I'd heard Gretchen mention it again.

"Yes. She was your sister . . . Gretchen's . . . uh . . ."

"Gretchen's biological mother. Yes. So you do know. She talked about it."

"Yes. A little," I said.

It was easy to forget — that Gretchen's parents weren't her biological parents. She barely ever talked about it — and when she did, she always stressed that as far as she was concerned, they were her parents and that was that. They had adopted her when she was very little. Shelly, her biological mother, was her mother's much younger sister, who had had Gretchen as a teenager, had a lot of drug problems, and died very young. It was sad, she maintained, but the woman had never really been her mother. And her father was the only father she'd ever known. It wasn't like she was orphaned.

"There's a lot in here about Shelly." Mrs. Waters picked up a stapled stack packet of papers and flipped through it absently. "Things she never asked me much about. But apparently she was back in our old hometown a lot, doing research. It was going to be another travel memoir, I suppose. This time going north, to New Hampshire."

"That's where you and Shelly grew up?"

"Yes. Emerson, New Hampshire. Gretchen visited there a great deal when she was little. Before Shelly died, and then, after that, just some holidays. Do you know how Shelly died, Jamie? Did Gretchen tell you that?"

"She had an abusive boyfriend?" I offered reluctantly.

"Yes." Mrs. Waters opened her hands and let the packet fall back into the crate. "That's right. He was an alcoholic. They fought a lot, and one day, he killed her. He beat her with an iron, and she died."

I nodded, horrified. Gretchen had never told me this detail, about the iron. She had never put it so starkly. She'd always made it sound like it was all a natural consequence of Shelly's hard-living choices. That something like that was bound to happen sooner or later. Hearing this now, I was shocked that Mrs. Waters was in as decent shape as she was. How sad to have a sister die that way — and now a daughter die almost as young.

"So Gretchen really didn't tell you much about the new book, I take it?" Mrs. Waters asked.

"Not really. She mentioned that this one was going to be kind of about the men of country music, rather than the women. That it was going to be a sort of companion book."

"Sort of . . ." Mrs. Waters said. "From what I've read, it looks to me like she started with that idea but got kind of . . . distracted. The book became much more personal."

"Hmm. Well, she did say it was pretty different from *Tammyland*. More serious, I guess, in a way. She did say that. But the last we really talked was a few months ago."

Mrs. Waters nodded.

"Yes. More . . . serious. *Tammyland* was so optimistic. I don't know how I, as her mother, feel about her wanting to write about these . . . darker topics. Ones so personal for me, not just for her."

Mrs. Waters stirred her coffee, then set her spoon aside. "Sometimes, as a parent, you can do everything . . . *everything* . . . but then you wake up on a day like this, and realize that it was never going to be enough."

She hesitated, then turned a little red — as if remembering that you're not supposed to say such things to women in my condition. I didn't mind, but I didn't feel I could say so.

"But . . . uh . . . Gretchen's manuscript." Mrs. Waters seemed flustered for a moment, then took a sip of coffee, which seemed to refocus her.

"She obviously put a lot of work into it, and, I suppose, wanted people to read it . . ." Mrs. Waters continued. "So I think it's important that someone take that on. Someone who cared about Gretchen and valued what she had to say."

She took another long sip of her coffee.

"I think of you as one of her best friends," she said quietly.

"Oh. Well, thank you for saying that."

"Maybe that's the wrong way to put it. I suppose in college you don't pick *best friends* anymore? But what I mean is, you were a solid friend to her. I was happy when she introduced me to you. It was what she always needed the most — solid friends."

"I'd be happy to take this stuff," I murmured.

"You shouldn't feel rushed at all," Mrs.

Waters said. "Just look through it at your own pace. I know you must be so busy, and I know you're only going to get busier. I picked you because I trust you. But I want you to take your time. It could be a year, it could be . . . well, I don't know. But eventually, I'd still like to feel that what she wrote is honored."

I cleared my throat. "Of course I'm glad to help."

"Her agent's name is Tracy Pike. I don't have her information. Nathan got ahold of her number, so I'll make sure you get that. You probably want to contact her yourself. She might be able to tell you more about what Gretchen's plans were, if she sent her a recent draft."

"Sure," I said.

Mrs. Waters closed her eyes for a moment. "Oh. Yes. I didn't tell you about Gregor and the laptop. When the police went and chatted with Gregor, they took her laptop. They haven't been able to locate her cell, and I suppose they thought her e-mails and things would give them a sense of who she's been communicating with."

"Why? Is there something they're looking for?"

"Not in particular, from what I've gathered. But I think they need to eliminate the possibility of . . . um . . . foul play, I guess they'd call it. Before they can say for sure if it was a random act of violence . . ."

"Or that she slipped and fell?" I asked uneasily.

"Jamie, they haven't made this public. But there are some reasons to think it wasn't just a fall."

I waited for her to continue. I wanted to know the details — at least, I thought I did — but didn't want to press her for them.

"She didn't have her purse on her," Mrs. Waters said. "And it wasn't in her car. The librarian and the cashier at the 7-Eleven both said that they were pretty sure she had a purse when *they* saw her. Just before. And there were bruises on her arm. Like someone might have grabbed her. A tear on her sweater in the same spot . . . that again, the librarian claims she doesn't remember Gretchen had at the talk beforehand. And it wouldn't be like Gretchen to wear a torn sweater to a reading like that."

"I see," I said softly. I disagreed, but perhaps Gretchen's habits had changed since we'd been close.

"Not enough to say for sure if there was a struggle. But enough to say there could've been one."

"I see," I repeated, my heart thumping hard.

What a horrifying possibility — for all of us, but especially for Mrs. Waters. Maybe it was a mugging — it was starting to sound like it. Maybe something else — but who would want to hurt Gretchen?

"The police have told us these things and asked us to be discreet about it for the moment," Mrs. Waters said softly. "But I wanted you to know."

Mrs. Waters stared out the window for a couple of minutes, watching a maple branch flutter and sway.

"Anyway . . . in terms of Gretchen's files . . . Gregor assured Nathan not to worry, he had everything of his and Gretchen's backed up on this thing called a Time Capsule. Does that sound right to you?"

I sipped my juice and tried to recover from what Mrs. Waters had just told me.

"Uh, yeah," I said. "It's a kind of external hard drive, I guess."

"He said it was saving both of their work every day. What exactly Gregor's 'work' was I don't know." Mrs. Waters used air quotes. "Anyway, he says if we bring up a laptop like hers . . . a Mac . . . he can easily transfer everything that was on her original right onto a new computer. It was a backup for in case one of their laptops got lost or stolen. Very easy replacement."

"Okay."

"Nathan's going to pick up a laptop you can use. He says he can get a good deal, and that he can go up to Gregor's and get all of the files."

"You know, I don't mind doing that. I'd kind of like to go up and chat with Gregor."

"Oh, I couldn't ask you to do that. You're already doing too much."

"How about Nathan contacts me when he has a chance to get a replacement computer, and he and I will work it out?"

I had a feeling Nathan would be easier to convince than Mrs. Waters. And I really did want an excuse to go see Gregor face-to-face. He would know a lot more about what Gretchen had been up to before she died. Whether or not I found it enlightening, I wanted a better sense of this. I had this sad notion that it might diminish some small wedge of my guilt.

"So," she said, leaning forward and trying her best to smile. "Tell me. How is the little one?"

"Very good. Pretty active, recently. I'd always heard of *kicking*. It's the somersaulting I didn't realize . . ."

I trailed off. Mrs. Waters was staring out the window again. As we sat in silence, a tabby cat came mincing into the kitchen.

"Is that Muriel Spark?" I asked. Muriel was one of Gretchen's two cats. She and Jeremy had gotten them together, but he'd let her keep them when they divorced.

"Yes. She and Theodore Roosevelt are staying with us now."

"Permanently?"

"Yes. I couldn't let anyone else take them. Gretchen would want me to baby them like grandchildren, I'm sure. I like having them here in the house. Even though it seems they don't actually get along."

"They never did, Gretchen said. Theodore used to tackle Muriel and take chunks of her hair out."

"We've already had one incident like that. Lots of cat screaming all of a sudden, and then I found Muriel hiding in a closet."

"I'd always be willing to take one, if it got to be too much," I offered.

I meant it, too. I missed having a pet. My own cat, Sadie, had died at age eighteen shortly before I got pregnant. I still missed her, and I'd feel comforted, somehow, to get to take care of one of Gretchen's cats.

"Sweet of you to offer," said Mrs. Waters. "But the last thing you need right now is a new pet. And to be honest, I want to keep them both. They're both Gretchen's."

I nodded, feeling insensitive for having offered. Besides, Mrs. Waters had already made it clear how I was to honor Gretchen.

"And anyway," Mrs. Waters said softly, almost wistfully, pointing at my stomach. "You have that one."

CHAPTER 7

It took me about a week before I could bring myself to look at Gretchen's stuff. Sam had kindly taken the boxes out of my trunk and lined them up in our coat closet, where they'd be accessible but not visible.

On the first day I was feeling motivated, I pulled out the box full of printouts and dragged it into the living room, in front of the couch. I had a couple of hours before work and intended to dive in.

First, I grabbed a stack of manila folders, thick with printouts. I checked out the subject labels Gretchen had scribbled on them: *Tammyland Three*, *Tammyland August*, *Patsy Cline*, *Tammyland Dolly Parts*, *Tammyland/Loretta*, *Endless Tammy*.

Clearly drafts of *Tammyland*. Still, I opened *Endless Tammy*.

"Your Memory's Finally Gone to Rest"

Woodlawn Memorial Park Cemetery, Nashville, Tennessee

I really came here to pay my respects. I dressed the part — black skirt and neatly ironed blue top — although I wonder if I've fooled anyone. I try to cut through the attached funeral home and am met by a somber, besuited gentleman at a desk who asks if he can help me — and to whom I blurt out the ridiculous response: "Um . . . yes. Can you please direct me to the crypt?"

After he points me toward the double white doors and tells me to take the elevator, I berate myself for not using the word *mausoleum*. That would have been the polite word, correct? I'm not experienced in these matters, as no one I know has ever been interred in one of these structures — only buried in a cemetery or cremated. Is it a southern thing? A celebrity thing? I'm not sure. Either way, this place feels sadder and less organic than a cemetery. As I walk through the third floor (where I know, from online research, Tammy lies), scanning for her name, I notice a strong, strange smell that reminds me of rusty pipes and stale dishwater. A series of misters blows perfume into the air, covering the odor momentarily.

By the time I reach Tammy's name stretched across a marble panel, I regret that I've come here. I don't know if this is respect at all, me here staring at the cards and letters and silk flowers of recent mourners, some of them clearly relatives and actual friends. I really didn't come here to gawk, but how else would it look to someone who knew her? As long as I've known the nature of her death, I've found it very sad. It is, admittedly, an outsider's sadness, however deeply I might think I feel it.

Tammy Wynette's death came after years of medical problems and a reliance on painkillers on a Michael Jackson scale. Versed — a medicine usually used only in hospital settings as a presurgery anesthetic — was found in her body during her autopsy. By the time she died, her physical existence had long since passed from unhealthy to freakish and terrifying. The details could easily break your heart.

You could say she performed herself to death. She had medical problems by the time she was in her mid-twenties. She started taking Preludin in the sixties to help ease her debilitating stage fright. And as she became more famous, her medical problems (primarily intestinal problems and adhesions) worsened. She had to have an emergency hysterectomy after her last daughter was born. For years, she had countless abdominal surgeries followed by rushed returns to stage aided by painkillers to which she quickly became addicted. She needed the drugs to keep up the act and they eventually killed her, as everyone close to her knew they would.

Tammy was perhaps an easy candidate for both performance anxiety and addiction. You can see it in some of her early performances — an uncertainty in her posture and her facial expression, a desperate deter-mination to present herself precisely and perfectly. De-spite all of the neediness and emotional inconsistencies her biographies expose, she always appeared — or tried to appear — the dignified lady.

I've seen footage of her last Grand Ole Opry performance once, and will never watch it again. It made me cry. And not in the "Tear in My Beer" kind of way you're supposed to cry when you listen to old country music — more in the "humanity is capable of such unbearable agony" sort that perhaps no art or music can capture. In this performance, she was fifty-four years old but she looks about eighty. By then, she was so thin and worn from the drugs that everyone in Nashville thought she had AIDS. She tells the audience she is "feelin' wonderful" when she is so clearly, painfully not. Her black satin jacket is buttoned incorrectly. She seems confused, is hoarse and gasping for air, and can't make it through "Your Good Girl's Gonna Go Bad." The younger country star Lorrie Morgan comes from off-stage to carry her through the song's final lines. Tammy was, according to her friends and staff, unhooked from medical equipment just before she went onstage — and then rushed away in an ambulance immediately after the performance. This was apparently not an unusual sequence of events in her final years.

Tammy died one year after that performance. As I watch the footage, it's surprising she even made it that long. Her final days and death are so horrifying I hesitate to draw a lesson from them.

There is something about a painful death that threatens so overwhelmingly to detract from our sum feelings about that person's life.

It is difficult for me to think too hard about Tammy's life without having it all point, ultimately, to such a sad and painful death. I think it is often that way when you know someone who has suffered so at the end. While, of course, I never knew Tammy, I *do* know what it is to carry that sort of weight for someone who's gone too early, too tragically.

With Tammy, there is still

her music. I can listen to "Till I Can Make It on My Own" and her version of "Gentle on My Mind" a few times and know she's left something here besides pain — know that she accomplished something of great value, even if pain was inevitably mixed up in it.

Most people don't leave any songs behind. Those of us left with the pain of an early death must be creative in hearing the other notes of that accompanying life — however soft, however low. You have to really listen for them. Train your ear to find them. Even if you have to strain. They might not be so loud and clear as Tammy Wynette's songs. Even if you find it impossible to separate the life from the death. That's simply your lot, having loved someone who died painfully — to endure that with each thought of her, for the sake of still hearing her echo.

This one hadn't made it into the final *Tammyland* at all. Probably a good call. In *Tammyland*, Gretchen had touched on how Tammy Wynette died, but seemed to avoid focusing on it too much. Probably because it could easily bring down the generally spunky, optimistic tone of the book.

Apparently I'd stumbled upon *Tammyland*'s gloomier "deep cuts." In a way, this piece felt more like the Gretchen I knew than the voice in *Tammyland* had.

When we were in college, she'd always had an obsession with the death penalty, and her senior thesis was about Karla Faye Tucker, a Texas woman who was executed for murder in the late nineties. The title was something like *That's Our Girl: Karla Faye Tucker and the American Media*. I still remembered her sitting at her computer, typing, saying, *A banana, a peach, and a garden salad. That was her last meal — can you believe that? Well, what a sweet, dainty little thing! Who eats salad when there's no tomorrow? I mean, how about at least a brownie for the road?*

Are you mentioning her last meal in your thesis? I'd asked her.

Are you kidding me? I've got a few pages about it.

I wondered then if she found the death

penalty barbaric or just strangely, morbidly fascinating. I was never sure.

Now, as I began to reread the Tammy piece, an uneasy feeling came over me. It felt almost as if Gretchen could be writing about her own death.

I thought of Mrs. Waters's words about Gretchen's purse, and the bruises on her arm and tear in her sweater. How long had she lain there on the concrete, bleeding alone, before someone came and found her?

I couldn't shake the image. I replaced the folder, put the box back in the coat closet, and took out my laptop. Googling "Gretchen Waters" and "accident," I found some of the articles about her. They all basically resembled the one I'd read two days after her death. None of them mentioned the details Mrs. Waters had shared with me. One of them mentioned what she'd bought at the 7-Eleven: a Mountain Dew and a small bag of chips. Another lamented the poorly maintained public steps, which were steep and crumbling.

I read the articles again. So she'd made it down the stairs just fine, gone to the 7-Eleven, made her purchases, and then headed back up the stairs. So Gretchen had fallen *backward?* How often does one fall backward while walking up stairs? I wondered. Had she been drinking? She'd confessed to me that she hated readings, and that she often had a drink or two beforehand to make them more bearable. But that wouldn't be enough to send her tumbling down a flight of stairs. Had she maybe forgotten something, then headed back down again?

More than one article mentioned that an autopsy was planned. Could one tell the direction she'd fallen from an autopsy? Her mother hadn't mentioned the autopsy, and I certainly wouldn't have asked. Part of me didn't feel ready to think about it yet. But another part knew I wouldn't be able to let go of Gretchen without knowing.

For now, I just pictured Gretchen in her final evening. Most young women, if they had any doubts about the safety of a neighborhood, would have gotten into their car right out of the library and driven home. Not Gretchen, though — no, she had a quirky cluelessness about her. Of course she went wandering across a dark, empty parking lot in an unfamiliar city, in search of junk food. Probably wearing her cute little camel coat and round-toe buckle shoes, looking a good decade younger than her thirty-two years.

I closed my computer and got ready for work.

CHAPTER 8

The next day, I forced myself to dive into Gretchen's manuscripts again. This time I went for the crate full of notebooks. The top one was a school notebook for kids, decorated with cartoon owls. Underneath that was a moleskin. I opened the owl one first and read the first handwritten page:

"Pretend I Never Happened"

Interstate 495, New Hampshire

What better song for a grown bastard child looking to find and stalk her biological father? Sure, the lyrics don't fit my situation exactly, but I've never found lyrics that fit my situation exactly.
Listening to it obsessively on my first trip to Emerson in

years, I quickly decide Waylon is my new Tammy for this project. My man-Tammy.

He's got a tear in his voice, just like her.

He's also, I've decided, the sort of man I hope to find on the other end of this — an outlaw with a beard and a black hat and sweaty long hair plastered across his forehead. A man so proudly badass he either didn't know I existed or was in jail for so much of my life it didn't seem worth finding me once he got out.

The sort of man Johnny Cash finds at the end of "A Boy Named Sue."

A man who couldn't be around for good reason, a man who thought it better for me and even Shelly that he wasn't. I want him to explain this to my face and charm me still with his fat old cowboy smile.

This is what I want to find. Because what's the alternative?

That was the whole piece. I put down the notebook, stunned.

The baby kicked.

"I know, right?" I said. "That's what this was going to be? Gretchen looking for him?"

As I said it, I felt myself faking an enthusiastic tone: feigning a calm, motherly voice so as not to stress out the baby with my grief. I'd found myself doing this since the day after Gretchen's death. I doubted my son was fooled.

"The Waylon Jennings part's kind of what I expected, at least," I continued anyway. "And the mention of Johnny Cash."

Still, I found it hard to believe where Gretchen seemed to be going with this. I thought of her father — Mr. Waters — thin, balding, and bespectacled, nodding politely to everyone who came up to him after the memorial service. He was a kind man, but the furthest thing from a cowboy that I could imagine. I wondered if he knew about this piece. Since it was on the first page of the notebook at the very top, I imagined at least Mrs. Waters had read it.

I turned the page and looked at the next piece.

"Judy and Diane" was what Gretchen had scribbled across the top of the page.

Shelly's old friends Judy Bacon and Diane DeShannon remind me of "Nan and Jan" — the women I was always encountering in Tammy Wynette's biographies and documentaries back when I wrote *Tammyland*. "Nan and Jan" are a pair of hairdressers — sisters — who worked for Tammy and became two of her closest friends. They often traveled on her bus with her and were among her most trusted confidantes.

When you read and hear their words about Tammy, you get the sense that they know entirely too much about the woman. They have things to say about her life and relationships, and they enjoy being experts on this most famous and controversial life. You get the feeling that they've overprocessed her life by now — among themselves and other friends of Tammy's who share their views of her difficulties.

So it is comforting, if a little disconcerting, to see

that Shelly had her own "Nan and Jan": Judy and Diane.

It's six days before Christmas, and I'm chatting with them both in Judy's living room. Judy's Christmas tree is weighed down with colorful, worn-looking felt ornaments: felt Santas, felt angels, felt reindeer heads with loosely glued red noses. There's a preponderance of felt ladies holding tinfoil cookie sheets full of teeny, tiny felt cookies. Judy resembles these ladies: plump and rosy-cheeked, with an apparent exuberance about serving holiday goodies. She's supplied us each with a mug of eggnog and outfitted her coffee table with ginger cookies and a box of glistening ribbon candy.

Glancing from the tree decorations to Judy, I realize I recognize her. I've been told I've met both Judy and Diane when I used to visit Shelly as a kid, but for the first time I feel something familiar. The roundness of Judy's face, perhaps, or her exaggerated smile — the oddly wide sort of smile one uses on a shy child.

One gets the impression that Shelly was the most interesting and yet unfortunate thing that ever happened to these women. They got to be the best friends of the youngest and most widely discussed of Emerson's few-ever murder victims. This wild and tragic friend had a baby at seventeen and did funny drugs and died very young. This is something these ladies will be asked to talk about for the rest of their lives. And both of these ladies — and I don't mean this badly — really like to talk.

Before any of that scandalous stuff happened, however — before Shelly was the Bad One or the murder victim — she was just a girl on their street with whom they'd ride bikes and play tag and walk downtown for ice cream.

"When we were little, she liked to collect pretty rocks and little pieces of colored glass," Diane informs me. "She kept them all in an old Easter basket in her room. It was very sweet."

As we chat, Judy is the only one drinking her eggnog with any sort of gusto. I'm shy about it, since I haven't seen these women since I was seven, and worry my behavior might be scrutinized later — for signs of my resemblance to Shelly, of my inheritance of the worst of her inclinations.

Diane — a stately, well-mannered woman — sips delicately at her eggnog only every so often. While I don't recognize her face at all, the thickness of her northern New England accent — the way she says "Eastah" — is familiar to me. Shelly's was the same. My mother — a suburban Connecticut resident for several decades now — lost hers long ago.

Both women agree Shelly

wasn't particularly wild until they all entered high school.

"The death of her dad — your grandfather — had a lot to do with it, I think," says Judy.

"Shelly and Linda had very different experiences growing up," Diane explains, and Judy agrees. "They were so far apart in age, and the situation was completely different when Shelly was a teenager, after he died. Harder than it ever was for Linda."

My grandfather died when Shelly was twelve and her sister, Linda, was twenty-one. Linda — my mom, or more accurately, the woman who raised me — had a relatively comfortable, if strict, upbringing. After my grandfather died unexpectedly of a heart attack, my grandmother had to find work and eventually move to a smaller house.

"She was pretty depressed, too," Judy adds. "It was all she could do to hold a job and keep food on the table. Keep herself together. Controlling Shelly just wasn't possible for her at the time. And Shelly changed slowly over those early teenage years. It didn't come all at once."

So, the ladies theorize, Shelly's "acting out" in high school was a result of her changed family situation.

"Kids didn't really get counseling then," Judy continues. "Not so much, anyway. I mean, we all knew she'd be sad. And teachers were understanding and all that. But what happened next, you couldn't have predicted."

"What happened next," according to Judy and Diane, was Shelly experimenting with alcohol early in high school and then other substances. And boys — lots of them — from the moment she stepped into Emerson High.

"Even when we were freshmen, she was invited to all of the parties with the older kids," Diane says. "She was popular because she was so outgoing."

"And she was so pretty," Judy adds. "I wonder, though, if it might have been better for her if she wasn't so popular."

Linda was just starting her new life out of college then — living and working in Boston. She was kind to her mother and Shelly when she came home, the women explain, but really didn't have a clear picture of what was going on with her little sister.

"Shelly was still sweet to her mother at home," Judy says. "She'd do a lot of the cooking and cleaning, she wouldn't talk back. She wasn't bad in that way. She knew her mother needed her like that and didn't complain. That's maybe what made her the way she was outside of that . . . finding a little escape by partying, or with the boys. Finding her affection that way. I didn't see it that way then, of course. Back then I thought she was so bold . . .

so . . . well, crazy, sometimes."

"But now, thinking
back . . ." Diane continues
for Judy, nodding.

"It just seems . . . a little
sad," Judy says. "She was so
young. And it should have been
so obvious."

I sniff at my eggnog but
don't sip it. The homey holiday smell of it is comforting
enough, and I'm growing more
comfortable here with these
women — women who knew Shelly
so well and who are willing to
share in a way my mother never
quite could.

"Obvious?" I repeat.

"Well, that it was more of
a . . . cry for help than her
being a typical bad girl."

Since what they've told me
so far didn't seem so bad . . .
a little alcohol and a lot of
boys . . . I ask them for
clarification. Was she really
such a "bad girl" for the late
seventies?

"Well . . ." Judy says. "She

was always sweet to her friends. I don't mean she was unkind. Nothing like that. It's just that . . ."

She looks at Diane.

"There were quite a few guys," Diane says, clutching her eggnog, glancing into it — I suspect to avoid eye contact with me. "A lot. Of guys. Many."

Judy nods.

"She started flirting when we were about twelve," Diane adds. "Honestly, I don't think I knew how to flirt till I was about eighteen. But little Shelly, she would flirt with Judy's big brother and his friends when he'd come home from college. Remember that?"

Judy nods again, shrugs, and finishes her second eggnog.

"Yeah," Diane says. "There were always a lot of guys, with Shelly."

I nod. I see. They are trying to tell me what my mom never quite had the heart to say, but that I was able to

surmise long ago. They are
trying to tell me that Shelly
was a slut.

I closed the notebook. Yes, it really did
seem Gretchen was heading in that direction — looking for answers about her biological roots. I supposed, now that I'd had a
few minutes to let it sink in, that it wasn't
such a crazy idea. It was only natural for an
adopted child to ask these questions eventually. In theory, it could fit with the men-of-
country-music theme — hence the little
Waylon Jennings piece. It certainly wasn't
the nuttiest idea Gretchen had ever had.

This piece didn't have anything about
country music, but maybe she was planning
to insert it later. It was just a first handwritten draft, after all.

Still, I felt like I needed a little guidance
here.

I found the phone number in my purse
that Nathan had given me — of Gretchen's
agent, Tracy Pike. I dialed it, got voice mail,
and left a message, explaining who I was.

When I picked up another notebook,
something slipped out of it and onto my
lap.

It was a faded snapshot of Gretchen wearing a fuchsia tank top, with her arm around

a little girl squinting in the sun.

For a moment, I wondered who the little girl was — then I looked back at Gretchen and realized it wasn't Gretchen at all. Gretchen had probably never worn a tank top in her life, and this young woman was a bit bustier than Gretchen had been, too. Of course, it was Shelly. And the little girl was Gretchen.

Still, Shelly looked shockingly like Gretchen. They had the same dark blond hair streaked with brown, the same whiteness of complexion, even the same tilt of the head.

The young Gretchen looked uncomfortable in the sun but was trying to manage a cringing smile anyway. There was something about the smallness of her lilac T-shirt, the innocence of its gathered little sleeves, that made me very sad.

My cell phone rang. It was Tracy Pike, surprising me with a quick call back.

"Thanks for taking the time to talk to me," I said after we introduced ourselves.

"Not at all," she said. "Of course. I wanted to say again how sorry I am. It must be such a shock. I'm terribly sorry."

"Thank you," I said.

I was surprised by the speed of her call-back and by the youthful efficiency in her voice. She didn't sound much older than me. Whenever Gretchen had mentioned her "literary agent," I'd always pictured a middle-aged Manhattanite with a smoky voice and a highball glass.

"So, I'm just starting to go through Gretchen's handwritten things." I spoke quickly so she wouldn't feel the need to offer more condolences. "And this weekend, I'll be getting the computer files from her boyfriend. Probably I'll know more when I see that, but I thought it might be good to touch base with someone who had a better idea of the scope of the book. So I'll know what I'm supposed to be looking for."

"Actually, I'll be curious what you find." Tracy paused. "She had kind of stopped communicating with me about her progress a little over a month ago. She was past deadline. I wasn't sure if she was powering through to the end or was so far behind she was reluctant to discuss it."

"But . . . what were you expecting to receive, exactly? What was the book she'd proposed? I mean, I know it was supposed to be like *Tammyland*, just about men this time. Men country stars. Johnny Cash, Willie Nelson, George Jones . . . Is that right? That was the last thing she told me about it."

"Um . . . yes." Tracy sighed. "That was

the general idea. First she started with just
that basic idea. But she was having trouble
making it go. So about six or seven months
ago she proposed a new direction."

"Which was what?"

Tracy let out a long breath, then I heard a
light tapping that I assumed was typing.
"Well, you and Gretchen were close friends,
right? I assume you know about her unusual
family situation?"

"Um . . . I'm not sure what you're referring to. You mean her . . . biological parents?
That situation?"

"Yes. Yes, that's what I meant. So, at first,
she was having trouble writing about all of
these country music men. Relating them to
her life. She said she wasn't feeling it the
way she had with the women. For obvious
reasons, I guess."

Tracy laughed a little.

"Uh-huh," I said.

"But the publisher really liked the idea of
a companion book to *Tammyland*. So Gretchen was struggling to *make* it relevant.
Then she proposed a way to make it more
personal. She was going to search for her
real father, and she was going to write about
that in terms of the country music guys."

"I see," I said.

"I mean, I asked her." More soft typing

noises as Tracy spoke. "I said, are you sure this is what you want to do? I know it's really personal. And she said yes, it was something she'd actually been meaning to do for a long time. That she was eager to do it. Then I checked in a couple of months later and she said it was going really well."

"So . . . does that mean she'd found him?"

"Oh. Um, I don't know. I didn't ask that. It didn't feel appropriate. As long as the manuscript was going well, the rest was none of my business."

I sank onto our couch, unsure how to respond. Then I heard a *bing!* on the other end. It sounded like Tracy had just gotten an e-mail.

"And I was trusting that I'd see it all in manuscript form," Tracy continued. "Sometimes, I actually like to be surprised. I like to experience the book as a real reader would, rather than having the author tell me what I'm going to get in advance.

"What I would do, if I were you," said Tracy, "is take a look at all her most recent files first. I mean, when you get them this weekend. See what she was writing most recently. By the way, her newest title was *My Favorite Lies*, I believe. It's a George Jones song. She changed the name a few times, but it was always a George Jones song. Before *My Favorite Lies*, it was *Accidentally on Purpose*."

I wrote down *Accidentally on Purpose* and *My Favorite Lies* on the newspaper on our coffee table.

"Good to know," I said.

"Yeah, and then I'd do key-word searches on all her files, using the men's names. You know, like Willie Nelson, Waylon Jennings, Conway Twitty, whatever the other names are. Look for stuff that has those words in the text that's dated within the last six months or so. That's about when she changed direction."

"And once I get a sense of what's there, what happens then?"

There was another *bing!* in the background. Busy woman, this Tracy.

"Well, that depends. You know, I've spoken with various people at the publisher and of course they're really saddened about Gretchen. Their main concern now is doing what's comfortable for her family. That might even mean the publisher will have to eat the loss on Gretchen's advance."

"Really?" I said. I didn't know the details, but my impression had been that Gretchen had gotten a pretty hefty advance for her second book, thanks to *Tammyland*'s unusually good sales.

"Well, I'm not certain. This is an unusual situation. I'm not sure, under the circumstances, if they'll pursue the family for the return of the advance. But if there is a full manuscript that was essentially done and her family wanted to move forward with publishing it, then we could take the initial steps. At that point the family would probably need to designate someone as the official literary executor."

"Yeah, that's the term Gretchen's mom used, but there's nothing official about it at this point."

"But that may or may not happen. You need to see what's there first. I wanted to say, however, that you should take your time. Don't worry about it. This is a very tragic situation, and the publisher understands that. I understand that. You and her family shouldn't worry about this. The publisher has already made arrangements to postpone the book. And they know they might have to cancel it altogether."

"Okay," I said. "I'll let you know what I can figure out."

"You take your time, okay, Jamie? This really isn't the most important thing at the moment."

"I know," I said, thanked her, and we said good-bye.

I slipped the photo back into Gretchen's notebook, then slipped the notebook into my shoulder bag. I'd read more at work.

Chapter 9

"In the Good Old Days (When
Times Were Bad)"

This is one of my favorite
of Dolly's oldies, but I never
wrote about it in *Tammyland* —
perhaps because it didn't
speak to my feelings about
divorce at all. It speaks to
something deeper — to memories
I've been hesitant to revisit
at any great length. Till
recently, that is.

The lyrics are about the
struggles of growing up poor
in a rural environment —
something I won't pretend to
relate — but the song generally reflects a familiar ambivalence many of us have
toward our past. Dolly trea-

sures deeply the memories of her youth, but recognizes, in the same breath, how painful those times were.

In general, I feel this way about my childhood. Certainly I didn't endure the sort of difficulties Dolly and her family did. Nonetheless, as almost every childhood is hard and mysterious in its own way, I think we can all point to memorable Good Old Days When Times Were Bad — beautiful and terrible times that seem so distant now that they feel like legend in your head.

For me those days are the last couple of weekends with my real mother. With Shelly, that is. I go over and over them and have wondered for years what exactly it is I want out of them.

It goes without saying that I'd pay any amount of money or make any hypothetical sacrifice to have her back again, but that's not what we're talking about here. What we're talking about is those days, and how they feel in my head, and what it would be like to relive them again. Because I remember Shelly giggling with her boyfriend Frank on the way home from Carvel. He was imitating someone they both used to work with, making him sound like an insufferable nerd. And I remember the easiness of her laugh, and thinking that the person must've really deserved the teasing, because Shelly wasn't mean like that.

I remember Shelly letting me pick the TV show that night — *Mr. Belvedere*. I don't remember the plot of the show but I remember that we watched it, and that Frank asked a few of his usual probing media-analysis questions ("So, this fat English guy lives with this American family and makes a bunch of jokes at their expense?") during the commercials, while he and my mother each nursed a beer.

And so far these memories are, I suppose, more about Frank. But then my mother put me to bed, and Frank stayed in front of the TV. During those last few weekends, she'd put me to bed like I was a little kid — like Linda used to when I was still really small. She'd watch me brush my teeth and then sit on the bed and listen while I read to her from the *Amelia Bedelia* books Linda had sent for me to keep at Shelly's place. I'd lie under the beautiful pink bedspread she'd bought for me at Kmart — it looked just like a big bridesmaid dress — and I wouldn't tell Shelly that I was a little too old to be put to bed anymore. I loved her smell — Prell shampoo and beer and a little bit of something else I'm pretty sure I'd recognize immediately if I ever got to smell it again.

I wondered what it would be like to be there with her every night. I wondered if I lived with her, if I'd ever tell her I was too old to be put to bed, or just let her do it. Let her till I was very old — till I was a teenager, even. Beautiful Shelly could put me to bed as long as she wanted. Young, beautiful Shelly who didn't seem any older than that girl Kelly my mom (Linda) had sit for me on the rare occasions when she and Dad went for a movie.

And before Shelly got up and turned out the light, did I really look at her? If I could do it again, what would I look for in her face, in her eyes?

And if I had it to go back to, what would I say to her?

Probably this: "Shelly, are you sure you know what you're doing?"

I suppose the answer to this and any other question is irrelevant now, since it wouldn't change anything.

So maybe only this: "Shelly, say one more thing to me. Just one more thing — anything —

before you turn out the light. Just one more thing, between you and me."

So Gretchen had reverted back to writing about Dolly Parton rather than sticking to the male artists. I wondered if she found herself doing that often, and how she planned to justify it in the final draft.

In all of the years I knew Gretchen, she never said as much about Shelly as she'd written here in this piece. And for some reason, I'd been under the impression that Shelly had died when Gretchen was four or five — that she didn't talk about her because she didn't really remember her. If Gretchen was old enough to read before Shelly died — old enough to think she was too old to be put to bed, old enough to remember later that she'd watched *Mr. Belvedere* — she had to be a couple of years older than that.

"How're you feeling, Jamie?" my boss, Patty, asked me when she caught me staring into space at my desk.

She said it with a hint of irritation. I could tell she'd grown tired of having to ask me this weeks ago, when I'd returned from my second hospital stay for dehydration.

"Great!" I said, returning my gaze to my computer. Exuberance and positivity always

101

seemed to throw Patty, so I'd taught myself to feign them when necessary.

Patty anchored her thick pink hands on my desk and leaned into my personal space. I think she was checking to see if I had Facebook or a game of solitaire on my screen.

"Um. Have you got Warren's article on the sewer bill?"

I could smell her Altoid breath. I wondered if she'd popped one in her office just for the occasion of coming out here and harassing me. Flattering, in a way.

"Yeah," I said, glancing at the clock. It was just before nine. "I've just got to shave another few lines off it, and I'll be done."

"Good." Patty leaned away from me again, folding her arms and giving me a single nod. "Because Erin just filed a story about that fire on Chestnut, and I need that next. I'm putting it on page one, where the budget story was going to be."

"Alrighty," I chirped. I could feel a couple of the reporters' sympathetic eyes on me, which I tried to ignore.

I finished my work early, but stayed late searching for articles on Gretchen on LexisNexis. I found some I hadn't read before, but none of them said anything new. The police apparently weren't releasing many details.

On the way home, I thought about a long-ago conversation Gretchen and I had had in college — the conversation to which Gretchen had referred in her last e-mail to me.

Gretchen had noticed that I seemed to get more mail than anyone else, and that I was always on the computer e-mailing this friend or that. In time she figured out that these weren't all high school friends — there was Penny from volleyball camp when I was thirteen, and Tara, who was in my homeroom all the way through junior high, but went to private school after that.

It started when I was a kid, I explained to Gretchen, when I became obsessed with the idea of having pen pals. And when I was a little older, I was just an obsessive keep-in-toucher.

I keep in touch with borderline friends and vague acquaintances as much as is possible without it being considered stalking. Often I don't particularly like the people I'm in touch with. It just comforts me to know they're still out there, still accessible.

Gretchen had asked if I was one of those old-fashioned letter-writing types. And I said no, it wasn't that. And it wasn't even friendliness either, although thankfully that's how most people perceived it. It was perhaps simply that I can't stand good-byes. That at the moment of good-bye — especially with someone who you know you'll probably never see again unless you come up with some excuse to do so — I always come up with the excuse. *Hey, why don't you give me your e-mail address, and I'll send you the title of that book I was telling you about.*

This is how I collect people. Not friends, exactly. Maybe just acquaintances. Maybe just names. Maybe even just avoidances of good-byes. It can be embarrassing, actually — I've known myself to start tearing up during partings in which I can't think of an excuse to be in touch quick enough.

It is a little weird, I have to say, Gretchen admitted. *Because you don't seem like a very sentimental person.*

What makes you think I'm not sentimental? I asked, wondering if she meant that I was cold and unkind.

Well. Okay. Maybe just not clingy at all, how about that? You're not clingy.

But I'm telling you that secretly I am.

But not with guys, ever, is what I was thinking of, said Gretchen, after some thought.

And she was right. Always, with guys, I'd been just the opposite. I was never interested in "staying friends" with boyfriends after a breakup. At the time of this conversation, I'd been dating someone for a couple of months and still didn't know his phone number. I always relied on him to call me. This had impressed Gretchen.

That's a totally different emotional category, I explained. *It's not about romance. Get that way about guys and you're doomed.*

Gretchen had nodded. *Yes. I imagine you are. But how do you keep from getting that way?*

I didn't wonder at the time — but wondered now — if she was really asking me. She didn't jump in and out of casual physical relationships like I did, but was equally casual about romance in her own way. When someone was interested, she took so long to decide if the feeling was mutual that the opportunity usually dissolved — often, it seemed, to her relief. It wasn't until after college that she and Jeremy really got serious. This was part of the reason it had shocked me so when she and Jeremy had divorced. She'd spent so long deciding about him — what, after all that, would make you change your mind?

I believe this blasé attitude about romance helped connect us as friends. There seemed to be a silent understanding between us that guys and relationships were not to be discussed for great lengths of time, or with too much emotional investment. We were smart, well-rounded young women who had a number of other things to talk about. A guy was rarely any more of a crisis than a cash-flow problem or a midterm exam. I recall letting my room phone ring while we were talking, saying, "Oh, it's just Will," or (with authenticating eye roll), "Probably just Jason — I'll let the machine get it." The apathy felt genuine even though I'd often call said male back within thirty seconds of Gretchen's leaving my dorm room.

Now I wasn't sure what part of that conversation Gretchen had been thinking of when she wrote to me. The part about my neurotic pen-pal habit? The part about men being in a separate category? Or some other facet of the conversation I'd long since forgotten?

Remember how smart we thought we were? she'd asked in that final e-mail. What, exactly, had she meant by that?

When I got home, Sam was still up — in bed, but propped up reading a Neil Gaiman book.

"What'd you have for supper?" I asked.

"Roast beef sandwich," he said. "And a salad."

"Really? You made yourself a salad?"

Sam shrugged. "I'm trying to be more responsible. Preparing for fatherhood, you know."

"Yes." I picked my pajamas up off the top of the hamper and began to change. "Every child deserves a dad who eats lettuce."

"I'm excited for when we'll get to have supper together again."

"Yeah. That'll be nice. While it lasts."

"While it lasts?" Sam repeated.

I meant that I'd be going back to the night shift after my maternity leave was over — and Sam knew it. But he was still holding out on the possibility that I'd quit my job and stay home with the baby for a while longer — six months, a year, maybe more.

"Let's not have this discussion again right now," I said. "I'm tired."

"The cost of day care just about breaks even with —"

"I know, I know. You've told me about twenty times. I don't want to talk about it tonight. We have a few months to talk about it."

"Not so many months now," Sam pointed out.

I ignored this comment, true as it was. As much as I disliked my job, I wanted to keep it. I needed to feel like I'd be keeping at least one foot in the real world after the baby was born. I feared for my mental health otherwise.

"If it's so soon," I said, pulling *What to Expect the First Year* off my bedside table and tossing it at him, "how come you haven't even cracked this yet?"

"Have *you?*" Sam asked.

"I read a couple of chapters, but didn't want to get too ahead of you."

"Oh," Sam said, gingerly putting down his own book and picking up the tome.

I slipped into bed and pulled *Tammyland* out from under my pillow. My signed copy. I stroked its smooth cover, sniffed the pages. I love the smell of paperbacks. So, apparently, did the baby, who gave a couple of exuberant kicks. Good sign, I thought.

I could feel Sam's eyes on me as I opened *Tammyland*. I tried to ignore them until I saw him, out of the corner of my eye, begin thumbing through the parenting book.

CHAPTER 10

"I Don't Wanna Play House"

"I Don't Wanna Play House" was, of course, one of Tammy's big hits during her golden year, 1968. The abandoned-wife narrator of this song laments at hearing her daughter proclaim to a playmate, "I don't wanna play house," because she's seen her parents play it and it doesn't look like much fun.

And those who find Tammy to be a bit "too much" are apt to point to this one as such, along with "D-I-V-O-R-C-E." It's all a tad too pathetic, a little too suburban and domestic, a little too manipulative of the audience, showing the harsh realities of a marriage from the viewpoint of the little kids.

But it perhaps could be an anthem of my generation, as well as the one before us. Not Tammy's narrative in the song, but that of the daughter she quotes. We're the little kids who've seen the marital wreckage of yesteryear and declared it unsuitable for ourselves. We see Tammy's expressions of suffering and reject them. We are too smart and too strong to be like her. We don't want or need a man — or any mate — in the same way women of her generation did. It is entirely different for us.

Because, you see, relationships between men and women have completely evolved into something that does not resemble Tammy's experience in the slightest. If you are a smart, modern woman, you will certainly never muffle your sobs into a pile of laundry, or spend a whole day worrying about the cold expression on your husband's face when he left for work that morning, or hear your four-year-old echo back at you some frustrated utterance that makes you realize how miserable you must sound to the rest of the world. No, our generation is too enlightened to ever be so domestically dysfunctional as all of that.

And I believe I thought this once. I was indeed a child for having that thought — or at least incredibly naive. To think one could love and marry and maybe start a family and never feel any of these sorts of things that Tammy always sings about so pitifully and so beautifully.

I really was a brat to think that once. "I don't want to play house." To think I could have everything I want and not have to play at all. A really clueless, insufferable brat, playing entirely outside of the house.

— Tammyland

CHAPTER 11

"Bedtime Story"

78 Durham Road
Emerson, New Hampshire

I sit outside my mother's old house on a weekday, when no one's home to feel creeped out to see the ghost of Shelly Brewer lingering on the side of the street in a Toyota. The little bungalow seems a bit prettier now than when Shelly rented it. The dark brown paint has been switched to a gentle blue. It still has thick white trim — brighter now, it seems to me. Gone, though, is the adorably lop-sided window box where Shelly used to plant her marigolds.

My last visit to Shelly's was in March 1985, a few days before she died. It was during a school vacation, and I went to see her before the weekend because I had a kiddie party that Saturday that I desperately wanted to go to. Shelly understood and accommodated.

If I'd been there on the weekend, I would've been there when she was killed. Maybe I would've been killed, too. Or she wouldn't have been killed at all. There's that to think about.

Anyway, there were a few things that were memorable about the visit. One was that I brought her a drawing I had done. I thought she might like it better than a ditto with a red "100" scrawled across the top.

So I drew her a picture of a crow. I loved crows, loved drawing them — pressing the crayon hard into the paper to make it dark and shiny, giving it the oily look of a real crow's feathers. And birds were easy, if you did them from the side and didn't try to make them too fancy.

When I was finished, I wasn't sure if Shelly would like it. Maybe a crow was too dark and gloomy. I had a friend at home who said so when we drew together. So I put a pink bow on the crow's neck and had it holding the string of a big, blue balloon in its claw.

When I presented it to Shelly, she said she loved it, and really seemed to mean it. She brought me to the drugstore and we picked out a plastic frame for it — black, to go with the crow. The pharmacist even admired it. When we got home, Shelly propped it up on her coffee table and said later she'd find a spot for it on the wall and hang it.

And then — I remember it being within minutes of her propping up the picture — Shelly decided to have a serious talk with me. She said she wanted to tell me that she'd made a decision about something. And I might hear people talking about it, and that it might upset me or my mom. But that she wanted me to know that she loved me, no matter what happened.

My first reaction was that she didn't really like the crow so much, after all, but was just trying to be nice, knowing that a serious conversation was coming.

Shelly continued. She said that the most important thing she wanted me to remember was that if someone was ever hurting you, it was important to do something about it right away. To either hit back or tell someone who would help you. Whatever you decided to do, the important thing was to do something immediately. Not wait and see if it would happen again. That was what she wanted me to remember from this.

I told her that no one was hurting me. And she said that that was good, she was glad. It didn't seem to me we understood each other, about her plans or about my crow. The conversation ended there, as Shelly suggested we make ourselves a little lunch.

That evening, though, I felt I understood a little better. There was a knock on the door, and my heart sank. Frank, I thought. He'd been completely absent this visit, allowing Shelly to focus all of her attention on me.

When Shelly opened the door, I heard her say, "My kid's here. She's asleep."

She let the person in anyway, and as they started to talk, I was relieved to hear it was a woman. This wasn't unusual. Shelly's friends seemed to know my bedtime — occasionally they'd come and visit with her after I was in bed. And I continued to busy myself fashioning my stuffed monkey into funny contortions, as I sometimes did when I couldn't sleep.

Then Shelly said something that made me sit up straight in my bed. She said, "It's more complicated than money. I don't really want money. And all the money in the world wouldn't even get me Gretchen back, anyway."

Get Gretchen back?! So it was true. Someday Shelly might bring me back here and be my mother. I couldn't imagine it. Would she start pretending to care about my dittos, my 100s? Would she let me take ballet? Did the Emerson school cafeteria have chicken nuggets?

The TV was burbling loudly, so I couldn't hear everything. Eventually, though, I heard the other lady say something loud enough for me to hear. Something like: "If you think you would hold up in a fight against him, you're wrong, Shelly."

This scared me. She was probably talking about Frank now. I could figure out that much, because I knew how much Shelly and Frank fought. She was warning Shelly about Frank. It seemed to me a lot of people didn't really like Frank: me, Nantie Linda, Aunt Dorothy, Grandma, the neighbors.

And yes, it was a relief to know that others knew what I knew. That Shelly and Frank fought. It was not a relief to hear someone else sound like they were worried Shelly should be afraid of him — like I was.

It seemed to me, after a few minutes, that Shelly and her guest were getting angry at each other.

Shelly said, "If he doesn't stop, I'll go to the police."

"You think the police will believe you?" her friend asked. And she told Shelly she should be careful.

A little while later, Shelly's friend left, and the

TV droned on into the night.

A few weeks after Shelly died, the framed picture showed up at my mom's house in a box of things her mother sent her, for her and me to remember Shelly by.

I had *seen* that bird drawing. In college. I thought about it on my way up to see Gregor.

I didn't remember what year it was now, but I came into her room one day after a holiday break and saw it sitting on her bookshelf. I asked who'd drawn it, thinking maybe a young cousin or babysitting charge. And she told me she had drawn it when she was a kid. I probably gave her a funny look. Displaying one's own framed childhood drawing was, fittingly, a decidedly quirky thing to do — but a bit on the egotistical side for Gretchen. I believe the drawing disappeared within a week.

CHAPTER 12

I have to admit, Gregor annoyed me before I'd even met him.

"Gregor? Like the bug in the Kafka story?" I'd asked Gretchen when she first told me about him.

"Yeah," she'd said. "But he's nothing like that guy, really."

That was true, I'd soon learn when I met him. I had to admit he was very attractive, but for his creative facial hair. He almost always wore a scarf with his dark, pec-hugging T-shirts — more often than not, a cowboy kerchief, which seemed to me pretty contrived, but with her later-in-life attraction to things country . . . who knows? Maybe Gretchen found it charming.

And I didn't care for his light red goatee. He looked like a leprechaun — a young, narrow-faced, hipster leprechaun.

Now, as he led me into his and Gretchen's chilly, high-ceilinged apartment, he seemed just a sad leprechaun. He wasn't wearing a scarf of any kind — only jeans and a loose green T-shirt that said THE JESUS LIZARD on it. His feet were bare, and he kept placing one foot over the other and curling his toes, as if he were self-conscious about them.

"How're you holding up?" I asked, handing him the laptop that Nathan had sent me.

"Okay," he said. "I'm trying to get a new place fast. Because it's hard to be in here."

"I can imagine. Did you two have a lease?"

"Yeah, but they're letting me break it. They understand."

Gregor led me to a spacious room with two desks — one slim and black, one heavy and oak. The black one had on it two neat stacks of magazines and had a clock over it that had the word NOW at each of the twelve hours instead of numbers. The wooden desk was dusty, scattered with paper clips. Over it was a framed poster of a mallard floating in brown, rippling water.

"We shared this office space, Gretchen and I," Gregor explained.

"Let me guess," I said, pointing to the second desk. "That one was Gretchen's."

"Yeah. Her parents didn't ask for the duck poster back."

Gregor paused while he hooked a couple of cords from the small drive on his desk to the Mac I'd given him.

"It's not any easier since the Waterses took Gretchen's stuff away. It's even more depressing. Like there's this big empty hole where she was." He pushed his leather chair toward me and gestured for me to sit in it. "I'm sorry. How are *you* doing?"

"Not so great. Reality's setting in, I think. It feels worse now than it did a couple of weeks ago."

He nodded, then glanced at my belly, as if that factored in somehow. I swiveled away from him slightly.

"Yeah," he said, looking away again. He glanced at the computer. "Um. Uh-oh. It says this is gonna take six hours."

"Oh, really?" I said.

"Oh, shit. I had no idea. I've never had to use the Time Capsule before. I don't know why I thought it would just be, like, zip-zap."

"That's okay," I said. "I can kill time around here for a few hours. There are some things I've been meaning to shop for — I noticed you have the big mall down by the exit. Is there any kind of a baby store there?"

"Uh . . . yeah." Gregor hoisted himself onto his desk, pulled up one leg, and grabbed his toes. "I'm not sure. But it's a pretty big-ass mall."

I felt silly for asking him this. Of course he didn't know. But I wondered if he regularly used terms like *big-ass*, and if Gretchen liked it.

"And maybe . . . I mean, I don't know what you had planned for today, but maybe you and I could get out of here for a little bit, grab coffee or lunch or something. I thought maybe we could chat about Gretchen's project some. I bet you know more about it than her family does."

"Yeah, prolly," Gregor said, picking at his pinkie toe. "Sure, that'd be a good idea. You hungry for lunch now?"

He glanced at my belly again.

"No," I said. "Is it even eleven o'clock yet? But if you want to talk now, how about coffee?"

Gregor let go of his foot. "Yeah. Okay. Let's do that."

I allowed Gregor to drive, and he chose a tiny coffee place with dim lighting, holey couches, and creaky wooden tables covered in African fabrics.

"Gretchen wrote here sometimes," Gregor told me as we waited in line. "But never for long. An hour, maybe two. She told me it was hard for her to concentrate in one place. She'd try coffee shops, she'd try the library, she'd try home. She'd even write at McDonald's sometimes. She could never settle into one place to write."

"Maybe that came from her experience with *Tammyland*," I suggested. "Since with that, she was always writing from a different place. At a Dairy Queen over a sundae, over a piece of key lime pie at a folksy diner, or whatever."

"That was more about the food than surroundings, though. She thought it would be cute to make it look like she was stuffing her face on southern food or road food the whole time. But half the time she was writing in her hotel room and just making up where it was written."

"She told you that?"

"Yeah." Gregor shrugged. "This time around, I think it had to do more with the fact that she was really having some kind of writer's block."

A similarly goateed guy behind the counter gave Gregor a nod of recognition before taking our orders: Gregor's cappuccino and my chai. Coffee still made my stomach turn, unfortunately.

At our table with our drinks, I prompted Gregor.

"So . . . you were saying. Writer's block. Gretchen was having a little trouble?"

"Um . . . yeah." Gregor dumped three raw sugar packets into his cappuccino. "You know, she wouldn't just switch places she'd write. She'd switch notebooks. I don't know how many notebooks the Waterses gave you, but it must've been a lot."

"Yeah. Piles and piles of them."

"I think the idea was that she kept starting over." Gregor stirred his cappuccino and then licked the little spoon before tucking it carefully next to his cup. "A new notebook was, like, symbolic. Or she'd try a more fun or more expensive notebook with a cool cover, to get her spirits up. Or she'd have a new idea while she was in a grocery store. Buy a cheap notebook there, go to the nearest Starbucks, write there for a while. So there were notebooks everywhere. She started to lose track of what she'd written where. One time she tore apart the whole apartment looking for some piece she'd written about Willie Nelson. When she finally found it, she was like . . . 'Oh . . . it's not as brilliant as I remember it.' And just tossed it aside."

I smiled a little. The process reminded me of watching Gretchen in the final hours of writing a paper in college.

"I don't know how much of the drafts and stuff you've read, what you've seen in her notebooks or whatever so far . . ."

"Well, I've gotten that she was playing around with another country music book. This time with the focus more on the male musicians, right?" I asked. "Or at least, that was the original idea."

"Sort of," Gregor said, putting his cappuccino to his lips and waiting for me to continue.

"And that she was getting a little more personal this time. There was more about her family's past."

Gregor put down his cup and scratched at his leprechaun beard. "So you know all about Shelly, I guess?"

"Yeah. She didn't ever keep that a secret. Didn't talk about it much, but it wasn't a secret. And I've read enough to know she was writing a bit about Shelly."

"Shelly and . . . what happened to her," Gregor added. "And who her biological father was. Did you catch on to that?"

"Yes. I read a little bit to that effect, and her agent confirmed it."

"I think the idea with that is that it would fit with the male musician theme. And she was feeling pressure from her publisher to write something that felt like a companion volume to *Tammyland*. Seriously, I don't think she had any daddy issues before she started on this thing. She had her dad. Mr. Waters, I mean. She didn't care about whichever of the punks Shelly knew in high school happened to sire her."

I shrugged. "That's the impression she always gave to me, but it was hard to ever really know what was going on in Gretchen's head. Maybe when she started to research the book, she started to care. Sounds like it."

"Maybe. But in the end, I think she was writing mostly about Frank. You know . . . the guy who killed Shelly. The boyfriend?"

"Right," I said. "Now, what was his last name?"

"Oh, man . . . I actually don't remember. She usually just called him Frank. But I'm sure his name is all over Gretchen's manuscripts. It should be pretty easy to find."

"Is he still in jail?" I asked.

Gregor looked surprised at the question. "No, Jamie. Gretchen never told you? He never went to jail."

"How could that be?"

"Well, the story is that he was partying all night that night, came home in the morning, and found her beaten and bleeding to death. Everyone thinks he made that up, of

127

course. That he beat her up. But just because everyone thought it doesn't mean it stood up in court. The case against him was weak, I guess. There were some odd circumstances that morning. The defense used them to their advantage."

"Jesus," I said. My heart sank a little deeper for Gretchen. Why hadn't she ever told me this? How was it that Mr. Lucky Charms here knew it and I didn't?

"There was something that really bothered her, that she learned about the morning her mother died. Her mother apparently said something as she was dying, to one of the medics or something, that implicated Frank. But it wasn't enough to convict. The last time we really discussed it, that's what she talked about."

Gregor paused for a moment, picking at his lower lip. "Her attitude about Frank was different than with the paternity stuff. It was almost like she found the paternity issue . . . I don't know, *amusing,* almost. But not the Frank stuff. Obviously. Not that."

"There wasn't a chance this Frank guy was her father?" I put my chai down. It was getting a little cold, which made it taste kind of sickening sweet. "Could that have been what disturbed her so much?"

"Uh . . . no." Gregor shook his head. "It

was pretty clear Shelly didn't know Frank till Gretchen was five or six or so. She met him when they both worked at the factory."

"What factory is that?"

"Emerson has a dog-food factory."

"Oh. I didn't know that."

"Yeah, I don't think Frank even grew up in Emerson. I'm pretty sure he moved there later, for the factory work. Gretchen never talked like he was even a possibility."

"Okay," I said. "That's good to hear."

"After a while she kept saying to me that she'd figured out that the real story wasn't about who her father was. The real story was about Frank and what happened that morning with Shelly."

"The real story . . . meaning . . . what she truly wanted to write about?"

"Write about and research, yeah," Gregor explained. "I mean, maybe that's just what she told herself. Cuz the whole father thing was becoming too close or too weird or something."

"So was she gonna somehow write about George Jones and Willie Nelson and those guys along with her mother's death?" I asked.

"Yeah, I don't know how well that theme held up as she got deeper into researching her mother's death. But researching that became her main focus. Kind of an obsession, maybe. For one thing, she was spending all of her time up there in Emerson. But there were other little things. Like, she bought this digital voice recorder. She showed it to me. She said she was starting to use it when she interviewed people. She was convinced she was going to catch someone in a lie, catch someone giving themselves away. And she'd have *proof*."

An uneasy feeling came over me as I thought of the casual P.S. in Gretchen's final e-mail to me: *In your days as a reporter, did you start to develop any skill for telling who is lying to you?*

"Catch someone . . . meaning Frank, I assume? Or someone connected to him?"

Gregor shrugged. "I guess. By then, she was getting kind of short with me in general. I'd stopped asking a lot of questions."

"Where's the voice recorder now?"

"I don't know. I assume her family took it with everything else. If you want to listen to what she got, you ought to ask her brother if he's seen it."

"Yeah . . . I guess I should."

It seemed to me that if Nathan had it, and had any inkling that it was part of Gretchen's project, he'd have given it to me. Maybe, I thought with a start, it was in

Gretchen's purse — the purse she'd supposedly had at the reading and the 7-Eleven but not when they found her.

"Did she play you anything she recorded?" I asked. "Tell you what she got people to say?"

Gregor shook his head. "Not really. She talked to me about it less and less in the last month or so. We were . . . having trouble. She was spending days, sometimes whole weeks, up there in New Hampshire with her aunt Dorothy. I almost got the feeling she was avoiding me."

Gregor hesitated, glanced at me, gulped the dregs of his cappuccino, and then glanced at me again.

"And I think she was talking to Jeremy more."

"Jeremy?" I repeated.

"Yeah. I don't mean like getting back together. Like, I think she liked talking to him more than me. About the book. About what was on her mind. Like he was smarter. Older. Maybe . . . knew her better, really."

"What makes you say that? Did you *hear* them talking?"

"Well, he called the house once or twice. And sometimes I'd hear her talking to someone quietly in the office, with the door closed. I'm not sure it was always him, but once I heard her address him by name. And I heard her saying once, 'Well, this book is going to be very different.' I'd hear her mention Shelly, and Frank . . . but I didn't mean to imply they were getting back together. Nothing like that. It was just a sign to me that she didn't feel close to me anymore — that she felt more like talking to *him*. She was tired of me."

"And you?" I asked. "How did you feel?"

"Me? No, I didn't get tired of her. It was like . . . she just woke up one day and decided I was too young, too naive for her. That she'd kind of run out of things to talk to me about."

Gregor shrugged. "You know, sometimes it seemed like she wasn't actually writing much. I know she was behind on her deadline. But I felt like the book was getting to her, and I'd say so. She didn't like that."

"Getting to her? How's that?"

"Well, it seemed like . . . going backward for her, somehow. Instead of coming up with, you know, a new topic, she was going into this old personal stuff that she'd supposedly put to bed a long time ago. I thought it was making her . . . unhealthy. She was in Emerson all the time. And that was her prerogative . . . whatever. I don't know what she was doing up there. But when she'd come back, she'd sit at her computer for hours, drinking wine while she wrote or . . . whatever she was doing. She'd stay up late. She wasn't eating much. It was like this project was driving her crazy. Spending so much time in that . . . space. Her mother's death. Shelly's death, I mean. And when I tried to talk to her about it . . . to at least say, 'Hey, maybe you need a break from this,' she'd gently push me away. Like, 'Whatevs, Gregor. You don't have anything like this in your life. You don't know what you're talking about.' "

"Would she say that?"

"No. But that was just . . . what it felt like."

"Right," I said. "I see."

"I don't know." He shook his head. "In general, I had thought she was losing her way a little. Wasn't really taking care of herself. And the fall. It was a shock, but part of me knew she'd been sort of . . . out of it lately. It could have been a little alcohol. Or just distraction. I dunno. I should have told her she should be taking better care . . ."

Gregor trailed off. I put my hand out on the table — not to touch him, but still as a gesture of support. I couldn't remember exactly what I'd disliked about him the first time I'd met him. He was a little on the dopey side, but a nice guy in general.

"Gregor, no one ever really told Gretchen what to do. That's not how it worked with her. She would've listened to you quietly and politely thanked you for your concern, and then gone ahead and continued whatever she was doing."

Gregor nodded. He stared into his empty coffee cup for a moment, then leveled his eyes at me. They were a nondistinct green gray, gentle to the point of drooping. I wondered still what Gretchen had seen in them.

"Yeah," Gregor admitted. "Yeah, I know."

CHAPTER 13

"Would You Hold It Against Me?"

Dollywood
Pigeon Forge, Tennessee

I was a hundred feet in the air on the Thunderhead roller coaster this afternoon, staring down at the trees and thinking of Dottie West. Probably I should have been thinking about Dolly. But no. Just as my car hit the top, I shut my eyes tight. My stomach dropped as the coaster went racing toward the ground, but I missed the view. As the car twisted around the ride's remaining curves, I thought, *Dottie West wouldn't close her eyes.* I opened my eyes at the bottom of the drop just so people watching from the ground wouldn't see what a chickenshit I am.

Certainly I had Dottie West on the

brain because I was listening to her in my car on my way to the park. I know I should've been listening to Dolly, but I hit a Dolly-wall when I heard "Me and Little Andy." (Sorry, Dolly — I love you, but I can't stand it when you do that baby voice.) Anyway, I switched to some early Dottie West (her album *Suffer Time*), listening to the title song and "Would You Hold It Against Me?" several times over. Both solid songs from Dottie — more to my old-fashioned taste, I must admit, than the adult contemporary style of her later career.

If you don't know country music outside of the biggest names, you might not know Dottie West. You might not know that she won country music's first Grammy for female vocalist, or that she's known to many as "the first truly liberated woman of country music."

Dottie West (born Dorothy Marie Marsh) grew up in poverty, helping her mother support her nine younger siblings. She endured sexual abuse by her father until she was seventeen, when she finally had enough. She went to the local police and reported him, and eventually testified against him and put him in jail for forty years. Despite all of the struggles, she managed to make it to college. She went to Tennessee Tech, where she studied music and met her first husband, Bill West, a steel-guitar player. By the time they moved to Nashville together, they had three kids (one more would come later). There they pursued their musical dreams together, befriending other aspiring songwriters like Harlan Howard, Hank Cochran, and Willie Nelson. Dottie and her husband often hosted and fed struggling musicians in their home.

In early performances, Dottie dressed in girlish ruffles and gingham and sang relatively demure songs. Like the early country music star Kitty Wells, she exuded the image of a dutiful housewife and mother who just happened to sing a little on the side. Still, in her early years she befriended Patsy Cline, who was breaking the country music gender barriers at the time.

Dottie got her big break in 1964, when her song "Here Comes My Baby" (cowritten with her husband) hit the top ten in the charts and won her a Grammy, leading to a regular spot for her in the Grand Ole Opry. While she continued to perform and produce albums, her sales and chart performances were spotty by the late sixties.

But things changed for Dottie in 1972. She and her husband divorced. Dottie did not waste much time feeling sorry for herself, however. She began dating younger men, much to the shock of the Nashville community. (She eventually married a drummer twelve years her junior, and after she divorced him, a sound engineer twenty-two years her junior — with a number of younger boyfriends in between, according to some.)

Her career took off again. Coca-Cola paid her to write a commercial jingle. She wrote "Country Sunshine," which became a big hit and earned her two Grammy nominations (plus a Cleo Award for the commercial). She began to record with Kenny Rogers, and the pairing proved commercially successful.

By the late seventies, her look and act had changed considerably. She became known for her painted-on spandex outfits and mane of red Farrah Fawcett–style hair. Her songs became more sensual. Dottie, who had famously refused to sing Kris Kristofferson's "Help Me Make It Through the Night" because it was too racy, went ahead and recorded it after her divorce — along with other sexy songs like "She Can't Take My Love Off the Bed." The sexual revolution was very real for Dottie West. While her career and family life before divorce were surely rewarding, she was willing to change with the new times and embrace everything they had to offer.

Her success continued. Her 1980 recording "Lesson in Leavin' " was number one on the country charts. She made appearances on *The Love Boat* and *The Dukes of Hazzard*, and posed for the men's magazine *Oui*.

But it ended rather sadly for Dottie. The hits dried up by the late eighties. Due to overspending and bad investments, Dottie filed for bankruptcy in 1991. She lost her house, and all of her personal possessions were auctioned off to pay back the IRS. That same year, she was in a car wreck that destroyed her Camaro. Her old friend Kenny Rogers gave her a car to use, but it crapped out on her on her way to a Grand Ole Opry appearance. An elderly neighbor saw her by the side of the road in her sparkly performance garb and offered to drive her the rest of the way. He lost control of his car, and Dottie died a few days later from injuries sustained in the accident.

She had plans to make a comeback with a duet album, but hadn't yet started recording it. After she died, a copy of *Women Who Love Too Much* was found on her bedside table, with sections marked for rereading.

I do wish she was in a happier state when it all came to an end, but at least she was on the way to the Opry, and at least she'd had a hell of a run. She'd packed in more after her divorce than most people do in an entire lifetime.

When I say that Dottie West didn't close her eyes, I mean that she allowed her life to change. After her divorce in 1972, she looked forward. She didn't cower in her old life or her old identity. She wasn't afraid of the future's possibilities (and it held so many for her, both richly rewarding and deeply tragic). After my own divorce, I wonder if I really have the nerve to proceed in the same way — to open my eyes both to what I've been *and* what I could be next.

After the Thunderhead ride is over, I get on again and try to keep my eyes open at the top. I fail. A little later, after an elephant ear and a ride on the Dolly-wood Express steam engine, I try again. I do it this time. Eyes open all the way down. It's terrifying. I suddenly have a newfound respect for all of the screaming teenagers around me. They see it this way every time. But of *course* they keep their eyes open for every ride. Because what are we all even here for, if we're going to just shut our eyes the whole time? I wonder how I might be at trying things that way from now on. If I can manage it outside of the magic butterfly gates of Dollywood.

Because I know these things are true: You must try, if the chance comes along, to sing your "Help Me Make It Through the Night." Sing it. Say the thing you've been wanting to say. Ask what you've wanted to ask. Don't worry about people petty enough to hold it against you. Don't try to anticipate how it all will end. Because that's not in your power anyway. So open your mouth. Open your eyes. Love too much. Wear gingham. Wear white spandex pants. Do *everything*.

— *Tammyland*

CHAPTER 14

"The Games Daddies Play"

In Aunt Dorothy's kitchen
Emerson, New Hampshire

I'm told there are two prime
candidates: Keith and Bruce.
Keith was Shelly's real boyfriend most of that year, but
her friends say that she'd
also been running around with
Bruce by the end of the school
year.
Bruce was the brains and
Keith was the brawn. Keith was
a good baseball player who had
to go to summer school every
year. Bruce was good at sci-
ence and math, and helped
Shelly with her trig homework.
That's how she got started

with him. Problem was she maybe didn't know how to stop with Keith before she got started.

My great-aunt Dorothy says there are two types of people in Emerson — the people who leave and the people who don't. (Shelly didn't. My mom, Linda, did. And brought me with her eventually.) Bruce was going places. Keith wasn't going anywhere.

That's how Shelly's close old friends tell it. Keith was one of those people you could just tell was going to stay here his whole life. His father had a plumbing and pipe-fitting business and Keith started working there after he graduated from community college. He pined after my mother long after she broke up with him (which was about three months later than she should have, her friends admit). She even returned to him occasionally for a couple of weeks here and there, and once, a couple of years later, when she was around nineteen and in her wildest, most destructive years — when there was no one else interesting to hang out with.

"Poor Keith," says my mom's old high school friend Diane. "Each time, he thought it was for real."

By the time my mother died at age twenty-four, Keith was happily married to another woman.

I can't tell which guy my mom's friends or Aunt Dorothy think is the one.

They all say I look so much like my mother — a mirror image, practically — that they can't see anyone else in me.

I say to them, "No, you're just saying that. You know."

Only Aunt Dorothy is willing to venture a guess.

"You're smart. You can't write a book if you're not smart."

I don't think this is true. What she means, nonetheless,

is that she's putting in a vote for Bruce. Bruce turned out to be a chemistry professor in southern New Hampshire. So he didn't go too, too far, but he left Emerson, anyhow.

My mom's friends Judy and Diane don't want to say. It could go either way. They think Aunt Dorothy has a point. But they also admit that the timing — and they believe they know a bit more about the timing than Aunt Dorothy would — points more to Keith. Poor Keith, one of them says again. I think that their affection for my mom — I mean Linda, not Shelly — makes them uncomfortable with this conversation. They wish I didn't need to ask. But no, they say, they won't tell her I was asking. They will leave it to me to have that conversation with her. They don't think she knows either.

Shelly just wasn't talking back then. In high school or ever after.

They say they think that Shelly's stubborn silence on the matter was very carefully reasoned: She didn't want to have to marry Keith and she didn't want to keep Bruce from Going Places. And frankly, by the time she was showing, she didn't particularly care for either of them anymore.

And what the hell does this have to do with Conway Twitty? Damned if I know! It's not the daddies playing games in this circumstance.

"Santa Looked a Lot Like Daddy"

Randy's Hot Dogs
Emerson, New Hampshire

Poor Keith proves relatively easy to get in touch with. I know where he lives, I've got his phone number, and Judy's brother's friend has even got his e-mail address. With all of these options available, I decide to take the gentlest approach. I send him an e-mail explaining that I am Shelly's biological daughter, that I'm writing my second book about her to some extent (a bit of a fudge, I guess) and talking with people she knew.

The ladies made him sound dumb, but I imagine he couldn't possibly be dumb enough not to read between the lines.

He responds quickly — within a few hours — to say he'd be happy to talk to me. He remembers my mother fondly and he's seen my book on display in the library and knows Shelly would have been very proud.

He suggests lunch at Randy's, Emerson's famous hot dog joint in a converted gas station. (Unless you're a vegetarian, he writes cautiously.) We're gonna do this real townie style. I'm really excited about this — it's gonna be some good cinematic stuff, meeting your potential biological dad in a hot dog joint.

I arrive early and can't decide what to listen to in the car while I wait. Something thematically appropriate? Like Red Sovine's masterfully cheesy "Giddyup Go"? No, too much. I look frantically through my "Daddy" playlist. (You'd be surprised — well, maybe you wouldn't — how many country songs have the word *daddy* in them.)

I decide on Buck Owens's "Santa Looked a Lot Like Daddy" — a ridiculous choice, to be sure, but it's upbeat and cheerful and it calms my nerves while I sit and tap the wheel and wait for noon to get a little closer. I'm loath to be the weirdo waiting by the tub of famous Randy's relish for her illegitimate father (wait — is he illegitimate? Or just me?). A few repeats in, I'm singing along softly and yelp when someone knocks on my passenger-side window while I'm looking in the other direction.

148

A middle-aged man is peering at me, looking uncertain. He has very tan skin and all-white hair combed back in a way that reminds me of Michael Douglas in *Wall Street*.

It's him. I hope to heaven he didn't hear what I was listening to. Please, please.

When I get out of the car, he tells me he didn't mean to scare me. He'd just recognized me right away.

"You really look so much like her," he says. "It's amazing."

He tries to pay for my dogs. Santa indeed. I don't let him. He's nervous and hesitant and doesn't know what the dining protocol is under these par-ticular circumstances, so he lets me trump his outstretched dollar bills with mine.

There is something Vegas about his appearance, but his manner is cautious and soft-spoken. He says he never met anyone who wrote a whole book before. Without much prompt-ing, he starts in with high school stories about Shelly.

He tells about Shelly scoring the winning goal at a girls' soccer game.

I gobble my first hot dog down while I try to listen, then start on my second. Sports stories bore me to death, even, apparently, when they involve my enchanting mother. I'm distracted by the large sign above his head that says NO DANCING. The sign is memorable to me. It's been here since before Shelly died. She brought me here at least a couple of times when I'd visit. *Why would anyone want to dance in here?* I remember wondering.

Keith feels my distraction and finishes the second story quickly.

He says, "Are you just writing about your mother? Or was there something else you wanted to discuss?"

"Yes," I admit.

I'm surprised by his forwardness. He quickly tells me that

one of my mother's friends told him I was asking.

I'm speechless for a moment. I realize that I had no clue how I'd bring it up and am now grateful to him for doing it. I like him.

"The truth is I don't know for sure. If anyone knew, Shelly did. And I'm not even sure she did."

"There are ways to find out," I say softly, focusing on the nub of my second hot dog.

"Were you interested in finding out?" he asks, and watches me, licking a bit of spicy relish from the corner of his mouth, then waiting, still openmouthed.

"I think so," I say. I hurry to add that it would be simply to know, to set it to rest, that I have a wonderful family who raised me and I don't expect anything of him.

"And I know it's a choice my mother made a long time ago."

I catch myself, realizing I said "my mother" where I meant

Shelly.

He didn't notice. He said he could understand my feeling of wanting to know. And he didn't want to deny me that. As far as expecting anything of him — we could see what happened. If the results were what he suspected they'd be, he'd like to spend a little time getting to know me. If I decided that was all right. Because he'd always wondered. He'd accepted Shelly's choice to stay silent and to grant guardianship to her sister and her sister's husband. They were good people. But he'd always wondered.

I nod and say okay. That we'd have to see.

I listen to "Santa Looked a Lot Like Daddy" a few times on the way back to Aunt Dorothy's.

I like Keith. I'm hoping for him without quite knowing why. He's not what I expected. And that might be kind of nice.

CHAPTER 15

I started mining Gretchen's Word files from Gregor on the following day — Sunday. In all of the files, there were only a couple under the name *Accidentally on Purpose*.

"Damn it, Gretchen!" I said. "How could you leave me hanging like that?"

I tried for files named *My Favorite Lies* — the other title given to me by Gretchen's agent — but found none.

Then I searched all of Gretchen's Word documents for *Keith* and didn't find anything besides what I'd already read. I also tried *Paternity* and *DNA* and still no new files came up.

I glanced over at her crate of notebooks. If Gretchen had gotten a test done, surely she would have written about it. Maybe not typed it in — but written about it, at least. What to do next? Flip through all of her notebooks, scanning for the name "Keith"?

I didn't feel like doing that just now, but

maybe soon.

Giving up on that subject temporarily, I tried her *Recent* documents, just to see what was there. I opened the most recently saved file, which was named *Library Talk 3.*

Thanks for the great introduction, Ruth, and thanks for having me. It's great to still have opportunities to talk about *Tammyland.* Now, I wanted to start with a piece about Tammy Wynette. But before I do, I'd like to talk a little bit about her. People always ask me how a person my age, who never heard any country music growing up, who went to a granola-crunchy liberal-arts college, could possibly become such a big fan of hers. And I always answer . . .

I clicked the file closed. I didn't think Gretchen would want me reading this. There was something embarrassing about it — how self-conscious it was. After all her success and surely about a hundred readings, she was still nervous before a little library book talk.

The next file was called *Emerson 1985.* It contained only these lines:

YOU TURNED OUT PRETTY

SMART. SMARTER THAN I THOUGHT YOU WOULD.

And then, underneath that:

Dr. Henry Platt — Pediatrician at
Emerson Pediatric
Group — Died 1984
Replaced by Dr. Katherine Wright —
1986

I paused there for a moment, finding the file's brevity and incongruous contents unsettling. Then I closed it and opened the third-most-recent document, which was called *Tracy Draft Letter.*

Dear Tracy,
I apologize for my late response on this.
I am sorry to have to tell you that I am far from finishing *My Favorite Lies*, in no small part because I am having a personal family crisis. I am not in a position to rush to the finish line at the moment. I hope we can work something out — like postponing my pub date.

Respectfully,
Gretchen

Personal family crisis? Was it true? Or just

Gretchen trying to buy herself more time? Based on her most recent Word documents, it felt like not a great deal of actual writing was going on. The addition of *personal* to *family crisis* smacked a little of desperation. I checked the date on the document. About a week before Gretchen died. I wondered if she'd actually brought herself to e-mail this.

I switched to her e-mail account and signed in easily as Gregor had instructed me.

I searched the account for *Tracy*. The most recent message was from Tracy:

Dear Gretchen,

I really need to know the status of *My Favorite Lies*. Bonnie's talking cancellation of contract if we don't give her something. I'm sure we can work this out, but we need communication from you.

I don't want to alarm you, but I do need to hear from you. Call me when you get this. I will be up till eleven at least — you can call me anytime you get in.

I hope everything is all right.

All best,
Tracy

That was about two and a half weeks before Gretchen's death. As far as I could tell, Gretchen had not replied.

I returned to her recent e-mails and glanced through them, starting with the day she died. There wasn't much that day besides junk mail and a last-minute confirmation with the librarian, who promised to provide wine and cheese. I wondered how much wine Gretchen had had after her talk — on top of her likely prereading drink. I sighed and looked at the previous few days' e-mails. A friendly e-mail from an old coworker, asking Gretchen what was new. Something from a book club in Florida. A couple of days before that:

Hey Gretchen,

Are you coming up to Emerson again this weekend? The spring carnival is happening Fri-Sun. Interested in coming along with me? Some real townie culture there that I thought you'd like to soak up for your book!

Cheers,
Kevin

Of course, I didn't know who Kevin was, but obviously he was some guy she'd met during her research trips to Emerson. I wondered how old he was, and if he had any connection to her research. And I was always wary of people who signed their e-mails with "Cheers." I scanned Gretchen's recent e-mails for more correspondences with him.

Two weeks earlier he'd written: *Really great to see you again. Let me know the next time you're in town — would love to talk to you again.*

I didn't see anything else recent. When I did a search of all of her e-mails, I found only one more — a much more formal one, from about six weeks earlier:

Dear Ms. Waters,

I'd be happy to speak with you. Tuesdays and Thursdays after six work best for me, but if it must be on a weekend, let me know and maybe we can work something out.

Kevin Conley

His note was a response to a similarly formal one from Gretchen, stating that she was researching Shelly Brewer's murder and requesting an interview with him. I scribbled down Kevin Conley as a possible contact.

Looking again at her more recent e-mails,

I saw that Gretchen had also been in touch with Jeremy about a week before her fall.

I'm glad you called me, Jeremy had written. *Thanks for letting me know. I don't know how I feel about it, but I'm glad you let me know. I'm glad to hear you're making headway with your book.*

There's still a lot of time to work something out, Gretchen had replied. *We'll talk again.*

How odd, I thought, that Gretchen was ignoring her agent's e-mails but meanwhile giving Jeremy the impression that her book was going well. Maybe it was just pride — wanting her ex to think her life was going swimmingly. Or maybe she was telling him something about the book others didn't know — Gregor had certainly suspected as much.

I wrote a quick e-mail to Jeremy, explaining to him a little about the situation — how I'd recently gotten Gretchen's manuscripts and files from Mrs. Waters and Gregor — and saying I'd like to chat with him soon, as we'd discussed.

Then I went back to Gretchen's e-mail account and searched for *Judy* and *Diane*. It seemed they were experts on Keith and Bruce and the paternity question, so I figured they ought to be useful. Gretchen had had some e-mail communication with

Judy. Most recently, Judy had written to Gretchen:

Hi Gretchen, When are you coming to Emerson next? Would love to see you again, have you for dinner if you're not too busy! Been missing you! Diane tells me she saw you at Subway. I didn't even know you were here last weekend. I hope you are well and making great progress on your book. Judy

Before that, Judy and Gretchen's communication had been brief and conversational, usually regarding Gretchen's comings and goings in Emerson, invitations to meet for coffee or have meals at Judy's.

I copied Judy's e-mail address into my own laptop and wrote her a message, introducing myself as Gretchen's friend, explaining that I'd been asked to get Gretchen's manuscripts in order and would like to chat with her about Gretchen's recent "research." (I didn't know what else to call it.) I gave her my cell number and asked her to call me if she was willing to talk. Then I did the same for Kevin Conley.

Sam knocked on the door as I was finishing up the message. His basketball game was apparently over.

"What's up, Madhat?" he asked. I hadn't heard this nickname in weeks, maybe months. There was a lightness to his step, a little smile on his lips. His team must've won.

"Oh . . . just trying to figure out what was going on with Gretchen. Just like yesterday."

"Anything new?"

I tossed the notebook onto the floor.

"Not really," I said. "Although she was apparently chatting it up with Jeremy lately."

"Jeremy? Really? That's weird."

"Kind of, yeah. I'm gonna write to him and get the scoop on that."

"Well, tell him I said hi. Um, anyway. I was thinking. You want to go shopping?"

"For what?"

"You mentioned a couple of weeks ago a baby registry, or something?"

"Oh. I forgot about that." "A couple of weeks ago" meant "before Gretchen died."

"Your mother just sent me an e-mail. She and some of your friends are cooking up some shower plans. I don't think I'm telling anything I'm not supposed to by saying that. I think they think I'm a bad guy for not making you do it sooner. Probably we should go now. Or tonight."

I glanced at Gretchen's notebooks, and then back at Sam. I didn't want to pull

161

myself away from Gretchen for Babies "R" Us. It's not that I didn't want my son to have a Björn or a swing or a hemp layette set. Maybe it was presumptuous of me to think so, but I was pretty certain he'd be okay without them.

"Well, right now I'm kind of busy," I said, staring at Gretchen's open e-mail account.

"Please, Jamie."

I looked up at him, startled by the pleading in his voice.

"Last time we went to Babies 'R' Us, I couldn't get my head to stop spinning. I left feeling like I'd just ridden a pink-and-baby-blue Gravitron for an hour or two."

"Gravitron?"

"You know . . . that amusement-park ride that spins you around and you stick to the wall?"

"Yeah. And the floor drops out?"

"Yeah. That's the one."

"Maybe that's how new parenthood is supposed to feel," Sam said. "Like the floor's dropping out."

"I wouldn't know," I said, closing my laptop. "Not really being a new parent yet. But that's very poetic."

"Yup." Sam rubbed his eyes. "Your mom is about ready to come here and drag you out to the mall herself. She's forty-eight hours away from that, I swear to you."

I sat up and shrugged, not quite ready to pull myself off the bed.

"It'll be fun. We'll run around the store with that little magic wand, scan a diaper pail, a high chair. Whatever looks good. Then bring back anything we change our minds about. No pressure."

I stood up. "Okay. Just give me a second to find something to wear."

CHAPTER 16

Judy called me on Monday while I was on my way to work.

"I'm sorry I didn't get back to you sooner," she said. "I don't check e-mail all that often. Now, did we meet at the funeral?"

"I don't think so. I'm . . . uh . . . short and pregnant?"

"Oh. I guess I saw you, but we didn't actually talk. Anyway, I'm happy to help."

She sounded warm and eager to please, just as Gretchen had described her. After we both stated several times how sorry we were, I started to ask her about all of the time Gretchen had been spending in Emerson lately.

"Oh, quite a bit. She usually stayed with Dorothy. I mean, her great-aunt Dorothy — Linda and Shelly's mom's sister. Spent a lot of time at all the local spots — the doughnut shop and Randy's Dogs and the playground."

"I see. Uh, Randy's Hot Dogs . . . that's where she met this Mr. Keith . . . Mr. Keith . . . um, I don't know his last name, but he was one of Shelly's boyfriends?"

Judy hesitated. I wondered if I'd made a mistake. She sounded approachable, but I was probably jumping into the personal details a little too quickly.

"She told you about that?" Judy asked.

"Well. No." I struggled to keep my phone at my ear as I turned on my blinker. "I read about it. I haven't read all of her work — it's kind of a mess. But I did read a little about Keith."

"Oh. Oh, okay. That makes sense. Of course she wrote about him."

"I read about her first meeting with him, but . . ." I stopped at a red light. "But I'm not finding any writing about what happened with that. If they did a test after that, she didn't write about it. As far as I can tell yet."

"Oh, dear." Judy paused again. "Well, I know that Keith's test turned out negative. Gretchen didn't share that with me, but I heard it from my friend Nancy, who happens to be very close to Keith's wife. It wasn't a shock to me. It had really seemed fifty-fifty, back then. But I think Gretchen was thrown for a loop. I think maybe we'd given her the idea that he was likely the one. Or it was that when she met him, she liked him. So she got attached to the idea that it was him. Maybe she didn't know what to write when it didn't turn out how she wanted?"

"Maybe," I said. "And what happened after she found out it wasn't him? I mean, writing aside, what did she do next? Did she move on to the other guy?"

"Well, I know that the next logical step was to go after Bruce. But she never talked about doing that. Or talked about it at all. It was like she was embarrassed how things worked out with Keith and didn't want to talk about it anymore. Maybe started to think it was a bad idea. Or maybe, now that it was certain to be Bruce, she was afraid of meeting him and disliking him. I felt like the experience with Keith maybe soured her on the whole thing."

"Uh-huh," I said.

The driver behind me honked, and I stepped on the gas.

"I'm not sure. She wasn't as . . . gung ho . . . when she found out about Keith. She got a lot quieter about the father issue. Didn't ask me and Diane and Dorothy about it so much after that. At least, not me

166

and Diane. Maybe Dorothy. She was closer to her."

"I see. Did you know Bruce at all?" I asked.

Judy let out a long breath. "Um . . . not all that well. Diane knew him a little better. You may want to ask her about him."

"I see. Well, anyway, it feels like the story sort of stops after Keith. At least, the part about trying to find who the biological father was."

"Hmm. Not a huge surprise. To be honest, I wasn't sure about what she was doing, writing about all of that. It seemed like it could be . . . harmful. Maybe she started to feel that way herself." Judy sighed. "You know, you really ought to come up here and talk with Gretchen's aunt Dorothy. She and Gretchen were getting pretty close during this whole thing. Dorothy's devastated, of course. But she's getting better by the day, and I'm sure she'd love to meet you — a friend of Gretchen's. I think it might be a comfort to her to know you're handling her work . . . that you care enough to do that for Gretchen."

"Of course," I said. "Well, if you don't think it would be too much of an imposition on Dorothy, I'd love to go up and talk with her."

"She's in her eighties, but she's quite sharp. You can't contact her on e-mail or anything. But I drop in on her every few days. How about I mention it to her, so you don't have to call her cold? That'd be better, because she's a little hard of hearing, and if she doesn't immediately recognize your voice, she'll think you're selling something and hang up. She's done that to me before."

"Um . . . okay," I said, turning into the newspaper parking lot.

"Yeah. That's what I'll do. And I'll call you back. If you're coming up here, you and I can talk a little more in person, too. If you'd like."

"Sure," I said.

"You let me know when you'd want to make the trip."

"How about next weekend? Saturday?"

"That should work," Judy said. "But I'll check with Dorothy."

"Sure. Okay."

After we'd hung up, I stared up at the brown brick of the newspaper building, with its neat rows of black windows. I remembered how I used to arrive in this parking lot in the late afternoons and evenings the first couple of years I was a reporter — always armed with a notebook and eager to pound out a story for the deadline. Or to get on the phone and ask a few more questions. Back then, it never used to cross my mind to linger in my car, or to dread going inside.

When I got home that night, I greeted my half-conscious husband with a peck on the cheek and then went rummaging through Gretchen's notebooks again, scanning for the name "Bruce" and words like *DNA* or *paternity* — just as I'd done with the Word file searches.

About three notebooks in, I came across a bright green plastic folder, unlabeled. It didn't contain Gretchen's usual Times New Roman printouts.

The first paper inside said *Emerson Police Department* at the top, followed by a bunch of boxes filled out by hand: a few inexplicable numbers, then an address (78 Durham Road, Emerson) and a date (3/10/85).

This was the police report from the day Shelly was killed. I skipped down to the narrative section.

At approximately 0825 hours, Officer James Dolan and Officer Nicolas Valenti responded to a call about a domestic incident and a gravely injured female at 78 Durham Road, home of Shelly Brewer and Frank Grippo.

We were met in the driveway by Laurie Wiley, who had placed one of the two 911 calls received by dispatch regarding this incident. She led us into the house, explaining that she had awoken to Frank Grippo's screams earlier in the morning. When she'd rushed outside, Grippo was already in his yard, screaming that someone had beaten Ms. Brewer and she needed an ambulance. According to Ms. Wiley, Mr. Grippo claimed to have discovered Ms. Brewer when he arrived home from a friend's house. After encountering Ms. Wiley, Mr. Grippo rushed to 90 Durham Road to request the assistance of Dr. George Skinner while Ms. Wiley called 911. (Mr. Grippo also called 911 upon returning to his home with the doctor.)

When we entered the house, we found Shelly Brewer on the living room floor, with large amounts of blood surrounding her on the carpet. She was not conscious. Her head injury was wrapped in towels and Dr. Skinner was speaking softly to her, pressuring a wound on the side of her head. Officer Dolan requested Crime Scene to respond to the location.

Frank Grippo was also present in the room. He was yelling at Dr. Skinner to do something. Mr. Grippo also stated that he was going to kill the person who did this to his girlfriend. Officer Valenti stayed with Ms. Brewer and Dr. Skinner while Officer Dolan brought Mr. Grippo into the kitchen in an attempt to calm him and ask him what had happened. Mr. Grippo said that he had come home at approximately 8:10 a.m. to find Shelly lying unconscious in her blood. He attempted to wake her but was unsuccessful. He had wrapped her head tightly with a tablecloth but then run to his neighbor, Dr. Skinner, for assistance.

Shortly after our arrival, at approximately 0835 hours, ambulance 42 arrived, which removed Ms. Brewer from the scene and transported her to St. Theresa's Hospital.

At this point, Mr. Grippo became violent, slamming cabinets and throwing dishes around the kitchen. Officer Dolan attempted to subdue Mr. Grippo verbally and Officer Valenti called for backup, as well as his supervisor, asking that he contact the New Hampshire Crime Scene Investigation Unit.

Officer Valenti then began to secure the crime scene by requesting Dr. Skinner to exit the house and wait in the driveway.

Officer Valenti then assisted Officer Dolan in the kitchen, telling Grippo that they would have to remove him from the house in handcuffs if he did not leave the home willingly. Grippo complied. Officer Valenti began to question him outdoors while Officer Dolan began securing the home with tape.

The details were unsettling. It hadn't felt real — this murder of Gretchen's biological mother, so many years ago — when Gretchen mentioned it offhand, as if it had been nothing. I wondered how many of these details she knew before she'd started researching.

The police report was followed by a series of newspaper articles from 1985 and 1986, describing Frank Grippo's arrest and trial and finally his acquittal. Shelly had died shortly after she arrived at the hospital, and Grippo was charged with her murder soon afterward. The final article summed up the case:

LACONIA DAILY NEWS
April 24, 1986

VERDICT DUE TODAY IN EMERSON MURDER TRIAL

172

LACONIA, NH - After four days of testimony in district court, jurors are expected to deliver a verdict later today in the murder trial of Frank Grippo, 29, of Emerson.

According to prosecutors, Grippo brutally killed his girlfriend, Shelly Brewer, 24, last March 10, 1985. Grippo claims that he returned home at approximately eight o'clock that morning, after a night of drinking, to find Brewer already bludgeoned by her own clothes iron, but still alive. He immediately contacted a doctor in the neighborhood and called 911.

The case for the prosecution rests on witness testimony that Grippo arrived home at least two hours earlier than he had told police, and that he and Brewer had been fighting over an alleged affair she had been having. Prosecutors have also focused on the testimony of Dr. George Skinner, who said he heard Brewer make statements implicating Grippo in her final moments. They've also highlighted a suspicious roll of $3,000 in cash that police found in Grippo's pocket that morning.

The defense has argued that Grippo couldn't have killed Brewer because he was at a friend's house when she was attacked. And they have also stressed a lack of physical evidence against Grippo, and sought to establish that Brewer had several other enemies who had motive to hurt her.

Key elements of testimony:

- **Arguments & Infidelity** — Neighbors and friends testified that Grippo and Brewer had been fighting in the weeks leading to Brewer's death, and several of them suspected domestic violence. Two of her friends testified that she was seeing Phil Coleman, a pharmacist for whom she worked at the time of her death. And three of Grippo's coworkers told the court that he complained angrily about Brewer's alleged affair.

- **Grippo's Alibi** — Two of Frank Grippo's friends, Bill Carnell and Steven Beaudette, testified that he was with them the night before the murder. Two patrons of the bar they attended and a waitress confirmed that he had been there until 2 A.M. Grippo then passed out on Carnell's couch, and Carnell's wife, Patty, testified that she saw him leave just before 8 A.M. But Brewer's friend and neighbor Diane Skinner (daughter of Dr. Skinner) testified that she saw Grippo's car in Brewer's driveway shortly after 5:45 A.M. during her morning jog. A twelve-year-old paperboy also reported to police that he saw Grippo's parked car at approximately 7 A.M.

- **Crime Scene** — Forensic detectives and the coroner concluded that Brewer was killed due to several strikes to the head made by her own clothes iron. The assailant had apparently wiped the weapon clean before leaving it on the kitchen counter. Additionally, police found trace amounts of the victim's blood in the bathroom sink, suggesting that the assailant had cleaned up after himself before leaving the house.

- **Brewer's Final words** — Dr. Skinner, who arrived at the scene shortly before the police, testified that while he was attempting to stop Brewer's bleeding, she said to Grippo, "I can't forgive you. I can't." The prosecution argued that this statement indicated Grippo's guilt.

- **Other Suspects?** — The defense argued that Brewer

had several enemies who could've been responsible for her death. Her friend Melanie Rittel testified that around 1981 Brewer had developed a cocaine habit. She owed a great deal of money to one particular dealer with whom she'd had a sexual relationship, and indicated she had been worried about him coming after her, Rittel said. She also described three other failed relationships Brewer had with men in the last five years, two of whom were married. Meanwhile, detectives found fingerprints on the kitchen counter and bathroom sink and doorknob that did not match Brewer's, Grippo's, Dr. Skinner's — or those of anyone else who had been known to be in her house in the preceding days.

- **Roll of Cash** — Throughout the trial, the prosecution raised questions about the $3,000 police found in Grippo's pocket — wadded in a roll and fastened with a hair elastic. Grippo claimed that he had seen the cash on Brewer's front hall table when he'd first entered her house that morning. He testified that he called out to Brewer, asking where the money had come from, and when he received no answer, he walked into the house to find her bleeding on the living room carpet. At that point he rushed to attend to her and did not recall putting the money in his pocket. The prosecution suggested that Grippo was intending to flee after killing Brewer. The defense argued that the money indicated some foul play on someone else's part, perhaps someone who owed Brewer money or someone who came to Brewer demanding a larger sum, and beat her when she couldn't offer more.

I closed the folder. How much of this had Gretchen known for years? I wondered. Had anything in this report shocked her? How much had she learned just recently? And what did she think happened? None of her writing so far gave much indication.

CHAPTER 17

84 Durham Road
Emerson, New Hampshire

"Shelly had a tired face for her age," says Laurie Wiley, Shelly's neighbor at the time of her death.

Shelly had moved back to the Durham Road neighborhood in 1983 (renting the house from an old family friend of the Brewers, as her mother had since moved to a small apartment). Laurie — who was relatively new to the neighborhood herself at the time — had heard some unflattering things about Shelly before she moved in, but found none of those things to be true. Shelly had clearly made some mistakes in her youth and had suffered as a result of them.

Laurie felt bad for Shelly — she could imagine it was hard for her working at the factory, and then the pharmacy, while all of her old friends in town were getting their first real jobs, planning their weddings, starting their real lives. But Shelly was clearly trying — woke up early for work every day, kept her yard up nice, even made a couple of attempts at being neighborly. She helped Laurie catch her runaway beagle once. She also befriended Laurie's teenage niece, Rachel, who was often babysitting Laurie's two-year-old son during the hours Shelly was home from work. Shelly and Rachel would sometimes take walks together, with Shelly helping with the unruly beagle. Laurie admits that Rachel actually talked to Shelly more than she or her husband ever did.

"Shelly really loved Carington," Laurie informs me, and I have to suppress a smile at the late hound dog's name.

Laurie was not in the room when Shelly spoke her last words. She was not, in fact, in the room for more than about thirty seconds that morning. She only got a glimpse of Shelly and then left the house, because the scene shocked her and she had a tendency to pass out at the sight of blood. She seems uncomfortable saying much about it to me — but yes, Frank Grippo knocked on her door that morning, and yes, she was one of the people who called 911. Frank called and she called.

Laurie was never sure about that Frank Grippo — from the very beginning. He moved in quickly after Shelly's last boyfriend, Winston Roland, moved out. He was a little gruff, but he seemed helpful to Shelly. He did lots of yard work, took the garbage to the dump every week, even seemed to cook for Shelly quite often, according to Rachel.

When Laurie would run into him, however, she found his manner unsettling.

"Something was always sarcastic about it. He could pass you gardening in your yard and say, 'Nice tulips,' in a way that was so . . . so snide, sort of, you weren't sure if you should thank him or spit at him."

And he seemed to drink a lot on weekends, but that was really none of her business.

"I did wonder how it was for you the weekends you were visiting, but it appeared that Shelly managed."

Worrisome, however, was that Laurie and her husband, Nelson, both heard Shelly and Frank fighting fairly frequently, especially in the weeks just before Shelly's murder. She says she doesn't know what they were fighting about, although she heard

Frank once say, "I know what you're up too, you little bitch," which alarmed her.

"It was really nasty, really bitter. I worried about her. Although — she always fought back. I heard her reply, 'No you don't, you stupid asshole.' "

She says at that point she did wonder if it was really the best idea for her young and impressionable niece to spend much time with Shelly.

"Rachel even said to me once, 'I don't know if that Frank guy is very nice to Shelly.' That kind of made me wonder — what she was taking in. And then when Shelly was killed, my God. We were all in shock, but Rachel was so young."

Laurie takes in a breath after she says this, realizing it is an error to say this to me. Her teenage niece was young. But I was younger.

"I'm sorry," she says.

CHAPTER 18

Dorothy MacKintosh's house was a tiny white Cape with cheerful green shutters and a side porch. As I got out of the car, I caught sight of a sign in the front lawn that said IF YOUR DOG POOPS, YOU SCOOP above a drawing of a squatting dog. I recoiled slightly. I've always found signs that reference dog poop a smidge more unsightly than dog poop itself.

I rang the bell and was greeted — after a couple of minutes — by a massive woman with tight white curls and drawn-on eyebrows.

"Hi . . . I'm Jamie Madden."

"Yeah, I figured. I'm Dorothy. What time is it?"

"Um . . . about two-thirty?"

"Come on in," Dorothy said, opening the door for me.

"Okay," I said, stepping into the covered porch, which smelled like lilac and baked ham. "Is Judy here?"

"No. Not yet. Judy's always late." Dorothy led me into a cramped kitchen with a worn wooden floor and brown appliances. There was a waddle to her walk, but she moved surprisingly quickly.

"How many months are you?" she asked, pulling out a chair for me.

"Seven," I said, sitting.

"Boy or girl, do you know?"

"Boy," I said.

With some difficulty, she settled in her own chair. "Ah. That's nice. Or did you want a girl first, hon?"

"I honestly wasn't hoping one way or another for the first. Next time — if there is a next time — I imagine I'll want a girl to even things out."

Dorothy nodded. "It's nice to meet a friend of Gretchen's. I'd only started to get to know her, but I miss her."

For some reason, hearing an elderly relative of Gretchen's say this was harder than thinking it myself. I opened my mouth to say "I miss her, too," but was afraid my voice would crack.

"Yeah," I squeaked.

Dorothy studied my face.

"I like your eye makeup," she said. "Is that supposed to be like Cleopatra?"

"I guess," I said, so startled that my tears receded.

"I haven't seen that look in a while. Is it coming back?"

"I don't know," I replied. "It's what I like."

Dorothy nodded. "Can't I get you something to drink? Coffee? Tea?"

"Tea would be great," I said, then regretted it because it meant she'd have to haul herself up again.

"Can't I help you?" I asked, standing as she did.

"Nope," Dorothy said, putting a kettle on to boil. "So Judy says you're a writer, too. You gonna finish Gretchen's book for her?"

"I don't think I could finish something so personal," I said. "I don't think anyone could. I'm just trying to see if we can put together what she had."

"You write any books?"

"I'm not that kind of writer. I was a reporter for about seven years. A health reporter for the last couple. Now I'm a copy editor."

"An editor. That's higher than a writer, huh?"

"Sometimes. Not in my case. There were cutbacks and they moved me to a part-time position, at the copy desk."

There was a knock on the porch door.

"Hellooooo?" said an upbeat female voice.

Two middle-aged women let themselves in. One was heavyset and red-cheeked with black hair that had a dramatic streak of white in the front. The other was tall and muscular, with soft blond-red curls framing her pale face in a puffy, outdated haircut, parted in the middle.

"Oh, good," Dorothy muttered, in a tone that reminded me of Gretchen: either perfect sarcasm or poorly expressed enthusiasm. "The girls are here."

Judy and Diane were very much as Gretchen described them: a couple of warm, well-meaning middle-aged ladies who seemed to have a great deal to say about Gretchen's mother, and now, sadly, about Gretchen herself.

"I have to admit, I thought it probably for the best that Gretchen didn't go after Bruce," said Judy, the plump one with the white streak. "I had a feeling that wouldn't go well."

Diane lifted the Saran Wrap from a plate of oatmeal cookies she'd brought. "Now, I don't know if that's fair. Bruce has always been a reasonable guy."

"But that son of his . . . he's had a lot on his plate. To just have Gretchen show up like that . . . not what he needed at the moment."

"What's this about his son?" Diane said. "I don't know what you're talking about."

"He's troubled. Into drugs." Judy broke off a quarter of one of the cookies and put it delicately into her mouth. "Suspended for dealing dope at the high school down there in Williamsburg."

"What was Bruce's last name?" I asked, my pen poised in the little notebook I'd brought along.

"Doherty," Diane supplied. "He's a chemistry professor now at UNH."

"Uh-huh. So to your knowledge, Gretchen never asked him to do a test?"

The ladies looked at each other, uncertain.

"No." Dorothy helped herself to a cookie and gestured for me to do the same. "I think she would've told me if she did."

"Makes sense," I said, breaking my cookie in half. "Gretchen's writing — at least the typed, polished stuff — seems to trail off after she found out it . . . uh . . . wasn't Keith."

"Kind of a shame," Judy said. "I think for a long time Keith wanted it to be him. Sweet of him, really."

"So when Gretchen would come up here these last few months, she was talking to

189

you three, talking to Keith and some of Shelly's other old boyfriends . . ." I hesitated for a moment. "Um, and Frank. The man named Frank? Do you think she ever talked to him?"

Dorothy took in a breath. Judy and Diane glanced at each other.

"If she did," Judy said, smoothing her hair behind her ear, "she wouldn't have told us. We would've told her to steer clear. My God. Did anything in her writing indicate that she did?"

Diane stared at me, waiting for an answer. Noticing a large cookie crumb stuck to her brown lipstick, I looked away.

"I haven't searched her files for that specifically," I said quickly. "Not yet. So, he's still around here?"

"Not in Emerson," Judy said. "But in Plantsville, which is just down Route 7. He lives with his brother. He's real sick these days, I hear. I'm not sure what it is."

"Probably liver disease," Dorothy added.

"I'm just assuming Gretchen had a lot of questions for a lot of different people," I said.

"Some," Judy replied. "She talked to her mom's old neighbors, one of the police officers who was there . . . and Diane's dad one time, too."

"Your dad?" I asked

Diane nodded.

"Yes," Judy put in for her. "Dr. Skinner. I'm sure you saw his name in Gretchen's notes."

"Oh . . . of course."

Dr. Skinner's daughter — the one mentioned in the article about her trial — had been named Diane. I just hadn't made the connection since her last name was, according to Gretchen's writing, now DeShannon.

"So your dad was actually at the scene of Shelly's murder right after it happened," I said, turning to Diane.

She wiped her mouth, removing the cookie crumb.

"Yes. Before she died, actually. When Frank came home that morning, he went screaming up the road. First went to my dad, because he's a doctor, and because he was so close. Which was a little odd . . . why not call 911? Then Shelly's neighbors, Nelson and Laurie Wiley, heard all the noise, and Laurie Wiley came over to see what was going on."

I nodded, remembering the name "Wiley" from the police report.

"So your dad — along with Laurie Wiley — was one of the few people who could give Gretchen a first-person account."

"Right," Diane said. "Although I don't know how helpful he could've been to her. He can easily switch between talking about the day he tried to save Shelly and the next sentence be talking about the day Amy Vaughn got hit by a car."

Diane finished her cookie before continuing. "He can't always follow the conversation so well since he's middle-stage Alzheimer's. My mother tells me Dad really enjoyed talking to Gretchen. I didn't know till after Gretchen had done it that they'd talked, or I would've come along and helped her. Talking to him can be a little frustrating."

"George isn't just a doctor," Dorothy piped up. "He's a talented fiddle player, too."

"Or *was*," Diane corrected her. "He's lost a lot of that with the Alzheimer's. But yes, I believe he and Gretchen talked about music some."

"So does he even remember the day Shelly died?" I asked.

"I wasn't there the day Gretchen spoke to him," Diane said. "I imagine it would all depend on if he were having a good day or a bad day. Chances are their talk wasn't that useful to her."

"Is he in a, um, convalescent home?"

"No," Diane said softly. "Still in the house where I grew up. My mother takes care of him."

She lowered her gaze and contemplated her plate of cookies. I felt tactless for pressing on the topic.

"And you, of course . . . she talked to you about being a witness in the case, also?"

Diane nodded. "Oh. Yes. Of course. Did she write about that, too?"

"Not that I've found yet, but there are some articles in her files that mention it. About Frank's car. You and the paperboy."

"Oh, yes," Judy said, shaking her head. "Not that it made much difference. Diane was Shelly's good friend, so her account wasn't taken as seriously as maybe it should've been. And Kevin was underage, so —"

"Kevin?" I repeated.

"Yes. The paperboy. I know his mother. Kevin Conley."

I took a sip of cold tea, trying to hide my surprise. Kevin Conley — the guy with whom Gretchen had recently become friendly via e-mail.

"Um. So Gretchen probably wanted to talk to him, too, I imagine," I said.

I knew the answer to that, but was curious how much the ladies knew about Kevin —

and about Gretchen's apparent friendship with him.

"I'm not sure," Judy said. "Maybe. She mentioned him once, but I don't know if she followed through. His testimony basically just corroborated Diane's.''

She glanced at Diane, who nodded in agreement.

I decided to leave the Kevin Conley question for the moment, since the ladies didn't seem to know anything else about Gretchen's contact with him. After that, the conversation turned a bit lighter. The ladies started talking about their memories of Gretchen from when she'd visit as a little girl, and significantly less frequently, after Shelly died.

Judy told a story about how Shelly once brought Gretchen to a museum in Vermont that had a display of antique toys and dolls. And then Gretchen turned around the following weekend and arranged all of her dolls in a dirty old fish tank and tried to charge everyone fifty cents apiece for a look.

"She even put a sign outside in the yard — 'Doll Museum — Fifty Cents.' She'd stand there with that sign, waving cars down, trying to get people to fork over cash to look at her half-naked Barbie dolls piled in a fish tank.''

"I remember that," added Diane. "Smart kid."

As they talked, it struck me how different Judy and Diane seemed in person than in Gretchen's piece about them; she'd made them sound like sisters in gossip — gabbing, finishing each other's sentences. But Judy was the real chatterbox. Diane seemed more tactful and thoughtful. I wondered if Gretchen had deliberately altered their dynamic to make her account of their conversation more entertaining.

Eventually, the ladies talked about how odd it was to see Gretchen after she'd spent so many years away. After Gretchen's grandmother — Dorothy's sister — died when Gretchen was around thirteen, Linda never brought Gretchen around, and they never saw her again — until recently. It felt very strange, said Judy, to have her suddenly appear: a thirty-two-year-old divorcée and best-selling author, asking lots of tough questions about Shelly.

"But the most startling thing about it," added Judy, "was how much she looked like Shelly. I swear I almost fainted the first time she showed up at my door. But then the moment she opened her mouth, you knew this was no ghost. So strange, a spitting image, but then the personality, so different."

"How so?" I asked.

"Don't take this the wrong way . . ." said Judy. "It's a good thing. But compared to Shelly, Gretchen was, like, an intellectual."

"She seemed kind of WASPy at first," Dorothy offered.

"*Dorothy*," Diane said, shaking her head a little, but smiling.

"I mean, not once you got to know her," Dorothy said quickly. "That was just my first thought the first day we talked. And I thought, wow, Linda's done a good job making this girl into the perfect opposite of her mother. So . . . quiet. So . . . careful."

Careful. The word stuck in my head for a few minutes, distracting me as the women reminisced about what a free spirit Shelly had been. *Careful* was a good word for Gretchen. I just wasn't sure it had applied to her in her final few weeks.

CHAPTER 19

After the younger women left, Dorothy asked me if I'd stay for dinner.

"I couldn't . . ." I said. "You don't need to make me anything."

"Oh, it's already prepared," Dorothy said. "I was planning on it. And I'm not going to let a pregnant woman walk away from my house hungry."

She opened the refrigerator, took out a casserole dish, and set it on the table.

"It's called a chicken and spinach bake. It's actually pretty healthy, if that matters to you. Gretchen liked it. I use some of the Cajun spice. Do you like the Cajun spice?"

"Sure," I said. "I like Cajun spice."

"Does that mean you'll stay?"

"Yes. Thank you."

"Good." Dorothy turned on her oven and quickly pushed the dish into it with a clatter. "It doesn't take too long to warm up. And I've made a little fruit salad for dessert."

"Sounds great. You didn't need to go to any trouble, though."

"I like to keep busy. That's what I was always trying to explain to Gretchen."

I nodded. As if to demonstrate her point, Dorothy set a fork, knife, and napkin at each of our places and then fetched some cups from a cabinet.

"Something to drink?" she said, pouring herself some root beer.

"I'll get myself some water," I said, getting up and going to the tap. Her sudden burst of activity was making me uncomfortable. It seemed to have been set off by the younger ladies' departure.

"I'm glad you stayed," Dorothy said, once she finally settled at the kitchen table. "You and I have some things to talk about."

"We do?" I replied.

"Judy and Diane don't need to know everything."

"Uh-huh," I said. I was surprised to hear this. Judy and Diane seemed like the kind of women who found out everything eventually.

"They'd like to know, but they don't need to know." Dorothy took a gulp of her root beer and licked her lips. "Gretchen and I were just starting to get a little close. And to be honest with you, I don't know how hard she was working on that book of hers."

"Yeah . . . I don't know either."

Dorothy sipped her soda again, and then her gaze met mine. Her eyes were like small, dark marbles buried in all her soft wrinkles.

"She said to me . . . 'I don't know where the idea comes from, that if you write one good book, the very next thing you have to do with your life is write another.' And I asked her, well, great idea or not, aren't they paying you a lot to do it?"

"And what did she say to that?"

"Not much, actually. I just don't think her heart was in it. But what she was going to do — give back all that money?"

"She didn't talk to me much lately, but from what I've gathered, I don't think she had very much of a plan."

"She told me, after the whole thing with Keith, that she wondered if she'd made a mistake, looking for her biological father. She said it was something that had never interested her before. And the negative test — yeah, she told me about it, even though she didn't tell the girls. She told me, 'Aunt Dorothy, this was a bad idea. I never wanted this.' The next morning, she woke up bright and early. When she and I had coffee, she said she'd done a lot of good thinking. And she decided what she really should be writing about was what happened to Shelly."

"And what'd you say to that?"

"I didn't say too much to encourage it. I didn't know if it was a good idea. On one hand, there was certainly a lot to write about, if Gretchen could stomach it. But on the other, it seemed like Gretchen would be setting herself up to relive a lot of grief and frustration."

Dorothy got up and checked the casserole in the oven.

"Getting there," she said, sitting again. The wicker seat of her chair whined under her weight.

"I didn't know all that much about Shelly's death before this," I admitted. "Gretchen never talked about it."

Dorothy nodded. "I think Linda did her best not to burden Gretchen with it. Gretchen was still quite young when the trial was happening, and Linda didn't involve her. Did her best to get Gretchen active in other things instead. School, friends, Girl Scouts. She was determined not to let Shelly's death shape Gretchen too much. It was important to Linda that Gretchen focus on being a normal kid instead. It was admirable. I think it became an outlet for Linda as much as Gretchen. Making Gretchen normal."

I smiled. I couldn't imagine Gretchen as a Girl Scout, nor had I ever quite thought of her as normal.

"Anyway, it was only natural she'd have questions about it as an adult. A *lot* of questions. In particular, why Frank Grippo wasn't convicted."

"And why was that, do you think?"

"Well, that's complicated. I used to say the jury box was filled with idiots. But the more I learned about it, the more I felt the prosecution just didn't have enough to really close it. And I think the jury didn't hear everything they were supposed to, everything they could have."

"Like what?"

"Frank Grippo had some assault charges from a few years ago that had been dropped, or something. So they didn't hear that either."

"Assaulting a woman?"

"Uh. No. I don't know the details, hon, but I think there was one about him beating up someone outside of a bar. Some signs he had a *very* bad temper when he was drinking."

"I see."

"But the worst thing was the way they treated Shelly's final words."

201

"I was going to ask Diane about that," I said. "But it didn't seem like the right moment."

"Yeah, I'm glad you didn't. It's a sensitive thing for the whole family. While Shelly was bleeding in Dr. Skinner's arms, she opened her eyes, looked right at Frank, and said, 'I can't forgive you. I can't.' "

Dorothy noticed me shuddering.

"I know. It's pretty chilling. But the defense lawyer ripped it apart. Made Diane's father look stupid on the stand. Called in a couple of other doctors and medical experts to say that with the head injury she had, and the amount of blood loss, there was no way she knew what she was saying. One of them even said it was doubtful she'd have been able to even speak at that point."

"But Diane's father is a *doctor*," I said. "And he was the one who saw Shelly's condition firsthand."

Dorothy shrugged. "I *know*. Preaching to the choir, hon. Dr. Skinner is — and was even then — a very well-loved guy around Emerson, and then to bring in some medical 'experts' and make him look like a fool. He wasn't able to save her, and then, insult to injury, he wasn't taken seriously enough in court to put her killer in jail."

"Wow. That sounds just . . . awful."

"But you can see why Gretchen was eager to talk to him. Even if his condition made it difficult. Anyway, my point is that the jury wasn't a bunch of idiots. The way the case was presented to them, there wasn't enough evidence. And part of it was that Frank had a sleazy defense lawyer. Said some terrible things about Shelly, implying that with her drugs and some of the men she'd been involved with, that there was no telling who'd have wanted to kill her. But everyone *knows* who did it. There just wasn't quite enough evidence to convict him, sadly."

"I wonder what Linda told Gretchen about that growing up. I'd think that would be a hard thing to explain to a kid."

Dorothy shrugged. "Yeah. I don't know what she told her."

"So Frank Grippo's always been hanging around here, despite what happened?"

"Well, no. Not exactly. Someone probably would've snuffed him out by now, if that were the case. He disappeared for a while. Seven or eight years, at least. Guessing he drifted off somewhere no one would've ever heard of Shelly Brewer — somewhere he could get work. Should've stayed there, wherever it was. But then he came back to live with his brother in Plantsville. Guess he couldn't hold a job anymore and went crying home to his poor brother. It's kind of a blessing that he didn't come back till after Gretchen's grandmother died. That would've been terrible — any chance of her ever running into him. Not that he comes around here anymore. Just stays at home in Plantsville, in a back room at his brother's house, mostly. They say he looks awful, though, when they see him around. And I hear it's filthy, that house. So Frank's gonna die alone like a dog. Like he always deserved."

Dorothy got up and shuffled to the oven again.

"Ready to eat?"

Dorothy let me dry the dishes as she washed.

"Will we see you up here again?" she asked while she worked.

"I think so," I said. "I'd like to. I mean, the more of Gretchen's stuff I read, who knows what I'll want to . . ."

I trailed off. Dorothy didn't appear to be listening as she scrubbed a plate vigorously, working off a crust of casserole sauce. When she was finished, she set it carefully on the rack. I picked it up, dried it, and set it on the counter.

"Yes," Dorothy said. "I'm sure you'll have

more questions. Anyone who learns about Shelly has questions. Just like Gretchen did. Lots of questions."

"That reminds me," I said slowly. "I had one other question, for now. I know I asked the ladies a little bit about this, but I just wanted to make sure . . . Did Gretchen ever say much to you about this Kevin Conley person? The paperboy who testified?"

Dorothy shook her head. "Not that I can recall."

"Do you remember him at all?"

"No. I *do* remember that a paperboy testified. A fairly young kid. The press didn't release his name, I believe. Leave it to Judy to know his name. But I didn't know him." Dorothy set a wet bowl carefully on the dish rack. Then she turned and squeezed my arm, making a little wet mark on my sleeve.

"Gretchen left some things here, upstairs. Some notebooks, some articles and things she'd collected. I'm assuming you want them."

I was surprised it took Dorothy this long to mention it. "Um. Yes. I'm sure whatever you have will be helpful."

"Come upstairs with me, then, will you?" Dorothy said.

I followed her through the cheerful living room — painted bright white, family photographs on the wall, a colorful braided rug on the floor, and a fresh feeling, as if it had been dusted that very day — to the stairway. When we reached the top of the stairs, Dorothy pointed to a basket sitting on a Shaker chair.

"Pick one out for the baby. No — pick two or three out."

I looked closer at the contents of the basket. It was filled with tiny baby hats, all knitted with pastel yarn.

"What are these for?" I said, lifting one up delicately.

"I knitted them. They're for babies in Africa. I read it in *Woman's Day.* There's an address they gave where you can send hats and socks. But I don't do socks."

"You knitted all these? They're beautiful."

"They're all the same pattern. It's a simple pattern. Now, pick some for your little boy."

"I . . . couldn't take them from the African babies."

"*Please.*" Dorothy pulled out a light blue-and-green one and thrust it into my hands. "I just do it to keep my hands busy. And your baby needs a hat, too. Plus it's colder here than in Africa. Don't worry — I'll knit a little faster tomorrow to make up for yours."

I held the hat gingerly as she led me past

the bathroom.

"In there," she said, pointing her chin toward the next door. "Go ahead."

I stepped into the bedroom. It smelled a little stale compared to the living room. The bed was made, but in a rumpled sort of way. The sheets were lumpy beneath the yellow bedspread. A country quilt was folded unevenly, tossed across the foot of the bed. There was a half-empty plastic bottle of Evian on the night table, pushed against a jumble of paperbacks and magazines, piled into a tippy stack.

"There on the desk," Dorothy said, pointing from the doorway.

The rustic desk in the corner was covered with papers, a few folders, a couple of notebooks. On one side of the desk, a leaking pen had run out across several papers, fusing them together. On the other, a black mug sat on a coaster fashioned out of an empty king-size bag of peanut M&M's.

"Oh," I said. The clutter was familiar to me from my college days with Gretchen.

"I haven't had time to clean up in here," Dorothy said. "But you should take all of that stuff."

I hesitated. There was a sad, lingering vitality to this mess that I didn't want to touch.

"Go ahead," Dorothy said, turning from me and extracting a bit of dust from the hall mirror with some spit on her finger.

"Okay," I said, gathering the papers and notebooks slowly into a pile, then pulling them to my chest. I stuck the leaked pen inside the M&M bag.

"I'll take the mug," Dorothy said, holding her hand out.

We went back down the stairs in silence.

CHAPTER 20

"Just Someone I Used to Know"

Nashville, Tennessee

I'm YouTubing past midnight in my motel after a day at the Ryman Auditorium and the Country Music Hall of Fame, eating a take-out slice of something called chess pie — a southern dessert that I'm afraid I simply don't understand.

Sweeter than the pie, though, are Dolly and Porter, singing and giggling me into the wee hours.

Dolly Parton began working for *The Porter Wagoner Show* in 1967. Porter Wagoner was a popular country star in the midsixties and early seventies. He was about twenty years older than Dolly, and he had a distinctive look: tall and lanky, with a long, horsey face, a goofy smile, and a red-blond pompadour.

And then there were his suits — bright-colored suits covered in rhinestone wagon wheels and cacti. Called "Nudie" suits (after Nudie Cohn, the tailor who made them), they reportedly cost several thousand dollars each.

In her earliest days on the show, Dolly looks like a cute secretary: tailored outfits and stylish (if slightly large) hairdos. In front of the camera, the two singers laugh a lot together (Porter with an aw-shucks guffaw and Dolly with an easy giggle) and flirt in an irresistibly folksy kind of way:

Porter: Thank you, Dolly. Fine job. A beautiful song, and mighty, mighty well done. You want to sing a duet with me?

Dolly: Why, I'd just be tickled to death to.

Porter (snorting self-consciously): 'Kay.

Dolly: I thought you'd never ask.

Soon after Dolly joined Porter's show, the pair began recording successful duets. But eventually things went somewhat sour between the two performers.

In a 1972 performance of one of their duets, "That Was Before I Met You," you can see a hint of Dolly's growing exasperation with her boss: She rolls her eyes at Porter's corny hand gestures, making similar but vaguely mocking gestures back at him. She points her thumb irritably in his direction, with a facial expression that seems to say "I'm with Stupid."

By this time, Dolly had tossed the cute secretary outfits and begun to take on the teased and top-heavy look that would become so iconic for decades to come. Her clothes were becoming more dramatic with each year on the show, her hair and figure more pronounced.

She was outgrowing Porter and his show. They apparently fought a great deal behind the scenes. While they had several duet albums together, Dolly was writing and cutting her own hits by then (such as "Joshua" and "Coat of Many Colors") and starting to cross over into pop. Tension grew between Dolly and her boss. According to Dolly, Porter became possessive, attempting to control Dolly's career decisions. Later, Dolly would admit that Porter often tried to put the moves on her. (In her biography, she describes watching Jim Henson give a Kermit the Frog performance on her variety show, and when her manager joked, "Isn't it amazing the way Kermit can sing like that with somebody's hand up his ass?," she replied, "Shoot, that ain't nothin'. I did that for seven years on *The Porter Wagoner Show*.")

Knowing about all of the trouble doesn't much taint my enjoyment of their performances — perhaps because we all know Dolly could handle it. My favorite of their duets is "Just Someone I Used to Know." It is, predictably, about love lost, love missed, and the accompanying regrets. The premise of the song is being asked about an old picture, and replying that it's "just someone I used to know," while privately feeling pained by the memory. And I think the song may have been a little prophetic for Dolly and Porter. They parted bitterly when Dolly left Porter's show in 1974, and later in the seventies, Porter sued Dolly over contractual issues. They eventually settled out of court.

Despite the troubles, Dolly wrote her hit song "I Will Always Love You" (probably more familiar to some for the Whitney Houston version) for Porter.

Penned affectionately and not romantically, she wrote it in 1973, when she was in the process of leaving his show. And the pair made amends a few years after the settlement. In fact, Dolly, who'd purchased the rights to some of Porter's songs while he was having financial difficulties, gave them right back to him. Dolly visited Porter when he was dying of lung cancer in 2007, and spoke and sang at his memorial service.

I can't say how Dolly and Porter felt about each other in the end, but clearly they had a connection that time didn't dissolve. I play "Just Someone" over and over again, trying to determine what about it makes me so damn sad — sadder than almost anything else on my classic country playlist. Maybe seeing Dolly so young and unsynthetic gives me a keen sensation of the cruel demands of time. Maybe looking at rhinestone wagon wheels simply makes me nostalgic for an era I never knew.

I'm still thinking of Dolly and Porter as I drift off to sleep, but when I wake up at 3 A.M. it's Jeremy who's on my mind. Where am I? What time is it? *Where's Jeremy?* Do I miss him? I don't know. I feel his absence, that's for cer-

tain. Is that the same as missing someone? He was here with me for so long,
and whatever happened to cause our
parting, it's unsettling that he's not here
anymore.

What does it mean to "used to know"
a person? Is such a thing possible? Isn't
"knowing" a permanent state of affairs?
Will I ever not know Jeremy? Or he not
know me? I don't think so. Clearly,
though, we are about to become "just
someones" to each other, rather than the
fundamental someones we vowed to be
a few years ago. And it seems to me so
sad how easily this can happen — as
much as we might want it to under some
circumstances.

It happens all the time. People we
thought we couldn't live without move
out of our lives, fade into mere
Christmas-card correspondents or Facebook friends or nothing at all. We're all
free agents. No one is guaranteed to you
forever — or even till tomorrow. I'm not
sure I have the heart or the indepen-
dence to really accept this. I wonder how
anyone can. And perhaps no one does.
Maybe we're all in denial about this
most of the time. Maybe that's how
we're able to find people to love anyway,

for as long as we're allowed. Maybe that's how we survive.

— *Tammyland*

CHAPTER 21

Before I got on the highway ramp, I stopped at a little convenience store called Smart-Mart and bought a Dr Pepper. I'd been avoiding the stuff for months because of the baby, but tonight I felt I needed a little caffeine for the road. Still parked in the store's lot, I took a few sips and flipped on the overhead light. I was eager to glance through the papers from Gretchen's desk at Dorothy's, just to get a sense of what was there.

There were a few notebooks. Among them, though, was a red plastic folder like Gretchen's green one that had contained the police report and newspaper articles.

I opened it. Seeing three envelopes with the return address *DNA Diagnostics*, I gasped and greedily ripped through their contents.

The dates on the three results reports were January 14, February 10, and March 26. The first one had tested Gretchen Waters and Keith Bergeron and said "Probability of Paternity: 0%." The next one tested Gretchen against a "Sample A" and a "Sample B." One said "Indeterminate result/Inadequate sample," the other "Probability of Paternity: 0%." The final one — the March one — tested Gretchen against two more samples: a "Sample C" and a "Sample D." Sample C was 0%. Sample D said "Probability of Paternity: 99.999%."

"Sweet Jesus," I whispered. She'd figured it out. After *five* tries. None of her writing — at least what I could find on her computer, or read so far in her notebooks — indicated she'd put in that kind of effort. Nor did anyone around her seem aware of it.

She'd gotten the positive result one week before she died.

I stared into the light of the convenience store. I didn't want to leave the Emerson area now. I wanted to stay here and figure out who Gretchen's father was — as Gretchen had.

And then, as if he'd somehow read my mind from a hundred or so miles away, Sam rang me on my cell.

"You on your way, I hope?" he asked.

"Just left Dorothy's house, actually," I said.

"*What?* Jamie, do you know what time it is?"

"Yeah. Um. It's just that Dorothy's a real sweet lady, and we got to talking about Gretchen . . ."

"I see. Well, I'm worried about you driving so late. It'll be after one by the time you get here."

"I'll be okay," I said, still staring at the lab reports.

"Are you sure you shouldn't get a cheap motel room and come in the morning?"

"Really, it's not a big deal," I assured him, although I considered this possibility. If I stayed around here I could chat with a few people in Emerson tomorrow, then take off later. Maybe I could make contact with that Kevin guy, for one.

"Either way, though, Madhat . . ." Sam sighed. "You've gotta get here by two tomorrow."

"Why's that?"

"I'm driving you to that little tearoom restaurant at two-thirty. That's where your mom's having your shower."

"Oh, *man*. Why didn't you tell me?"

"Because it was supposed to be a *surprise*."

"Crap."

"It's not *crap*. This isn't a bad thing. If

you don't feel up to driving tonight, just stay over. I can book a motel from here on-line, if you want. As long as you leave by ten-thirty or so, you'll be fine."

"I'm driving home tonight, Sam. In fact, I'd better get on the road now. Okay?"

"Okay."

I chugged my Dr Pepper and started my car.

CHAPTER 22

My mother had reserved a private room for us at the tearoom.

In the middle of the table was a Martha Stewart–style wedding cake fashioned out of diapers, ribbon, receiving blankets, and tightly rolled-up onesies — all hip and cheerful fabrics, alternating stripes and polka dots of dark brown, baby blue, and white. A stuffed monkey emerged from the top, one fist raised. A revolutionary monkey.

"Isn't it gorgeous?" my mother said. "Abby made it. Abby has been amazing with all of the preparation. Wait till you see the favors she's giving out at the end."

Abby — my closest high school friend. We hadn't talked as much as we used to since she'd had twins four years earlier. You'd think my pregnancy would have made us feel more connected, but it really hadn't. We'd only talked twice since I'd announced it, and she was as busy as ever with her children and her full-time marketing job. Still, she'd insisted on arranging my shower.

My mother led me to her. We hugged while my mother continued to rave about the diaper cake.

"I know it's not really your thing," Abby admitted. "But when I looked up baby-shower ideas, I just couldn't control myself. So many cool little ideas. Gives me a chance to explore my crafty side."

My mother said something about how cute the invitations were, then wandered off to greet a friend of hers who had just walked in.

The mention of invitations made me think of Gretchen. Had Abby sent her one? Without thinking, I asked Abby if she had. She didn't seem surprised at the question, however.

"Yeah. I invited her on e-mail, through her author Web site. Since I didn't know her address." Abby glanced at the floor. "She RSVP'd. Seemed excited about it."

I almost asked her when exactly that had happened, but thought better of it.

"I'm so sorry about Gretchen, Jamie," Abby added softly. "If you need anything, you should call me."

"You're already doing so much," I mumbled.

"This is kind of for your mom, aside from the presents," Abby said, "which I'm hoping will come in useful. Don't get me wrong. But I mean, what else can I do for *you*?"

The question overwhelmed me with a wave of emotion so strong it felt like nausea. To prevent myself from bursting into tears, I changed the subject.

"Where are the twins today?" I asked.

"Everything's ready!" my mother announced before Abby could answer.

Abby showed me to the head of the table, where a large chair was stuffed with polka-dot pillows. A sock monkey was perched on one side of the chair's high backing, wearing a blue sweater vest.

After that was a blur of tea sandwiches and cupcakes and gifts in Gerber and Graco packages. There were lots of coos and smiles from both me and the guests, accompanied by the general feeling of being someone else. I tried to grin and remark at every sleeper and swaddling blanket that passed through my hands. I believe I even said "Cool!" when I opened a box containing a breast pump, though I couldn't remember later if the word had actually come out of my mouth. I couldn't think of what else to say, since cooing didn't seem appropriate for that item.

Two gifts stood out. One was Abby's. In addition to a Diaper Genie, she'd wrapped up a copy of *The Little Prince* — which I'd been enamored of in high school.

Some part of my Sparkly Pregnant persona cracked just then. It seemed like I could keep up the act unless someone tried to address the person behind the belly. When that happened, I could feel it all coming apart.

I thanked her and quickly reached for the next gift.

Two gifts later came a framed poem from Aunt Paula, my father's brother's imperious second wife. It was a fabric picture frame, covered in light blue polka dots and brown elephants, with a long poem inside.

"It's for the nursery," Aunt Paula announced. "Read it, honey."

I began to read aloud:

A baby boy is a gift
From heaven above
For his mommy to kiss
And to hug and to love.

"Did you write this?" I asked.

"No," Aunt Paula said, crossing her bony arms. "I found it on the Internet. I thought it was nice."

It was clear I was supposed to go on. The poem was endless. Eight stanzas.

Soon he'll be playing
And climbing up trees
And running to Mommy
To kiss his skinned knees.

I looked up self-consciously and noticed an empty chair between Abby and my mother's friend Irene. Probably that's where Gretchen would've sat if she'd come. She knew Abby from college visits and she would have liked Irene's quiet and unassuming manner.

But I could just see Gretchen sitting there, staring down at the floor, embarrassed by this poem, embarrassed for me. Maybe she was uncertain if I was ever supposed to have children. She was so unsure for herself — how could I be so presumptuous as to think I was any different? Cold and prickly women like her and me had no business having babies. Who did I think I was? The wounded expression on Aunt Paula's face confirmed this sentiment — I didn't know what I was doing. I didn't even have a clue how to pretend to be a sweet and grateful pregnant woman, even for an afternoon.

He'll outgrow his teddies,
Sweet bunnies and ducks
And ask for trains and LEGOs
And baseballs and trucks.

By the time I got to the appropriately
capitalized LEGOs, I'd started to giggle
through the words. I wondered if Aunt
Paula got this poem from a corporate
LEGO site.

By the end of the next stanza, my eyes
were starting to water with the strain of trying not to laugh. I didn't know why I was
laughing, but I couldn't stop. I looked up
for some kind of assistance. Aunt Paula's
mouth was open now, her eyes wide with
disbelief. I glanced at the empty seat again
and imagined Gretchen there, rotating her
left foot around in a circle, then her right.
She'd be wearing her clunky-heeled sexy
librarian shoes. Picking at her cuticles. Smiling just a little in spite of herself.

"Aww . . ." someone whispered. Some of
the guests seemed to think I was getting
weepy.

I struggled through the next stanza, stumbling on the words, still tittering.

When I looked up again, my picture of
Gretchen was gone. I glanced up at Abby,
who was staring at me sympathetically. *She*

225

knew I wasn't crying, but laughing. Did she know it wasn't a gleeful laugh, but a nervous, negative one? She blinked and smiled a little. Then her mouth straightened, as if to say, "Just finish it, Jamie."

I hurried through the last few stanzas — which had my son growing a foot taller than me and lettering in football — and thanked Aunt Paula, telling her how cute the poem was, that it was just right for the nursery, for which I hadn't any wall decorations yet. Which was true. Because I hadn't stepped into that room for weeks.

I glanced gratefully at Abby as I reached for the second-to-last unopened gift.

It was a relief to remember that there had been something of me before this sadness and this baby. To have someone there — someone besides Gretchen's ghost — who at least remembered it, too.

CHAPTER 23

Loretta Lynn's Ranch and Museum
Hurricane Mills, Tennessee

Admission to Loretta's museum is ten bucks. It's still early and I've got the place to myself. It feels like Graceland here, except emptier of guests and yet somehow less sad. I move slowly around the dark maze of glass cases, at first attracted to Loretta's various sparkly stage outfits, many of which I recognize from my obsessive YouTubing of her performances.

There are two significantly less flashy sets of cases, however, that eventually draw me in much more.

First, there are the cases full of random gifts from other celebrities. There are some expected items: Patsy Cline's earrings, and the nightie she gave Loretta shortly before she died (just as documented in *Coal Miner's Daughter*). But then there are the unexpected ones: A note and mug from Ellen DeGeneres, thanking her for being on her show. A Kermit the Frog stuffed animal and *Muppet Show* jacket. An apron that says DOMESTIC GODDESS on it, signed by Roseanne Barr. Little things from people arguably less famous than Loretta — the sort of swag someone who understood herself to be a legend might toss into the trash on her way to her next gig. There are also signed books from Jimmy Carter, both George Bushes, and Caroline Kennedy, plus a Bush-Cheney campaign sign and a cheerful pair of yellow pumps that once belonged to Barbara Bush.

I feel humbled by the gratitude exuded by this odd collection. There's a sense of every opportunity treasured, and little taken for granted.

Even more striking to me is the wall-length display case labeled simply FAMILY. Again, there are the expected items: a scrip from the Van Leer Mining Company that belonged to her father, an apron of her mother's with hands clasped in prayer embroidered onto it, a butter churn from her family's old home in Butcher Holler — artifacts of her famously humble roots. Her rags-to-riches story is partly what makes Loretta so beloved, so it's not surprising that it's documented here in these cases.

More startling to me are the cases a few paces down, which are devoted to her children. Here are her children's baby books, bowling trophies, prom dresses, sequined gymnastic leotards, baseball mitts, a blue-and-white high school cardigan that says WAVERLY WILD-CATS, even a crusty old signed cast from a child's broken arm.

And then my gaze settles on Loretta's daughters' report cards. Year after year, arranged into a fan. I bend down to squint at the grades. They're average.

As I straighten up, I feel myself begin to lose it. So this is what it's come to: I'm tearing up over Loretta Lynn's daughters' mediocre report cards.

I take a few steps back to a bench in front of Loretta's brother's leisure suit. I sit down, cover my face, and weep. Good thing it's too early for other tourists. And my quiet sniffling is drowned out by the video of Loretta highlights that plays on a loop around the corner from this case.

It's not that I've not had enough

maternal admiration in my own life. My mom has kept all of my report cards, too. She'd put them in her museum, if she had one. And surely she'd put in my sweaters and my favorite stuffed turtle and my good citizenship award from sixth grade.

It's that there are two sides to mother love, and I know that I'll only ever experience one. The decision for me was never about wanting to attend cocktail parties and sleep late on Sundays in my thirties and forties, or traveling to India or maintaining my girlish figure. It's not a decision that gives me pleasure; it's simply how I know it has to be — how I simply know it will be. It isn't about selfishness at all. In this moment I see that clearly. Because certainly there's part of me that would like to be the warm, nurturing collector of trophies and outgrown toys. There is part of me — as there is part of almost everyone — that wants to love someone in that way. It doesn't make me happy that I can't and won't. There is a difference between happiness and acceptance.

So I sit on the bench before Loretta Lynn's daughters' report cards and weep.

I sniffle quietly for a couple of minutes. I wonder if there is a surveillance camera. Probably not. Just as I reassure myself of this, the young woman who took my admission approaches me.

"Sorry, I'm almost done here," I say. I've spent an awful lot of time here, surely more than your average customer. And an obsessive amount of time in the "Family" section, which most people probably pass through quickly, on their way to look at Loretta's colorful dresses, or the suits of Ernest Tubb, Ray Price, George Jones.

"Take your time," she says uneasily.

She hesitates, then says, "Did you see that we have Johnny Cash's black coat? And his Folsom Prison shirt? On the other side?"

"Yeah," I reply. "I saw that."

"Where are you from?"

I realize I don't want to fulfill some stereotype of the sniveling Yankee who comes down here and doesn't know how to act. I don't want to say "Massachusetts" of all things.

"Pennsylvania," I say, since that sounds much more neutral to me.

"Oh. Whereabouts?"

"Pittsburgh area."

And the lie brings me out of my melancholy, refreshes me. I shove my stringy, sweaty tissue back into my pocket and hope the young woman never saw it. I'm reminded that you can be — or feel — whatever you want to be, if you can get yourself to say it enough times. If you can convince yourself of how convincing you are.

"I'm almost done here," I say.

— *Tammyland*

CHAPTER 24

78 Durham Road
Emerson, New Hampshire

All I really remember about Frank Grippo is the fighting and *The Smurfs*. I wouldn't say one is any more memorable than the other, so I'll start with *The Smurfs*.

A couple of times, Frank watched me on Saturday morning because Shelly had to go into the pharmacy for a couple of hours. I remember her asking me not to tell Nantie (what I used to call Linda, my mom), and I understood why even then. Nantie had certain ideas about child rearing. They didn't include leaving the kid with a boyfriend during a monthly weekend visit. But Shelly liked her job at the pharmacy — so much more than the one at the factory — so when her boss asked her to do something, she always said yes. Daughter visit or no. She was trying to be responsible. She knew I'd be okay for a few hours with Frank and the TV.

So I remember watching *The Smurfs*. I'd gotten up and poured myself a bowl of Cap'n Crunch's Crunch Berries, my absolute favorite sugar cereal that Nantie wouldn't ever buy except on my birthday. I always ate the yellow Cap'n Crunch first, saving all the red Crunch Berries for last.

"Good idea," Frank said to me when he came in the room and saw my bowl of fuzzy red rounds floating in pink milk. "That looks good, Gretch."

He poured himself some other cereal while I finished mine, confirming my suspicion that he was just joking that my Crunch Berries looked good.

Which was fine, I thought. More bowls of Crunch Berries for me.

Frank sat with me on the couch. I remember the squeak of that couch, and how its brown upholstery was threadbare on one arm. He watched with me for several minutes, slurping up his cereal noisily but saying nothing. I remember his big brown eyes and his chiseled jaw, even though at that age I didn't know the word *chiseled*. He grunted at one point in the show, glanced at me, but then waited till a commercial to make a comment.

"Why's there only one girl?" he wanted to know.

"Who? Smurfette?"

"That's her name?"

"The girl with the blond hair? Yeah. She's Smurfette."

"Looked to me like she was the only girl. All those little blue people, and only one girl. Why's that?"

I shrugged. "I don't know."

"That seems kinda weird, Gretch."

I told him I'd never thought about it before. He put a hand up defensively. "I didn't say it was bad."

"You said it was weird."

"That's not the same thing. It is weird. What if there's a prom, or something? What then? And don't you wish there were more girl Smurfies?"

"They're *Smurfs*," I corrected. "Not *Smurfies*."

"Okay. Don't you wish there were more girl Smurfs on the show?"

"I don't know," I said, growing annoyed that he had to point out everything he didn't like that I did — the Crunch Berries, the Smurfs. I wanted Shelly to get home.

"I didn't mean anything by it," Frank said, which struck me as a dumb thing to say. If you don't mean anything, why are you even saying something?

Then he excused himself to go take a shower.

That's all I remember about *The Smurfs*.

As for the fighting, I remember hearing two different fights while I was in bed at Shelly's. One started when Frank came home late, after I'd gone to bed. One after Shelly had taken me out for pizza, and she couldn't get her car started in the parking lot, so he picked us up. One might have been the very night before *The Smurfs*, but I don't recall exactly. I don't remember much but the screaming and yelling. I don't remember him ever hitting her, but I remember her calling him a drunk. I knew the word *drunk* by then, so I remembered it. But I didn't understand their words well enough to know why they were angry with each other.

Later my mom would ask me if I had ever seen or heard Frank hit Shelly. And if he'd ever hit me. I would not fully understand the context of this question until I was thirteen, when I was told that Frank had killed her. Till then I'd been told there had been a car accident, and it was Frank's fault. I guess until that point my parents thought that was close enough, a little gentler of a story for a child to swallow.

In any case, to the second question, I'd always say no. On the first, I said no for years. Until I was thirteen. Then I'd say I didn't think so. I wasn't sure. Maybe. With all that screaming, I think maybe I did hear a slap or two in there somewhere. I couldn't remember anymore. And I heard some thumps and bumps around the TV room as they worked themselves up. Maybe it was Frank pushing her around. Maybe. I couldn't remember anymore. Probably. It was a long time ago. I was seven years old.

McDonald's Parking Lot
Plantsville, New Hampshire

Frank Grippo now lives in Plantsville, just a couple of turns off the highway.

The Plantsville exit is about ten miles south of the one that leads to the more remote Emerson. When you first turn off, there's a strip of stores and restaurants that probably survive largely from the traffic drawn in off the highway: McDonald's, Subway, the Ninety Nine, Motel 6, and the creepy, inappropriately named All Tucked Inn.

Turn off onto Route 5 and it already starts looking pretty rural. Thomas Grippo's house is right on Route 5, a mile and a half down from the McDonald's metropolis. Here the houses are spread pretty far apart, but traffic whizzes by on the busy road. Number 140 is made of cinder blocks, painted a clean but nauseating baby blue. I park at the very end of the driveway, next to a slightly crooked mailbox on a thin metal pole. The snow has a narrow, crooked driveway shoveled out of it, with piles of snow so high on each side, they appear to be closing in on the black Taurus sitting between them.

I don't spend any time sitting there in my car. I'm afraid that if I think too hard about this I'll turn around and go. The steps and doorway are dilapidated wood, incongruous with the rest of the house — a dark little termite-gnawed vestibule to the institutional concrete.

I try the doorbell twice but don't hear it ring inside. Then I start knocking. No answer. I step down off the steps and stare up at the house. No light from the windows. As I turn to go back to my car, I hear a door swoosh open.

"Can I help you?"

The voice is soft, rasping.

I ignore the sudden hammering of my heart, take a deep breath, and turn.

"Hello," I say.

With effort, the man takes a step out of the house. He is skeletal and pale, with a delicate blond fuzz growing on his mostly bald head. There is a nasty brown mark high on his forehead — either a birthmark or some kind of abrasion. None of this is familiar, but his ears and his eyes are. Big ears that stick out. Small, dark, close-set eyes.

"Can I . . . ?" he begins to repeat, then stops and stares at me.

"My name's Gretchen Waters," I say. "I believe you knew my mother."

At that moment, while I wait for his response, the words *"My name is SUE. How do you DO?"* run through my head.

"Oh my God," he says. "Last time I saw you . . . you want to come in?"

"I want to talk," I say. "But

I want to talk out here."

I almost feel bad saying it. He looks terribly unsteady on his feet. Still, I'm not going into that cartoon-insane-asylum house, not in a million years. Not with Frank Grippo.

Frank sighs heavily and lowers himself onto the stoop. I stay standing.

"What do you want to talk about, Gretchen?" he asks.

"Shelly," I answer. "What else?"

Frank rubs his head, then his eye. He looks very tired.

"It's good to see you," he says. "You look good. You look just like her. It's nice to see you turned out good."

"You don't know I turned out good."

"Yeah, I do. Linda wouldn't have it any other way."

This makes me angry. As if raising someone well were a tedious or bourgeoisie sort of goal.

"I wanted to talk about Shelly, not Linda."

His face goes blank for a moment, his eyes dull.

"I'm going to go in and get my coat," he murmurs. "It's too cold out here."

When he returns, he asks, "What about Shelly, then?"

"I want to know why you two fought so much. I remember you fighting. The neighbors heard it, too."

"That's what you want to know about?"

"To start."

Franks shrugs. "She thought I drank too much. She said she was going to have to get rid of me if she was ever going to get custody of you back."

"That's all?"

"No."

"What else, then?"

"I was pretty sure she was spending some time with her boss."

"Spending some time?"

"Yeah. With Phil Coleman. The pharmacist."

"Cheating?"

"I didn't say that. I don't

speak ill of the dead like that."

"But you thought she was cheating."

"Isn't that what all the lawyers and the newspapers said?"

"What do you say?"

"I say she was looking for an upgrade. She was trying to change her life around. She wanted you back. A man like that fit with the plan better than me. Put her in a whole different financial category."

I shiver but try not to look cold.

"And that made you angry?" I ask.

"Yeah," Frank replies simply. "Yeah, it did."

"So what happened that morning?"

"She and I both went out that night. Me with my friends. Shelly with hers. I wasn't in a rush to get home to Shelly. It wasn't fun between us anymore. Because I could tell she was fixing to break up with me. Just a matter of time. And when I got home, she was lying there in front of the couch, blood coming out of her head. The worst thing I'd ever seen."

We are both silent. A dog barks in the yard next door. A weird, howling bark that makes me think the dog might be in pain. Or maybe smelling that he is about to see someone murder someone else.

"So I couldn't stand to let her be with someone else, is that what you think? Is that what Linda told you all these years?"

"Linda's never said much. This isn't about Linda. Linda didn't send me here."

"No. No, Shelly's sister wouldn't do that. What do you want, Gretchen?"

"I want you to tell me what really happened that morning."

"I just told you."

"I need you to tell me. Just between you and me."

He shakes his head, scoffing.

"If I had some big confession to make, do you think that's all it would take? You showing up here and asking? That's almost as dumb as the idea of me killing her, running off for a couple of hours, then coming back home and calling the police."

"Not so dumb. That way you could look oblivious. Your friends are the ones who said you weren't at home all night, but what did they know? They were drunk, too. And maybe you figured that was a better bet than running and getting caught. Seeing how the verdict went, looks like it was a good bet."

"Sure, Gretch. Things turned out real well for me."

"Better than for Shelly."

Frank rubs his eyes with both hands, then stares at me again. His eyes are ringed with purple. He really does look awful.

"Jesus, you look so much like her. You must hear that all

the time."

"Only around here. Where I live, where I grew up, no one ever knew Shelly."

"I'm sorry for what happened to your mother, Gretchen. I never would have wished something like that on her."

An old, sick feeling comes over me in a wave. I stand there for a few seconds trying to determine what this feeling really is. Anger? Fear? Do I want to punch him? Stab him? Run?

"So you really found three thousand dollars on my mother's mail table, huh? Just before you found her body."

"I don't know if I should answer the question, if you're going to ask it like that."

"Like what?"

"Like you don't care what answer I give. You're not going to believe me anyway."

"Tell me, Frank. Did they let you keep it when the trial was over?"

"Of course not. It was evidence. It wasn't mine." Frank stares at me. "Any more questions?"

"No. I think I should leave," I say. "It doesn't seem like this is a good idea."

Frank coughs. "Probably not."

I turn and take a few steps toward my car. The dog continues to bark — less desperately, less painfully now. Just a mindless woof woof woof.

"Just like that, huh?" Frank calls hoarsely. "That's all?"

"That's all," I say softly. I'm sure he doesn't hear me.

I get in my car and drive to the McDonald's, parking so I can take a minute to stop shaking.

It's not fear or hatred, I decide. It's frustration.

It's the same frustration I'd feel, deep down, whenever I'd hear the Smurfs theme — years and years after that morning with Frank in my mother's TV room. La LA la la la laaaaaah! The feeling was frustration at Frank for being right when I didn't want him to be. That a man so horrible could be right. But truly, what the fuck was up with *The Smurfs?* What the fuck was *up?*

CHAPTER 25

The night after the baby shower, I found a few files in Gretchen's computer that had *Grippo* in them. *McDonald's Parking Lot* and *78 Durham Road* were the only ones that described direct contact between Gretchen and Frank Grippo.

Rereading the second file, I had a wary feeling. I thought of what Gregor had said about Gretchen's voice recorder. Had she gone to Frank with the idea of recording him, hoping he'd confess something to her? What on earth had Gretchen been thinking, going to this man's house alone?

After reading this piece, I called Gregor's cell number, and he picked up.

"Hey, Gregor," I said. "Thanks again for helping me out the other day."

"No problem," he replied. "Glad I could do something."

"I wanted to ask you about something you mentioned."

"Yeah?"

"Yeah. You said something about Gretchen using a voice recorder for some of her interviews lately?"

"Uh . . . yeah?"

"Did you say she was recording people without their knowledge? Or did she generally ask their permission?"

"I don't know. I just assumed she asked people. And I remember she said it kind of helped her relax . . . knowing she could access it later. Knowing she wouldn't have to remember everything."

"So she didn't say if she recorded anyone without the person knowing?" I asked.

"She didn't mention anything like that to me. But . . . um . . . in the end, I don't know if she would have, anyway."

"I see."

"Have you checked with Gretchen's brother about that?"

"No. I will, though."

"Yeah, I haven't looked around here again. Don't think it's here, but I'll check again for you."

"Okay. Thanks."

After we'd hung up, I considered the small size of a digital voice recorder, and wondered how long it might take us all to dig up such a thing in all of Gretchen's clutter.

Would she have put such a thing in a prominent place, or buried it somewhere deep? But then another possibility dawned on me — one I should've thought of from the beginning. If she used it often, likely she kept it close. Like in her purse. If she'd had a purse on her the night she died, that voice recorder was probably in it.

CHAPTER 26

"The Rubber Room"

Dunkin' Donuts
Emerson, New Hampshire

A first for me today:

Talking about my mother's death to someone who at ten-minute intervals appears to think I *am* my mother.

His name is Dr. Skinner. He was with my mother when she died. He tried to save her, and heard her last words. I've come here to talk about those words, and anything else that Dr. Skinner can tell me. The trouble is that Dr. Skinner has midstage Alzheimer's disease. He's still basically functional, but conversations about the past can be hit or miss, his wife tells me. I am welcome to try. She certainly understands why I would want to, she adds kindly.

She asks me what kind of tea I'd like, then leaves me alone with her husband in the sweet living room, all cherry and colonial but for Dr. Skinner's leather recliner.

In the beginning of the conversation, the doctor seems quite lucid.

"I heard you're a writer now," he says. "You write about music."

I tell him about my book and he seems excited. He tells me about his fiddle and calls for his wife to bring it to him. She calls back that it's upstairs, and that she's sure this young lady has more important things to talk about than his fiddle.

He accepts this response, shrugging.

"So what are the more important things?" he says, half

smiling, not sure if he's said
something funny.

"I wanted to talk to you
about Shelly. Shelly Brewer?"

"Oh. Shelly. Yes. Diane's
friend."

He studies me and his eyes
widen.

"I'm her daughter," I say,
even though I know his wife
already told him this.

"Oh," he says. "Oh, yes."

"I wanted to know what you
could remember about the morning she died."

"Oh, dear."

"Can you remember much about
that?"

"Oh, dear. Yes, yes. Very
much. But why would you want
to hear about that? It's very
sad."

"I think it's important," I
say, "that I know all the
facts. To make peace with it,
you know?"

He pauses, then nods. "I see.
I understand. Yes."

"So are you okay talking
about this?"

"I think so, Shelly."

I am stunned, although I shouldn't be. I know how much I look like her.

"I'm Gretchen. Shelly was my . . . my mother."

"Oh." His eyes are blank. I start to wonder about the wisdom of this interview.

"You remember Shelly, don't you?"

"Yes. It's so sad. And I saw her just the other day. We were chatting."

"Just the other day?" I say.

"I mean, a few days before she died."

"Oh. I see."

His wife comes in with a tea service then — cream-colored cups and saucers with roses and golden rims.

"It's hard to remember Shelly like that," he adds.

"Of course you remember Shelly," Mrs. Skinner says to him, handing me a teacup. "She was over here all the time when she was a little girl, always playing tag with Diane. And in the pool. And of course you remember the morning you tried to help them save her. I know you remember that. A very sad day, George, but I know you remember it."

"Yes, yes, I do," he says, seeming to brighten. "That fellow Frank came pounding on our door early in the morning. My wife said, 'What in the world?' He was screaming and yelling that he needed a doctor, so I went over in my pajamas. I put my shoes on and went in my pajamas."

Mrs. Skinner nods approvingly and hands him his teacup. Then she sets out a plate of sugar wafers — the kind that come in vanilla, pink, and chocolate, that I didn't realize still existed.

"I went down there and I followed him into the house and she was there in the living room. It was terrible. Bleeding with a tablecloth all tied around her head. I said to him, 'What happened here? What

HAPPENED?' "

"You did?" I ask.

"Yes, and he didn't have an answer. He said he didn't know. He started yelling at me to do something, do something. I was the fucking doctor, do something."

Mrs. Skinner sighs.

"Well, that is what he said."

"I know," Mrs. Skinner says.

"So he was maybe more angry than upset, you think?" I ask.

"I don't know. Maybe."

"So what did you do?"

"I unwrapped her head and her neck, to look for the source of the bleeding. I asked him to bring me some clean cloths."

"Did he?"

"Yes. She had several injuries. She was bleeding from a laceration in the back of her neck, and there was a deep wound in the back of her head. Also, her collar-bone was broken, her shoulder bleeding. After I made sure nothing was obstructing her breathing, I focused on the head wound, because that was where she seemed to be bleeding out."

I notice him becoming slightly clearer in his tone as his words become a bit more medical.

"And I've heard she said something."

"Yes."

Dr. Skinner stares longingly at the sugar wafers.

"It's okay, George," says Mrs. Skinner. "Gretchen here's a big girl. She just wants to hear what happened."

"Gretchen?" Dr. Skinner gazes at me. "Oh, dear. Shelly?"

"What did Shelly say when you were with her, helping her?"

Dr. Skinner sighs, leans forward, and picks up a strawberry wafer. Then he eats it carefully, not looking at either of us.

"I'm sorry," I say to his wife. "Maybe this is too upsetting."

Mrs. Skinner shakes her head.

"He used to talk about it all the time. I'm sure he remembers."

"Are you two talking about me?" Dr. Skinner asks.

"We're talking about the day Shelly Brewer died. Such a sad day, remember?"

Repeatedly hearing about the sadness of that day — without any actual information — is starting to make me feel dizzy. I decide I need a sugar wafer, too, and grab a vanilla one.

"It was sad," Dr. Skinner says, nodding. "I wonder . . . if I'd gotten there earlier."

"She was so badly beaten, George."

"Yes, but maybe she could have said something more, too. Even if I couldn't have saved her."

Dr. Skinner is beginning to look very distressed.

"We don't need to keep talking about this," I say.

"Yes," Dr. Skinner says. "Maybe we ought to take a

little break."

He pauses, then sips his tea. "Did you say you're a blue-grass fan?"

"Well, country, yes. Country is what I wrote about. But I love bluegrass, too."

We talk music for a little bit longer. His wife won't let him go upstairs for his fiddle, but lets him play me a couple of Ralph Stanley songs off a CD. I tell him I was already a fan of Ralph Stanley, but he doesn't seem to believe me.

Later, in the kitchen, his wife apologizes for him, say-ing he's having a particularly bad day. I'm welcome to come back another time. She's sure he would do better on another day. I wonder if this is a line she's been telling her-self for a while.

But she insists, further, that he's always talked about that terrible morning a great deal — what he wishes had gone differently, what he thought of Frank's behavior. And if I try again and it doesn't go well, I can always ask her what I need to know. Do I have any questions for her now?

I say no and thank her for the tea and cookies. She seems disappointed to have me leave and asks if I think I'll come back. I say probably I will.

I've chosen Porter Wagoner's "Rubber Room" to write this to as I sip coffee at Emerson's Dunkin' Donuts. Not because I mean to poke sarcastic fun at Dr. Skinner's condition, which I absolutely don't — but because talking to him has made me feel like I'm in one.

Porter Wagoner's song is about his experience drying out in Nashville's Parkview Hospital (the same facility of "Committed to Parkview," which Johnny Cash, once a patient there himself, wrote for his friend Porter). It's one of the spookier songs of classic country, with an unaccustomed psychedelic feel to it. The final words of some of the verses echo dramatically, making the song very creepy, melodramatic . . . rubbery. That is, despite the obvious pain in it, there's something ridiculous about it.

At the Skinners', I felt myself losing all sense of what the conversation really was about — what was past for the doctor, and what was present? The "echo" for me in Dr. Skinner's living room was hearing him call me Shelly more than once. Did he think I'd returned from the dead to talk about my death? Was that the unfortunate impression I'd given this poor man? And more personally, more selfishly, do I echo Shelly somehow? We look alike, yes, but I've always heard what a loose cannon she was, how messed up, how sadly destructive and out of control. (Though I will always maintain that that is not the person I remember from when I was seven.)

I was always a good kid and a good student and, aside from a little too much alcohol in certain social settings, stayed away from the drugs. I went to a snooty school and got married at the age I was supposed to (twenty-seven) and never did an unpredictable thing in my life till I got divorced and wrote a book — still relatively careful, buttoned-up rebellions when you look at Shelly.

But now . . . here I am making a half-demented elderly doctor talk about such a sad and sordid thing. Stealing mail. Confronting my mother's accused killer. All the strange things I've done in the last couple of weeks — how odd that I can know how deranged they might be but have no interest in stopping. I'm starting to think that I'm crazier than Shelly ever was.

I think there's supposed to be a kind of horror in the echo, but I don't mind it.

Maybe I've been listening for it my whole life.

Bar at T.G.I. Friday's
Plantsville, New Hampshire

Kevin is tall and thin with deep eye circles under soulful gray eyes. His clothing seems to contradict his boyish features and gentle voice. He's got on jeans and a crisp, textured black shirt that strikes me as something a high-class pimp might wear. Over that is a black leather jacket with white stripes down the sleeves, which strikes me more generally as something an asshole might wear.

While we talk about 1985, he drinks a Sam Adams. I sip on a weak margarita and munch on the stale bar popcorn.

He doesn't remember me at all. He remembers being told that Shelly — the woman whose killer he was helping to put in jail — had a daughter.

Being a "witness" definitely

265

affected his adolescent years, he says. Mostly in a good way. He felt a tremendous sense of responsibility, of doing something important that no one else his age usually got to do. Kids in school looked at him with admiration. He tried not to talk about it in a gossipy way — after all, a lady was dead. His mother always reminded him of that. It wasn't something to brag about. He understood that and tried his best to act accordingly.

He tells me this with his eyes focused on his beer. No matter what he says, I'll bet he got all puffed up and self-important about it. He doesn't want to admit that to me, because the dead lady who made him a little Emerson celebrity is my mother. I want to tell him I don't hold it against him. I remember what it's like to be twelve.

We don't talk much about the actual car in the driveway.

Kevin was not, of course, so familiar with his customers that he'd know which was Shelly's car and which was Frank's. What is important is that he remembered, when asked, that there were two — Shelly's little red hatchback and Frank's large gray Chevy.

He knew about Shelly within hours of her ambulance ride away from Durham Road. Judy was a friend of the family — used to babysit him when he was very small — so small he doesn't remember it. But she came over that very day in hysterics, sharing the news. It didn't take long for the adults — and soon after that, the police — to start asking him what he might have seen by that little brown house that morning.

He only had a couple of encounters with Frank and Shelly, while collecting his paper-route money. Sometimes they remembered to leave an envelope for him. More often he'd have to knock.

He usually hoped Shelly would answer. Shelly always seemed surprised to see him, as if she forgot every two weeks that she received the paper at all. Frank tipped better, but he was "a little weird about it," says Kevin.

He says Frank would always take out his wallet and pay him the exact amount first, then hesitate and say, "You want a little tip?"

And then after a chuckle and another pause: "Well, here's a little tip."

He'd hand Kevin a dollar. And sometimes, if he had an excess of quarters, he'd take out two or three and say, "And here's another little tip. How about that?"

To which Kevin never knew what to say besides thank you, because it always felt like Frank wanted something more, some sarcastic exchange Kevin wasn't sure he could pull off. Shelly was sweeter and less confusing, though she usually gave him exactly seventy-five cents extra.

I tell Kevin that other neighbors have mentioned Frank's strangely ironic manner as well. I tell him my story about the Smurfs — really the only Frank story I have. Kevin seems strangely riveted by it.

"You actually remember him, then?" he says. "I didn't realize. I can't imagine."

It occurs to me that I've not told this story to anyone. Not because it is particularly sensitive — but maybe because of how neutral it is. It's just the Smurfs. Me and Frank and the Smurfs and breakfast.

I say to him that I wish it were more of a story. What I mean is that I wish it were a memory that told me better how I should feel about the man. I don't tell Kevin that, of course. Too much.

But my abbreviated admission is enough. Kevin seems to

relax a bit. I'm not a seven-year-old girl with a lost mother anymore. I'm a thirty-two-year-old with a dumb story. Dumber even than his. (Because frankly, "You want a little tip? Well, here's a little tip!" sounds to me like something any old beer-guzzling doofus would say to his paperboy.)

Kevin was just a kid in 1985, just like I was. I don't expect much from him.

CHAPTER 27

I found Gretchen's piece on Dr. Skinner rather odd. First of all, given the outcome of her first visit, I couldn't imagine Gretchen wanting to return. Had she? It seemed so sad and futile. But maybe Mrs. Skinner had encouraged her. And the reference to stealing mail? What the hell was that about? Whose mail? Frank's?

"Good idea, Gretchen," I muttered as I read it.

And a couple of things made me linger over the Kevin Conley piece, too. First of all, there was Gretchen using the word *soulful* to describe Kevin's eyes. Gretchen wasn't one to use such words. I wondered if she meant it — and if she did, it probably meant she liked him. And clearly, based on their e-mails, they'd grown comfortable with each other. How comfortable? I wondered.

Kevin hadn't said much in his response to my e-mail, but he had written back with a phone number. I decided it was time to make use of it.

"Hi, Kevin?" I said when a guy picked up, then explained who I was.

"Can you talk for a few minutes?"

"Sure. I'm on a break period right now and I can't talk long. But I have a few minutes, yeah."

His voice was low and his words slow, but he sounded friendly.

"Oh . . . where do you work?"

"Plantsville High. It's a high school. Here in Plantsville. I guess that's . . . obvious."

"You're a teacher?" I asked.

Kevin yawned. "Not quite. An aide in the special ed room."

"Oh. Well, I'm sure you're busy. Should I call back sometime?"

"I've got a few minutes. It's okay. I . . . uh . . . want to help."

"All right. Well, I was recently there in Emerson . . . unfortunately I wasn't organized enough to talk to everyone I should. I started with some of Gretchen's family and
—"

"Dorothy, right? And the ladies?"

"Judy and Diane, yeah. You've met them?"

"No." Kevin paused for several seconds. "Gretchen talked a lot about them."

Kevin sounded vaguely stoned to me, but

given his job description, I decided to give him the benefit of the doubt. Maybe he was, like many teachers I knew, perpetually sleep-deprived.

"I think I'll be going up there again soon, by the looks of it," I continued. "Listen, when was the last time you saw Gretchen?"

"Oh . . . a couple of weeks before the accident. And I should say how sorry I am. I really miss her. And I know you were close friends. She talked about you."

"Uh-huh," I said softly.

"Anyway . . . uh . . . she came up here for a weekend and we hung out that Saturday night. She stayed at my place that night, actually."

"Oh," I said.

"We'd had a few drinks. And she crashed there."

I didn't reply. I wanted to ask if this meant what it sounded like — that they were seeing each other? Behind Gregor's back?

"You know, it's good to hear from you. As I said, she talked about you. Did you have your baby yet?"

"No," I said, surprised. "Not yet."

"Oh. I'm sorry. Is that a rude question?"

"Um . . . no. Not at all. Not over the phone, anyway. Uh, anyhow . . ."

"Anyhow," Kevin repeated, and I wondered if I should interpret his tone as mocking.

"It sounds like you guys started seeing each other more frequently in the last few weeks . . . talking a lot?"

"Yeah. I don't know how much she had written, about her and me talking . . ."

"I've only come across a little bit of that. It looks like the first time you met. Before you started to become . . . friends."

"Okay. That doesn't surprise me. The more time I spent with her, the less it seemed she was writing very much. But, um, did you have any questions about that? The little bit she wrote?"

"No. Seems pretty straightforward. The stuff about you being the paperboy and seeing Frank's car . . . I was more interested because you guys seemed to become friends . . . Is that right?"

"Yeah. Definitely. For a few weeks, anyway."

"So I just thought you'd have some insight into what she was up to . . . what she was writing."

"Yeah. Sure." It sounded now like Kevin was chewing something while he talked. "Whatever you want to ask."

"Well . . . I don't have any questions organized right now . . . so I think I'll want to talk again, maybe in person, if I can manage it, but . . . oh, just for example . . ."

"Yeah?"

"I was recently reading these pages where she went to Frank Grippo's house. Did she actually do that? Just drive right up to his house?"

"Yeah. Well, sort of. Actually, *I* drove her."

It took me a beat to recover from my surprise. "She doesn't write it like that. She narrates it like she went herself."

"Well, I didn't get out of the car. I had told her, look, if you need to do this, write it like I'm not with you. But don't be stupid. Don't do this alone. She agreed to that. I waited outside in the car while they talked."

"Well, that's a relief," I said, before realizing what a dumb comment it was. Gretchen was still dead. "Um. Were there other incidents like that? Where you were there and she didn't say?"

"Not that I know of. I knew she was harassing all kinds of people her mother used to know, but that was the only one I was worried would get her into big trouble."

"Did she bring a voice recorder with her?" I asked. "And record her conversation with Frank?"

Kevin was silent for a moment. "Not that I know of."

"Okay. So . . . the part about her going and parking in the McDonald's lot . . . that's not true?"

I heard a long, high beep in the background on Kevin's end, followed by a woman's voice saying, "Courtney Howell, please report to the guidance office."

"I haven't read anything she wrote," Kevin said. "What does it say she did?"

"Just parked in the parking lot. And thought about Frank. Her ambivalence about her memories of him."

"Well, then, that's basically true. We parked at the McDonald's together and talked about that for a few minutes. Before I drove her home. Just a little fudging, I guess. To make it look like she didn't have a chauffeur. Um, I'm sorry, but I have to go to class in a few minutes."

"No problem. It sounds like you were really close to what she was doing. I'd really like to talk more."

"Anytime. But as I said, I didn't know much about what she was *actually* writing. We'd just started . . . uh . . . hanging out. We didn't talk about the book much."

"I understand. But I think I'll still have a lot more questions for you. If you don't mind."

"Do you want me to call you back to-night?"

"Uh . . . I won't be home tonight. But sometime soon, I'm sure. Plus I'm thinking I might come up to Emerson again in the next few weeks. We could meet in person, maybe."

"Um. Sure," Kevin said. "Nice talking to you, Jamie. Let me know."

"Thanks," I replied. "I will."

Kevin seemed nice enough. Why would Gretchen want to write Kevin out of the scene? Wasn't it, in a way, more compelling that she had the old paperboy witness in the car with her? As I hung up the phone, I wondered what else Gretchen had left out.

CHAPTER 28

The hospital elevator was crowded with distressed men clutching pillows to their chests, and pregnant women trying not to bump bellies in the tight space. We'd just finished our second childbirth preparation class on the fourth floor, and everyone was reeling from a relatively graphic birth video, complete with a naked and delirious woman screaming and grunting on her hands and knees. After the video, people seemed to have lots of questions about epidurals. But the nurse teaching the class waved off most of those questions, saying she'd talk about "that stuff" in a week or two.

We'd all brought our own pillows on which to practice labor positions. Now someone put out a shaky hand and hit the ground-floor button. Just as the elevator door closed, a young man in a baseball cap, the youngest in the class — he was about twenty, his pretty pregnant partner probably even younger — smiled broadly and whispered, "Pillow fight!"

A few people giggled, including me. No one moved, of course, but I could feel the tension leave me as I pictured hospital security cameras capturing an elevator full of expectant parents swatting each other with pillows, feathers flying. It seemed to me a pillow fight might have been more therapeutic for us all than the class we'd just experienced.

Sam, however, didn't seem to derive any relief from the young guy's little joke. He was silent as we filed out of the elevator, walked to the car, and started out of the hospital lot.

"Well, that was intense," he said, after a couple of minutes of driving.

"Yeah," I answered. I didn't particularly want to discuss what we'd just seen — not at the moment, anyway. I turned on our CD player and played his favorite Radiohead.

As he pulled into the driveway, I said, "If it's any comfort to you, I'm probably going to take full advantage of the drugs available."

"It's not *my* comfort I'm worried about," Sam said as we got out of the car. "So whatever you decide will be okay with me. Really."

"Best not to overthink it," I said. "It's just one day, and then we'll have Charlie here. What's going to happen is going to happen, and worrying won't change *how* it happens."

This was something I'd been telling myself for a while. I wasn't sure I believed it.

"I guess you're right," he said, unlocking our front door. I noticed he didn't remark on my use of the name "Charlie" for the baby — my favorite name so far, though I knew Sam was lukewarm about it. He headed into the living room ahead of me while I hung up my jacket.

"Is this some kind of joke?" he called from the living room.

"What?" I called back.

"Jamie, come in here," he yelled, his voice sounding more frantic now.

I rushed in behind him, and found our television cabinet open, our DVD player and his Wii gone, leaving neat, clean rectangles in the dust.

"Did you move the DVD player?" he asked me.

"No," I answered. "Why would I?"

"Oh my God," he said, glancing around. "Has someone . . . ?"

He ran into the kitchen. "Someone's broken in!"

"Why wouldn't they take the TV?" I called to him.

"Looks okay in there," he said, taking my arm. "But we're gonna go into each room together, and check. In case . . ."

He didn't finish his sentence, but led me into our office. Drawers were open, both of our desks in disarray.

"Fuck," he whispered. "My laptop. Where's yours?"

I indicated the bag still on my arm. Lately I'd been hauling it around almost everywhere I went, reading Gretchen's stuff whenever I had a free moment.

"Isn't that the one you got from Gretchen's brother? Where's *yours?*"

"Um . . . last time I used it, I think I was in bed."

He nodded and led me to the bedroom.

"I can't remember if I put it on the bureau or left it on the bed."

Sam pulled the duvet off the bed.

"I don't think it's here," he said.

"But that's weird," I said. "Why didn't they take the TV?"

"Who cares why they didn't take the TV, Jamie?" Sam bellowed, then slapped his hands over his face. "They took everything else!"

I glanced around the room, then let my

eyes come to rest on my bedside table. There I had left two notebooks of Gretchen's — but now they were gone.

"Uh-oh," I whispered.

" 'Uh-oh' is right," Sam muttered, picking up the phone. "I'm calling the police right now."

I headed out the bedroom door, ignoring Sam as he called, "Stay in here with me!"

"I'm sure they're long gone," I yelled back.

"Now, how the *fuck* did they get in?" Sam bellowed, kicking something, then lowered his voice. "Um, hello. I need to report a break-in . . ."

I tiptoed back down the stairs and headed straight for the coat closet, where I still stored Gretchen's crates. I peered in and found them still there, piled high with Gretchen's notebooks. I let out the breath I'd been holding.

When I rejoined Sam in the bedroom, he asked if I noticed anything else missing. I glanced at my nightstand and wondered if I'd been mistaken about where I'd left the two notebooks. I told him no.

CHAPTER 29

"Hello Trouble"

Williamsburg, New Hampshire

The man who is probably my father is a divorced professor of chemistry at UNH, living in a modest, crisply painted gray saltbox house in Williamsburg, New Hampshire. He shares custody with his ex-wife of a seventeen-year-old son who, if gossip has it right, is in drug rehab.

And he doesn't answer my e-mails. I don't know how to respond to this lack of enthusiasm. I called his home phone once, got no answer, and chose not to leave a voice mail.

So I've been forced into the

"show up at the doorstep" bit. I don't like it — it reminds me of selling Girl Scout cookies. But I'll have to take it. It is, after all, more like a country song than corresponding via e-mails.

I knock on his door and pray his son's not around this evening. That would be awkward. While I wait, I notice that there are three stamped envelopes clipped to Bruce's mailbox, ready for tomorrow's mail.

I hear slow footfalls. The man who is probably my father opens the door. I'm surprised at his stature. He's at least six feet tall, relatively thin, and rather dark in his features. His hair is thick, almost black, with specks of white on the sides and the front. He looks more Distinguished Gentleman than I expected. (Perhaps when I heard "university chemistry professor," I just pictured squat, pale, bespectacled.) His dark, deep-set eyes study me carefully.

"Hello," I say. "Um. My name is Gretchen Waters."

His face doesn't change.

"I figured. I thought I recognized you when I peeked out the window. You look so much like . . ." He trails off.

"You peeked out the window?"

"Yes. I get a lot of Mormons."

I nod, encouraged that he'd seen me and opened the door anyhow. "I don't know if you've gotten my e-mails."

"I have," he says. "I hadn't decided yet how to respond."

"Do you need more time?" I ask.

"No," he answers. "It seems my time is up, is it not? Do you want to come in?"

This startles me. It's not what I expected. (What did I expect?) But it's chilly out there on the doorstep and not conducive to conversation.

I follow him to his living room, where I sit on his black

285

leather couch. He sits across from me in a matching black chair. He asks me if I want something to drink, and I say no, I'm okay.

He tells me he looked up my book after I first wrote to him. Hasn't read it, but has been meaning to. Wanted to read at least a little of it, to get a sense of what kind of books I write, before agreeing to anything.

I tell him this next book isn't going to be anything like the first. This book is going to be about Shelly, not about music. I've been in and around Emerson, I explain, learning all about Shelly.

He crosses his awkwardly long legs and asks me who I've spoken to so far. I list off a few people — Dorothy, Judy, Diane, and then . . . hesitating first . . . Keith.

He nods. None of this surprises him. He's very cool with all of this.

"I imagine they were all very

helpful. They all cared about Shelly a great deal."

It's clear he's going to be a tough nut to crack. I want to say "And didn't *you* care about Shelly a great deal?" Because everything the others have told me indicates that he did.

But instead I say yes and start to tell him a couple of the stories — the more flat-tering stories — that Judy and Diane told from high school.

After a while he's warmed up and he tells me one. Shelly was his date for the junior prom. It felt like a pity date at the time — he was a nerd and she was out of his league. It was the one night a year that most kids were allowed to stay out all night — some kids went to the local diner, some went to private parties. Shelly didn't want to do any of it. She wanted to drive to Cape Cod. Or rather, she wanted Bruce to drive her to Cape Cod. She didn't have a car. She'd never been there. She wanted to see the sun come up on a nice beach. Wouldn't that be nicer than getting drunk? And Bruce, who wanted to get drunk in the worst way, said yes anyway, because he was a pushover.

And they watched the sun come up on a nice beach and had breakfast together. And it was one of the most memorable evenings of his high school years. (He doesn't say why, but I wonder . . . was it just the beach and the breakfast? Is he telling me the story of my conception?) And when they got home, everyone else was hungover.

I'm not sure what to make of this story. I don't know what it says about Shelly except that she probably kind of liked the beach, and that she was good at manipulating males to do what she liked, which I already knew.

The man who is probably my father saves me from having to

come up with a response, however.

"I would say she was sponta-
neous, but I think she'd been
planning on going to the Cape
since I asked her out."

I nod.

"You seem a lot quieter than
she was," he says. "More
reserved. Maybe that's just a
first impression. And I don't
mean it in a bad way."

I smile. Always a pleasure
to be told how quiet you seem
by people who've known you
less than an hour. It ir-
ritates me enough to pounce on
him.

"People think that may have
come from my father," I say.

"Linda's husband? Bob?" he
says, without blinking. "He's
a good man. I remember him."

"No," I say. "Not Linda's
husband."

Bruce sighs and repositions
his long legs, staring at his
sturdy brown shoes.

"But Linda and Bob are your
real parents. They raised you.

That's how Shelly always wanted it."

"That's how she wanted it sometimes, I think," I say.

There was a long pause then.

"Are you sure you don't want a soda or anything?"

I can't believe this dapper, sensible man keeps soda in the house, and I almost take him up on it just to see.

"No," I say, because I don't want to let him off the hook. "No, thank you."

Bruce sighs again.

"I see. The gossips have gotten to you."

"No one was gossiping. I came asking questions."

Bruce cocks his head and gazes at me, then covers his chin with his hand, rubbing his clean-shaven face rather aggressively.

"You know, your mother . . . I mean, Shelly, was smarter than most people gave her credit for."

"I know that. I remember her."

"You know that."

"Yes, I do."

This man who is probably my father is starting to irritate me, unfortunately. I think sympathetically of his son in rehab. If I'd been raised by this slippery fellow, perhaps I'd be self-medicating a little myself.

"She was sure she wanted things a certain way . . . because . . ." Bruce sighs yet again and scratches his salt-and-pepper head.

"Because?" This is going to be interesting. I can tell.

"Because she didn't want anyone to be hurt."

"Anyone? Who's anyone?"

"The idea was that you were given . . . you had . . . two committed, caring parents. She didn't want anyone to get in the way of that."

"But in these situations," I say, adopting a professorial tone of my own, "when an adopted child becomes an adult, there is often a natu-

ral curiosity about understanding the facts. And I
think she was smart enough
that she would have understood
that. She wouldn't have denied
anyone that."

Bruce shifts his gaze away
from me. "I suppose you're
right about that."

And then there is another
long silence. It had to be
about five minutes, at least.

Then Bruce says, "I guess I
do need a little more time to
think about this. I wasn't
prepared for this discussion
tonight."

So I tell him I'd be happy to
set up another time to talk.
I'm sorry to have startled
him. I just wanted to make
that first contact.

He says that he has my e-mail
address. He will contact me in
a few days.

We make small talk as I
slowly head out the door. He
asks me how the publishing
business is going. Is my book
available as an e-book? Do I

get paid well for e-books, or is that bad business for authors?

I tell him it's complicated. As I head down the door-step, he says, "Gretchen. Uh. It really was nice to see you. Thank you for coming."

I turn — I must've given him a funny look, because then he says, "Really."

And then he closes the door. What I do next happens very quickly, impulsively, although I admit I was thinking about it the whole time we were talking — how the licks on the envelopes clipped to his mailbox could make good DNA samples.

I yank the three envelopes from his mailbox and slide them into my coat. I'm impressed with myself at how swiftly and quietly I manage to do it. Still, I half expect Bruce to come back to the door and yell at me that he saw what I've done — to bring his mail back. But he doesn't.

And on the way home, I listen to Gram Parsons's "Hickory Wind."

I don't listen to it for any real connection between the song and Bruce or even myself. Unfortunately, I really wouldn't know a "Hickory Wind" from a whiff of an "Autumn Wreath" — scented Yankee Candle, and I doubt Bruce would either.

I suppose I just listened to "Hickory Wind" all the way home because I fucking well like it, but if you want con-nection, let's try this: "Hickory Wind" is full of longing, full of the question *How the hell did I get here, so far away from home? How did I turn into this and how can I get back to what I was?*

I'm not sure I have such a nostalgic sense of what home is, but I know I've moved far away from what I was ever sup-posed to be. I've sold myself pretty cheap this time.

And the funny thing is, I

wouldn't have minded it so much if it turned out to be Keith. Keith is a gentle soul with bad hair who seemed, oddly, to really want to be the one. It seems he really loved my mother — loved her so much that even though he's clearly moved on, he'd have liked to have this connection with her now that she's gone. A tangible thing to reassure him it was real. A little piece of her sending him a Christmas card every year.

Bruce, on the other hand, feels like some tricky part of myself I probably never should have wanted to know about. Still, I can't help myself.

There are some people who think Gram Parsons actually stole "Hickory Wind" from a blind folksinger named Sylvia Sammons, who performed the song in South Carolina coffeehouses in the midsixties, around the time Gram Parsons was doing the same circuit. So be it, either way. I still love it, and love him singing it. And maybe it shows how heartfelt and how fraudulent some of us somehow manage to be at the same time.

CHAPTER 30

On the morning following the break-in, I took a few more notebooks out of the closet and found the Bruce piece. I read it over my peanut-butter-and-banana-sandwich breakfast.

For real, Gretchen? I thought as I came across the mail-stealing part. It seemed out of character for her, but technically, it fit: She had to have gotten her other DNA samples somehow or other. Had this mail theft led to that 99.9 percent result eventually? If so, what were the results in between Keith's negative and that final positive from Bruce's mail? Failed samples? Did she test all three stolen envelopes?

Bruce sounded a little strange — just strange enough to be Gretchen's biological father. His oddly forward, slightly creepy way of holding a conversation kind of reminded me of some of Gretchen's more bizarre social habits. Perhaps the physical resemblance wasn't quite there (Gretchen was tall, yes. But dark? Not by any stretch. She often looked like she had an iron deficiency.) It hadn't been there for Keith either, apparently. Gretchen, everyone thought, was all Shelly in her looks.

I decided I'd like to get a glance at this Bruce myself sometime.

On my way out for work, I made sure all of our doors and windows were locked. Our deck door in the back was likely how our intruder had gotten in, we'd determined. After we'd called the police, Sam had discovered several of our back windows — looking out onto our deck — unlocked. We didn't know how long they'd been that way. Probably for weeks. It made me worry about our mutual carelessness. Maybe this was how we were going to be as parents — accidently leaving stairs ungated, outlets unplugged, Quentin Tarantino movies playing on the TV in an empty living room.

CHAPTER 31

Hi Jamie,

Yes . . . actually, my mother did find a digital recorder recently — in an overnight bag of Gretchen's. She didn't know what it was at first, so when I told her what you'd been asking about, the mystery was solved. I've listened to a little bit of it, and you're right — she used it for her recent interviews for her book. I'll FedEx it to you this week.

Please don't work too hard on this. My mother keeps telling me to tell you that. Take your time. There is really no rush. We are not in a hurry to resolve the issue of Gretchen's book soon — she just wanted to put it into good hands. We know you have a lot going on right now.

Sincerely,
Nathan

Nathan's e-mail took me by surprise. I'd

thought Gretchen's voice recorder was long gone, probably in her purse. I also thought it might be a good item to hand over to the police. In spite of myself, I made no such suggestion to Nathan. I wanted to get my hands on it first. But I promised myself I'd give it to the police if I heard anything I thought they should hear.

I tore into the FedEx package when I got home from work a couple of nights later. It was after eleven, but I was eager to start listening.

I brought it up to the baby's room and sat in the rocking chair. It wasn't much of a nursery yet. There was a crib, a changing table, my grandmother's rocking chair, and a ton of shopping bags full of boxed baby gear. I hadn't looked at the stuff since the shower.

Now I thought I might sort through some of the gifts while listening. I pulled one of the shopping bags onto my lap, then clicked play. On the recording, there was a little bit of a clunk, then a man's voice.

"So where were we?" he said.

"You were talking about Linda and Shelly's dad," said a soft female voice.

"Your grandfather, yes," replied the man.

"I never knew him," said the female voice. It was Gretchen.

I pushed the shopping bag off my lap and hit pause.

I hadn't anticipated what it would feel like to hear her voice again. I rocked silently in the chair for a moment, shaking. The words I'd hear come out of this machine were the last ones I'd ever hear her say.

The baby gave a couple of kicks, which was both sad and comforting.

"You'll never meet her," I whispered. I wondered if Gretchen would've been into being "Aunt Gretchen." Probably not. She'd have tried, though, like she always did.

The kicking stopped and I started to cry: loud, gulping sobs that woke Sam up.

"What time is it? What's wrong?" He was squinting as he came into the nursery, blowing his overgrown bangs out of his eyes.

"I don't know," I said.

Sam sat on the carpet and looked into the bag I'd dropped onto the floor. He pulled out a box, and out of that a mobile with stuffed clouds and a bear dressed in baby blue, hugging a stuffed moon.

"Oh, good," he said. "I was hoping someone would buy this."

He pulled the cord and it started to tinkle out Brahms' lullaby.

"I don't remember putting that on the registry," I said.

"I think I put it on," Sam admitted.

I nodded and snuffled back my last tears as the mobile slowed and plinked out a few last gasping notes.

"Lots of nice stuff," Sam said, looking around. "We're lucky."

"Yeah," I agreed.

I gazed over to the corner of the room, where the changing table was. There were five tiny onesies there, all washed and folded and placed carefully on the shelf beneath the changing area. I'd done that the week before Gretchen died. I couldn't remember now what had been going through my head then. I think I was wondering how long my son would wear those tiny clothes, and once he graduated to the next size up, if it would seem like the time had gone by quickly. But I couldn't remember if I'd felt serene and maternal at that moment. Had I ever? Would I ever?

Now nothing seemed to matter but Gretchen and the soft kicking in my stomach. They seemed strangely linked somehow — Gretchen gone, and this new person arriving. To think of them together was painful, but lately, that was the only way I thought of them. And there was nothing serene about it.

Everything else felt insignificant, and far

away. I wasn't sure how to explain this to Sam — that I loved the baby already, and that my disinterest in this baby-blue fabric and tinkling music took nothing from that. And I loved Gretchen. And I couldn't concentrate on anything else.

"Gretchen's recorder," I said. "Her brother FedEx'd it."

"I saw," Sam said. "It was by the side door when I got home."

"I had forgotten what her voice sounded like."

Sam put the mobile back in the box. Then he leaned his head against my knee and put his hand over my stomach.

"I wonder how it is for him. You being so involved in this sad thing right now."

"For who? For Charlie?"

"Oh. Are we still considering that?"

We'd already had several discussions about the name "Charlie." I thought it was a charming old-fashioned name for a good honest fellow. *Are you sure you aren't just thinking of Charlie Bucket?* Sam always asked, referring to the character in the Roald Dahl books. Sam, for his part, couldn't shake his strong association of the name with Charlie Chaplin.

"He'll be okay," I said. "I wouldn't worry about it."

"Have you thought more about Andy? That's a lot like Charlie."

"It's really not much like Charlie. It's not as gentlemanly. And I don't like that it rhymes with 'candy.' "

Sam nodded uncertainly. "Are you going to listen to this for a little while? Should I join you?"

Sam and I stared at each other for a few moments. I could tell he was trying to find something recognizable in my expression — some happy sense of camaraderie we had a few months ago. I, meanwhile, was looking for something else entirely in his black eyes — a certain cleverness, a certain almost mean mischievousness that had been the first thing about him I'd fallen in love with. It seemed to have dissipated as I'd ticked off the weeks to my due date. I knew it was in there somewhere, but he seemed to save it, now, for other people, or for times when I wasn't around. It had been part of a desperate strategy, perhaps, to protect himself from my deepening prenatal crazy. Or to cure me of it.

"I'll try again tomorrow," I said. "Don't worry about me. I've got one more thing I've got to do, but I'll come to bed in a few minutes."

After he returned to the bedroom, I took

out Gretchen's computer and opened up her e-mail. I searched for the words *Jamie* and *shower*.

Oddly, after hearing Gretchen's voice, I wanted to see Abby's invitation and Gretchen's response. In Gretchen's box, I found the invitation but no reply. I wondered if Abby had lied to me about Gretchen's enthusiasm — another instance of coddling to protect the poor pregnant woman's feelings?

I took out *shower* and searched just *Jamie*. The most recent message that came up was the one she'd sent me two weeks before she died. After that was a message in her draft folder — not to Abby, about a shower, but to me. There was no greeting or salutation, but Gretchen had written it to my address:

It seems to me there are things we should have talked about. Like, what happens if you think you've found the love of your life, but you notice, whenever you go into the city together, that he walks ahead of you in the subway station, and doesn't look behind for you until after he's gotten on the subway? And what if you find yourself wishing you did not have to tell him to wait for you? What if being with him starts to mean having to say those things . . . "Honey, wait for me?" And you start to resent him making you do that in order to keep him walking by your side?

If I never wanted to think about these things, and still don't, why in the world did I think I wanted to be a wife?

And how come you and I never talked about that? How come we still don't? Does Sam ever walk ahead of you in the subway station? Would you ever admit it to me if he did? Or that you cared?

She'd written this a couple of weeks before the message she'd actually sent. It wasn't much, but it was more than she'd ever actually said to me about her divorce. I wondered if there had been a great deal more she'd wanted to say about it. And I remembered Jeremy at the memorial service, saying, *I'd like to talk to you a little more. Just about Gretchen. About Gretchen and me.*

Jeremy. He hadn't answered any of my e-mails yet. I'd actually written him again just yesterday. But he was still grieving, too. Probably I should give him a few days before badgering him again.

I closed Gretchen's e-mail and followed Sam to bed.

CHAPTER 32

"Too Far Gone"

The Mall at Green Hills
Nashville, Tennessee

Nashville's Mall at Green Hills is pretty swanky — there's a Tiffany and a Louis Vuitton and an Apple store. It's so damn classy it doesn't even have a food court, so I've been forced to write in a Cheesecake Factory. Not that I'd ever be so ridiculous as to resent having to order a coffee and a slice of Turtle Cheesecake. It's being the sniveling pale Yankee weirdo — dining alone while scribbling in a notebook — that I don't like.

I deserve to look like a creep, I suppose. I've come to the Mall at Green Hills because I'm rather a sick woman — because ever since I started being interested in these women's lives, I've

307

been obsessed with a particularly dark part of Tammy's history — her "kidnapping," which happened right here at this mall.

It occurs to me, as I sit here licking caramel off my spoon, watching all of these beautiful people eat Cobb salads, that I'm a shameless student of people's worst moments: lies, violence, melodrama, fraud. I have been since I was a kid. I like to hold them up like baubles and examine them every which way. When I was young, I thought that would make me understand them and become immune to such moments myself. Now I'm older and smarter, and study them purely out of gratuitous habit.

It happened on October 4, 1978:

Tammy's story went like this:

She'd gone shopping at the mall for a birthday gift for her daughter Georgette. When she returned to her unlocked car, there was a man inside, wearing panty hose over his head and wielding a gun. He told her simply, "Drive." That was the only word he said to her during their sixty-plus minutes together in her yellow Cadillac. They headed down Highway 65 for a while. After about twenty minutes, he had her pull over and tied panty hose tight around her neck. Then he took the wheel, gesturing her onto the floor of the backseat, and drove for about forty more minutes.

Then he pulled to the side of the road near Pulaski, Tennessee, beat her up, and fled in another car, driven by a mysterious accomplice.

A few minutes later, a young man in a pickup truck saw Tammy stumbling along the highway, bruised and with panty hose tied tight around her neck. He didn't recognize the unfortunate woman, but picked her up and brought her home to his stunned mother, who happened to be a Tammy Wynette fan. The family politely held back their questions and their disbelief, helping her cut off the panty hose, letting her rest on their couch, calling the police.

The Tennessee Bureau of Investigation was perplexed by the case. The assailant hadn't stolen anything from Tammy. There was no sexual assault, no ransom demand, no motive. Tammy herself didn't seem that interested in cooperating with the investigation, or finding the culprit. Some claim that the bruises on her face appeared to be enhanced by makeup in the days immediately following the incident.

There are a number of theories about what really happened. Some thought George Jones (her third husband) hired a couple of thugs to frighten Tammy into submission over a $36,000 child support dispute they'd been having. Some thought it was just a media stunt, cooked up by Tammy for a little attention since, for the first time in almost a decade, she hadn't been nominated for any awards at the upcoming CMAs. Still others thought her new (fifth and final) husband, George Richey, had beaten her, and the whole thing was a ploy to explain why Tammy, who had several concerts scheduled, was so bruised up.

Indeed, after Tammy's death, one of her daughters claimed that her mother confessed this to her twelve years after the incident — that it was fabricated to cover up Richey's violence. A couple of Tammy's friends say she told them the same thing. While my gut tells me this is the closest thing to the truth that Tammy fans will ever get, there are a couple of reasons to doubt it. For one, Richey passed a lie detector test about the kidnapping, while Tammy refused to take one. Also, Tammy's daughters hated

Richey and he hated them, particularly after Tammy died. Richey managed to keep most of Tammy's money from her daughters. While there is ample evidence that he was a controlling and temperamental man, it seems Tammy's daughters also had every reason to demonize him after her death.

Some other confounding factors are these:

In the year preceding the incident, there were break-ins at Tammy's mansion, in which people left threatening notes and words like *slut* and *pig* scrawled on her mirrors. There was also a mysterious fire in the house. After the kidnapping, more threatening notes were found — one stuffed into the gates of her house, another backstage at a concert. The latter notes were analyzed by a handwriting expert who said that they were written by someone who was trying to distort his or her handwriting, and could not say conclusively that they were not penned by Tammy or George Richey.

Also, in the early 1980s, Tammy mentioned offhand in interviews that she discovered later that her phone was being tapped in the days before the kidnapping, and that someone was doing surveillance on her house from the nearby woods. She said she knew who it was, but preferred to let the matter drop. She did not elaborate much on this claim or mention it again in subsequent interviews. And it does not appear to have been corroborated by the police, who hadn't ultimately pursued the case at great length.

Friends and family all confirm that, kidnapping aside, Tammy had an unusual tendency to exaggerate stories and invite drama into her life. She apparently had a deep need for sympathetic attention.

So here I am at the scene of the crime, asking myself, *How the hell did this happen?* Love Tammy as I do, I don't believe her version of the events of that October day. But if her daughter's version is essentially true, how did Tammy come to this? How is it that desperation and dysfunction could converge so perfectly with absurdity to create such a cinematically pathetic incident in Tammy's life?

It's no secret that Tammy had a lot of hardships and made a number of very bad choices. But the kidnapping incident has a special kind of insanity to it. And it feels like a turning point for Tammy. It was a step away from the merely melodramatic and toward the sadly, scarily delusional. After this point, Tammy never had the kind of success she'd had in earlier years. Skeptical fans mocked her story, and this is where Tammy's "pathetic drama queen" reputation really started to take shape. (In 1980, a punk band called the Maggots released a song called "Let's Get Tammy Wynette!" mocking the kidnapping incident, singing from the point of view of the supposed kidnappers.) Her reliance on drugs grew steadily more serious, her relationship with her enabling, controlling husband more entrenched.

A clear, factual explanation of that day can't be had. Tammy's the only person who could have clarified it, and she's gone. So all one can do now is try to understand it on some broad emotional level. And in order to do this, you need to resist the impulse to laugh at Tammy, to scoff at her fakery and her flailing recklessness. Like her music, understanding it requires — fancy this — a totally sympathetic heart, a total, if momentary, absence of irony.

Strip off the details that make it worthy

of a punk-rock song: a whiny diva who trades in her sequins for painted-on bruises, kidnapping herself in her own yellow Cadillac. Take away the stardom and the fancy car (and the distraction of the silly panty-hose head), and you see a battered woman who didn't know where to turn and who, sadly, had vowed never to get another divorce. Get a little closer, and she's just a terribly confused individual who never had a clue how to pursue her own happiness. In the last analysis, she's someone who so desperately needed love that she did things that brought her the very opposite. What exactly made her this way isn't the point. The point is that everyone knows people who operate this way. And that most of us know that at our worst moments, that is how *we* operate.

Tammy's life — like her music — conveys a vulnerability that I think many of us are not comfortable with. You can hear the "teardrop" in her voice, and think, *That's beautiful and honest.* Or you can hear it and opt for the safer response: *That's pathetic and maudlin, to which I am too cool and self-assured to relate.* And for that reason, Tammy will never be hip like Johnny Cash or Loretta Lynn have become.

There is nothing ironic or sassy about Tammy Wynette. There is nothing cool about being as desperate for love as she was. In the metaphor of American celebrity as high school, Johnny Cash is the badass with the motorcycle (and therefore acceptable in a hipster's musical library), but Tammy's that cheesy girl who tries way too hard. She wears too much clumpy mascara and the wrong color lipstick and fucks a guy who doesn't like her much on the off chance it'll make her feel popular and loved. She cries easily and will do anything for attention. She downs five aspirin and tells everyone she attempted suicide. Really, nobody wants to be that girl.

In Tammy's case, that girl has, in spite of all of her flaws, a disarmingly powerful, beautiful voice. To enjoy her voice, however, one must believe it. And to believe it, one must admit that it's possible to be that vulnerable oneself. That, in fact, you could be that girl. That your worst moments could potentially be as sad and confused as hers. That you, too, have a tender, needy, crazy, and distinctly uncool heart.

— *Tammyland*

CHAPTER 33

The next morning, after Sam had left, I settled at the kitchen table with a mug of tea and Gretchen's recording. I felt ready now — ready to hear Gretchen's voice without dissolving into a hormonal-existential mess. I started the recording at the beginning again.

"So where were we?" the male voice was saying.

"You were talking about Linda and Shelly's dad," Gretchen replied.

"Your grandfather, yes," replied the man.

"I never knew him," said Gretchen.

"Well, he was a good guy," the man continued. His voice had a nasal quality. "I knew the whole family from church. But I got to know him pretty well from the Knights," the man was saying.

"The Knights?" Gretchen repeated.

"The Knights of Columbus. I was the youngest one in there. I didn't stay long.

But I had fun selling Tootsie Rolls a couple of times with your grandfather, outside of the IGA. It was to raise money for various charities. Handicapped kids."

"Uh-huh," said Gretchen.

"So your grandfather, he was pretty welcoming to me. I was a bachelor then. Didn't know anyone in town for a while, really. Your grandparents took pity on me, had me over for dinner a few times. That was before he got sick, though. That was so sad. He left us way too soon."

"So you felt like you knew my family," said Gretchen, sounding slightly impatient. "That's why you were willing to give Shelly a job years later."

"Well — yes. I knew her since she was, uh, eleven or twelve or so. I liked your grandparents, liked the whole family. So when she came in for that clerk job, it felt like the right thing to do, to give her a chance. She'd had a rough go of it, but clearly cleaned up her act. And I wanted to help her get out of the factory. It seemed like it was dragging her down."

Gretchen cleared her throat. "Still . . . a pharmacy clerk. For someone who'd had a drug addiction, that was a quite a . . . favor. Quite a leap of faith."

So this man was Shelly's last boss — the

pharmacist, with whom she was supposedly flirting or maybe more. I looked back at my notes to remind myself of his name. Phil Coleman. Of whom Frank was supposedly jealous.

"I guess so," answered the pharmacist. "But I felt like I knew the real girl, from before all of that. She'd been off the stuff for a year or two at least. And my impression was she'd mostly abused alcohol, actually, and some cocaine. It wasn't like now, where I'd be concerned about someone lifting oxycodone, or whatever."

"But still, it was a risk," Gretchen said.

"I had faith in her. I wanted to give her that chance."

"So it all worked out."

The pharmacist sighed. "She only worked here about nine months before she was killed."

Gretchen didn't respond immediately to this statement. There was a shifting sound on the recording for a moment. I wondered if this guy knew he was being recorded. I supposed it didn't really matter. He probably wouldn't have agreed to talk to Gretchen if he had anything too illicit or explosive to share.

"But it all worked out?" Gretchen repeated.

"For the most part."

There was another pause.

"So . . . there were problems, or no?" Gretchen nudged.

"Just a few growing pains on the job. But nothing related to her addiction recovery, of course. Nothing like filching medications. I'd have had to let her go for something like that, absolutely."

"So what . . ." Gretchen began.

"Well . . ." There was a pause, then what sounded like another sigh from the pharmacist. "We had sort of a strange incident once. I caught her rifling through some of the recently filled prescriptions, from about a month earlier."

"Not part of her job?"

"What? No. Not at all. Not prescriptions that old. When I asked her what she was doing, she couldn't really come up with an answer. She said something about being worried about some teenagers . . . When I pressed her on it, she said that she thought they were maybe forging prescriptions, or something. But the more I asked about it — like, what did she think, that one of them lifted a prescription pad from one of the pediatricians? And didn't she realize I knew all the town doctors' handwriting like the back of my hand?"

"So you weren't convinced there was a problem," Gretchen said, after a moment's pause.

"No. Not at all. In fact, I pointed out to her that no young kids had come in with prescriptions for anything narcotic recently. Antibiotics and antifungals and the usual things. Really, I'm pretty sure it was something she said to cover up being . . . well, maybe being nosy, or maybe checking up on someone in particular. She didn't seem entirely convinced of her theory herself. She didn't really try to sell me on it."

"But you didn't fire her for that?"

"No. She'd done really well, up till then. She was a great worker. And I thought to myself — hey — maybe she *did* really think that happened. With her history, maybe she was a little overly concerned about the kids getting drugs on her watch. I don't know where she could've gotten that idea, but I wanted to give her the benefit of the doubt."

"It never came up again, after that one time?" Gretchen asked.

"No . . . not that I can remember. But that was maybe a month before she was killed."

There was another pause.

"So that was the only problem you had with her on the job. Otherwise, I hear you got along pretty well."

I held my breath for the pharmacist's answer. I knew Gretchen was probably trying to hint at their supposed flirtation. She said it so casually, so sweetly, he apparently didn't pick up on it.

"Yes. She was very patient with customers. Very careful."

"Okay," Gretchen said uncertainly.

There was another long silence, then the pharmacist asked, "Did you have any other questions?"

"Um . . ."

I bit my lip. I wasn't sure if I wanted her to ask him or not. Surely he knew it was something people had talked about?

"Did Frank ever come in when she was working?" Gretchen asked.

"Frank Grippo?"

"Yes."

"Um . . . No, not really. Once or twice. And never for long."

"What was your sense of him? Of their relationship?"

"Oh, I really couldn't say. He brought her her lunch once. Maybe stopped in to buy a soda and say hello a time or two. Not enough for me to make a judgment at the time. I knew his face. I knew he was her boyfriend. He seemed a little old for her, and maybe a little gruff. But I didn't ever speak more than about five words to him, so I couldn't say I knew much about him. Until he was arrested, of course, and in the papers . . . then I learned all sorts of things about him. But I'm sure that's not what you're talking about."

"Yeah, no," Gretchen replied. "I know all about what people said about him *afterward*."

"It really was very tragic, and I'm sorry. How old were you then?"

"Uh. Seven."

"*Seven.* Oh my God. I'm so sorry."

I wasn't expecting this, and it seemed Gretchen wasn't either.

"It's, uh . . ." she stuttered. "Thank you. I appreciate that."

"I wish I knew more. But I just never got much of a read on Frank Grippo."

"That's okay," Gretchen said.

There was some more rustling on the recording.

"So, have you been in town long?" the pharmacist asked.

"Oh, since Friday this time. I've been up a few times, talking to family, Shelly's old friends."

"Do you like Emerson? Do you remember it well from when you were a kid?"

"Some spots that I went to a lot back then. Like the playground on Kipling and Randy's Hot Dogs."

"Ah. Randy's. Gotta love Randy's dogs."

I rolled my eyes. All of these references to that blasted hot dog stand were making me want a hot dog in the worst way. I wasn't supposed to eat them — *What to Expect* had told me so.

The rest of the conversation was similar small talk and ended with a discussion about the weather. Gretchen said good-bye to the pharmacist. That was followed by a series of rustling sounds, some clicks that sounded like heels on pavement, and a car door. Then the recording stopped.

I waited a few seconds to see if there was anything else. Then there was a slightly different kind of hiss, then a little clunk.

"You mind if I record this?" Gretchen asked.

"You're something else, you know that?" said a soft, vaguely familiar male voice.

"Is that a yes?" Gretchen teased.

Gentle laughter. "*No*, Gretchen. Give me that."

That recording stopped there. I had to replay it three times before I could place the voice: Kevin Conley, the grown-up paperboy. They certainly sounded comfortable with each other. And Gretchen sounded so lighthearted.

I let the recorder run to the next interview.

"It might take me a minute to get used to that thing," said a gravelly female voice.

"I don't need to use it. Really," Gretchen said.

"No, no," was the response. "It'll just take a minute. Then you won't be able to shut me up, hon."

"Okay. Well, then. Should we start with that night? Or something easier?"

"We should just get right to it, hon."

"Okay. So you and Shelly went to the movies."

"Yup. Me and Shelly and her friends Judy and Diane."

"Were all four of you friends?" Gretchen asked.

"Not really. I only knew them through Shelly. I knew Shelly from the factory, you know?"

"Yeah."

"I got the feeling those girls didn't usually associate with folks from the factory. It was just they knew Shelly since she was a kid."

Hearing this, I thought about Judy and Diane and their disdain for Shelly's friend Melanie. I guessed this was her speaking.

"Uh-huh," Gretchen said softly.

"And actually, I never really spent much time with them. It was just the movie we'd picked for that night. *The Color Purple.* Shelly mentioned it to her other friends, and they decided they wanted to go along. Kind of invited themselves, I think."

"Just the movie? Did you guys go out after?"

"Me and Shelly and Diane did. We all met at the movie. Judy went home after. We were going out for a drink, and Judy wasn't into that. Judy was engaged, planning a wedding for that spring. Shelly would say all Judy ever wanted to do was sit at home and dog-ear her brides' magazines."

Melanie laughed a little.

"Was it a late night, with the three of you?" Gretchen asked.

"No. We were home by about midnight. I think it was awkward for Shelly, trying to keep the conversation going between her and Diane and me. We were very different, you know? She and Diane talked mostly about their old high school friends and stuff. Me and Shelly, more about the factory and the guys we went out with. And she knew I was self-conscious around those friends of hers. I probably shouldn't have been — they were nice girls. But I think it made Shelly uncomfortable, too. She was uncomfortable that night. After one drink, she said she was tired, and we all went home."

"Did she talk about Frank at all that night?"

"Not really. A little. Same old stuff."

"Which was what?"

"She was worried about his drinking. She thought she'd probably have to ask him to move out soon if it didn't improve. I mean, Shelly was no Goody Two-shoes about alcohol, let's be honest about that. Even when she went to rehab and everything, it was to get off the drugs. And the drinking, after that, she cut down. Got it under control. But she never gave it up, did the AA thing or anything. Back when we both worked at the factory, she'd go to happy hour sometimes with the rest of us. She liked to have a good time."

"Uh-huh," Gretchen said.

"But Frank . . . I think she felt Frank was over-the-top. That that kind of drinking she shouldn't be around. Especially now that she was trying to hold a job and see you more. And she hadn't realized the extent of it before he moved in."

Gretchen hesitated for a moment, drawing in a breath.

"Why *did* Shelly let him move in? What

was the attraction in the first place?"

"Well. That's a good question. You know, I knew Frank a little bit from the factory. And he could be funny. Laid-back. It was easy to be around him. No pressure, I guess. But I think what Shelly liked about him was that he was strong. Not just muscle strong, but sort of stoic about things.

"And honestly, I think the girl had a problem being by herself. After she and that Roland guy broke up, I think it was hard for her being in that house alone. She was one of these girls who always thinks she needs a man around. Like she thought she needed the protection. Kind of ironic, I guess. That that was what he was there for."

"So do you think he was the one? Who killed her?" Gretchen asked.

Melanie sighed. "Wow, honey. I didn't expect you to ask me that straight out."

"Well. It's kind of the point of the whole thing, really," Gretchen said softly. "To ask that question."

"Well, you know . . . the first couple of weeks . . . knowing Frank just as an acquaintance, even . . . I thought, no, it couldn't be. It didn't seem like . . . you know, you want to feel like you could *know* that about a person, when you looked in his eyes. I couldn't quite believe it. And that's maybe just because you can never believe someone you know could do something like that. But some people *do*. And Shelly *did* talk about how he was unpredictable when he was drinking. And that they'd fight. She never said that he hit her, but she never said he didn't either. I'd like to think that she'd have told me. We confided about a lot of things. I didn't know what to think. And the trial left a lot of questions. I don't know about Frank. It took me a while to decide it was possible that it was him. And I still feel it's possible. I'm not like some of her other friends, though. I'm not *sure*."

"You say you guys confided in each other a lot. Do you think there was any truth to the rumor that she was getting involved with her boss?"

"Phil Coleman?"

"Yeah."

"Yeah. Hon, I don't want you to have a bad memory of Shelly. Shelly was a real sweet girl, and smart about a lot of things. Just not men. You know? She was still young. A lot younger than you are now, even."

"So you say yes. Why? Did she tell you she was involved with him?"

"Uh. Yeah. It wasn't going to go anywhere. She went out with him one night after work.

For a drink, or whatever. And I don't know what else happened, but it sounded to me like things got romantic. I was honest about that when the lawyers asked me. I know some of her family and friends thought I was helping them destroy her reputation. But that's never what I wanted to do, hon. When people ask me questions about my poor friend who was murdered, what am I supposed to do but tell the truth? I felt the truth was the best way to find out what really happened. Even the unflattering parts of the truth. Do you mind if I smoke, hon?"

"Not at all," Gretchen said.

After a pause of about fifteen seconds, Melanie continued. "I told you, Shelly's way of dealing with men was kind of warped. I think it always had been, since she'd started getting in trouble with the boys in high school. I think this time it was that Shelly was afraid of losing her job. There were a couple of incidents at work where Phil was unhappy about some mistakes she'd made, or something. And getting a little flirty or romantic with Coleman . . . I think that's how she'd always dealt with problems like that. Really, I loved Shelly. But it was true. That's how she tried to solve her problems a lot of the time. I'm sorry to say it. As I said, she was young."

"It's okay," Gretchen said. "So, this idea that Frank had, that she was looking for an upgrade, someone who'd make her look like a more responsible parent . . ."

"That's crazy. Shelly had some crazy impulses with men, but she wasn't dumb. She wouldn't have rationalized going out with Coleman — who was engaged — as a good parenting choice."

"But Frank obviously knew *something* was up between Shelly and her boss."

"Yeah. Yeah, obviously he did."

"And that could've been enough to make him really, really angry."

"Yeah. That's all true."

"Do you think that's what happened?"

"Probably, Gretchen."

The interview stopped abruptly there. There was a silent spot on the recording, and I hit pause again, to take it all in. Melanie was certainly different from Shelly's childhood friends. I wondered if I should track her down and talk to her, too.

I hit play.

Gretchen was saying, "Thanks for talking to me again."

"Oh, no, no, no. It's my pleasure," said a hoarse male voice.

"How are you feeling today, Dr. Skinner?"

"Oh, pretty nice."

"That's good to hear," Gretchen said loudly, enunciating.

"You said your name is Shelly, right?" Dr. Skinner asked.

"No, I said Shelly was my mother. My biological mother, you know?"

"Oh. Then what's your name again?"

"Gretchen."

"Yes, that's right," Dr. Skinner said good-naturedly.

"But I wanted to *ask* about Shelly. That's probably why you were thinking of her name."

"Yes. Probably. That and . . . you look just like her."

"Yes! That's what everyone says," Gretchen replied.

"Everyone is right," said Dr. Skinner.

"Maybe it would be easier if we started with what you knew about Shelly before she died," Gretchen said. "I know she and your daughter spent a lot of time together. At each other's houses."

"Oh, yes. All of the girls liked to come over and go in the pool."

"Diane's friends, you mean? Judy and Shelly?" Gretchen asked.

"Yes, Judy and Shelly. Nice girls, both of them. Shelly was the prettiest, though."

"I see."

"Judy had excellent manners," Dr. Skinner continued. "Still does, really. Knows how to talk to people."

Gretchen coughed. "Shelly didn't have good manners?"

"Oh, sure. Just not exceptional. Each of the girls was exceptional at something."

"What about Diane?"

"My daughter? She's very athletic. She's very good at basketball."

"Does she still play?" Gretchen asked.

"Oh, that's silly. No."

"So, getting back to Shelly. You knew her a long time."

"Oh, yes."

"What did you think when she moved back into the neighborhood? When she was in her early twenties?"

"I can't say I thought much. I was glad to see she was doing better. It was generous of Bill to rent her that little house. I'd have been afraid of druggies going in and out at all hours. But he felt he owed it to Florence to be nice to her daughter. Florence was Shelly's mother, you see."

"I know," I said.

"Yes, I guess you would."

Dr. Skinner was starting to sound a little confused. Gretchen continued anyway.

"So you didn't have much interaction

332

when she was older, when she moved back in?"

"Nope. Not at first. But after a little while."

"Tell me about it," Gretchen said gently.

"I'd see her around the neighborhood. Ask her about her job. Try to catch up. She was still a sweet girl, despite all of the trouble."

"Did you have any impressions of Frank? Frank Grippo?"

Dr. Skinner sighed. "I heard he was bad news."

"Uh-huh, anything specific?"

"Hadn't he been to jail?"

"Well, no. He'd been arrested a couple of times in the past. He'd beaten a guy up once while he was drunk . . ."

"Shelly could have done better."

"I agree," Gretchen muttered.

"Shelly was usually so sweet."

"That's what they say," Gretchen said, with a sigh still in her voice.

"But she did give me some trouble," Dr. Skinner said, his tone suddenly different — clearer, more confident, as if he'd just remembered something. "When Dr. Platt died, she started giving me trouble."

"What kind of trouble?" Gretchen asked.

"She wasn't happy. She wanted me to do something."

"What could you do about it?"

"I don't know." The doctor was quiet for a moment. "You're right. I don't know. What could I do but take on some of the kids? Help out by taking some of the kids as patients? What else could I do?"

Gretchen paused. "Did she have questions about his death?"

"No. He had a heart attack. That was that. The man smoked like a chimney and had three rib eyes a week. No one who knew him was surprised."

"But Shelly was surprised? Was she close to him, or something?"

"Close? Uh, not that I know of. Why would she be close with *him?*"

"I don't know," Gretchen said quickly. "I'm just trying to figure out what you're saying. You mentioned to me last time that you chatted with her a few days before she died. Was this the chat you were talking about?"

"Yes, dear. What else would it be?"

"Okay."

"It was me she gave a hard time to. She gave me a hard time, when he died."

Gretchen sighed. "But why?"

"Because nothing I said would calm her down. I offered to do this or that to help, but no. Nothing."

"Like what else did you offer?"

"Oh, I don't know." Dr. Skinner sounded exasperated. "Everything I could think of. I'm getting a little tired, dear. Forgive me."

"But why was Shelly so upset when Dr. Platt died?"

"Because, then, there weren't enough doctors."

"I don't understand. Enough doctors for what?"

There was a long pause then.

"Shelly?" the doctor said hoarsely.

"Yes?" Gretchen replied quietly.

"There's nothing to worry about. The kids will be fine."

"Why wouldn't they be?" Gretchen asked.

"Exactly. That's what I said. They're fine."

"Dr. Skinner?"

"Yes, dear?"

"Can we talk about the day Shelly died now?"

Then there were some shifting sounds.

"I'd rather not," Dr. Skinner said. "Forgive me. I'm tired, and it was the saddest day."

"Okay," Gretchen said, sounding disappointed.

My cell phone rang just then. With some relief — this conversation with Dr. Skinner was depressing me — I stopped the recorder and rolled off the couch to go answer it.

It was Gregor.

"Um . . . sorry to bother you," he began.

"You're not bothering me."

"It's just . . . I wanted to ask you about something. Um, is Gretchen's ex gonna be helping you with the whole literary executor thing?"

"Jeremy? No. Not that I know of. I mean, I've tried to contact him a few times to chat . . . but so far we haven't talked. Why?"

"Well . . . It's just . . . he showed up here yesterday, saying that Gretchen's parents had asked him to help, too. Wanted the same files you got. Asked if that could be arranged."

"No one in Gretchen's family told me about that."

"Huh. You'd think they would've."

"Did you call them and ask them?"

"No. They . . . uh . . . I just don't think they like me much."

"Did you let him have her files?"

"No. I was headed out. Didn't have time. Wasn't sure if I should, anyway."

"Maybe I should call the Waterses and ask them."

"Yeah. That'd be great," Gregor said.

Five minutes later I had Mrs. Waters on the phone.

"Jeremy?" she repeated. "No. I haven't

spoken to him at all. Why, dear? Do you need help? Maybe you should slow down? What're you now, seven months? More than that, right? Just put it aside for a little while and relax. Really, I don't care if you wait a *year* . . ."

"No, it's not that," I said. "I don't need help."

I hesitated, realizing I didn't wish to worry her. "Jeremy's been asking if I need any help, and I didn't know if he'd spoken to you."

"Oh. No," Mrs. Waters said. "He hasn't. No hard feelings with Jeremy, dear, but I'm not sure if Gretchen would've wanted that."

"Okay. Really, it means a lot to me to be reading Gretchen's stuff. I don't need help. I was just asking, is all. To make sure."

"Well, thank you for that, honey," Mrs. Waters said with a sigh.

After I'd hung up I called the newspaper and told them I was sick.

I knew I was pushing it — with all the days I'd had to call in during my early pregnancy. But I had a few things to say to Jeremy. And I wasn't willing to wait.

CHAPTER 34

Jeremy's condo was in a boring but well-manicured complex in a quiet central Massachusetts town. The place was a mass of gray paint and white balconies, each unit with the same red-brown door.

I could hear some kind of video game playing behind Jeremy's door — the revving and crashing of a driving game. The noise stopped after I rang the bell. As the door opened, I pulled my cardigan over my stomach and buttoned the button over the roundest part. Jeremy stood in front of me in a light blue work shirt and a pair of navy sweats.

"Jamie!" He put his hand on his head and rubbed his hair. "What's going on?"

I put an indignant hand on my hip. "I need to talk to you."

"Huh? Do you, uh, want to come in?" Jeremy said. He glanced over my shoulder and squinted at my car in the parking lot.

"Is Sam here with you?"

"No. And no. I'll talk to you out here. What the hell is going on, Jeremy? Did you break into my house?"

Jeremy's mouth hung open for a moment. "What're you saying, Jamie?"

"I heard you wanted to get your hands on Gretchen's manuscripts."

Jeremy ran his hand through his hair again, but said nothing.

"Gregor called me, Jeremy. He told me about your conversation the other day. And I *know* Gretchen's parents don't have any intention of getting you involved with her book."

"Right," Jeremy whispered, pressing his glasses up his nose. "Jamie, won't you come in so we can talk?"

"Nope. Right here."

"I hate to have you standing out here . . ."

"Spare me the fragile condition bullshit, okay? Just tell me what's going on. Did you try to *steal* Gretchen's notebooks?"

"Her notebooks? From whom?"

"The laptops? Did you think her work would be in those laptops? Because it's not."

"What laptops? Jamie, you need to help me out here. Did someone steal Gretchen's drafts from you?"

I didn't reply. He pushed his glasses up

his nose.

"I really *don't know*," Jeremy said. "I *did* ask Gregor for the files, yes. I shouldn't have done that. But I wanted to see them before I talked to you. I needed to know what kind of conversation we were going to have to have."

"You haven't answered my e-mails. Why didn't you just answer me and ask to see them?"

"There's a bench outside." Jeremy tugged at his sweatpants' drawstring and tied it tighter. "Will you at least sit out there with me? We obviously need to talk, and I have a feeling it's going to take more than a couple minutes."

"Fine," I said, and he led me to an island of hedges in the middle of the parking lot, where there were three granite benches surrounding a small fountain with no water.

"Nobody ever sits here," Jeremy informed me before sitting.

I plopped myself down on the bench opposite his and waited for him to speak. Instead, he watched as a white Hyundai drove up and parked by the condo next to his. A young couple — a beefy guy and a pretty redhead in low-rise jeans — got out. The guy opened up the back and started sliding out a large box from IKEA. His lady friend grabbed hold of the other end of the box. He talked and she giggled while they worked, but I couldn't hear what he was saying.

"What is it you wanted to tell me?" I prompted Jeremy.

Jeremy gazed at the couple until they'd disappeared behind their red-brown door with their box.

"I've wondered often, especially lately, what she told you about the divorce," he said finally.

"Not all that much, really," I admitted.

I watched him play with his sweatpants drawstring for a few moments, wrapping it around his thumb.

"She tell you I hit her?" he asked quietly.

I stared at him. "No."

He put his palms on either side of him, flattening them against the granite as if he were about to spring up. But he stayed put.

"You mean once or you mean a lot of times?" I asked.

"More like once."

"More like once?" I repeated.

The red-brown door opened and the couple returned to their car, pulling smaller IKEA boxes from it. This time, when they returned to their apartment, they left the door open. I watched them intently so I wouldn't have to look at Jeremy.

"I want to tell you what happened between her and me," he said.

I hesitated, distracted by the obvious question: Why hadn't *Gretchen* told me what happened between them? Why was this the first I was hearing of this?

"Okay," I murmured. "So tell me."

"My dad was real sick. He died of lung cancer, did you know that?"

I nodded. "Yes. I'm sorry."

"And Gretchen and I, we'd been talking a lot about how we'd have kids soon. I mean, around the time he decided to refuse any more treatment. A really hard time."

"Okay," I said again.

"And, not like she has it in the book. In the book, she makes it sound like some kind of agree-to-disagree thing we had going. But she basically had said yes, we were doing this. She'd stopped taking the pill and everything. Did you ever tell you that?"

"No," I said, feeling vaguely inadequate for not knowing that either. Not that Sam or I told anyone when we were at that stage.

"Okay. Well, she did. We were trying, you know? And with my dad, there were some days when that was the only thing that kept me going. Knowing there'd be this other life . . . knowing there'd be something to look forward to. I know it sounds weird from me, the guy, to be so sentimental about it. It was like we were reversed. The woman's usually the one who's all excited about it."

"I don't know about that," I said. "I've known a lot of couples where the guy's the one who really goes crazy over the kids."

"How is it with you guys?"

I had to think about this before answering. It was a good question.

"We're both equal, I guess. We both knew we'd do this eventually. But, um, it gets more complicated when it becomes a reality."

Jeremy seemed to hear only the first part of my response. "Well, that was kind of how I thought we were. That we both wanted it. But one day I got home early and took in the mail. And there was this notice for Gretchen from the medical center. It pissed me off, because she'd had some X-rays done like eight months before for a back problem she'd been having, and the insurance was supposed to pay for it. We kept getting the bills. And then we thought we finally got it squared away with the insurance, but here was a bill again. At least that's what I thought. I tore it open, and what was in there wasn't a bill for an X-ray. It was a reminder notice. It said that Gretchen had to come in for her next Depo-Provera shot. Do you know what that is?"

"Yeah," I said. My heart did an extra little hard thud. This was starting to sound like a sordid story — the kind Gretchen probably wouldn't have wanted me to hear.

"Women get them every three months —"

"Jeremy, I know what they are. I don't know if we should be —"

I'd been gazing at the open red-brown door of the young couple. Now I was watching as a long-haired tuxedo cat pranced out of their apartment.

"I just want you to *understand* what happened." Jeremy was staring at me, trying to reestablish eye contact. I let him. "I need someone who was close to her to know. I thought it was a mistake. I thought, this stupid hospital fucks *everything* up. I think that's what I said when I showed the notice to her when she got home. And then the look on her face . . . And she starts telling me that she just couldn't handle it yet, it was impossible for her to even think of kids yet. Oh my God, Jamie. I was so angry."

"So you . . ."

"I kind of pushed her into the wall. Hard. When I heard that, I was just, like, out of control for a couple of minutes there. Like there must be something terribly wrong with both of us for her to do that. To do that and let me think we were trying for all that time, rather than just *talking* to me. To make me think that any minute now we'd be —"

"It had been three months?"

"Six."

"Okay. So how did Gretchen react? When you did that?"

"Well, she was shocked. And she kept trying to explain . . . That she wasn't ready, she was terrified, but I had been so sure, and so stressed about my dad, she didn't want to upset me. It felt like crazy talk to me, though. I mean, who *does* that?"

I shrugged. "Maybe a lot of women? I mean, not with such extreme measures. Maybe for a lot of people, though, *controlling* the situation is easier than talking about it?"

"I don't know. But I thought we could talk about things. I mean, I'm not some insensitive prick. I mean, that day aside. We talked about everything. Or . . . I guess . . . I thought we did."

"So was there another time?"

"A few days later. After I visited my dad in the hospital, I went for a couple of drinks. When I got home, I was getting all up in her face. I was like 'When do those magic shots wear off, Gretchen? When are you going in for your next one?' I was following her around saying that, while she was trying to dry dishes and put them away. I kept getting in front of the cabinets wherever she was trying to reach, blocking her way. And then finally she looked right back at me and said, 'So you're an asshole now? This is who you are now? Because I'm not ready to be your baby machine?'

"That's it. That's when I hit her."

"In the face?"

"Yes."

"With your fist?" I asked, not sure I wanted to know the answer.

"No. With my hand, though. The other side of her face kind of slammed into the cabinet door. Then she pushed me away. She ran into the living room, and I followed her, trying to apologize. She started pulling books off the shelves. Big ones — the biggest she could find. Dictionaries and stuff. And throwing them at me. She was screaming, 'Don't you EVER hit me! Who do you think you are? What the fuck do you think this is? A turn-of-the-century whorehouse?' "

I bit my lip, stifling a snort. "She said that?"

Jeremy's face was purple by now. He stared at his hands. "Yeah. And she kept throwing those books. Till one hit me in the head. Then she ran upstairs and locked herself in the bedroom. She wouldn't let me in to talk. I could hear her crying in there all night long. The next day she had a bruise on her face. I think she may have called in sick so people couldn't see her. And she spent that night away. I don't even know where she went. A couple of days later she tells me she thinks we should separate."

"DAMN IT, ANGELA!" A yell came from the open apartment, and the IKEA guy came outside, looked under his car, then under the bushes nearest his door.

"And did you agree that you should?" I asked.

"My head was kind of still exploding from everything that had happened, so I didn't know what to think. But we met for dinner a couple of days later. And she was like, 'I had to tell the people at work I bumped into a door. I had to be one of *those* women.' And I didn't know what to say to that. I was sorry I put her in that position. I kept apologizing. But I guess I expected her to apologize, too. She didn't, really. Should I not have expected her to?"

"I don't know. Apologizing after you hit

her . . . why would you expect that?"

"Um . . . I didn't mean it like that. Of course that sounds terrible. I was sorry. I can't tell you. Really sorry. I still am. But I mean, I expected her to acknowledge the other thing. That was never really resolved, though. She started saying stuff about how if we broke up now, and didn't stretch it out, there would still be time for me to find someone I could have a family with. Because she was pretty sure it wasn't going to happen with her."

By now both the young man and the young woman were outside, looking under cars for their cat.

"And I started to see that she was right. It was like we'd both seen each other's absolute bottom. Lying and sneaking and hitting and shit. It was, like, who wants to try to be in love after that? We'd already seen how bad we could be to each other. It was like something was erased after that. There wouldn't be any joy in getting back together.

"And she started talking about Shelly a lot. I think, in a way, it was always about Shelly. At one point, when I was trying to get her to come back, she said to me, 'I never really knew how to pretend to be a daughter. I don't really want to try to pretend to be someone's mother either.' "

348

"I see," I said slowly. It sounded like Gretchen also found it difficult pretending to be someone's wife.

The tuxedo cat ran out from under my car just then. The guy leaped at him but missed. The young woman tried to chase him back into their apartment, but the cat ran right past the door.

"Should we help them?" I asked, turning to Jeremy.

Jeremy shook his head. "They do this at least once a week. Even if the whole baby question wasn't about Shelly, then the, uh . . . incident between me and her . . . what I did . . . *that* was. I think it sort of triggered something in her. I'd flipped a switch. She couldn't give me another chance, because that was the sort of thing Shelly was always doing. And she couldn't make the same mistakes as Shelly, cuz look where that led."

"But her life was so different from Shelly's."

"I know. I tried to argue that point. And that she and I had so much more history than just those two bad nights, but . . . that was that for Gretchen." Jeremy shrugged. "I think that whole thing always weighed more on her than she was ever willing to say."

I watched as the cat hopped up on a

garbage barrel, looked at his owners as they crept toward him, lifted his paw, and licked the fur between his toes.

"Now, we didn't talk much after the divorce."

"Right. I know."

"Except when she was in the middle of this new book. We had coffee a few times. Because there was something she was writing about that she wanted me to know about."

"Which was?"

The young woman snatched at the cat's tail, then scooped him into her arms. She marched haughtily to her door and slammed it behind her. The guy followed her, opening the door for himself and slamming it as she had.

"She said that she wasn't sure how she was going to do it in a way that was fair to both of us. But she found herself wanting to write about what really happened between her and me."

"Why now?" I turned back to Jeremy. "Why all of the sudden, after skipping over it so nicely in the first book?"

"That's what I wanted to know. At first I accused her of just wanting to sell books. She said it wasn't about that at all. She said she'd learned some things about Shelly that made her reconsider certain feelings she'd had about her own life."

"Did she explain what that meant?"

"Well. Yeah. She said she'd found out, she was pretty sure, that she was wrong about some of the choices that Shelly had made. Namely, that she didn't think Shelly's death had anything to do with her choice of men. That it was never about that guy Frank. Never about her choice to stay with him."

"Meaning that she didn't think he did it?"

"Right. So that made her feel better about Shelly. Relieved, in one sense. And she said that made her want to write about herself. The influence Shelly's memory had had on her own choices. Her own relationships. And she wanted to be more honest about that in this next book."

"Did you give her permission to do so?"

Jeremy bit his lip and gazed into the shrubs behind me. "She didn't need my permission."

"I know. But did you give it your approval?"

"I told her I'd think about it. In all honesty, I was hoping she'd change her mind. Gretchen was a pretty private person. I had a feeling that even if she wrote that stuff down for herself, she'd eventually edit it out for publication."

"So you wanted to see what she'd actually written, because you were afraid I'd just go ahead and publish it as is, and never speak to you about it?"

"I just needed to see what was there. What I needed to be prepared for. And how I was going to talk to you."

"Gretchen hasn't even been gone a month. All things considered, you couldn't wait a little while longer?"

"It kept me up at night, knowing it was out there. This thing that I'd done. Out there when Gretchen wasn't anymore."

Charlie Bucket jabbed me at that very moment. I put my hand on my side and rubbed away the soreness. His strikes seemed bony and sharp lately. I was starting to feel like I was housing one of those boxing nun puppets they sell in novelty stores.

"People make mistakes," Jeremy said, maybe mistaking my distracted silence for anger. "People can change."

"I'm aware of that," I told him, pressing my fingers gently against a second jab. "Do you think you're one of those people?"

"I'd like to think so. But I guess I shouldn't expect you to believe me."

"Why's that?"

"Because your loyalty lies with Gretchen."

"It sounds like Gretchen still had some

faith in you, if she'd sit you down and tell you her plans to write about what happened. And expect you to be perfectly civil about it. Which you were."

Jeremy was silent, fiddling with his drawstring again.

"So you don't know who broke into my house, then?" I asked. "You know anything about that?"

Jeremy took off his glasses, closed his eyes, and rubbed the bridge of his nose. "No."

"Okay," I said.

I didn't know what I believed about him anymore. Or about him and Gretchen. But I was pretty sure I believed his answer to my question.

"Someone broke into your house and stole Gretchen's things?"

"Just a couple of notebooks. And two laptops, but not the one with Gretchen's files on it, because I had that one with me. But I think that was the intention. They just didn't find the rest of the stuff. They stole some other things, but I think that might have been to hide what they were really looking for."

Jeremy put his glasses back on. "Do you know how serious this is, Jamie?"

"Of course I do."

"If someone went to that extreme to get

their hands on something Gretchen wrote, they probably have something a lot worse to hide than I did. Something Gretchen knew."

"I know, Jeremy."

Jeremy stared at me through the finger smudges on his lenses. "Should I be worried about you?"

I gazed back at those smudges and smiled a little. His glasses were never clean in college. I tried to remember how young the rest of his face used to look back then, when we were all twenty-one. But couldn't quite.

"No," I answered. "I don't think you should."

CHAPTER 35

"Stand by Your Man"

I'm not sure if every Tammy Wynette fan should be required to come to the defense of that single song, or even to like it in particular. The song, like so many of her hits, was mostly written by her producer, Billy Sherrill. And there is so much more to Tammy than this song — which isn't a particular favorite of mine — that I find discussions of it rather boring. Still, I suppose my liberal background requires I address it before I proceed any further on this trip, before I sing Tammy's praises along with those of Dolly and Loretta.

Admittedly, before I started listening to more country music, this was my uninformed view of Tammy Wynette: a country-western Phyllis Schlafly in sequins. All I knew of her was that she sang that particular song.

Since then, I've watched the same early television performance of "Stand by Your Man" countless times. In it, Tammy is wearing a red-sequined dress that's all wrong for her figure. Her hair is an absurdly high helmet of whorled light blond. In this Opry appearance, she is clearly a very nervous performer — you can see it in all of the videos from early in her career. She barely moves her body as she sings. Her face looks stiff, almost pained. She rolls her eyes back slightly between lines, as if trying to remember the words. She looks like a kid in a spelling bee, just trying to get it right. I have immediate sympathy for her — for her discomfort, for the care she puts into the song. And for most of the song, the meaning of the words dissolve in this sympathy. I like her regardless of whether she or I believe in standing by our men, on traditional principle or otherwise.

I also feel bad that her signature song happened to come out at the height of women's lib. Later, similar songs of hers might have been more defiance than coincidence. But with "Stand by Your Man" — there she was, still a struggling mother of three, her career still new and fragile, trying to take her one shot at stardom, trying to get her song perfect, when these northeastern intellectual types come flying out of nowhere (at least, nowhere Tammy knew or understood) and pick on her, her dream, and her developing act.

People often point out that Tammy was simply singing about values with which she was raised. Aside from that, in the context of country music history, it seems odd that feminists singled out Tammy. Sure, the song seems to command an attitude that is offensive to feminism, but country music is full of songs about people who stick with their mates (male or female) even though their behavior confuses them, depresses them, drives them crazy ("You Win Again," "[I'm Not Your] Steppin' Stone," "You Can Always Come Back"). Tammy was singing about something her fellow country musicians — male and female — had sung about hundreds of times before. It was just the particular wording and timing (and the skill with which she sang it) of "Stand by Your Man" that got it noticed.

As for Tammy's sad, sad delivery, it is, again, a part of the tradition of a genre of music that has always stressed that love can be painful and depressing and motivates men and women to do unhealthy and irrational things. No one's ever begrudged her onetime partner George Jones his unrelentingly pathetic hits: "He Stopped Loving Her Today" (really, just listen to it), "When the Grass Grows over Me," "If Drinkin' Don't Kill Me." You don't have to like the genre, but it doesn't make sense to isolate one artist and song for being pathetic. And a woman is, I believe, allowed to be just as pitiful in love as a man.

To be fair, though, Tammy did have a few subsequent songs that cross the line for me. After feminists exploded at "Stand by Your Man," Tammy and her producer seemed to enjoy thumbing their noses at them, producing "Singing My Song," "Run, Woman, Run," and the ridiculous "Don't Liberate Me (Love Me)," which thankfully never went up the charts. (Also good for a laugh is the embarrassing "Good Lovin' [Makes It Right]," although frankly I don't think all of the advice in that one is entirely off the mark.)

So while I don't think the reaction to "Stand by Your Man" was fair, I can see how some of Tammy's subsequent music and fake-eyelash-batting persona would have chafed at feminists of the day. Truly, I am grateful for the feminists who came before me — the very ones who found Tammy's music offensive. And I am grateful for Tammy, her voice and her heart. Thankfully, I was not alive in 1968 and therefore do not have to choose between the two.

And by the way, if we are to accept that gender and sexuality is a spectrum, I believe we have to accept that some people are going to fall on the traditional side of it. Oddly, I think it can be harder for someone of my generation and background to accept a woman who dresses and acts in the bleached-blond feminine tradition of Tammy Wynette than a man who does the same for a gay pride parade. But how is that fair? Hasn't the point always been freedom of choice in one's lifestyle, one's relationships?

This is a freedom that Tammy actually exercised — at least, for much of her life. Everyone who knows the basic facts of her life knows she wasn't into standing by a man at all costs. She married her first husband rashly, despite the protests and disapproval of her family. She left him even though she had two kids, one on the way, and no job — because she realized she didn't love him and she wanted more for herself — in particular, a shot at being a singer, which he didn't support. She left number two for George Jones. She left George Jones because, although she loved him, seven years of his drunken high jinks had taken a toll. Marriage number four was a three-week farce. Husband number five was the only one she stood by, though he surely didn't deserve it. But that's another story, too long and sad and perplexing for this piece on a song she sang before she'd even met him.

In the end, more than standing by her man, I think Tammy stood by her song. She insisted that "Stand by Your Man" was "just a pretty love song," and despite growing tired of having to defend it, she clearly drew great joy from its popularity. Her autobiography was titled *Stand by Your Man*. The doorbell of her mansion played the tune. She sang the hell out of that song and loved the hell out of the success that it brought her. Whatever she was personally, professionally, this was a woman who knew what she wanted, worked her ass off for it, and refused to apologize for it when she got it.

Does she really need any more defense than that?

— *Tammyland*

CHAPTER 36

Nathan's message showed up on my cell while I was at work the following evening.

"Jamie. Please call me," was all he said on the voice mail.

I noticed it during my break and called him right back — thinking he wanted confirmation that the FedEx package had been delivered.

"I've been calling a few people." Nathan sounded drained. "A few people I didn't want to hear this on the news. It's hit a couple of news stations. Not where you are, probably, but . . . Jamie, they found Gretchen's purse."

My heart jumped. "Where?"

"In Youngs Lake in Emerson."

"Emerson? There's a lake there?"

"A little one, yeah. Near the state park."

"Were the police diving for evidence, or something?"

"No. Not at all. Little kids fish there all

the time. Some girl was with her dad and caught Gretchen's purse. It seemed empty at first, but they found an expired credit card in one of the inside pockets. The dad recognized her name from the local papers and turned it in."

"So . . . what does this mean?"

"Well, they don't think Gretchen put it there, that's for sure."

I took a breath. "Oh my God, Nathan. I'm so sorry. How's your mom holding up?"

"About the same. It doesn't change much for her. We already knew Gretchen's death might not have been an accident."

I had more questions, but didn't want to make this any harder for Nathan.

"Thank you for calling me," I said.

When we'd hung up, I went back to my desk and did a few searches on news stories with Gretchen's name in them in the last forty-eight hours. Sure enough, a posting from a New Hampshire news station had a brief story about it. The author Gretchen Waters, who'd died falling down some stone steps in Willingham, was presumed to have died an accidental death.

Now the discovery of her purse in an Emerson lake was causing police to suspect foul play. Her money, credit cards, and ID were gone from her wallet, but police had been able to identify it as hers because of a loose, expired credit card zipped into an inside pocket of the purse. Her boyfriend Gregor Bachman also confirmed that the purse resembled Gretchen's.

Police weren't releasing many new details, but said that an investigation of some "unusual circumstances" of Gretchen's fall had already been quietly under way before the purse discovery: Her head injuries had suggested a backward fall. There were hairs on her sweater that didn't match her own (likely from someone at the reading or anyone else she'd encountered recently, but still being given "a closer look" by police). And there was bruising on her arm, with a laceration possibly made by fingernails — suggesting Gretchen had been grabbed and thrown. The details were essentially the same as what Gretchen's mother had told me, with only a few new specifics.

The article mentioned that Gretchen's family was originally from Emerson, and that she'd been in Emerson a great deal recently, researching her next book. It also mentioned that Gretchen was the daughter of the 1985 murder victim Shelly Brewer.

I sat back in my chair and closed my eyes. So Gretchen's purse was found in Emerson, when she'd died forty miles away in

Willingham. That was quite a coincidence. It was unlikely that a random mugger would end up in Emerson in order to chuck her purse into Youngs Lake. Almost certainly her killer had been from Emerson or its vicinity. Likely someone she'd spoken to in recent weeks.

P.S. Also, in your days as a reporter, did you start to develop any skill for telling who is lying to you?

Remembering Gretchen's last e-mail to me, I wanted to scream. I got up and ran to the bathroom. There, I stared at the stall door, saying to myself over and over: *Who was lying to you, Gretchen?* I had a feeling she'd figured it out herself. And that that was the somebody who pushed her.

I stayed there for about twenty minutes, figuring no one would call a pregnant woman on a lengthy bathroom break. When the question finally grew stale in my head, I returned to my desk. My break had ended a while ago, and now I had a seventeen-inch story I had to reduce to fifteen inches. I glanced at the reporter's name. Someone not particularly diva. Good. I did the edit within fifteen minutes, then went back on-line to find more stories about Gretchen. I was waiting for one of the reporters to turn in his story about school budget cuts.

There was one article about Gretchen from her hometown in Connecticut, in which Nathan was quoted as saying that the family was saddened, but hoped that the finding of the purse would bring them closer to the answers about Gretchen's death. In another, the Willingham librarian who'd hosted Gretchen's event was quoted as saying how shocked she was.

Her name was Ruth Rowan — she'd been quoted in earlier articles about Gretchen's death. I scribbled her name down, then searched the library's Web site for her e-mail address.

My e-mail dinged: the school budget article had arrived.

CHAPTER 37

"I'm getting up at six tomorrow," I told Sam two evenings later. "My alarm's gonna go off before yours."

"Why?"

"I've got an appointment."

"They gonna do another ultrasound ever? Are they gonna let you bring home the pictures?"

"Not that kind of appointment. I had my last doctor appointment yesterday morning, and it was uneventful. She basically just listened to the heartbeat and told me my belly's getting sufficiently bigger. No, I've got something set up in New Hampshire. A little south of Emerson. Forty minutes less of a trip. Willingham's this little city not far from UNH. And you know where that is, right? Didn't your friend Alex go there?"

"But . . ." Sam looked confused. "Wait, that's all they did for the appointment? What'll they do for the next one?"

"I don't know. Probably the same thing."

Sam looked dubious. "You're driving all the way there and back before work? For what?"

"Someone's agreed to talk to me. It's about Gretchen."

"Well, I figured that. Another one of her sources?"

"Sort of."

"This couldn't wait till the weekend? I could help you drive on a weekend."

"This lady doesn't work on weekends. I could only catch her on a weekday."

"What does it matter when she works? Did you tell her you're over seven months pregnant?"

"Why the hell would I tell her that?"

Sam shrugged. "I don't know. But, Jamie . . ."

"Yeah?"

"How long is this going to last?"

"Till my time runs out, Sam."

"You make it sound like you're about to die. You know, you don't need to give up on Gretchen once the baby's born. I'll be helping you. It'll be both of us. You'll still have time."

I pulled one of Gretchen's notebooks from the small stack on my bedside table, deciding not to bother reminding Sam that *time* was going to be a different animal for us in a couple of months. He would have time to "help" after work. I would have time to take an occasional shower. There didn't seem much sense in holding this against him, since it was biology and our current financial situation that dictated the terms, not him.

"It feels urgent *now*, though . . ."

I stopped myself before elaborating, unsure whether or not I should tell him about Gretchen's purse in the lake. I hadn't yet. I hadn't wanted him to worry. And now I was pretty sure it wouldn't convince him of anything, except that I shouldn't go anywhere near Emerson again in my condition.

Sam closed his eyes.

"Okay," he whispered.

I examined the notebook. It was red, with an especially worn cover. On the first page, Gretchen had scrawled *Tammy 2?*

Sam rolled over and turned off his lamp.

"I love you," he said.

"I love you, too," I answered.

I opened Gretchen's notebook. After a few minutes, Sam began to snore softly.

CHAPTER 38

"Till I Get It Right"

Perhaps more than any of her songs, this was Tammy's real anthem. Certainly more than "Stand by Your Man," which made her famous, but, as everyone knows, did not reflect her real approach to relationships.

In "Till I Get It Right," Tammy declares that she'll "keep on fallin' in love" till she gets it right. This summary makes her sound plucky, but anyone who's heard it knows it's more of a sad song. Tammy describes herself as "a wounded bird," and it's essentially a breakup song. The narrator has been hurt again, but knows she'll give love another try, again and again.

When I listen to it, tiny, embarrassing tears form at the very corners of my eyes. Not so much because I can relate — but because the song is so Tammy, and, really, so Shelly, too — although I'm fairly certain that Shelly would've found it cheesy and old-fashioned.

Like it or not, she and Tammy had a few things in common. In particular, the habit of jumping naively from man to man in hopes that one of them would magically make everything better. This habit can be pretty frustrating to those close to such women — surely it was for Tammy's family, as it certainly was for my mom and Shelly's friends. Even for me, remembering what I do and trying to understand.

But this song brings me closer to understanding. It doesn't explain anything, of course. It simply makes me feel the sadness of it, and along with it, the hopefulness of it. The words hint at what it feels like to want romantic love with the same kind of compulsion that some of us have for our next promotion, our next mixed drink, our next piece of chocolate.

No one knows exactly why Tammy was that way about men. Some theorize that it had to do with the death of her father when she was a baby. She never had a father, and perhaps she was always looking for the perfect masculine prince and protector.

I think this explanation is too simplistic. For one thing, Tammy's grandfather played an important and protective role in her life through high school. What's more, there are plenty of women who grow up without fathers but don't become man-crazy, and in any case, I prefer not to reduce most behaviors to a direct cause-and-effect relationship. If you can simplify Tammy's behavior that way, you can simplify Shelly's in almost the same way: She lost her father when she was twelve. I never knew her father, but I knew her, and I know nothing of hers could ever be that easy to explain.

I believe a lot of Tammy fans think they know who was the best man for Tammy: George Jones. He was her true love, they say, but he threw it all away with his alcoholism. Personally, I like to point to Burt Reynolds as the true love. Sure, it didn't last long and wasn't likely to, but accounts of their time together make me think it was the most fun and uncomplicated relationship she ever had — something she certainly could've used more of. Her daughters and others close to her, however, claim that neither of these men — nor any of the men she was ever with — was her true love. She never really got it right.

And of course, I wonder about Shelly, and if any of those guys she was with was ever the right one. And if she found something she was looking for in any one of those relation-ships. Or if what she wanted was fixed but unattainable, or simply kept changing.

The guys I've picked out as her possible real loves are Bruce and Roland. Bruce be-cause he was an atypical choice for her. From what I've heard, he was a kinder, gen-tler, more thoughtful kind of guy than she usually went for. Why she dated him I don't know — but there must have been something different there that kept her with him for all of those months. They say that the two of them remained friends long after high school — after he went to college and she stuck around here. And I remember meeting him once, when I was six or seven. We ran into him at Kmart in

Plantsville, where she'd always take me to buy cheap candy before a movie. He was in the candy aisle, too, with a package of black Twizzlers in his hand: this gangly, suntanned man with poufy dark hair. He was doing the same thing we were — buying candy ahead to avoid the theater's prices — although he was going to a different movie than us. I remember Shelly laughing at the coincidence, and telling me, "Honey, this is my friend Bruce. We're old friends."

The other is Roland. One of those cool guys who went exclusively by his last name. He was with my mother when I was around four or five, and apparently I even met him a couple of times on visits, though I don't remember it. The thing about Roland is that he helped Shelly get off drugs. Brought her to meetings and even helped her pay for a short clinic stay, at one point. My mom has told me this about Roland more than once. And I remember her telling it with a wistfulness in her voice, as if she wished Shelly had stayed with him. Whether or not this was a great match, Roland must have cared a great deal about Shelly. And Shelly must have, on some level, trusted him.

Did she ever get it right? I like to think she did. Maybe not with her last romance, if you can call it that — but maybe with a couple of the others along the way.

"Jolene"

Route 2, southern
New Hampshire
Winter 1985

It was actually Shelly who introduced me to country music. She did so unwittingly, while she was driving me back to Connecticut from Emerson one Sunday night in the winter. In those days I visited

her about two weekends a month
— whole-weekend visits that
had started less than a year
before.

I remember it as the last
drive we had together, but I
know that can't be true. She
was killed in March, and I
know we must've seen each
other in between.

Shelly wasn't even a country
fan, but she was flipping
around on the radio that
night, and stopped at the
song. She may have been distracted by the road, just
wanting to settle on one station for a moment — but I
remember her singing along
softly with it.

I remember the *click-click
click-click* of Shelly turning
her high beams off and on
again when other cars came
along. With the road winding
in front of us as we glided
through the dark, the song
felt almost scary to me — with
that low guitar and the lady I
didn't yet know was Dolly

sounding so sad as she repeated that name: "Jolene."

"I like that name, 'Jolene,' " I said, after it was over.

"Do you?" Shelly said. "It's not a name you hear much around here."

"I like the name 'Stacey' even better, though."

All the girls in my first-grade class loved the name "Stacey," I explained. We all wanted to change our name to "Stacey."

"Well, you can't all be Stacey," Shelly said. "That would be weird if you were all Stacey."

Still, I wanted to know how a person changes her name. A girl in my class had said her mother was going to let her change her name to Stacey, but I suspected she was lying. And I wondered, if it were really true, how they were going to do that. Would they change her birth certificate?

Shelly said yes, that girl

was probably lying. Little girls aren't allowed to change their names. If I still loved "Stacey" when I was much, much older, I could change my name.

"But it doesn't suit you, though," she said. "You don't seem like a Stacey."

I remember being a little sad because it was surely better to seem like a Stacey than almost anything else. And did Shelly think I seemed like a Gretchen? I wondered. And what did it mean to seem like a Gretchen? Was it a little like being Gretel in the fairy tale? (Did she even pick that name for me? I wondered years later. Or did someone else? It was everything my aunt Nantie — later, Mom — wanted me to be: buttoned up and classy, but gentle, like her.)

Shelly was none of those things. From everything people have told me about her since, she could've been a Jolene. She could have any man she wanted, and she did. Since high school. She was woman enough to take just about any man. Which is how I came into the world, with ambiguous paternity.

She could've been a Jolene, but she was Shelly. I always called her Shelly. Not Mommy. Not Mom.

My aunt raised me from the beginning, but no one ever kept it from me that Shelly was my mother. My dear aunt didn't want to upset Shelly, I suspect, by forcing the issue. She had me call her Nantie. When I was nine I switched to Mom because I was getting older now and Nantie was weird and that's what everyone else had: a mom.

I suspect that during the period when I was five to seven, when I was visiting Shelly more, it was a sort of "trial run" for her. She'd been getting her life together. She was thinking of asking for me back, and my aunt knew it. Everyone probably knew it but me.

But then she died. She died before I could know it for sure.

That "last drive" — I remember it so well. I remember Shelly telling me about the pet-food factory where she used to work. She never told me about the actual job. Instead, she'd make up stories about the dogs and cats who'd write letters of appreciation, letters of complaint. The snooty white longhair cat who was always complaining that the kibble wasn't quite crunchy enough. The cheap little wiener dog who typed his letters on an old-fashioned typewriter, always trying to get free samples.

I remember the bittersweet promise of school the next day. I loved first grade. I loved bringing home to Nantie dittos with 100s and star stickers on top of them, putting them on the refrigerator. I never showed these things to Shelly when I saw her — it didn't seem the sort of thing that would interest her.

And I remember Jolene. I remember that guitar haunting me like Halloween. Jolene, Jolene, Jolene, Jolene.

I've only heard the song again a handful of times. It's not the kind of song that just pops up on the radio in New England — or maybe anywhere — these days. And I've only begun to listen to it deliberately lately — this song that first made a conflicted country fan of me all those years ago, before I knew that there were different types of music for different types of people. This song that will always remind me so painfully of the only woman who I would ever really think of as my mother.

CHAPTER 39

I was dreading arriving at the Willingham Library parking lot — seeing the place where Gretchen had actually fallen. I even considered parking down the road from the library so I wouldn't have to be in the actual parking lot. But I'd programmed the GPS for the library address, and it ordered me toward the library lot in its clipped, efficient female voice — like a stern mother reminding me of my responsibilities.

I pulled into the lot, took one of the front spaces, then headed straight into the library, without looking around much.

Ruth Rowan — a petite woman in her forties with a soft, mulletlike hairdo — sat me down in her windowless office behind the reference desk. While Ruth herself smelled sharply of soap, her office smelled like old coffee.

"You said in your e-mail that you're a

friend of Gretchen Waters?"

"Yes. And I'm a journalist."

"I see. And you're here in which capacity, then?"

Oh, librarians. Always so sharp.

"A little of each, I guess."

I explained about being Gretchen's sort-of literary executor, and that seemed to put her at ease a bit.

"I know the police have asked you all about that night. But I was wondering if you'd be willing to tell me about it, too."

"Are you going to put this information in her book?"

"I'm finding it helps me feel a bit better," I explained, "to know as much as possible about what happened."

Ruth nodded. "Fair enough. Shall I start with her reading?"

"Okay."

"She seemed a little nervous. I mean, she did a good job. But she didn't seem totally happy to be here. She was . . . maybe . . . uncomfortable. Especially when someone asked her about her second book."

"What did she say about it?"

"She said that she was in the process of doing a major overhaul of the book. That she wasn't sure what kind of book it was going to be yet. That she didn't want to say

384

a lot about it. Which struck me as a little odd. That's a pretty standard question most authors get, you know? What are you working on next?"

"Maybe she didn't want to jinx it," I said.

Ruth gave me a sad look. "Maybe so."

"Also . . . Gretchen just didn't really like public speaking."

"I see. Well, she did a fine job. I'm not saying she didn't."

"Did anyone in particular make her nervous?"

"Well, that's a good question. When she went up to the podium, she said, 'Oh. Hello,' to someone as if she recognized a guest she wasn't expecting. I didn't see who, it wasn't clear. I didn't think much of it at the time, although I did tell the police about it later. And that didn't seem to make her nervous. On the other hand, there was someone in the crowd who asked her why *Tammyland* didn't have hardly anything in it about Kitty Wells. He said anyone who knew anything about women in country music would've given a big chunk of the book to Kitty Wells. It seemed like he wanted to give Gretchen a hard time about that."

"What did Gretchen say to that?"

"She said she appreciated the contribution of Kitty Wells to country music, but that her book was a personal memoir, and none of Kitty's songs happened to speak to her in the way the others had."

"And was he happy with that response?"

"No, not at all. But this particular patron isn't happy with anything. He's a terrible curmudgeon. He writes a letter to the editor nearly once a month explaining why the school or library budgets should be cut. He likes to attend our events just to poop on them, if you'll excuse my language. I'm sure he didn't mean anything personal with Gretchen. I'm pretty sure he doesn't care a whit about Kitty Wells either."

"So were most in attendance people who regularly come to these book events?" I asked.

"Oh, I recognized about half of them." Ruth straightened a pile of books on her desk. "We have our regulars, certainly."

"How many people were there in all?"

"About eighteen or so. Which is pretty good for a book event like this. It's usually a fairly middle-aged crowd at these things. There were a few young women this time, since *Tammyland* is a little more of a young women's book."

"Any men? I mean, aside from your curmudgeon?"

Ruth sat back in her chair. "Um . . . yes.

Two others. A short, bald man. I believe he was the husband of one of the ladies. And one other man, who was by himself. A very tall, middle-aged gentleman. I'd never seen him before. He had what they call 'big hair,' which is why I noticed him."

The description took me by surprise.

"Dark hair?" I asked.

"Yes." Ruth studied me worriedly.

"With some white in it?"

"I think so," Ruth said slowly.

"And how long did the event last?" I asked, deliberately changing the subject.

"A little over an hour, if you count the refreshments afterward. Gretchen chatted with several of the attendees, had some wine. Then she and I chatted for a little bit while I locked up the library."

"You two were the last out?"

"Yes. We were behind the other guests by a few minutes."

"That was still enough time for most of them to start up their cars and leave, probably?"

"I suppose. As I told the officer who came and spoke to me, I didn't see Gretchen get into her car. I didn't see exactly where she was parked at the time. I usually park on the side of the building, away from the main lot. Most of the staff parks there."

I hesitated, not wanting to sound pushy or critical. I wasn't blaming her for not walking Gretchen to her car.

"So you didn't see any of cars in the main lot?"

"I caught a *glimpse*. As I came down the steps. But then I circled around to the side."

"Were there a lot of cars in the lot?"

"A few." Ruth sighed. "There are usually a few, even when the library is closed."

"Why's that?"

Ruth shrugged. "There's often overflow from the Dragon Buffet half-price nights. We don't enforce patrons-only parking. It's usually not a problem, since our lot's pretty big and we don't have a lot of patrons around dinnertime anyway."

"So what kind of cars did you see there that night?"

"I described what I remembered to the officer who came."

"Can you tell me, too?"

Ruth looked frustrated. "Well, okay. I don't have a photographic memory. I don't remember everything. But there were a couple of SUVs. As usual."

"Do you remember the colors?"

"One tan — a really huge one. One was smaller and a dark color. I don't quite remember. There are lots of SUVs in our town. There might have been more than two. It wouldn't have been remarkable to me. There was a black VW Bug, I think. And there was a cute orange compact car. I noticed that one because I've been wanting one of those myself. I test-drove a Honda Fit recently."

"Okay," I said.

"There was a pickup truck near the back of the lot, close to the Dragon Buffet side. Blue. Kind of old-looking. But that's all I remember."

"There were more cars than that, though, you're saying."

"A few, yes. Those were the ones that were memorable to me the next day, when the police questioned me. I certainly didn't remember any license plates, or anything like that that would've been of great use to them."

"Do you know if the police tracked down other patrons who'd been at Gretchen's reading? People who were leaving the lot the same time as her?"

"Yes. I gave them the names of the patrons whose names I knew. I don't know how much they were able to tell them. I know that Susan Sparks — she's one of our regulars at the readings — before she pulled out, she saw Gretchen head down the stairs to the 7-Eleven, which she thought was a little surprising, since it was dark by then. But you know, it's really not that odd. I've done it — after my shift is over, swing down there for a quart of milk or a Diet Coke."

"Are those steps down tricky?" I asked. "Dangerous?"

"They are a little steep, yes." Ruth glanced at me, then out the window at the parking lot. "I tend to hold on to the railing. You could . . . um . . . go out there and see for yourself. If that would help. Or have you done that already? On your way in?"

"Um . . . no. I haven't. I suppose I should."

Ruth nodded. "I *am* sorry about Gretchen. She was clearly a kind and interesting young woman. It must be difficult for you."

"Yes," I said.

She glanced at my belly. "Would you like me to go out there with you?"

Often I was exasperated by the pregnancy-inspired concern, but this time I was grateful for it.

"Okay," I said.

Ruth Rowan and I stared down the cement stairs together, silent for at least a minute or two. The steps were cracked in a few spots, with dandelions growing out of them.

At the bottom, the black pavement looked relatively new, with fresh white lines for the 7-Eleven parking spaces. I looked beyond the pavement and watched an elderly man in a driver's cap emerge from the store with an armful of ice. I didn't wish to focus on the spot where Gretchen had lain bleeding.

"Do you know where Gretchen was parked?" I asked, turning to Ruth.

"Yes. Not far from the steps. That space, I believe." She pointed to a space a few feet from the steps. "The police had this area blocked off the week after it happened."

"So she probably was headed for her car, and then saw that there was the 7-Eleven down there, and decided to grab a snack."

I didn't look at her, but instead at the patchy grass on either side of the cement steps leading down to the lower parking lot.

There was a simple metal pole railing running alongside the stone steps. I stood on top of the first step and gripped the railing. It was scaly with chipped paint and rust, and it moved toward me when I pulled it — a little wobbly, but firmly in the ground.

"Why are these stairs even here?" I asked.

"That used to be a town building as well," Ruth explained, pointing at the 7-Eleven. "So these stairs connected them. But since the town sold the building about fifteen years ago, the steps haven't been maintained by the town."

I nodded.

"You know it was a bit rainy that day, right? I believe it was kind of muddy. Slippery. So . . . so before they found her purse, we thought that may have contributed. Maybe it still did."

"Maybe," I said softly. It certainly would make it easier for someone to push Gretchen, if that's what she meant.

Ruth gave me a robotic pat on the upper arm. I got the feeling she was grasping for the right thing to say. I decided to relieve her of that burden and let her go back to her job.

"Yeah," I said. "I think I've seen enough. Thank you for coming out here with me."

Ruth didn't react immediately. For a few minutes, we gazed down the steep stairs together. Then she walked me to my car.

CHAPTER 40

"The Darkest Hour Is Just Before Dawn"

Twenty-First Avenue
Nashville, Tennessee

I'm sitting on a bench on the west end of Nashville, on a pleasant little chunk of grass that might be a park or might be part of a condo complex in which I shouldn't be loitering. Either way, no one's paying attention. The sky is turning a little gray. I wish it would rain, but it's been threatening for a few hours.

I've been listening to Emmylou Harris and Ricky Skaggs sing "The Darkest Hour Is Just Before Dawn" and "Green Pastures," alternating between them.

This is really my favorite of Emmylou's work — her beautiful, respectful treatment of classic bluegrass gospel songs. I particularly like these two, both of which she performs with Ricky Skaggs. "The Darkest Hour" was written by the bluegrass duo the Stanley Brothers. "Green Pastures" was written by Ralph Stanley (half of the Stanley Brothers) and Avril Gearheart — and Emmylou and Ricky Skaggs's performance feels like the embrace of one big happy country music family, with Willie Nelson playing guitar and Dolly Parton singing backup vocals.

When I listen to either of these songs, I feel like somewhere, someday, somehow, there is a home out there for me.

Is this a sort of Christian thing to say? It might be a little, even if I am not Christian. By "home," I don't mean heaven. I don't mean Jesus' open arms, necessarily, as I can't say I've understood exactly what they signify. I mean some sense of peace, some sense of being forgiven. I can't say I know where these will come from, only that when I listen to this music, I feel their possibility as something real.

These songs bring me back to what originally drew me to this music — this music that none of my friends ever listened to (except maybe when Jack White sang with Loretta, or just after

Walk the Line came out). Music that puts words in my mouth and my head that would embarrass us all.

There is a simple acknowledgment of pain and struggle here that speaks to me. Surely most music has that, but this song is the one that draws me in, that changes my experience of that pain. This one comforts me, sings me home.

The people who originally listened to these songs certainly suffered more than I ever have, but I believe the song's promise applies to me regardless. It doesn't require of me a childhood in the cotton fields, wifely obedience, or even Sunday church attendance.

It does require something of me, though. It requires that I be honest about what's in my heart and my soul. That I stop pretending. That I want to find my way home, and that I under-stand what that really means. And what that means to me is not necessarily something pastoral, or conservative, or even Christian. It's just a rare feeling of trust that comes over me when I hear it. Trust not so much in my judgment, but something entirely outside of it. That everything, in the end, will come to rest. That everything will end, and that is okay, too. Rarely do I ever feel that way, and that is the gift of these songs.

Part of the beauty of Emmylou Harris is that she gracefully and unassumingly delivers songs like this to people like me — who never have and never will stand in an old Appalachian country church on a hill, but who need their stark, simple assurances all the same.

— *Tammyland*

CHAPTER 41

Once Ruth had gone back into the library, I sat in my car for a little while.

I thought about "Till I Get It Right," the piece from a notebook I'd read the night before. There Bruce was mentioned so casually and even a little bit fondly — unlike in their more present encounter, where Gretchen had conveyed him as cagey and odd. In both past and present descriptions, Bruce certainly sounded like one of the men who'd shown up for Gretchen's reading — tall with a lot of puffy dark hair. I wanted to look back at Gretchen's more recent description of him, but I didn't have it with me. Also — I grew anxious as I remembered this, alone in my car — Willingham was pretty near the University of New Hampshire, where Bruce worked.

In any case, I thought again that I might like to just get a look at the guy myself. Just to get a feel for what kind of person he was.

Plus a few of the other people Gretchen had interviewed in the last days of her life. But especially him.

Now hungry, I wandered over to the Dragon Buffet.

"How much is it for lunch?" I asked the rail-thin hostess.

"Eight ninety-nine," she answered. "Just one?"

"Um . . . well. I'm not sure. Do you have those little fried doughnuts? Those little puffy appetizer doughnuts with the sugar on them?"

"Sorry? You want sugar?"

"Never mind. It's okay. Yes, one person for the buffet," I said.

I discovered, to my relief, that they had the little doughnuts. I piled my plate with five of them and ordered a glass of milk. The doughnuts were gone before I'd had a chance to reconsider. Then I went back and guiltily filled my plate with a bunch of broccoli, plus several strips of chicken breast for protein. I thought of asking about the MSG, but decided I probably didn't want to know. During this second trip to the buffet, I noticed a woman — about my age, and dining with a toddler — staring at me, watching me carefully as I refilled my plate. Probably she'd witnessed my doughnut run. I stiffened as I returned to my table.

Since becoming pregnant — and particularly visibly pregnant — I'd considered printing up "None of Your Business" cards. I could wordlessly hand them out to people staring at me as I purchased beer for Sam at the grocery store, or gobbled down an order of Wendy's french fries at my desk at work. I'd have special embossed lettering for acquaintances who feel they can suddenly ask me about personal or medical-type matters — like whether I'm going to breastfeed. A special limited-edition card — perhaps reading *None of Your Fucking Business* — would be reserved for anyone who asks me if I plan to have a water birth.

I ate my broccoli more slowly than the doughnuts, reading one of Gretchen's notebooks so I wouldn't feel so self-conscious about being the conspicuous pregnant lady dining alone.

CHAPTER 42

"Rachel"

D'Angelo's sandwich shop
Plantsville, New Hampshire

Rachel can't believe I'm thirty-two.

She's only ten years older than me, but in her head, she says, I've always been the little blond girl — Shelly's girl, who she saw a couple of times and who disappeared after Shelly died. The little girl she worried about sometimes, asking herself, *Whatever happened to her?*

Rachel picks up her jumbo fountain soda, sips, and jiggles the ice before going on.

She can't believe I'm a writer, that I have a real book. She confesses she's not much of a reader, so she hasn't picked it up. Her aunt Laurie — Laurie Wiley — says it's good, though. And her aunt Laurie's kind of picky, so that's saying something.

She doesn't remark on how much I look like Shelly, which is kind of nice.

She says she's not sure quite why she and Shelly started a casual friendship that year.

"I was only sixteen. She was . . . what? Like, twenty-four? It was kind of weird at first. It started when she was outside once, watching me walk by her house. I was trying to hold on to my little cousin's hand while my aunt's stupid dog was practically pulling my arm out of its socket."

And so Shelly helped her, and started chatting with her. Asked her about school, about her friends.

"I liked her. And I guess I

liked the idea of hanging out with a twenty-four-year-old. It was kind of cool, like. And the fact that she'd had some, you know, pretty serious life experience? That made it cooler."

Rachel says they talked mostly about Rachel. Rachel was dating a guy named Jay at the time and they talked a lot about him. Rachel often tried to get Shelly to talk about her boyfriend, too, but Shelly didn't offer much. Only in the last few weeks of their friendship did Shelly give the occasional eye roll when Frank's name came up, indicating that she wasn't happy. By then, though, Rachel knew better than to ask.

"She was still a lot older than me and I understood, after a while, that I wasn't supposed to ask about certain things. If I'd realized how grave it was, I would have asked anyway. The week or two before she was killed, she was different. More serious. Maybe I'm just remembering it that way. But it did seem like something was going on. I was maybe just too young to know how to ask."

"Now you think it was trouble with Frank?" I ask.

"Probably," she answers.

"Was there ever any sign that he was violent with her?"

Rachel tilts her oval face to think about this, then raises a sculpted eyebrow.

"No physical sign," she says. "If that's what you're asking. It was all her. She said some things to me that were . . . well, sad, now that I think about it."

"Which were?"

"Well, there was this one point when I was whining about something my boyfriend had said to me. He didn't like my new haircut, or whatever. I was implying that he could be kind of mean. And Shelly stops me and says, 'You have to figure out if you think he was being mean or if you think he was being stupid. And if you think he's mean, you get rid of him, and don't give it another thought.'

"And I told her that that was very easy to talk about, but not very easy to do. And she just laughed at me, like, no shit, girl. You think I don't know that? And then she said something like, 'You know, this is where it starts. You start at your age, deciding how much crap you're going to put up with. And if you're not careful, you'll end up tolerating a lot more than you should. And you won't know how to cut it off, because that'll be what you're used to, what you've convinced yourself you deserve. You want to end up like me? How do you think I ended up where I am now? How old do you think I was when I started taking shit from men?'

"Something like that. I was speechless. Because she'd never talked about herself like that before. We both knew she'd messed up her life big-time, but it was the elephant in the room. We never . . ."

Rachel trails off, blushes, shakes her giant soda cup again. "Sorry."

It takes me a moment to re-alize why she's apologizing. She thinks I've never heard before that my biological mother "messed up her life." Or she's self-conscious about talking to one of the messes.

"It's okay," I say. "I know all about Shelly. I know all about the stuff people said about her."

"Okay. Well, I'm still sorry."

"You were saying?" I prompt her.

"Well. It was the first time she talked about me in terms of herself. And it felt like she was talking about *her* life now. Not just past boyfriends. Like she still felt trapped."

I hesitate. "I wonder if she really felt trapped, though?

She didn't need Frank for money, really. He wasn't helping her raise any kids, or anything."

Rachel shrugs. "Yeah, I don't know. That's a good question."

After some thought, she says, "There was this sadness about her, around then. This one afternoon, I was hanging out with my friend Denise, and we went walking downtown to buy some candy and go to the drugstore, because she had a prescription she needed filled. I was excited that I could introduce her to my cool older friend Shelly, who was working the pharmacy counter. She took Denise's prescription and asked her a couple of questions about it. I don't know what the issue was — a minor picking up her own prescription, or something? Is that illegal? Or was it back then? Anyway, the pharmacist came in and helped her resolve the issue, whatever it was.

"And as soon as they were

done talking, I leaned over the counter, all casual and girl-talk-like, and I said, 'So, Shelly . . . how's Frank these days?' You know, like she and I talked about our boyfriends all the time, me and this cool friend of mine in her twenties. And she looks up from what she's doing . . . and the expression on her face. She looked . . . horrified. And she said, 'Excuse me?' like she didn't understand what I was saying. Even like she didn't know me. And I shut right up. I had crossed some line. I remember walking home feeling embarrassed. Denise saying to me, like, 'I thought you said she was cool. She seems like kind of a grump.'

"That was the second-to-last time I saw her."

"What was the last?"

"We did one more dog walk together."

"Was that friendly?"

"Yeah. We didn't talk about

the drugstore. We didn't talk about Frank. But she seemed tired. I think we baby-talked to my cousin most of the time, paid attention to her instead of each other. That's how I remember it."

"And how did you hear she died?"

"My aunt Laurie called my mother the day it happened. My mother told me."

"What was your first reaction? When you first heard she was killed, did you think of Frank first?"

Rachel considers this. "Hmm. Right away? No. My aunt claims she suspected him the moment she saw Shelly there all beaten and bleeding that morning. But I didn't know enough about him to think that immediately. For the first few days, it felt more like a mystery. Scary, in that way. Like, who came into our neighborhood and did this? Could they do it again? But the more

we heard, the more it seemed
like Frank."

CHAPTER 43

I called Shelly's old friend Judy the following morning.

"You must be about ready to pop," she said cheerily.

"Oh. No . . . not quite there yet. Still about six weeks to go."

"You must be excited. Aren't you excited?"

Excited. That felt like a good word for a trip to Disney World or a kitchen renovation. For now the feeling felt more akin to anticipating jumping out of an airplane, which required a stronger word. But I was willing to go with *excited* for the sake of comfortable conversation.

"I am . . . but in the meantime, I'm trying to get as much done as I can on Gretchen's . . . manuscript."

"I see. That's kind of you, sweetie. Did you have more questions? It's funny you called. Dorothy was asking for you just the other day. She wanted to know if I could get your address through e-mail. She's not on e-mail. I told her I'd write you, it just slipped my mind."

"My postal address?"

"Yes. She wants to send you a package. I believe she knitted something for you."

"Oh. That's sweet, but . . . she doesn't need to do that."

"She actually does. She has a sort of knitting compulsion. I think since Gretchen died, she's picked up even more speed. I guess it's therapeutic for her."

"Well, I'm thinking of coming up to Emerson again," I said. "While I still can."

"Really? Would you like to meet again?"

While I appreciated Judy's friendliness, I wasn't sure I needed to do tea and cookies with her a second time.

"Oh, I don't want to impose. Unless you want to meet. I've come across a lot of interviews Gretchen did with other people from the area . . . and I'd like to touch base with a few of them. I thought I'd stop in and chat with Dorothy, because I had a couple more questions for her. But I wanted to check in first, see if you thought she'd be up to it."

"Absolutely. She always likes visitors, and she really enjoyed meeting you. Otherwise she wouldn't have knit you something."

"Well, should I call her? Or do you want to chat with her?"

"I'll talk to her. When do you think you'll come?"

"This weekend, actually."

"Just a day trip? Last time I was worried about you driving all that way by yourself at night, in your condition."

"Well, I'm thinking of spending a couple of nights in a motel in Plantsville this time, so I won't get tired. And I like driving, generally. So that's not a problem."

"Do you know where you'll be staying in Plantsville? Because I'd suggest staying away from the All Tucked Inn. The Motel 6 is probably okay, though."

"Okay. Thanks. I'll keep that in mind."

"Your husband coming?"

I found this question slightly irritating. What difference did it make?

"I'm not sure," I answered.

"Oh. I see. Well, do you want my help getting in touch with some of the other folks you want to interview? Anyone I should give a heads-up to?"

"No, that's okay. Gretchen left pretty clear contact information for most of these people."

"Okay. Well, good," Judy chirped. "But let

412

me know if you need anything."

"Actually . . . there are just a couple of things that have come up in my reading that I was wondering if you or Diane would know about. Um . . . if you have time to talk now."

"Sure I do," Judy said.

"First, I was wondering about Shelly's friend Melanie."

I heard Judy suck air between her teeth. "Is she one of the people you're going to talk to?"

"I'm gonna try," I admitted.

"Well, be careful with that. Did Gretchen interview her?"

"Yeah."

"Because she didn't help prosecutors any, during the trial. She said some terrible things about Shelly. And she was supposed to be her *friend*."

"Things like?"

"Oh, like Shelly sleeping with her boss. About Shelly being into drugs and getting involved with shady characters who supposedly would've wanted to kill her. All of that was *over*. Shelly had cleaned up her act years ago. It was like Melanie liked to talk about those things to make herself seem more edgy and interesting. Well, look what it got her — her friend's murderer walking."

"So . . . um . . . you don't think Shelly was involved with Phillip Coleman?"

"Nope. I don't. Shelly made some mistakes when she was young. And she had some problems. But she was committed to cleaning her life up by that time, for her own sake and for Gretchen's. She wouldn't have gotten involved with a man who was engaged. One who had given her that nice job, no less."

"So you don't think Melanie was trustworthy?"

"Well . . ." Judy's voice was high-pitched, hedging. "At the time I just thought she wasn't very smart. You talk like that about your murdered friend, it's going to have consequences. She was maybe too naive to know that. I don't think she had any malice toward Shelly. Maybe she's improved. Where is she living now?"

"Manchester."

"Hmm."

"And what did you think of Shelly's boss? Phillip Coleman."

"Nice guy. He was a friend of the Brewers, I believe. Which, I think, is how Shelly got that job. I know his wife a little bit. Our sons are the same age. You going to talk to him?"

"Um . . . I'm not sure. Gretchen documented her interview with him pretty well. At some point, if it looks like her book is publishable, I'll probably have to talk to all of her sources and verify everything. But I'm not at that stage yet.

"Also, there's something that's come up a couple of times in Gretchen's notes that I'm not sure how to interpret . . . And in some of the recordings she did."

"Excuse me. The recordings?"

"Yeah. Some of her sources. Like Melanie. She recorded her interviews with them."

Judy was quiet for a moment. "I see. That's interesting."

"I'm not sure if she always told her sources she was recording. I can't tell."

"Did she record anything with me and Diane? Or Dorothy?"

"Not that I've found, so far."

"Uh-huh," Judy said.

"Anyway, there are a few people who come up and I'm not sure how they're connected to Shelly or anything. There's some vague stuff related to prescriptions . . . which I assume has something to do with Shelly's last job. But then there are a few mentions of a couple of doctors. Pediatricians, I guess. She has notes about a Dr. Platt and Dr. Wright. And they seem to come up elsewhere in her . . . research."

"Oh. Hmm."

"Do you know either of them?" I asked.

"Dr. Platt was my own pediatrician. I mean, when I was a kid. Not for my own kids. I imagine he was Shelly's, too. He was basically everybody's my age at that time in Emerson. He was here forever."

"According to Gretchen's notes, he died in 1985."

"Hmm . . . That sounds about right."

"Do you know if it was before Shelly died, or after?"

"That I can't remember. Gretchen wrote about him?"

"Um. A little. I just can't figure out why. Was he practicing right up until he died?"

"Yes," Judy said. "I believe he was."

"Because I'm thinking maybe he treated Gretchen at some point, so she had some memory of him . . ."

"I guess that's possible, if she got sick while she was visiting Shelly, or something. But I'm sure Linda had a regular pediatrician for Gretchen at home."

"Yeah. It was just a thought. The other thought was that maybe he was still Shelly's doctor when she got pregnant."

"Hmm. You know, he probably was. That's kind of how it was around here. No one went to the adult doctors till after high school. I mean, usually. Things are a little different now, of course, but —"

"Is it possible that Shelly told him who the father was?"

Judy was silent for a moment.

"I never would have thought of that. I suppose it's possible. But not likely. He was a nice old man, but not the sort of person you'd confide in about that kind of thing. And I know that after the initial discovery, Shelly, of course, went to an ob-gyn. I remember her dreading it. Riding into Plantsville with her mother every month. She said they were all very disapproving there at the doctor's office."

"I'm just throwing ideas out there," I admitted. "I have no idea. Maybe it's none of those things. And she made a note of the doctor who replaced Dr. Platt. A woman named Katherine Wright."

"That name rings a bell, too. She's not around anymore, though."

"Interesting that Dr. Platt died the same year as Shelly, though."

"Hmm. I suppose. But he had a heart attack. He was quite old. He probably shouldn't have been practicing anymore.

But everybody loved him, so no one complained. You know, Dr. Skinner knew him pretty well. I can ask Diane about all of this, if you want."

"Okay. Sure. You can give her my e-mail if she remembers anything."

"Sure thing. Anything else?"

"Not for now. Thanks for talking."

After we hung up, I got on the computer and started making my plans for the weekend. I made a motel reservation near Emerson, wrote to Kevin Conley, and started a list of other people I planned to drop in on — like Bruce, Melanie, and Phillip Coleman.

CHAPTER 44

"Why didn't you tell me?" Sam demanded. "We could've gone together. We could've shared the driving."

I slipped my shampoo into my canvas bag. "Because I knew you had that thing with your boss this weekend. You've been talking about it for weeks."

"I can't get out of it," he said, pulling himself up on the bed next to my bag.

"I know. That's what I'm trying to explain. That's why I didn't ask. But I really need to go this weekend."

Sam watched me as I waddled around the room, looking for my one pair of maternity tights.

"I've made several appointments to talk to various people. And my time when I can travel is *really* running out."

"How about you postpone it just till next weekend? We could make it into, like, a babymoon."

I straightened and looked up from my packing.

"A *babymoon*, Sam?"

"Yeah, it's when the new parents go away for a romantic trip before —"

"I know what it is. I'm just surprised to hear you say it. Trust me. Emerson, New Hampshire, is not a very romantic place."

Sam was silent.

"Besides, I think that babymoon thing is for yuppie parents, you know?" I reassured him.

"That's not what we are?"

I slapped one more shirt into my bag and zipped it up. "God, I hope not. Don't even joke about that."

"Wow, Jamie. What's wrong with you?"

"What's wrong with me?" I repeated. "*What's wrong with me?*"

I was, on some level, only pretending to be offended by the question. Because it was actually a reasonable one. I just didn't know how to answer it.

"Nothing is wrong with me. One of my best friends died six weeks ago and I need to do this for her. How's that?"

"Do you need to do it right now? Do you need to do it *this weekend?* Is that really what Gretchen would have wanted?"

I rolled my eyes at the second question. I

never liked this assumption — that once someone died, "what they would've wanted" suddenly becomes sensible, altruistic, knowable. I wasn't sure Gretchen's desires had ever been any of those things.

"How about this," I said, taking Sam's hand. "I'll do this trip this weekend. Then next weekend, not a word about Gretchen's book. We'll go away together for a night, maybe to that bed-and-breakfast we liked in the Berkshires? Something like that. Make it a *real* break for both of us."

Sam shook his head. "That's not necessary. It's not about me needing a vacation. And I would never ask you to stop talking about Gretchen."

Sam stood up and picked up my bag for me. "If you need to do this, I can't ask you to stay. I guess I should let you go now if you don't want to be driving in the dark."

We walked down to the front door together. I said nothing, as Sam's resignation was making me feel terrible — no less resolved, but terrible nonetheless.

"Promise me you'll call as soon as you get there?" he said after he'd tossed my bag into my backseat.

"Promise," I said, kissing him.

CHAPTER 45

"It's All Wrong, but It's All Right"

Howard Johnson
Gatlinburg, Tennessee

I love country music autobiographies. Maybe this is obvious by now.

Loretta's famous *Coal Miner's Daughter*, and her awesomely titled follow-up, *Still Woman Enough*. Dolly's *My Life and Other Unfinished Business*. Tammy's *Stand by Your Man*.

They all sit next to my bed at home, and I've read them in repeated rotation.

They help put me to sleep. Not because they're boring — they're not. But because I find them oddly comforting — with the possible exception of Tammy's, which has fallen out of the rotation and stays on the bottom of the pile. That one makes me sad — but that's a different essay.

I've just finished with Dollywood today in Pigeon Forge, but decided to stay in this area for a night longer. Tomorrow I'm taking a break from the country ladies to stop by Ripley's Believe It or Not, one of Gatlinburg's many tourist traps. Supposedly they've got Old Sparky there, and that's a can't-miss for me. But for tonight, I'm exhausted from the hot sun and manufactured fun of Dollywood. Instead of walking up and down the streets of Gatlinburg with all of the other tourists, I'm holed up in my motel. Huddled in a blanket and eating a couple of éclairs from a brilliant place in town called the Donut Friar, I'm rereading my favorite parts of *Still Woman Enough*.

Loretta's books tell some pretty hard stories. The first, *Coal Miner's Daughter*, is a rags-to-riches story about her hardscrabble life growing up in Butcher Hollow, Kentucky, her marriage at fourteen, her life as a young mother, and her road to stardom. As tough as some of those stories are, her second book tells all of the harsher stories that she kept out of the first — stories that detail the extent of her husband's alcoholism and violence early in their marriage. And further, this book has much more in it about loss — loss of her son by drowning, loss of her husband, loss of music friends like Conway Twitty and Tammy Wynette.

Maybe *comforting* will seem an odd word for this material. There is something reassuring, however, about knowing someone is being completely honest with you about her life. There's no attempt to sound clever or PC, or to play it one way or another, or even a suggestion that the reader should learn something from Loretta's stories. And it goes without saying that marriages like hers were not unusual in the time and place in which she grew up. But that's really not the point, from Loretta's perspective. For Loretta, it's not history or sociology or sexual politics.

This is what my husband was like. He drank a lot. He cheated on me. He hit me and I hit him back. And I loved him.

It's disconcerting. But it's her life. Is she supposed to put it in more palatable terms for the comfort of her readers?

Loretta doesn't advocate that women enter or endure marriages as she did. She simply explains how it was for her, and doesn't try to frame it with a lesson or a message. And somewhat disarmingly (to this reader, at least), she never says she wishes it had gone any other way. I don't fully understand why I find this comforting. Maybe it's because her autobiographies read like an admission that life is painful and complicated, and that relationships require complex thought and, usually, a fair amount of suffering. Of course I was aware of this before I cracked Loretta's books. Perhaps this message still feels novel to me, as a child of the eighties. I grew up on health-class role plays and sanitized sitcoms, everything After-School-Specialized, categorized as healthy or unhealthy, easily identifiable as one or the other. The generation that came before us learned all of that for us, so we didn't need to figure it out for ourselves.

Which is, of course, ridiculous. Some of us will have desires or relationships that fall slightly out of others' comfort zones. You ultimately decide for yourself what is Okay and Not Okay.

Though less stark and less grim, Dolly's bubbly memoir carries a similar message for me. Although she does not go into great detail, she implies that she and her husband might have sometimes turned to the affections of others while she was on the road — that they had an open marriage. That was fine by both of them, she explains, as long as it didn't get in the way of their relationship when she was around, and they respected each other by keeping their dalliances private. She's so coy about it I suspect there weren't really any dalliances, but she's not willing to say one way or another — or apologize one way or another, for that matter. That's as much as she's willing to say, and the details are nobody else's business.

When talking about her weight issues, she says offhand that while she doesn't advocate making yourself throw up, chewing up your food and spitting it out might not be a bad idea. In her own words:

" 'That's disgusting,' you say. That may be, but what's more disgusting? Spitting out food or being a lardass?"

I love it. Where I come from, chewing and spitting out your food as a weight-loss technique would definitely be considered a gateway behavior to disordered eating, a sign of poor body image, and definitely Not Okay.

Dear reader, at this point, you probably think I don't get out much — at least, much outside my sterile little liberal bubble. And this isn't the case at all. I get out a fair amount. It's that I admire these women for the relative purity of their voices. Perhaps they occasionally filter their experiences. But I doubt that either of them, Dolly or Loretta, ever finds herself, before fully settling into an opinion about something, pausing for an almost instinctual second to wonder, *But do we agree with this? Is this Okay?*

I admire these women for deciding what their own boundaries are, and for being willing to detail them without apology. I'm not about to spit out this delicious éclair or arrange an open marriage or live with a volatile alcoholic. My boundaries will be different from theirs. Still, unless I define them myself, Okay and Not Okay is bullshit.

— *Tammyland*

CHAPTER 46

Dorothy's house was my first stop, once I'd checked into the motel. She'd had me promise I'd come for dinner, and I had agreed, provided she let me bring the food this time: pizza and salad and root beer.

"Did Judy tell you I had something for you?" Dorothy asked, after we'd eaten.

"Yeah, she mentioned that."

"I figured. Judy can't keep her mouth shut. It was supposed to be a surprise," Dorothy said, handing me a small shirt box. "Open it."

I did. There, laid out in tissue paper, was a tiny blue-and-white sweater, with white elephant buttons.

"Oh, wow," I said. "It's gorgeous. I can't believe you did this in just the last couple of weeks."

"I like to keep my hands busy. I do it while I watch TV."

"What about the hats for the African

babies?" I asked.

"I got sick of doing the same boring hat over and over. I finally boxed them up and had Diane send them off."

"Well, thank you so much."

"I love knitting baby things. It was my pleasure."

As she said this, there was a knock on the door, and then a sing-song "Hellooo?" echoing into the kitchen.

I expected the stout, chipper Judy to appear, but to my surprise, Diane stepped into the room, a tin canister in hand.

"Hello, dear," Dorothy said. "Jamie's here."

"I can see that," Diane replied, giving me a little wave. "Good to see you again, Jamie."

"You, too."

"I heard you were going to be here this evening." She took a seat and folded her thin hands on the tin. "And I heard you had a couple of questions for me."

"Oh," I said, remembering my questions to Judy about the pediatricians. "Yeah, that's right."

Diane opened her tin, showing the contents to Dorothy.

"Hermits," she said proudly. "Your favorite, right?"

"One of them," Dorothy said, taking the

tin from her. She took one and then offered the tin to me. I took one reluctantly. I'd been eating too much sugar since Gretchen died. True to his nickname, Charlie Bucket was probably having a Willy Wonka sort of experience in the womb lately.

"So," Diane said, "I can't stick around for long, but Judy told me you were asking about some notes Gretchen made, about the pediatricians in town? Particularly Dr. Platt, right?"

"Yeah. And the name seemed to come up when Gretchen was learning about Shelly's last job. At the pharmacy. There was maybe some problem with her job, and certain prescriptions."

Diane looked puzzled and clicked her tongue against her teeth while she considered this.

"Ohhhh," she said softly, after a moment. "I remember now."

She nodded as if in recognition of the memory. "You know what that probably was about? I don't know if Shelly would have told Judy this, but she made a pretty serious mistake at that job. The switching around of young patients to different doctors — I mean, when Dr. Platt died . . . I think that confused Shelly, and it caused her to mix up a kid's prescription with someone else's

— an adult with a similar name. I don't remember the details, but it was something that could've been a real disaster. The kid had a lot of serious health problems."

"How'd they catch the mistake?"

"Um, I think the kid's mom caught it. The kid had taken maybe one dose, not enough to do anything serious yet, but . . . you know, it was scary."

"Was Shelly shaken by that?"

Diane nodded gravely. "Very."

"Do you remember the kid's name?"

"No. I think the last name was Johnson, something like that. A common last name, so it was easy to mix up."

"Was your dad by any chance the prescribing doctor? Dorothy and I were chatting about it earlier, and she said there was a time, after Dr. Platt died, when some of the kids went to him."

Dorothy nodded. "That's right, isn't it, Diane?"

"Yeah, that's true. But no, he wasn't the prescribing doctor. I don't recall who that would have been. I guess it would have had to have been Dr. Copalman or Dr. Silver. I think those were the only other two general practitioners in Emerson at the time. Maybe Schreiner was here, too. I don't remember. Do you, Dorothy?"

"No, I really don't," Dorothy said. "Sorry."

"So . . . but Shelly was a little fearful for her job after that?" I asked.

"Oh, yes. She was really scared."

"I don't remember this," Dorothy admitted.

"But you remember when Dr. Platt died suddenly, right?" Diane turned to her.

"Yes. That was sad. All the kids loved him."

"Well, all of his patients had to use other doctors in town for a bit, while the pediatric group found a replacement. Which took a while."

"I see." Dorothy nodded. "I got that."

"And that was about the same time Shelly was working at the pharmacy. It was the switching of doctors, I think, that made it easy to make a mistake. Before that, you'd never mix up a kid's prescription with an adult's, partly because Shelly — like everyone in town — knew who the kids' doctors were versus the adult ones. But, anyway. It worked out. It blew over. She kept her job."

"Huh," said Dorothy, rising from her chair. "She must've not told her mother about it. Because I've never heard that story."

Dorothy excused herself to go to the

bathroom, and I used the opportunity to ask Diane a more sensitive question.

"But do you think her relationship with her boss . . . I mean, with Phil Coleman, may have protected her a little?"

Diane studied me before answering. I studied her back, noticing that the perfect ivory quality of her skin was partly an illusion. Beneath her eyes, purple-brown pouches shone under powdery makeup.

"Maybe," she said, biting her lip regretfully. "There may have been some truth to that. I think Melanie Rittel was a bit of a drama queen, but I don't think she was as off base as Judy sometimes makes it sound. As I've said, Judy is very protective of Shelly's reputation — I mean, where it's possible to be. And I think sometimes she didn't want to believe some of the things people said about Shelly. Like, I believe Shelly and Judy's brother had a little thing going, for a time, and Judy just didn't want to see it . . ."

Diane stopped talking for a moment, her eyes widening. "Is there any mention of *that* in your recordings?"

"What recordings?" I said, surprised.

"I mean, Gretchen's recorded interviews. Judy mentioned them to me. I hadn't realized till after she talked to you earlier this week — that Gretchen had recorded some of her interviews. Judy hadn't either."

"Oh. Um . . . no. I haven't heard anything like that. I haven't listened to all of them yet. They can be kind of hard to hear."

"I see." Diane nodded and reached into her tin for another hermit. "That makes sense. But on the question of Coleman . . . I'm not sure. Knowing Shelly, it was definitely possible. I didn't feel it had a place in Grippo's trial. It wasn't fair. It was a distraction."

"And Coleman never admitted to it."

"No. Certainly not. It's possible it happened and he didn't want to own up to it, though, even under oath. He had a fiancée at the time. Now his wife."

"And he's still a pharmacist in town. The rumors didn't hurt his business?"

"Not so much. People didn't like to see Shelly maligned so badly at trial. It was really hurtful to her mother, who people really loved and supported. People sort of saw Phil Coleman as yet another person hurt by all the gossip, when it was Grippo who really should have suffered. So, no. People left Phil Coleman alone."

Diane sighed and broke her hermit into four even pieces, then ate one reluctantly.

Dorothy returned, and Diane asked me if

I had any other questions. I said no, for now. Diane left soon after that. After a cup of tea with Dorothy, and a few more cookies, I thanked Dorothy and retired to my motel.

CHAPTER 47

"My Favorite Lies"

Upstairs at Aunt Dorothy's
Emerson, New Hampshire

So it seems Shelly was smarter than everyone realized. She thought of a little charade to carry on when she was only seventeen years old. That charade was the "Bruce or Keith" conundrum. It was one or the other of these two guys — the doofy, good-hearted one or the smart and serious one. Everyone who knew her stared and squinted when I was a kid, trying to figure out which. Odds were on Bruce because I'd turned out more academic than my mother. But she would never tell.

Reader, it was apparently neither of the two. Yes. Neither!

I don't think Judy or Diane or even Dorothy ever had any clue. Or even my mom (Linda). No, part of Shelly's trick was to convince them of it so naturally they'd easily repeat it themselves, long after she'd gone. They'd repeat it like a secret, like real gossip.

They'd find it delicious for years to come — that Shelly didn't know who the baby daddy was, didn't want it to be either of them, so was never willing to find out, or perhaps, just knew and would never say.

So that years and years would go by, and once the two had been ruled out, the real one would have slipped away. He'd be long gone, never to be found out.

Is this how you always wanted it, Shelly? Or was it everyone

else — Judy and Diane and
everyone they spoke to — who
created and perpetuated that
myth for you? How much did you
actually say, and how much did
they assume? Where am I supposed to go from here, Shelly?
Who am I to ask when everyone
close to you tells the same
phony secret?

And who to look for when it
could be anyone? They say
there was a time when you'd
happily lay a guy for the
price of a few drinks. Or do
it in the car on a second
date. (Should I believe them,
Shelly? Was that really you?)

And I choose to take this as
a gift from you. My favorite
lie — of yours, or of those
told about you, I can't even
determine anymore. Because
either way, I can be anyone
now. My father is the man married to your sister. The
genes, for what they're worth,
come from the clouds, from
some nowhere man I'll never
meet.

I've named this page after a George Jones song. But guess what, Shelly? I'm not listening to it as I write. And I'm not eating a Twinkie or a Twizzler or any of the shit you and I used to eat together, though when I revise this I'll probably say I was.

No, I'm just sitting upstairs at Aunt Judy's, sucking on a stale cough drop, wondering if it was you or someone else who decided to spin it this way. How much control did you have, Shelly? How can I ever know?

CHAPTER 48

"My Favorite Lies" floored me.

I'd brought a stack of Gretchen's notebooks to the motel, and found this piece sitting alone in a brand-new-looking Muppets notebook. It was followed by about ninety-seven sheets of spotless college-ruled white paper. Gretchen gave no indication she was sure of what she was saying. I imagined she was, given that she had lab results — however cryptic to me. So who did she try next? After Bruce? After this resolve to accept the unknown as a "gift," she'd obviously changed her mind at some point and pursued the father question again. What had made her decide to do that? Regardless, I remained very curious about this Bruce character who had perhaps attended Gretchen's final reading. I still intended to meet him.

The following day at noon, I had an appointment to talk with Kevin Conley over lunch, which left me a little free time in the morning for one impromptu interview.

I didn't really have time to set out for Bruce's town of Williamsburg, so I set my GPS to one of the addresses I'd looked up beforehand: Clark Street Pharmacy. I doubted Phil Coleman worked Saturdays, but I'd start there.

Once inside the store, I pretended to examine wrapping paper in the back, trying to steal a look at the pharmacist behind the little window. When I saw that it was a woman, I left the store and returned to my car. There I went to the White Pages on my iPhone and looked up Phillip Coleman in Emerson, New Hampshire. I got an address: 422 Cider Mill Drive. I put that into my GPS and drove.

Cider Mill Drive was a cute street with a few miniature McMansion-type houses and a cul-de-sac. As I approached 422 Cider Mill, I realized I had no plan for what I was going to do there. All I wanted was to get a look at Phil Coleman, for now. I could ring the doorbell and try to think of something creative to say. In my condition, I wouldn't pass for a Girl Scout. And what were the chances Phil Coleman himself — and not a wife or a kid — would answer the bell?

I decided efficient and honest was the best

way in and out. I struggled out from behind the wheel, then made my way down the brick steps.

"Can I help you?" someone asked from the general direction of the manicured hedges.

"Oh!" I jumped as a woman stood up from behind them, holding a small shovel in her gloved hands.

"Can I help you?" she asked again, lowering her eyes to my stomach, which was looking particularly prominent today in the unfortunate plum-purple cami I'd chosen. It looked like a giant blueberry poking out from under my black cardigan.

"Um. I'm looking for Phil Coleman. Is he in?"

The woman, who appeared to be about fifty, pulled off her gloves slowly. "Yes. Who shall I say is . . . visiting?"

"My name is Jamie Madden. Mr. Coleman doesn't know me. It's regarding the Gretchen Waters case?"

"Oh." The woman gave me a blank look. "Are you with the investigation, or . . . ?"

"No. I'm her literary executor," I said, figuring that had an air of officiality to it.

"Oh," the woman said. "Um. I'll grab him, then."

A few seconds later she led out of the

house a tall, overweight man with thinning gray hair. He was wearing ill-fitting navy dress pants and a white undershirt.

"Hi. I'm here about Gretchen Waters. I'm assuming you know who that is?"

The man nodded. I tried to take in his features as I babbled on. Thin lips. Thick neck. Big, dark eyes. Full, expressive eyebrows. Not bushy, though. Relatively pale skin tone. Not superpale — but pale enough.

"She was working on her second book, as I imagine you know, because she interviewed you as one of her sources." Wide face, slightly jowly. Straight nose kind of like Gretchen's. "You had an interview with her, correct?"

"Correct," Phil said, glancing at his wife.

"Now, I'm asking people generally. Do I have your permission to use all or portions of that interview in a final version of her book? Provided I sent you the relevant parts of the book to look over for verification?"

"Uh . . . sure, I guess. Are you close to that point? You must be working awfully fast."

I could feel the woman's eyes on me, which I tried to ignore.

"Getting there," I said. "I'm sorry to bother you at home here. Gretchen had your address in her files, but I couldn't locate an e-mail contact. If you give me that address, I can send you material that way, when the time comes."

"Sure," Phil said. "Let me just go get a pen."

After he'd slipped back into the house, his wife said to me, "Literary executor. Did Gretchen's family hire out for that, or are you close to the family?"

"I'm an old friend of Gretchen's," I said. "That's why her mom asked me."

She nodded. "I'm sorry for your loss."

Phil came out with a slip of paper and handed it to me.

"Happy to help," he said. "Did you have any other questions for right now?"

"No . . . well . . . actually. Now that you ask. Someone just told me a story about Shelly at the pharmacy, and I was wondering if you could confirm it."

Both Phil and his wife stared at me. I had a feeling I'd made a mistake. Still, I quickly explained.

"I'm told that at one time Shelly gave the wrong prescription to the wrong patient. Gave something to a kid that was supposed to be for an adult with a similar name. Got mixed up. Could've made the kid really sick, but the kid's mom caught it just in time?

Shelly nearly got fired for it?"

Phil's wife glanced at Phil.

"No." Phil shook his head. "That never happened."

"I know it was a really long time ago, so —"

"Shelly only worked for me for a brief period of time. That never happened. I would remember if it did. Because that *would* have been a fireable mistake. Who told you that? Was it something Gretchen wrote?"

"Oh . . . no. It was a story someone told me about Shelly. Probably they were mis-remembering. It *was* a long time ago."

"Yeah," Phil said. "I'm sorry, but that story's just not true."

"Well . . . sorry to have bothered you."

"It's no bother," said Phil, rubbing the back of his fleshy red neck. "Let me know if you have any other questions."

The woman put her gardening gloves back on. I got the distinct feeling she didn't want me to linger.

"Thank you," I said to both of them, and then got back into my car.

CHAPTER 49

Gretchen was right that Kevin Conley's eyes were "soulful." There was a wounded quality to them, intensified by the thin appearance of the rest of his face. He had a dark stubble that didn't appear in Gretchen's description, but his royal-blue shirt had a slight sheen that reminded me of her characterization of his clothing as "pimpy."

We met in front of a downtown Emerson diner. He'd recognized me right away ("I'll probably be the only five-foot pregnant lady there," I'd told him on the phone ahead of time).

"I'm glad to see you," he said, his urchin face breaking into a wide smile.

"Thanks," I said. "Me, too."

Looking around at the diner's wood paneling and crusty brown griddle, I asked, "Did Gretchen like this restaurant? Seems like the kind of place that would've appealed to her."

"We came here together once," Kevin admitted. "She wasn't impressed. She thought the grilled cheese was soggy."

"I'll be sure not to order that, then."

"If you don't want real food right now," Kevin suggested, pointing at a small chalkboard listing pie varieties, "the pie's good. I mean, if you're not a fancy person."

"I'm not a fancy person. But I'll probably get soup." I didn't say so, of course, but I was still worried about Charlie Bucket's temple of sugar. Still, I glanced over at the pie options. *Sweet Jesus*, I thought. *Tollhouse pie.*

After we ordered (I strained not to order the pie), Kevin asked me if I'd finished reading Gretchen's manuscript yet. I admitted I had not — that it was in pieces, and it would be a while before I felt confident that I'd read everything.

"I'll be curious," he said, "if she wrote about this one particular conversation we had. About the day Shelly died."

He studied me with his big gray eyes. I'd never known Gretchen to be into the vulnerable type before, but maybe after Jeremy she'd wanted to try something entirely new.

"Well, all I've seen is that first one," I explained. "Where she interviewed you. Before you started hanging out together. Is that what you mean?"

"Uh. No. Maybe once we started to become friends, she didn't feel it was appropriate to write stuff down that I said, like it was just part of the story. But there was one thing I said that probably *needed* to be part of the story."

"Okay," I said.

"No idea what I'm talking about? You haven't seen anything she wrote that gives you a hint?"

"No," I said, trying to keep the agitation out of my voice.

"After we went to see Frank, it was different between us . . . after we talked in that McDonald's lot."

Our waitress came and plunked down our drinks wordlessly. I waited for her to slip away before replying.

"Because?" I asked, picking up my water glass.

"Well." Kevin scrunched down his straw wrapper, making it into a tiny, tight accordion. "Because I saw that she didn't come here to prove anything. It wasn't about getting Frank or avenging Shelly. See, she didn't have a lot of preconceived ideas about Frank. I'd have assumed she would. Because of who she was. But she told me, that day and other days, that she had trouble thinking of him how she was 'supposed' to."

I watched as Kevin took a bit of iced tea out of his glass with his straw and squirted it onto the wrapper. It popped into a light brown worm, writhing on the table.

"How was she supposed to think of him?" I asked.

"You know . . . as pure evil. As the man who killed her mother. But she said . . . maybe it was because they kept the manner of Shelly's death from her for so long . . . she was never quite able to believe it. When everyone else in her family did, she always had trouble with it. She thought Frank was a loser. But she didn't think he seemed like a killer."

"But she was only seven when she knew him."

Kevin shrugged. "That's just how she felt, I guess."

"And did she feel differently when she showed up at his house?"

"No. Not at all. That's the thing. And that's not what I expected. I'd expected her to go there because she wanted to spit in his face. But that wasn't how it was for her at all. I realized then that she wanted to go primarily to get a good look at him, to confirm or contradict her feeling."

Kevin captured a bit of iced tea in his straw and squirted it into his mouth. Watching all of this, I started to wonder how much, as a parent, I was going to focus on table manners.

"And that changed your opinion of her, I guess?"

"Not of her. I already knew I liked her by then. If she hated Frank and wanted to see him fry, I would've understood."

Kevin shook his head. "No, it wasn't about liking her or not liking her. I'd already decided about that. I think I was already hopeless pretty quickly in that respect."

"And was she?" I asked.

"Oh. Um . . . no. Hopeless, no. But willing to give me a chance."

We were both silent for a moment.

"But that's not what I meant to get at. Talking about the conversation in the McDonald's parking lot. I was meaning to tell you about something I told Gretchen after that. That I wasn't sure she'd written about or not."

"Okay," I said. "Did you want to tell me, then?"

"Yes. I . . . uh. . . . told her a little more about the day Shelly died. How that afternoon Judy came to our house and sat in our living room and cried hysterically and told my mother what happened. It was like being in a movie, that day. I mean, I didn't say that to Gretchen because I know how tacky that would've sounded to her."

"She would've understood if you said that. She didn't mind if people were tacky, as long as they came by it honestly."

Kevin grunted. "Ha. Yeah. I'm sure you're right about that. But anyway, *nothing* like that ever happened here. It didn't feel real. I think in my little early adolescent brain, I expected Columbo to show up."

"When did people start asking you what you saw?"

"Not till the next day. But of course, I started thinking about it before that. I started thinking about it ten minutes after Judy showed up. I could tell by what she was saying that they'd start asking me soon. I stayed up late that night, wondering what they were going to ask me. Because of course, I hadn't heard any screams or seen any blood or guts. I was expecting they'd ask me about stuff like that, and I wouldn't have an answer."

Kevin bobbed his straw up and down in his iced tea. "And the next day, Judy came and talked to me. Before the police ever got to me. And *she* asked me first the question about the cars. She told me that her friend

Diane, the lady who jogs every day around the same time I delivered the papers . . . she told me she'd seen Frank's big gray car there next to Shelly's. And she wanted to know if I had, too.

"But I didn't answer right away. And that seemed to upset Judy — that I had to take some time to stop and think about it. Because the thing is, when there was enough room in someone's driveway, I'd usually ride my bike right up it to get closer to the doorstep and toss the paper, and not even get off my bike. We weren't really supposed to do that — the yard toss. But I did it when I could get close enough without stopping. That was my system. I tried to be conscientious. If I missed big-time, I'd stop and re-deliver it."

"So whether there were one or two cars in the driveway was actually something you *would* remember."

"Yes. Not for days and days, of course, since I'd be likely to mix the days up. But I might remember for a day or two."

"And could you remember for sure this time?"

"I thought so. I was pretty sure."

I waited for him to continue. Charlie Bucket kicked with anticipation.

"But Judy told me how sure that lady Diane was. And she was sure of the opposite. The opposite of what I remembered."

"You remembered his car *not* being there?"

"Yeah. That's what I remembered." Kevin lowered his voice so much I had to lean forward to hear him. "One car. But that other lady was so *sure*. And Judy was so sure she was sure. And Judy was so sad and so clearly wanted *me* to be sure of the same thing . . . I thought . . . I must have it wrong. No, there were two cars there that day. The red one and the gray one."

"What time did you deliver the paper?"

"My alarm always went off at six thirty. I always set out around six forty-five. That's why I was sure it had to be about seven."

"You even testified, didn't you?"

"Yeah. I don't think anyone put too much stock in what I said . . . obviously. But yeah, I did. By then I was so deep in . . . I knew that I was doing the right thing. The way everyone was so sure . . . it just *put* that car there for me, in my head. Easy."

"Not so much that you remembered it differently, though? If you can say it that way now. Somewhere in the back of your mind, you must have always known that you . . ."

"Yeah. You're right. Somewhere, I always did."

The waitress brought my chicken soup and Kevin's hamburger. He stared at his food for a moment while I slurped down several spoonfuls.

"Did you tell anyone?" I asked. "I mean, before Gretchen?"

"No. It's not like anyone asked about it again, after the trial was over. It was like . . . a little sore spot I always had . . . that I didn't think about unless someone pressed on it somehow. And that was rare."

"Till Gretchen came along."

"Right. And when she did, I couldn't help thinking . . . thank God that guy didn't go to jail . . . at least, on my word. And I didn't know if that was the right thought for me to have, because maybe he did it, but Gretchen opened it all up for me . . . I was so ashamed of myself . . . even though I was a kid, I should've known better . . . but I was so grateful Gretchen came along and asked. Grateful to tell someone . . . and not just anyone . . . but someone it *mattered* for."

I opened my package of saltines. "And what did Gretchen say?"

Kevin sighed. "She wasn't as surprised as I thought she'd be. She wasn't like, 'Oh, I knew it.' But there was no shock at the confession."

"What'd she say, though?"

"The first thing she said was, 'I'm glad you told me.' "

Kevin finally picked up his burger and took a big bite.

"And then later?" I asked.

"We never talked about it too much later, after the initial conversation. But it felt very much . . . there. Between us."

"In a bad way?"

"No. Not in an especially good way either. Just . . . there."

I nodded. Gretchen had an unusual gift for allowing uncomfortable realities to simply exist in her presence without acknowledgment, to silently work themselves out. Until recently, perhaps.

"I haven't seen anything she wrote about it," I told him. "I've still got quite a few of her notebooks to read, and there might be something hidden on her computer I haven't seen yet. But I don't know if it's there."

"I wonder if it meant all that much to her. If it changed anything about how she was going to write about it."

Kevin tried picking up his burger again, but a pickle and some ketchup drips leaked out. He grabbed a napkin and mopped his plate self-consciously.

"I'm sure she meant to write about it

eventually," I said. "It seems to me she got so caught up in the research, she'd stopped writing."

"If you and her family decided to publish her story . . . would you put this in?" Kevin asked.

Kevin watched me carefully for a moment. He seemed to be looking at my stomach. I looked down and saw that an ample scattering of saltine crumbs had settled there.

"Well . . ." I said, wiping them away. "Do you think Gretchen felt this was an important part of the story?"

"I think so," Kevin said, mushing his napkin into a moist little ball. "Yeah. But I think she wasn't sure where it fit."

I put down my soup spoon. I liked to think he was wrong. Gretchen *had* figured out where it fit. She just kept it to herself and didn't write it down.

"I guess I'll have to figure that out," I said, "before I can answer your question."

"Right," Kevin said, and picked up his hamburger again.

CHAPTER 50

After I got back to the hotel, I debated for a while before calling Judy. I didn't want to offend her, but I wanted to see if Kevin's memory of how he'd come to be a witness was, in her view, accurate.

Judy didn't sound surprised to hear from me, and said she'd be happy to talk to me for a few minutes.

"I'm not sure if Gretchen would've asked you about this," I said. "But I'm getting from her notes that you were actually the one who first spoke to the paperboy, Kevin Conley, about what he'd seen in Shelly's driveway the morning of her death."

"Yes," Judy replied. "That's correct."

I asked her if that topic naturally came up in conversation, or if she had gone to Kevin specifically to ask what he'd seen.

"The second," Judy admitted. "Maybe that sounds like I was overstepping my bounds. Remember, though, that Diane knew she saw Frank's car there early that morning. That was a good start. But what good would that do on its own? One account of a good friend of the victim? That wasn't going to be enough. Not even close to enough.

"So, yes, I put my head to who else would've seen what she saw. And Kevin was one of the people who came to mind. I didn't want the police to overlook anyone. Even a kid."

"But you went and talked to him first," I said. "And by the time you were done with him, he was saying *he* saw what Diane saw."

"I only asked him what he saw." Judy's tone was stiff now. "Did Gretchen have the impression something else happened?"

I hesitated. "Um . . . Well, did you know that Gretchen was spending time with Kevin Conley in the weeks before she died?"

Judy took in a breath.

"No . . . You mean she interviewed him?"

"Well. Yes. And they started . . . dating, I guess, would be the word for it."

"I didn't know he was still around."

"Yeah. He works as a special ed aide in Plantsville."

"Oh." Judy was quiet for a moment. "Did he say something that concerned Gretchen?"

"Well . . . let's just say he was twelve when it happened, and he maybe wasn't as confident of what he saw as he'd like to be now."

"Well. I've certainly never heard that. If that's how he felt, what took him so long to say so?"

"Maybe it was simply a matter of someone asking," I suggested.

Judy paused, then sighed. "Maybe it was a matter of someone *writing a book* asking. Maybe he wanted to please Gretchen? Give her something to write about?"

"It's possible," I admitted. "I'm not making a judgment. I just thought I would get your take."

"Well. My *take* is that I loved Shelly and I did what I could for her case. I knew it was Frank, and I needed to do *something*. It was like Diane was at least doing something — some small thing. I was *really* Shelly's best friend, and I needed to help, too."

This was the first I'd heard of this — of Judy being Shelly's "best" friend. I wondered how accurate this label was.

"Jamie, you've got to realize. There were some things Shelly said to me a week or two before she died . . . that when I thought about it later . . . made me think that things were worse between her and Frank than I realized."

"Can you tell me what they were?"

"Yes. I spoke to Gretchen about it several times . . . I don't know if she wrote about it. Maybe you're already familiar . . ."

"I don't think so."

"Well, it was just me and her one night. Having a bite to eat. That was rare in those days, with her working so hard, and dealing with Frank, and spending so much time with Melanie. And Gretchen every other weekend. And I was working and planning a wedding, so I was pretty involved in those things. But I remember very well that Shelly made a point for us to have dinner together one night.

"And she was talking about making some changes in her life. Granted, she was always talking about making changes in her life around then. Some of them happened and some of them didn't. That's how it was with Shelly. This time, at first, I thought she was talking about Gretchen. About getting Gretchen back. But then I realized she was talking about something else.

"She told me some things were going to change for her in the next couple of weeks, and she didn't want me to think any less of her. She said I might be surprised by some of the choices she made.

"The thing that I remembered so well

later was how she looked straight at me and said that she'd regretted how she'd let men treat her in her life. That she let men hurt her. And she was ready to take a stand about that. Maybe she'd never felt worthy of that before. 'And maybe I still don't,' she said. And it's painful to remember her saying that, even now. She said she could maybe take a stand if she was doing it for someone besides herself.

"I assumed she was talking about Gretchen. That normally she might tolerate how Frank treated her, but for the sake of being a good role model for Gretchen — or maybe for the sake of getting her back — she was going to leave Frank. That's what I figured she was trying to say. And she talked about how it was important to her, now, to expose a person who hurt her. That she spent a lot of her life being ashamed of it when someone hurt her, and that's what always kept her from letting the shame fall where it really belonged. Listening to her say this stuff, I wasn't certain she believed it. But it seemed like she wanted to.

"The part about not wanting me to think less of her . . . I assumed that at some point soon I was going to hear that he'd been hitting her. That she was too ashamed to tell me straight out. Yet, anyway."

"And you didn't make her talk about it directly?" I asked.

"Well . . . no. She already seemed to be in a lot of turmoil. And resolved. I encouraged her resolve. I said, 'Listen, Shelly, whatever you have to do . . . of course I'll support you.' And she seemed satisfied and relieved to have the conversation end there. Of course, I shouldn't have been satisfied. If I'd known how serious it was, I would have said a lot more."

"Did she talk to *anyone* about it directly that you know of?"

"Yes, actually. Diane."

"Really?"

"Yes. I don't know how much Gretchen talked to her about it, or how much Diane would've wanted to say. But around the same time Shelly talked to me, she had a similar conversation with Diane. But she talked straighter, apparently. She actually came out and told Diane about the hitting."

"Okay," I said. Although I wasn't sure I could totally trust her, I had a wave of sympathy for Judy. I thought about Gretchen, and how she'd never told me what happened between her and Jeremy. Probably Judy had wondered, all these years, why Shelly had talked frankly to Diane but not to her.

"I think Diane struggles not to feel guilty about that," Judy said with a sigh. "She's confirmed it, but doesn't like to talk a great deal about it. I don't know if she ever discussed it with Gretchen. She probably wouldn't have unless Gretchen knew to ask."

"Did she testify about it in court?"

"Yeah. She did. But since hers was the only account . . . and she didn't witness it firsthand or have many details . . . it didn't have a great deal of impact. Disappointingly, the prosecutor never stressed the pattern of domestic abuse as much as he should've. I suppose he just didn't have enough concrete evidence. No previous hospital visits, no eyewitnesses to anything but yelling and screaming."

Judy sighed again. Then there was a silence so long I thought we might have been disconnected.

"Hello?"

"Hello. I'm still here," Judy said. "You know, Jamie . . . If you find out who killed Gretchen, won't you do everything you can to make sure that person rots in hell?"

"I . . . think so."

"If it happens, you *will*. Maybe you or Kevin Conley or someone else thinks I didn't play fair. Well, Frank Grippo certainly had not played fair either. Frank killed my friend and then let his lawyer call her a slut and an addict and a bad mother in court for everyone to hear. So am I going to feel guilty that I tried to help her side a little bit? No. I'm not. And if you see Kevin again, you should tell him he shouldn't feel guilty either."

Judy was silent for a moment more.

"Now. Did you have anything else you wanted to discuss with me?"

"Um. No. Thanks for your honesty."

"Of course," Judy snapped. "Goodbye, Jamie."

I decided, for the time being, not to make too much of Judy's tone. She had a point — if someone questioned my loyalty to Gretchen, or my efforts to find answers about her death, I might start sounding the same way.

Her revelations about Shelly reminded me of a piece in one of Gretchen's notebooks that I'd read early on. I rummaged through the ones I had in the motel room — I'd brought about half of them — to find it. It was called "Bedtime Story." It started with a story about a picture Gretchen had drawn for Shelly and ended rather incongruously with this:

Shelly decided to have a serious talk with me. She said she wanted to tell me that she'd made a decision about something. And I might hear people talking about it, and that it might upset me or my mom. But that she wanted me to know that she loved me, no matter what happened.

My first reaction was that she didn't really like the crow so much, after all, but was just trying to be nice, knowing that a serious conversation was coming.

Shelly continued. She said that the most important thing she wanted me to remember was that if someone was ever hurting you, it was important to do something about it right away. To either hit back or tell someone who would help you. Whatever you decided to do, the important thing was to do something right away. Not wait and see if it would happen again. That was what she

wanted me to remember from
this.

I told her that no one was
hurting me. And she said that
that was good, she was glad.
It didn't seem to me we understood each other, about her
plans or about my crow. The
conversation ended there, as
Shelly suggested we make ourselves a little lunch.

That evening, though, I felt
I understood a little better.
There was a knock on the door,
and my heart sank. Frank, I
thought. He'd been completely
absent this visit, allowing
Shelly to focus all of her attention on me.

When Shelly opened the door,
I heard her say, "My kid's
here. She's asleep."

She let the person in anyway,
and as they started to talk, I
was relieved to hear it was a
woman. This wasn't unusual.
Shelly's friends seemed to
know my bedtime — occasionally they'd come and visit

with her after I was in bed. And I continued to busy myself fashioning my stuffed monkey into funny contortions, as I sometimes did when I couldn't sleep.

Then Shelly said something that made me sit up straight in my bed. She said, "It's more complicated than money. I don't really want money. And all the money in the world wouldn't even get me Gretchen back, anyway."

Get Gretchen back?! So it was true. Someday Shelly might bring me back here and be my mother. I couldn't imagine it. Would she start pretending to care about my dittos, my 100s? Would she let me take ballet? Did the Emerson school cafeteria have chicken nuggets?

The TV was burbling loudly, so I couldn't hear everything. Eventually, though, I heard the other lady say something loud enough for me to hear. Something like: "If you think you would hold up in a fight against him, you're wrong, Shelly."

This scared me. She was probably talking about Frank now. I could figure out that much, because I knew how much Shelly and Frank fought. She was warning Shelly about Frank. It seemed to me a lot of people didn't really like Frank: me, Nantie Linda, Aunt Dorothy, Grandma, the neighbors.

And yes, it was a relief to know that others knew what I knew. That Shelly and Frank fought. It was not a relief to hear someone else sound like they were worried Shelly should be afraid of him — like I was.

It seemed to me, after a few minutes, that Shelly and her guest were getting angry at each other.

Shelly said, "If he doesn't stop, I'll go to the police."

"You think the police will believe you?" her friend asked. And she told Shelly she

468

should be careful.

I supposed, if Judy's words were accurate, that this conversation had probably been between Shelly and Diane — because Diane, it seemed, was the only one with whom Shelly had ever discussed Frank's violence directly. And what was this thing about money? What did money have to do with it? Could Shelly perhaps have stood to lose money somehow in leaving Frank? I wondered if Gretchen had ever figured out if this friend was indeed Diane — and if she'd ever asked her about that night.

I tried Diane's number but got no answer. Then I wrote her an e-mail, asking her if we could chat again before I left town.

CHAPTER 51

I shut off CNN when Sam called me that night.

"Jamie. We need to talk," he said sharply.

His tone made me uneasy.

"Okay," I said.

"You didn't tell me they'd found new evidence in Gretchen's death."

"What, you mean her purse?" I tried to say it casually.

"Yes, I mean her purse! Christ, Jamie, when were you going to tell me?"

"How did you find out about that?" I asked.

"Chris from work told me. He saw it on some news or other. And he was asking me, 'Didn't you say that was a friend of your wife's? How tragic. How is your wife holding up?'"

"I'm holding up fine."

"Uh-huh. So this is why you were in such a hurry to get up there?"

"Kind of," I admitted.

"Jamie . . . are you researching Gretchen's book . . . or are you *investigating?*"

"Well . . . A little bit of both."

Sam groaned into the phone. "Don't you think you're putting yourself in harm's way a little bit?"

"A little bit," I admitted.

"And is that a smart idea right now?"

"When is it ever a smart idea?" I asked.

"Jamie, I think you should come home."

"I've got a couple of people I'm talking to tomorrow," I said. "I'm here now and I may as well just get it done."

"I was thinking I might come up and join you."

"It'd be a complete waste of time. If you drive up tomorrow morning . . . by then I'll be nearly done."

Sam was quiet for a moment.

"How about you call me a couple of times tomorrow, at least," he said reluctantly.

"Absolutely," I said.

I felt a twinge of guilt as I hung up — and even considered calling Sam right back to apologize. But I wasn't confident he wouldn't keep trying to talk me back home. So I put my phone aside and took out *Tammyland* to take my mind off him.

I reread Gretchen's piece on Patsy Cline,

which I liked — and then felt compelled to open my computer and find some of Patsy's music online. I wasn't really a fan of much of the other music Gretchen wrote about — but I did like Patsy. I went online and started with the song Gretchen used for the title of her piece, "The Heart You Break May Be Your Own," then moved on to some of Patsy's more famous tunes. Halfway through "She's Got You," Charlie Bucket started to move around very animatedly. I played the song again, then turned it all the way up and stuck my stomach as close as I could to the laptop microphone.

"You're right," I said. "That voice is really something."

It seemed to me he was kicking in tune to it. The poor boy hadn't heard much very pleasing in the past few weeks. Just me crying and whining and asking lots of grim questions about two dead women. He deserved to have someone sing to him, as I'd done occasionally before Gretchen died.

Then the kicking stopped and I tried "Sweet Dreams." Nothing more from Charlie. Maybe Patsy had sung him to sleep.

I returned to Gretchen's favorite and played it again.

"The heart you broke was not your own, turns out, Gretchen," I whispered.

I closed her book and turned the TV back on.

Chapter 52

"The Heart You Break May Be Your Own"

*Plane Crash Site Memorial
Camden, Tennessee*

You have to drive through residential Camden and then walk down a gravel path into the woods to get to it: the site of the 1963 plane crash that killed Patsy Cline, Hawkshaw Hawkins, Cowboy Copas, and Randy Hughes. Their names — along with musical notes — are engraved on a large gray stone that marks the spot.

A few steps back from it, among the trees and poison ivy, someone has fashioned a cross out of PVC piping. There is a spray of silk flowers poking out of the top, and a rosary, a worn peppermint-striped ribbon, and a red cowboy handkerchief hanging off it.

There are two Patsy Clines in my head. First, there's the immortal one — the one that I thought of when all I knew of her was "Crazy" and "Walkin' After Midnight." This is the untouchably legendary Patsy with the chilling voice, who looks out from her final album covers with a sultry gaze and striking red lipstick. This is the Patsy I see in footage of her performances, looking serene in her perky button-down dresses and sculpted eyebrows, saying little but singing so big and so full of expression.

Then there is the human one I've learned about in various biographies. This is the Patsy who loved performing in the cowgirl outfits her mother made, who enjoyed yodeling during her performances, and said she felt like a prostitute when singing pop songs instead of country. This is the Patsy with the foul mouth and supposedly voracious sexual appetite. She also liked to cook and be a homemaker and loved her babies.

Perhaps it is artificial to separate the two, because it sometimes seems that the phenomenon she was meant to be was always somehow a part of her. She craved stardom from a young age, and sought it out like someone who almost knew, deep down, her time to achieve it was short. In her teen years, she had to drop out of school to support her family, working at a drugstore and waitressing. In those years, however, she was already singing at local nightclubs and variety shows, showing up at radio stations asking to sing, and writing letters to the Grand Ole Opry requesting an audition.

Her early auditions were not the cinematic, record-producer-drops-his-cigar-and-exclaims-"this-little-gal-can-SING" sort of affairs. She had to work at it. She had to develop a distinctive style. Her early recordings were not successful. Her ambition, however, was tireless and obsessive. Her mother, to whom she was very close, found her drive perplexing and exhausting.

Was it just that she wanted fame and money and applause? Or was there something else pushing her? Perhaps she had a deep, subconscious sense that she was destined to create something beautiful and timeless, and that she had limited time in which to fulfill that destiny. Indeed, friends of hers, such as Dottie West and June Carter Cash, claimed she had premonitions of her early death. In the months before her death, she gave away some of her belongings and made sure others knew her wishes regarding who would raise her children. She was only thirty years old.

I know her death at thirty is immensely tragic. She left behind two small children, not to mention her brokenhearted mother. Yet her short life is, nonetheless, inspiring. How many of us pursue our potential with that kind of intensity?

I know I don't have a legendary Gretchen hiding somewhere inside of me. There was a moment, however, when I was deciding whether to stay in my old life or break out of it, when something that felt outside of me said, "There is something else you are supposed to be doing."

Am I doing it now? I suppose a mere trip to Nashville isn't going to be enough. That'd be a rather sad destiny if it was. I don't think mine will result in anything as beautiful or lasting as Patsy's. But I do have one that's more than this, more than the life I was living. And it's not up to me whether it's a breathtaking, transcendent legacy or simply a legacy. That's not for me to ask, or to ask for. I can only follow it, as she did, and have faith that it will mean something.

It is when I think of this that I'm reminded of one of Patsy's lesser-known songs, "The Heart You Break May Be Your Own." There is probably no "may be," about it. I think in the end, it always "will be." Because you can only go one way or another, can't you?

— *Tammyland*

CHAPTER 53

The man who answered the door had to be Bruce. He was tall, with superlong limbs — like an awkwardly drawn stick figure. His hair was fluffy, black with white streaks, and his skin was indeed quite dark. He reminded me of the covers of my mother's old Neil Diamond albums.

"Hello?" he greeted me.

"Hi," I said. "I'm here on behalf of Gretchen Waters's family. I'm wondering if you have a few minutes to chat."

Bruce slouched against his door and stared at me. It was nine o'clock on Sunday morning. I had figured that was early enough for him to be up, but unlikely to have gone anywhere yet.

"My name is Jamie Madden," I said. "And I'm Gretchen's literary executor."

"Oh." Bruce looked puzzled for a moment. "Oh, I see. Did she have a number of unpublished manuscripts stashed away?"

"Just . . . uh . . . one. But I'm in the process of reading through all of her material and verifying it with some of her sources."

"And I'm . . . one of her sources?" Bruce smiled a little, as if I'd said something amusing.

"Yeah."

Bruce stepped out onto his porch and gave me a once-over. Reflexively, I took a step back.

"Did you hear they found her purse in Youngs Lake?" he asked me.

"Yes."

He nodded. "Very unsettling."

"Yes," I agreed.

"What's your name again?"

"Jamie."

"Don't you want to sit down?" Bruce opened his door to me.

"I'm okay, for now. I was thinking of asking if you'd be willing to talk to me at that Dunkin' Donuts, over there on the Main Street. I don't want to impose, but I think there are some things I need to clarify before going forward with her book."

Bruce looked perplexed again. "Dunkin' Donuts?"

"Just . . . uh . . . a neutral place. I don't want to impose, but I want to talk to you."

"Dunkin' Donuts is neutral?" Bruce gave a reptilian smile.

I didn't reply. His dark features and Gretchen's declaration of her mysterious paternity notwithstanding, I almost sensed a bit of Gretchen in his general weirdness.

"I'm happy to talk to you," Bruce said. He stared at my middle for a moment, then looked up to meet my gaze. "But are you sure you should be doing this *now?*"

"Excuse me?" I said, irritated. Where are those "None of Your Business" cards when you need them?

"I mean . . . I mean . . . they found her purse. In Emerson. That means it likely wasn't an accident, what happened to her."

"Yes, I know what it means."

"I'll talk to you. Sure. I hope, however, that you'll be careful who else you try to talk to."

"If you meet me at the doughnut shop," I said, "maybe you can tell me what you mean."

Bruce drank his hot coffee in tiny, careful sips.

"I do hope you're being cautious," he said, before I'd had a chance to ask him anything. "Who you're choosing to interview right now. If I were you, I might hold off on this until the police have a better handle on the Gretchen situation."

"Do you think there is someone in particular I should be afraid of?"

"Probably. Unfortunately, I don't know who that would be."

"But you think someone around here might have killed Gretchen?"

Bruce took a big bite of his chocolate-frosted doughnut with rainbow sprinkles — a doughnut selection I'd found incongruously creepy.

"It looks that way, doesn't it?" he said softly, after he'd swallowed.

"Any guesses?" I asked, trying to sip my tea casually.

"I don't know enough about the situation to have a guess. All I know is that Gretchen suddenly showed up in Emerson — and here — asking all kinds of sensitive questions, and a month or two later she's dead, with her purse thrown in the lake."

I shuddered at this, but hoped he didn't see it.

Bruce paused. "Showed up asking questions. Like you're doing now."

I wasn't in the mood for any more scolding — in fact, his attempt at it made me feel particularly bold.

"Were you by any chance at Gretchen's

reading the night she died?" I asked.

"Yes." Bruce crinkled his forehead and pressed a few stray sprinkles onto his fingertips, then slipped them between his lips. "I've spoken to the police about that."

"You have?"

"Of course. As soon as I heard what happened, I went and spoke to them. Unfortunately, I didn't have much to offer them, in terms of what I saw. I left right after the program."

"Was anyone else you knew from Emerson there?"

"No. I didn't recognize anyone. The police know all of this. I was surprised at being the only one, since her reading was announced in the Emerson paper."

"A reading so far away?"

"Yes. They had a feature about her being local . . . or sort of local. And it mentioned her reading. That paper is often hard up for stories, you know."

"Why were you there?" I asked.

Bruce opened his coffee and blew on it before answering.

"Gretchen piqued my curiosity. Frankly, it was nice to see a child of a good friend, all grown up. So much like Shelly, in some little ways. For the most part, though, so different. And I liked her, when I met her. When

I saw she was doing a reading not too far from my job, I wanted to go give a little support. And I was curious about her writing. Plus, as an academic, I know what it's like to give a talk and wonder if anyone will show up."

This guy's smoothness was really irritating me.

"Do you think maybe you were curious about her because she might be your daughter?" I asked.

Bruce winced with surprise, then smiled. The many little lines around his mouth folded in gently. "No."

"And you're sure of that?"

"You know, she was a lovely young woman, and I admired her forwardness. I went to her reading as an old friend of her mother's. But no. She wasn't my daughter. Shelly was always certain of that. As was I."

"It didn't sound like Shelly was sure."

Bruce was silent. I couldn't decipher the expression on his face: The left side of his lip curled, his right eyebrow arched. Was it anger? Embarrassment? Deception? I remembered Gretchen's question about not being able to tell who was lying, and realized I had no skills in that area. All I could think to do was keep throwing him curveballs.

"Gretchen stole your mail, you know. She stole several pieces of your mail to get your saliva and do DNA tests."

Bruce's coffee cup wobbled in his hand. "What?"

"A mortgage payment, a *Rolling Stone* subscription . . . one other piece, I think. Right out of your mailbox. And sent them to a genetics lab."

Bruce put down his coffee cup and folded his arms. "Is that right?"

"Yes."

Bruce nodded. "She was certainly an interesting girl. You must miss her."

This wasn't the response I was expecting.

"And the results were negative," Bruce said quietly.

"I don't know because . . . uh . . . she didn't write about it and she didn't . . ."

I looked down at my sticky hands. I'd been nervously breaking my glazed doughnuts into little bits.

Bruce handed me a napkin, then bit his lip.

"I assume they were negative," he said, "because I *know* they were negative. I loved Shelly as a friend. But I was never *with* Shelly."

I stared at him. He seemed to be blushing a little.

"It's true," he said.

It took me a moment to recover my voice.

"Why didn't you tell Gretchen that?" I asked.

Bruce rolled his eyes toward the ceiling, thinking. "It's complicated. It's not what Shelly would have wanted."

"I'm sorry. That sounds ridiculous. Shelly would have wanted you to string Gretchen along, thinking you might be her biological father?"

"No. Shelly wouldn't have wanted Gretchen to ever ask the question. She didn't want *anyone* to ever ask. But most of all, Gretchen, I'm sure."

"And how do you know this?" I asked.

"Because Shelly was my friend. She told me. When we were just young kids. When she got pregnant, we were just friends. But I think I was the first person she told. She was afraid of what would happen. And she was afraid of people finding out who was responsible. Later, mostly for Gretchen's sake. She clearly *wanted* people to think the field of possibilities was so open, it wasn't worth finding out the answer."

"And you were okay with being one of the possibilities? For all of this time?"

"For Shelly, yes. She was my friend. She'd been through a lot."

Bruce's fluffy hair fell forward as he looked mournfully into his coffee.

"Then why are you telling me this now?" I asked, after a moment.

"Because Shelly's dead. And Gretchen's dead. And I'd rather not see you dead as well."

I dropped the doughnut bit in my hand. The bluntness of his words startled me.

"I'm just afraid," he hurried to say, "that Gretchen may have asked the wrong person the wrong questions."

"The wrong person? Who would that be?"

"I don't know," Bruce said, frowning.

"Which was the wrong question? Who killed Shelly, or who was her father? Or something else?"

"I don't know that, either."

Bruce gazed at the last bite of his sprinkle doughnut wearily.

"But you might know the answer to the second question, sounds like."

"No." Bruce shook his head. "I don't. But yes, I know a little bit about Gretchen's father. I just don't know his name."

"What does that mean?"

Bruce ignored the question and took another sip of his coffee. "Who made you Gretchen's 'literary executor,' anyway?"

He used air quotes when he said "literary

executor."

"Her mother. I mean, Linda. Shelly's sister."

"Yes. Of course I know who you mean. Have you told her everything you've found in your research so far?"

"No."

"Do you plan to?"

"I don't know. It depends on what comes out."

"Well, Jamie. I don't know who Gretchen's father was, but I always knew it wasn't me and it wasn't Keith. Shelly told me that it wasn't Keith. It was someone older than her. Someone who'd . . . taken advantage of her situation."

He paused, and I waited for more. I put my hand on my stomach. The artificial hazelnut smell of this place was suddenly making me sick.

"When Shelly was very young, she never had a chance. She told me all about it one night. I'll never forget. We went to a movie and I parked my car behind the dog-food warehouse, hoping to get to 'neck' as they called it then. Of course we talked instead. It was clear that night that was all we were ever going to do, she and I.

"And then that prom night. All night together, far away from Emerson. She'd planned it all along. She needed to tell someone. And she knew I would keep her secret. She was right. I always have. But there's no sense in it, now."

Bruce glanced around the doughnut shop. There were only a few other customers in the place, most of them of the white-haired variety. None of them was sitting very close to us or paying us much attention.

"It started when she was thirteen years old. *Thirteen*. She told me that much. It was a family friend, someone older. That's all I could get out of her. She was confused. Her own father had just died. It went on for years. She finally put an end to it when Gretchen came. But by then, it had already done so much damage to her life. It was tragic."

"Gretchen . . . I think Gretchen figured it out before she died. Who it was."

"Really? What makes you think so?"

I hesitated. "Just . . . some things she wrote. But didn't you worry about what it was doing to Shelly? Couldn't you have told someone?"

"My loyalty was to her, and she didn't want me to. And I was young, too. By the time she told me, it was over. She resolved never to be alone with him again. And she was old enough to make sure that happened."

"Who do you *think* it was?"

"Her parents . . . her family . . . had a lot of friends. It could have been anyone."

"You didn't try to guess?"

Bruce shook his head. "She never let me. She didn't want to have that conversation. And I won't guess now either. I'm sorry."

"What about other girls? What if he did something like this to other young girls?"

"Shelly told me that if she ever suspected anything like that, she would say something. But at the time, no. She wasn't ready to say anything for herself."

"Seems unlikely she'd have *known* what he was up to when she was off drinking herself to death for years after that."

"Are you going to hold that against her? That she was too troubled herself then to save anyone else?"

I was silent for a moment. Gretchen was right. Bruce did seem to have a great deal of loyalty to Shelly.

"No," I said.

We were both silent.

"It must have been someone pretty terrible," I said, "for her not to want Gretchen to find out."

"Anyone who would do that to a grieving

thirteen-year-old girl would have to be pretty terrible," Bruce said.

"Yeah. But you know, I think Gretchen could've handled it. If you told her."

Bruce's puffy hair waved gently as he bobbed his head from side to side a few times, considering this. "Hmm. Perhaps. I had that sense. I was thinking about it. On the other hand, I'd made a promise."

CHAPTER 54

"Forever Yours"

Red Bay Museum
Red Bay, Alabama

The Red Bay Museum in Red Bay, Alabama, isn't just about Tammy Wynette. While about half of the creaky upstairs is devoted to the First Lady of Country Music, the rest of the museum is about the town of Red Bay itself. Downstairs you can look at the original cashier's desk from the Bank of Red Bay, the neon sign and re-created lobby from the historic Red Bay Hotel, or a hospital bed from the town's favorite doctor, who delivered most of the Red Bay babies in recent decades.

The museum is funded, in part, by the profits from the consignment store next door.

The tour guide lets me walk around by myself for about twenty minutes (she has to man the consignment store, which gets far more visitors), then comes to check on me in the Tammy section.

I've looked at several of Tammy's blouses and jackets, several sequined dresses, and her makeup case. I scowl at the donation letter accompanying it, from her last husband, George Richey, explaining that the contents of the case show that Tammy was "in many ways . . . an ordinary woman like many of you." There is also endless Tammy "fan" paraphernalia: concert posters, ticket stubs, baseball caps with her name on them, Tammy figurines.

When the guide finds me staring at a pair of Tammy Wynette playing cards, she asks me quietly if I've ever heard of Tammy Wynette before.

I'm surprised by the question — uncertain what she thought would bring me into this museum and keep me here for longer than five minutes if I hadn't heard of her. I say that I am a fan, and that's why I came.

She seems surprised and delighted. Maybe no one of my age and accent ever comes in here claiming to be a Tammy fan.

After I confess that I am one, she opens up. She tells me sheepishly that her husband is one of Tammy's cousins, and that many of the items here were collected by her family members and old friends. (The bulk of Tammy's estate is now in the hands of the young widow of Tammy's final husband, who, sadly, inherited everything of Tammy's.) She points to a red blouse with fringe in one of the cases, and tells me that it's her own contribution. It was a hand-me-down from Tammy.

"But I hardly ever wore it," she confesses. "The neck was too wide for me."

Gazing into one of the other cases, she says, "It's kind of sad . . . but . . . anyway. We do the best we can."

She doesn't say exactly what's sad. The collection? Or Tammy's life?

Either way, it *is* kind of sad. Up here in this attic room, Tammy's life seems to have happened so long ago. But there is something so sincere about how her memory is preserved.

As we go down the stairs together, the guide asks me where I'm from. I go ahead and tell her Massachusetts. There is an earnestness to this place that makes me want to tell the truth.

Whatever fame Tammy gained or lost, however tragically her life ended, it's clear here that she was loved, and still is. Maybe that's all that any of us can ask for after we've gone — whatever we've accomplished, wherever we've failed, whether we've achieved success or fame — that there are a few people left behind who wish to honor us in strange and humble ways.

I linger there in the museum for as long as I can. I ask the guide what she thought of the latest Tammy biography. She thought it was decent, but maybe contained a little "too much information." I think I know what she means. Tammy doesn't come across so well in parts of it — in the same way none of us likely would under such intense scrutiny.

I hope she'll tell me a story about Tammy — something that would never appear in any book. Of course she doesn't. Like family, like a true friend, she knows better than to give a stranger something like that. When she is clearly tired of me, I put several dollars in the donation jar and step out onto the hot sidewalk of downtown Red Bay.

As I start my car, Tammy's "Forever Yours" comes on. I'd been listening to her album *Stand by Your Man* on my way here, and despite my ambivalence toward the title song, this is a pretty stellar album for Tammy. She's clearly in top form here, well before everything went to shit. I love this simple song, in which one can appreciate the crystalline power of Tammy's voice, without the distraction of her cheesier lyrics.

I open my window and blast Tammy on my way out of town. It's three and a half hours of driving back to my Nashville hotel. The heaviness that accompanies me is not for Tammy. It's not even for the eerie feeling one gets at leaving a place to which you know you will never return. It's for the odd look Tammy's cousin's wife couldn't help but give me as I left — and for my own obvious distance from home.

— *Tammyland*

CHAPTER 55

I hurried back to the motel because I wanted to listen to Gretchen's recordings again. In particular, I wanted to listen to the Phil Coleman one.

A family friend. Shelly had known him when she was thirteen. And seventeen, for that matter. And in 1985, she'd let him back into her life. For a good job? For Gretchen's sake, even? It seemed potentially sick and sad. I felt a wave of sympathy for Shelly. Up till now, I'd perhaps been a little wary of her. What had taken her so long, I'd wondered, to decide she really wanted her daughter in her life? Had she ever considered how that might have damaged Gretchen? Now, though, her ambivalence made sense, sad as it still was Gretchen was, after all, the child of her abuser.

My motel room had been made up by the time I arrived. I opened the shades and the window so it wouldn't feel so dank, then propped myself up on some pillows with the recorder. I hit the back button till I got to the first recording — remembering that Phil Coleman was Gretchen's first recorded interview.

I didn't know exactly what I was listening for, but I figured I'd know it when I heard it. The first thing I noticed was that Coleman was a little defensive when Gretchen asked him about the wisdom of hiring a former drug abuser for a pharmacy job. Clearly he'd wanted to give Shelly the job because he already knew her and was justifying the decision rather weakly.

But I felt like I knew the real girl, from before all of that. She'd been off the stuff for a year or two at least . . . I had faith in her. I wanted to give her that chance.

The next thing I noticed was that the bulk of their conversation was about Shelly's snooping — her concern about teenagers and their prescriptions. It seemed to me that Gretchen kept that part of the conversation going just as much as Coleman, if not more. Was she really interested in that subject, or was she trying to manipulate the conversation somehow? And was Coleman's view of what happened accurate? Was it really in Shelly's nature to care that much about a bunch of small-town stoner teenagers she didn't know?

I'd never met Shelly, of course, but on the basis of what Gretchen had given me, it seemed to me the answer was probably no. More of a concern for her — as it would be for anyone — would probably be a mistaken prescription given to a sick child. So whose account of the screwup was accurate? Diane's or Coleman's? It seemed Coleman had more to lose in telling the mistaken prescription story, if it was true. On the other hand, how ashamed could he really be of the incident — a clerk's error over twenty years ago?

Or was it *Shelly* who'd knowingly given Coleman a story that sounded kind of clunky? Maybe she'd told Diane about her mistake but told Coleman something else? Maybe he'd caught her rifling through the prescriptions to check on her error, and she'd made up a story offhand to cover it up?

But was any of this indicative of an abusive relationship that began when Shelly was thirteen years old? No. But then, they'd likely both learned to cover that up long ago. I hit play again.

Soon came the awkward moment when Coleman asked Gretchen, *Did you have any other questions?*

And then Gretchen, after a particularly lengthy pause, asked about Frank.

This still perplexed me. She hadn't been afraid to ask Keith straight out, or Bruce. Well, at least as straight out as was possible for Gretchen. With this guy, though, she seemed more reticent. Maybe she thought it would be dangerous to ask. Or maybe the point of their meeting was not to get answers to Gretchen's spoken questions. Maybe the point, for Gretchen, was to get physically near him and to get information off his clothing, his hair, his mail, or one of his other possessions — samples. As she'd done to Bruce.

The interview ended shortly after that, then skipped to the one with Shelly's friend Melanie — the one who was as certain that Shelly had had a relationship with Coleman as Judy was that she hadn't. Who was right? Who knew Shelly better? Diane and Judy? Or Melanie? And if Shelly really revealed to Melanie that she was involved with Coleman, would she have mentioned that it had started in her youth? If it had? Would she feel able to be honest about that in a way she couldn't with an old friend like Judy? And what was it about her friendship with Diane that made her better able to confess Frank's abusive treatment to her than to

Judy *or* Melanie?

I let the Melanie interview run. Melanie seemed to be honest about what she thought about Shelly and Coleman, and didn't seem to be holding anything back for Gretchen's sake.

Near the end of that interview, my mind began to wander. I wondered if this motel had a vending machine. Something salty would be nice right now. I got up from the bed and started rummaging around for some change. My purse, my pockets, the pockets of yesterday's jeans.

I gathered up about eighty cents and stuck it in my pocket as the Melanie interview ended and the one with Dr. Skinner began. I hoped they had Doritos. Original flavor. Not Cool Ranch. I've never quite understood the appeal of Cool Ranch. I paused the recorder, then went to the motel lobby to check out the vending options. They had the original flavor I was so craving. I opened them on my way back to my door.

Walking and munching, I noticed a car at the back of the lot that matched the color of my Doritos: a cute, rusty orange hatchback. Now, who was it who was telling me recently she wanted a car like that? My mother? My boss? My old friend Abby?

Back in the room, I pressed play and tried

to pace myself with my tiny bag of Doritos.

Dr. Skinner was saying, *Oh, yes. All of the girls liked to come over and go in the pool.*

Diane's friends, you mean? Judy and Shelly? Gretchen replied.

Yes, Judy and Shelly. Nice girls, both of them. Shelly was the prettiest, though.

I see.

Something about that exchange made me put down my Doritos bag for a moment. I sat on the bed and listened some more. But of course they were just having the same old circular conversation as in Gretchen's earlier written interview. I picked up the bag again, half listening until this part:

But she did give me some trouble. When Dr. Platt died, she started giving me trouble.

What kind of trouble?

She wasn't happy. She wanted me to do something.

What could you do about it?

I don't know. You're right. I don't know. What could I do but take on some of the kids?

I paused the recorder. What was up with that? What was Shelly's issue with the doctors of Emerson, New Hampshire? Gretchen had clearly picked up on it at some point, as she'd written those pediatricians' names in one of her most recent Word documents.

I hit play again.

Did she have questions about his death?

No. He had a heart attack. That was that. The man smoked like a chimney and had three rib eyes a week. No one who knew him was surprised.

But Shelly was surprised? Was she close to him, or something?

Close? Uh, not that I know of. Why would she be close with him?

I don't know. I'm just trying to figure out what you're saying. You mentioned to me last time that you chatted with her a few days before she died. Was this the chat you were talking about?

Yes, dear. What else would it be?

Okay.

It was me she gave a hard time to. She gave me a hard time, when he died.

But why?

Because nothing I said would calm her down. I offered to do this or that to help, but no. Nothing.

Like what else did you offer?

Oh, I don't know. Everything I could think of. I'm getting a little tired, dear. Forgive me.

But why was Shelly so upset when Dr. Platt died?

Because, then, there weren't enough doctors.

I don't understand. Enough doctors for what?

Shelly?

Yes?

There's nothing to worry about. The kids will be fine.

Why wouldn't they be?

Exactly. That's what I said. They're fine.

Dr. Skinner?

Yes, dear?

Can we talk about the day Shelly died now?

I'd rather not. Forgive me. I'm tired, and it was the saddest day.

Okay.

This is where I'd stopped the recording the first time I'd listened to it. This time, I let it run beyond that.

Okay, Gretchen said. *Maybe we could talk about something else.*

Maybe. Maybe that would be better.

I think you were about to tell me why Shelly was so upset when Dr. Platt died.

Oh. Yes. She was worried there weren't enough doctors. Because where would all the kids go?

Was there a particular kid she was worried about? Her daughter, or something?

Her daughter? No . . .

Then, who?

*Well, all the kids. No. The girls. The teen-
agers.*

So, just the teenagers?

*They were sending a lot of the teenagers to
me. In the meantime. It really wasn't too much
trouble.*

Then why did Shelly care?

*She wanted me to say no. No teenagers.
No girls.*

Why not?

There was a long silence.

*Nothing I would say would calm her down.
She didn't even want the money.*

And you took those patients?

Oh, yes. Certainly.

I see, said Gretchen. *And how did that work
out?*

*Fine, fine. Of course. Shelly, there was noth-
ing to worry about, see? You were always different.*

How was I different?

Oh, you know.

It's been so long I've forgotten.

"Jesus, Gretchen," I whispered. "What the
hell is going on?"

*No, you haven't, Shelly. You told me you'd
never forget.*

What *wouldn't I forget? Just tell me.*

How are we doing in here? A different
female voice piped up. She sounded elderly.

Anyone hungry?

I am, said Dr. Skinner.

Gretchen, I've got a chicken roasting in the oven. If I knew you were coming, I'd have made something a little more elegant, but —

Oh, that's nice of you, but — I'm sorry. I shouldn't have just dropped by like —

No, that's fine. But we never eat the whole thing. The whole chicken, I mean. Can you stay?

Oh . . . no . . . I can't, but thank you for offering. I should let you two get ready for your dinner.

Oh, it's about twenty minutes away yet. I think George is up to carving it this evening, right?

Well, it's just a chicken, dear.

Is that a yes?

Gretchen quickly excused herself again and said her good-byes. After a couple of shuffling noises, the recording stopped.

My Doritos bag floated to the floor. I rubbed my temples, trying to take it all in.

Shelly didn't care about teenagers faking prescriptions. Or about some mixed-up prescription. What she'd noticed — what disturbed her — was simply who was writing prescriptions for whom. That Dr. Skinner was suddenly treating young girls because another town doctor had died. *That's* what she was concerned about.

"My God, Gretchen," I whispered. "That's horrible."

Another recording started. I didn't recognize the voice at first, because of its distance from Gretchen — but recognized the words. It was Frank Grippo, outside of his house. Gretchen seemed to have transcribed the conversation exactly as it unfolded. I skipped it.

Next was Dr. Skinner again, talking endlessly about some fiddler named Vassar Clements. Then Gretchen and Dr. Skinner talking about the Nitty Gritty Dirt Band.

Finally, when Dr. Skinner seemed to lose some steam, Gretchen said, *You said if I came back you'd tell me about the day you tried to save Shelly.*

Did I? Dr. Skinner said.

Yeah. You did. You know, this won't take long.

I thought you were going to ask me to play a tune on my fiddle. That's what I thought you were gonna ask.

Let's do that after.

Okay. Shelly?

Yeah?

Before we get into that . . . I was wondering . . .

Yeah?

507

Did you steal our toothbrushes?

What?

Diane says she thinks it must've been you. Once she heard you were here.

Now, why would I want to do that?

I don't know. She says you're the only one who's been in the house. The only one with a reason.

Let's talk about that later. Come on, now. We're talking about the day you tried to save Shelly.

I don't think I could have. She'd already bled so much.

Yeah. I understand. I'm sure you tried everything you could.

Yes. I suppose so.

Everyone knows you did. I didn't come here to question that. I just wanted to ask you about what she said to you before she died.

Yes.

Are you ready to talk about that?

Maybe.

It was just a few words, wasn't it?

Yes.

She said, "I can't forgive him." Right?

No. She said, "I can't forgive you." You. Right?

Right. And who was she talking to, Dr. Skinner?

I don't know, Dr. Skinner whimpered.

Are you sure? Was Frank Grippo in the room?

Yes.

Was she looking at him?

There was a long silence.

Was she looking at Frank when she said it? Gretchen asked again.

Dr. Skinner said something inaudible.

What? said Gretchen.

No, he said.

No, she wasn't looking at Frank.

She was looking at you, wasn't she?

Yes. I believe she was.

Do you think she was really talking to you? Or to someone in her head?

Another long silence.

How could I know that? She'd lost so much blood.

Gretchen didn't say anything.

I don't know, dear. Dr. Skinner sounded very hoarse now. *I don't know what happened. I don't know how it happened.*

Sure you do. She looked at you and she told you she couldn't forgive you.

Yes.

Why would she need to forgive you? You're not the one who beat her up, are you?

No. No! Dr. Skinner exclaimed. *Don't say that. Of course not.*

C'mon, now. Maybe you just don't want to

remember.

No. No! Dr. Skinner was shouting now.

Then why . . .

I would never do that to her. I loved her.

Gretchen sighed. *Of course you wouldn't. Of course you did.*

I'm very tired, dear.

Gretchen didn't reply.

Forgive me, Dr. Skinner said. *But I'm —*

I heard you, Gretchen said. *No one is going to forgive you. No one's left who can.*

Oh, dear, said Dr. Skinner.

Yes, Gretchen said dully. *Oh, dear.*

I'm awfully tired. Do you think you could come back again?

I'm not sure, said Gretchen. *What for?*

Oh. Well. I've missed you, dear. And you turned out pretty smart. Smarter than I thought you would.

Yeah. Didn't I? Gretchen said.

And then the recording stopped.

I waited for more. Nothing. I skipped to the next recording. Nothing. It skipped back to the first recording, with Phil Coleman.

"Oh God," I said, getting up from the bed quickly. The baby kicked lightly. "Oh God, Charlie. What am I supposed to do now?"

No response from either God or Charlie Bucket.

I threw the recorder down on the bed and grabbed my keys.

Chapter 56

The Skinner house was the nicest on Durham Road. It was a colonial-style brick house with white-framed windows and a pretty, elaborate doorway: a house befitting the town's beloved old doctor.

A petite elderly woman pulled the door open. Although her hair was white, she didn't appear nearly as old as Dr. Skinner had sounded. Her complexion was smooth and pink, her bright green eyes complemented by a similarly colored twinset.

"Hello, Mrs. Skinner?" I asked.

"Yes?" She smiled at me, then picked up the black Pomeranian who'd been yipping at her feet. "Shut up, Libby."

"I'm Jamie Madden. I've met your daughter . . . I'm a friend of —"

"Oh, dear," Mrs. Skinner interrupted me. "Yes. You. I didn't know you were expecting."

"How would you know that?" I asked,

then regretted how abrupt I sounded.

"Diane's mentioned you. Gretchen Brewer's friend, right? Please, come in."

Libby gave a little snarl of protest, but Mrs. Skinner squeezed her a bit, which seemed to silence her.

"Well . . . Gretchen Waters . . . but yes."

"Gretchen Waters. Yes. I always forget."

"I was wondering if it would be possible to talk to Dr. Skinner?" I asked.

"I'm afraid not," Mrs. Skinner said, leading me to the kitchen and offering me a chair. "Not right now, anyway. He's sleeping. And I don't know how much you know about my husband's condition . . . but won't you sit down a minute? I was about to have a little snack here. Would you like a slice of banana bread?"

Did these Emerson women do anything besides bake? "Um . . . no thanks."

"Here . . . please. Just sit a minute, at least."

I did. "You don't anticipate Dr. Skinner will be up for a while, I guess?"

"Oh . . . one never knows . . . I'd hate to have you sitting here for hours and hours, but . . . are you sure I can't get you something to drink at least? How about some tea? I'm having some. I have a lemon kind. No caffeine."

"Well . . . sure. That would be nice. Thank you." I figured with a tea in my hand, I could sit here for longer — wait for Dr. Skinner to wake up.

Mrs. Skinner put a kettle on the stove. "Diane's told me a little about you. Friend of Gretchen Brewer's. That was a real shame, what happened to that girl. I'm sorry."

"Thank you. Yeah, it was."

"So it's the doctor you want to talk to, then?" Mrs. Skinner asked.

"If possible. I understand if it's not —"

"Gretchen talked to him a great deal. I don't think it could've been all that helpful, though."

"Yeah, I'm not sure if it was."

"But I kept letting her come back. He seemed to enjoy it, and if she didn't mind, then, well . . ." Mrs. Skinner touched her white hair gently as she sat at the table with me. "I didn't see any harm in it."

"I see," I said, wondering if Mrs. Skinner could possibly know so little that she truly believed what she was saying.

"Diane didn't care for it, though," Mrs. Skinner said. "When she found out. *She* thought it might become a problem."

"For whom? Your husband, or —"

"Yes. My husband. She thought it was

stressful for him."

"Did you agree?" I asked.

"I didn't so much at first. But since Gretchen's not come anymore, he asks for her. 'Where is that girl? That girl who was going to listen to me play the fiddle?' And I have to tell him she's not coming back. I'm not sure if I should tell him why, though. I don't see any sense in it."

"That sounds difficult."

Mrs. Skinner got up and took a teapot out of her cabinet — it was a delicate white, decorated with little strawberries. She threw three tea bags into it.

"Yes. I suppose it is difficult." She returned to the table with the pot. "He's easy enough to distract, though."

"I've wondered . . . how much did Gretchen talk to *you?*"

"Me? Oh, not very much. I didn't know Shelly like Diane did. Just what she was like as a girl, coming over our house. And I think she was most interested in George's experience that day . . . the day of the murder."

"I'd think at this point your memory of what he'd said about it over the years would've been more useful to Gretchen than what Dr. Skinner could manage to put together."

Mrs. Skinner shrugged. "You'd think, but

that's not what Gretchen chose to focus on. And I'm not the writer, so what do I know?"

"If *I* wanted to ask you some questions, to clarify what Gretchen had written . . ."

Mrs. Skinner looked surprised — then flattered. "Oh. Yes. I'll talk to you about it, dear. Of course."

"Well . . . Do you mind telling me about that morning? I mean, before we get to what your husband said about it . . . what you remember? Like, when did Frank come to the door?"

"Well, it was relatively early in the morning for a Saturday, I remember. I was dressed, but George wasn't. We'd gotten a late start that morning."

"Were you out the night before?"

"Yes. Quite late. We'd been to a dinner party at these people's house, the Kings. Wilbur King always made his cocktails way too strong." Mrs. Skinner chuckled self-consciously. "It always took an extra hour or two to recover enough to drive a car."

"So you got in late the night before?"

"Yes. Anyway, when Frank Grippo knocked on our door, George was still in his robe and slippers. Which is how he ended up at Shelly's that way."

"Uh-huh. So you two were having breakfast when he came?"

516

"Yes. Well. Having coffee. Reading the paper. I don't remember if we were really eating breakfast yet."

"You'd been up for a bit, though?"

Mrs. Skinner shrugged. "Yes. Far as I remember."

"Okay. So Frank Grippo comes to the door . . ."

"Yes. Ringing the doorbell and banging on the door all at once. I opened it and he pushed by me into the living room, yelling for the doctor. 'We need a doctor!' he was saying. And he had blood on his shirt. George heard the ruckus and came into the living room to see what it was all about. I was a little scared, because Frank seemed crazed. Still, George just followed him right out the door."

"You didn't think of going along?"

"No . . . he asked for a doctor. I guess I was afraid of him. And if he really needed a doctor, I knew I couldn't help."

"He did say that it was Shelly who was hurt, though, right?"

"Yes."

"Were you worried about Shelly when you heard that?"

"Of course. It was a confusing moment, though. I didn't know if Frank was telling the truth, or just going a little crazy. I never trusted that Frank Grippo."

I studied Mrs. Skinner's earnest emerald eyes and felt she was telling the truth as she knew it.

"Um . . ." I struggled to remember my next question. "Diane was living here at that time, wasn't she?"

"Yes. She was in grad school, living at home to save money."

I nodded. "Where was she during all of this?"

"She was sleeping, actually."

"Hadn't she been out jogging?"

"Yes. In fact, I was already awake when she came home. I was picking up the paper when she came in, I remember. But she said her knee was hurting her. She took something for it and went back to bed for a bit. She's always had that bad knee, but that morning I ended up being grateful for it."

"Why's that?"

The teakettle began to whistle, and Mrs. Skinner poured the water into the pot.

"Because if it hadn't been for that, she would've gone with her father to Shelly's. I know she would've. But she was asleep when Frank came over. Didn't wake up till her father came back, and Shelly was off in the ambulance."

"How long did it take Dr. Skinner to get back?"

"Oh . . . I don't recall exactly. About forty-five minutes. And when he did, he was like Frank — blood all over his clothes. It was terrifying. And he looked so terrible. He told me later that in all his years as a doctor he'd never seen anything so brutal. He didn't say that in front of Diane. Just later. But it was clearly terrible for even him to see. He was quite shaken. Just imagine how it would've been for Diane, having to see her old friend . . ."

"But when your husband got home, how did he describe what he'd seen?"

"He told both Diane and me that Shelly had been beaten very badly. So badly he thought someone had tried to kill her. That he thought it was Frank. Diane kept asking, 'Did you save her, Dad? Did you save her?' And he had to say that he had tried, but he wasn't sure. It didn't look good."

Mrs. Skinner got up and took two mugs out of the cabinet, handing me one.

"Diane was in shock. She stared at him like he was crazy, like she didn't know what he was saying. Like . . . 'Did she come over here asking for help? Was she bleeding? What are you talking about?' It was so awful. And he had to start over, telling about

Frank coming over, and trying to save her, and the police and the ambulance. And she kept asking him, 'Did you save her, Dad?' And he had to keep saying he'd tried his best and he was hopeful, but it didn't look good."

Mrs. Skinner shook her head, gazing at the teapot. I wondered if Gretchen had ever heard this story. I suspected not.

"But the news just wouldn't quite sink in for Diane," Mrs. Skinner continued, sliding her mug between her hands. "Because then she started pushing her father, hitting him. She started screaming at him, 'Why, Dad? Why?' She was hysterical for a few minutes. I had to pull her away and sit her down. Got her a drink of water while her father went and changed out of those bloody clothes."

Mrs. Skinner stood up and pulled the teapot toward her, gripping the handle. It seemed to me the graphic detail of the bloody clothes disturbed her, so I changed the subject slightly.

"I would think the police would've wanted to talk to your husband right away about what he saw," I said.

"Yes. They did, right on the scene. Then a couple of times later."

"Did Dr. Skinner tell you about what

Shelly said right when he got home that day?"

"Oh . . . that." Mrs. Skinner poured my tea carefully. "Gretchen did seem terribly interested in that. No. I think he was too much in shock about everything he'd seen. And maybe it didn't seem as significant till after she died. I don't think he would've talked about that in front of Diane, anyway. Not right away, I mean."

"So what Shelly said . . . that didn't come up right away. Do you remember the first time he talked about it?"

"No." Mrs. Skinner put a near-empty squeeze bottle of honey on the table and got us each a spoon. "I believe it wasn't till a few days later. He told the police one of the times they questioned him about that morning, and he came home and told me."

"And what were her words . . . to your recollection?"

Mrs. Skinner paused to attempt squirting honey into her tea. The bottle wheezed a few times and finally produced a few drops.

"She looked up at Frank standing there, and said, 'I can't forgive you. I can't.' "

"He talked about that a lot, didn't he?"

Mrs. Skinner stirred her tea, considering the question.

"Well. He talked about that morning a lot.

521

Her saying that, actually not so much. Just . . . what she'd looked like, how brutal it was."

"And he pretty firmly believed it was Frank?"

Mrs. Skinner took a thoughtful sip of tea, then nodded.

"Yes. And me, too."

"Why?" I asked.

"Well. Maybe this doesn't sound very smart, but who else would it be? She'd taken up with this alcoholic who didn't treat her well, and maybe she was cheating on him. Not that that excuses it at all, of course not. But all the signs were there." Mrs. Skinner sighed. "I . . . um . . . hope that doesn't sound too harsh. Shelly was a lovely girl. She was trying really hard. I didn't mean to say she deserved to be killed. Frank Grippo was an animal and should have gone to jail for the rest of his life."

I nodded. Duly noted. It was the sort of line everyone around here had about Frank Grippo. Then another question occurred to me.

"Your newspaper. Was Kevin Conley your paperboy?"

"Yes. Oh. You must have read about the trial. The business about the cars."

"Yeah. You said you were just picking up

the paper when Diane came home. What time was that?"

"I don't know, dear. I don't check my watch every minute. And it was over twenty years ago."

"I'm sorry," I said. "I guess it's not important."

The paper couldn't have been delivered until around seven, according to Kevin. Mrs. Skinner went out to get it at that time or later. And Diane was just coming in from her jog then? After seeing Frank's car in Shelly's driveway at five forty-five, just five houses down? Either she wasn't as certain of her timing as she'd claimed to be, or that must have been one hell of a bad knee to take her over an hour to make her way home. But maybe Mrs. Skinner's memory of the timing was, understandably, shaky.

"Won't you have a slice of banana bread with me?" Mrs. Skinner asked.

"Okay," I relented. "That sounds delicious."

I stayed for only about fifteen minutes more. Dr. Skinner wasn't likely to wake up, and even if he did, I wasn't sure what I'd ask him now — or if I'd be as effective in drawing him out as Gretchen had been. Besides, Mrs. Skinner had given me more than enough to think about.

Stopped at a red light on my way back to the motel, I thought now about Mrs. Skinner's description of Diane's reaction to her father's bad news on that morning. She had lost it, hitting him, screaming, *Why, Dad, why?* Mrs. Skinner clearly heard these words one way — the natural way one would hear them. Why did this happen to Shelly? Why couldn't you save her?

But there was probably more than one way to hear those words. If one knew about Dr. Skinner and Shelly.

The person behind me laid on his horn. The light was green.

I hit the gas hard. I wanted to get back to the motel room, where I could look at Gretchen's piece "Bedtime Story" again. I was certain now that the friend of Shelly's in that piece was Diane, and I had a feeling their conversation was not about Frank, after all.

The conversation was really about money, and keeping certain information secret:

If he doesn't stop, I'll go to the police.

You think the police will believe you?

Doesn't stop what? Seeing young female patients?

If this was what that conversation was really about, it would mean Diane first knew

524

about Gretchen's paternity in 1985. Or even before that. She knew Shelly was about to tell everyone, and was trying to keep her from doing so.

CHAPTER 57

I could tell the moment I stepped into the motel room that something wasn't right. When I closed the heavy door, the breeze from outside followed me in. I whirled around. The front window was wide open. I remembered opening it a crack, but not that much.

All of the covers were pulled off the beds. At first, I thought the housekeeping service was there.

"Hello?" I called.

No response.

Both of my laptops — my Gretchen one and my new personal one — were gone. My overnight bag was gone, too, as was the pile of notebooks I'd left in the corner.

"Shit!" I whispered.

I rummaged through the covers, but knew it was no use. Everything was gone.

I dialed Sam's number.

"Hey," he said. "I was hoping you'd check

in. I was trying to call you this morning."

"Sam, someone's broken into my motel room and taken everything."

"What're you talking about? Who?"

"I'm not one hundred percent sure. But I have a feeling it was the same person who broke into our house. Sam, when our house was broken into, some of Gretchen's notebooks were taken."

"Jesus, Jamie. What're you saying?"

"I didn't mention it at first because I wasn't sure, but I think whoever broke into our house was after Gretchen's research, not our stuff."

"Jamie, call the police. I don't know who you're talking about, but *call the police*! Are you sure the person isn't still around?"

"Yeah. I think so."

"Can you please call the police right now? Or go to the police department. Do it right now, will you? Promise me. Should I come up there? It's in Emerson, New Hampshire, right? What did you say it was, a Motel 6 or something? I can look up the —"

"That's not necessary," I assured him. "I'm leaving for the police department right now."

After I hung up, I took out my iPhone and looked up the address of the Emerson police station.

"That motel is not very secure," the balding police officer informed me. "The staff should have advised you not to leave any valuables there. It could've been anyone."

"True. But I don't think it was *anyone.* This is *murder* evidence. I'm pretty sure it was someone who knew about Gretchen's research."

"But you didn't see a license-plate number on this orange Honda?"

"No."

"What made you notice that car out of all the cars in the hotel lot?"

"There actually weren't very many cars," I said, but then tried to explain about the similarity to the orange car Ruth Rowan had seen in the library lot.

The policeman, who had previously introduced himself as Officer Rice, folded his arms. "Ms. Madden, are you conducting your own investigation of Ms. Waters's death?"

"I'm Gretchen's literary executor," I said. "The family gave me all of her manuscripts."

"Literary executor?"

"Yes. I'm just doing what her family asked

me to do. Organizing her writing. You know she was a writer, right?"

Officer Rice raised an eyebrow. "Of course, Ms. Madden."

"So, I have . . . well, *had*, before it was stolen . . . the material she was writing right before she was killed."

"As you may know," Officer Rice said, "the state investigator has been looking at some recent drafts on her computer, talking to some of the people she'd encountered for her research on her mother's death. We're aware that she was involved in that."

I nodded. "Okay. Yeah, I did know that. But she didn't write exclusively on the computer. More often, she wrote her stuff out longhand. There was much more in her notebooks than on her computer. And either way, it looks like someone was eager to get at it. And I guess I should've been more careful."

The officer sighed and put his chin in his palm, thinking.

"Do you have any thoughts on who, specifically, it might have been?"

"I have one idea," I said, and then mentioned Diane.

"Diane DeShannon?" Officer Rice looked bemused. "Dr. *Skinner's* daughter?"

With Emerson being such a small town, I

wondered how well Officer Rice knew Diane. I wondered how well he knew all of the players in Gretchen's book.

But he didn't say anything more about Diane.

"Why don't you sit tight for a minute?" he said instead.

"Okay."

He was gone for a while.

When he finally came back into the room, he handed me a plastic cup full of water.

"Thought you might want this," he said.

"Thank you," I said, shifting in my chair. I wished he'd skip the prenatal chivalry and focus on getting back Gretchen's manuscripts, but I couldn't tell how seriously he intended to take me.

"So," he said. "We'll be talking to Ms. De-Shannon shortly, Ms. Madden, just to clear the air. And of course we'll let you know if we find your things."

"Okay."

"But before you go . . . just a question, Ms. Madden. This additional material you say you have . . . we'd like to take a look."

"I can't let you look at it if someone else has it. That's why I'm here, sir. But yes, of course."

"All right, Ms. Madden."

■ ■ ■ ■

I sat in the police department parking lot for ten minutes and I didn't see any officers leave the building or approach any of Emerson's three police cruisers.

"Jesus," I muttered, thumping my steering wheel with my palm. "Take your time, folks."

Then I sat for a few more minutes, thinking about various conversations I'd had with or about Diane.

First, there was her certainty about seeing Frank's car that morning in 1985, when Kevin was certain of the opposite. I thought, too, about her story about Shelly's prescription blunder, which neither Dorothy nor Judy could remember and Phil Coleman wouldn't confirm. And then there was this business about Diane being the only one Shelly had ever told about Frank hitting her. No one else seemed to have seen or heard this firsthand from Shelly, and Gretchen, based on her childhood observations, had never been able to fully believe it.

Also, in your days as a reporter, did you start to develop any skill for telling who is lying to you?

It took me a moment to realize that my

gentle thumps at the wheel were turning into loud, painful wallops. I stopped so as not to upset Charlie, then glared at the police station's white steps and glass doorway. Still no movement. I took out my phone and called Dorothy.

After I convinced her I was indeed Jamie Madden, and not someone selling something, I asked her where Diane lived.

CHAPTER 58

Diane's house was a green raised ranch on the opposite side of town from her parents' place. The yard looked modest but was impeccably kept. To the left of the house were two square garden boxes, already sprouting rows of lettuce and herbs. Beyond that were three woodpiles — one of thick logs, one of slimmer ones, and then a remarkably symmetrical pile of kindling.

And there was a little orange Honda parked in front.

I had to catch my breath at the sight of it. Then I struggled out of my car and made my way up the walk.

When I rang the doorbell, no one answered, and I heard no movement in the house. As I pressed it again, I smelled something funny — a burning smell.

As soon as the thought registered, I found myself flying off the front steps and onto the lawn, following the smell.

When I got to the backyard, I saw Diane standing over a trash barrel and heard a crackle. Over the top of the barrel, I could see flames.

When Diane saw me, her face twisted in surprise.

"Burning some brush," she said with a little smile.

As I rushed at her, smoke flew in my face.

"I knew it," I tried to shout through my coughs.

"Knew what?" she said softly, when I'd finished coughing. "It seems to me you know very little."

I hesitated, uncertain how to interpret the smirk playing at her lips, the ferocity in her stare.

"I know Gretchen was your half sister," I said. "I know that much. I know you didn't want anyone to find out."

Diane didn't look surprised to hear me say this. She didn't move.

"Did he do it to you, too?" I asked, because I'd wondered that on the way here. And because I thought it might disarm her. "Did your father abuse you?"

Diane made a guttural noise. "No. There was no *abuse*. It was all Shelly."

"What does that mean?"

"Shelly would go after anyone. Shelly

didn't have any clue who was off-limits."

"Shelly was thirteen years old," I said softly.

"Seventeen," Diane said, folding her arms. "You really *don't* know so much. What does this have to do with you? Why don't you focus on your own . . . business?"

She waved her hand at my middle as she said it. I ignored her words and the gesture.

"Shelly was thirteen when it started."

"Who told you that? It's not true. She was seventeen the time I caught them, and I would've known if it started any sooner. I would've *known.* She was seventeen and by then she'd already been a slut for years. Ask anyone. They're all too polite to say it at first, because she died young. But they'll all say it eventually. They were even willing to say it to her own daughter, weren't they?"

"And what did *you* say to Gretchen?" I heard a car door slam, but kept talking. "When you confronted her in Willingham. When you realized she figured it all out? 'Welcome to the family, sister'?"

Diane's face turned a painful red. "I would never use the word 'sister.' And neither would she. Gretchen was all Shelly's. She was just another Shelly. She didn't have anything to do with us."

I took a tiny step closer to Diane. "I'm

535

pretty sure Gretchen felt the same way. About not having anything to do with you."

Diane didn't reply, but poked at the burning notebooks with her rake.

"So much so that I don't know if she would've written about it. But Shelly . . . Shelly was going to say something, and your father was trying to stop her."

"My father never would've been able to. I heard him try. He never knew how to handle her. *I* did, though. I knew her since we were little kids. I knew how she operated. I knew she would take the money and be quiet if someone explained it to her right."

"But she didn't," I said, feeling my voice grow shrill. "She surprised you. Shelly really was getting herself together. She knew how to tell you no. She knew it was the right thing. You didn't know how to handle *that* Shelly, did you?"

Diane shook her head. "There was no *new Shelly.* Shelly was never going to change. Not really. Everybody knew that."

"Is that why you had to bludgeon her with an iron? Because you realized there was no other way to shut her up?"

The wind picked up and Diane began to cough violently. Still, I kept yelling.

"Gretchen was even worse. She might not have been wild about telling people who her father was, but she would've if she had to. If that meant helping people understand why her mother died. And who killed her. And once she knew one thing, she was pretty damn close to the other, wasn't she? You didn't have much choice but to push her, did you?"

Diane dropped her rake and stared at me.

"I just went to *talk* to her. That's all. I didn't even know there were stairs in that parking lot, or that she'd decide to go down to that convenience store."

"No," I said, trying to steady my voice. "But nonetheless, that was when you decided to get out of your car and talk to her. Take her by surprise in the dark. Maybe intimidate her a little bit. Just a bonus that she somehow ended up dead at the bottom of the stairs. Silent and bleeding, just like her mother. Eerie, huh, how they both ended up that way? Tell me, Diane — they looked so much alike, was the second one easier? Was it just like killing the same woman over again?"

Diane lunged at me. I shoved her aside and pushed over the barrel. Several notebooks — most of them already burning, but a few not — scattered across the grass. I began stomping on the ones that seemed salvageable. Diane grabbed me by the sweater and threw me to the ground. I felt a sharp pain in my wrist as it hit the ground, crushed under my own hip.

"Ms. Madden!" someone called to me.

I looked up.

Officer Rice and a female officer were approaching from the side of the house.

"Help!" I screamed. The female officer ran to me and knelt beside me.

"Not me! The notebooks!"

She looked confused. I pulled myself up and began stomping on the flames again.

The lady officer grabbed my hand and pulled me back. Despite her thin frame, she had a strong grip. My wrist ached as she did it.

"Don't, honey," she said. "You're gonna hurt yourself."

She held me aside and stamped out the flames with her heavy black boots.

Officer Rice, meanwhile, was holding Diane gently by the elbow.

I stared at the torn, half-charred leftovers of Gretchen's notebooks.

"Oh God," I whimpered. "Gretchen . . ."

The female officer picked up one notebook, black on the cover but still intact inside.

"This one can be dried out and it'll probably be fine. There are a few like that here."

She said it with a sweetness I didn't expect from someone in a uniform. But I stared at the notebooks that weren't fine and started to cry.

Diane stared at me, her mouth straight and her eyes dull. She shook off Officer Rice's grip.

"What use is it, anyway?" She was screaming now.

I couldn't reply. I was sobbing too hard.

"What exactly is it you want to document? It was just hurtful. Hurtful stuff. Don't you understand? What would it do to my mother? And what does it have to do with you?"

I watched her pick up one of the charred notebooks. She stared at it as Officer Rice stepped toward her again.

"Your mother . . . I'm not sure that's who you ever cared about protecting," I whispered.

Diane flung the notebook at me.

"What would you know about *protecting?*" she howled. "Just look at yourself."

"Diane, I think we need to sit down and talk," Officer Rice said, putting his hand on her shoulder and leading her away from the pile.

"Yeah," I mumbled. "You two ought to do that."

I sat in the grass and touched the notebook Diane had just tossed down.

"They're not all burned," I whispered. "Not even half. It takes a while for the fire to eat all the way through . . ."

"Miss . . . um . . . Miss . . ." the female officer said.

"Madden," Officer Rice supplied as he led Diane into the house.

"Miss Madden. Mrs. Madden," the lady officer groped. "Can you get up?"

"Jamie," I said. "Yes, I can get up. If you'll let me take my friend's things with me."

"I'm not sure if you can, Ms. Madden," the officer said.

Chapter 59

"By the Moonlight Alone"

Almost Midnight
Bristol, Virginia

I've meandered off Highway 81 to stop in Bristol, Virginia, the purported "Birthplace of Country Music." I hadn't planned on stopping here, and it's nearly midnight. But I'm thinking that later I might want to say that I did.

Since I've got the GPS, I allow myself to get lost a little, looking for a place that's open for maybe a coffee, maybe ice cream. I don't find anything but a convenience store, but I'm not in a King-Cone-in-my-car kind of mood. It's a little actual humanity that I'm after. But I can't seem to find it. I feel small and lonely in the dark of this unfamiliar town.

I turn into a residential neighborhood, just to see. It's full of neat, modest brick houses with white doors and trim that practically glow in the dark. As I turn-around, I hear a train hooting some-where close. I pull over. I want to listen to the train — a bit of manufactured travel reverie, yes, but I indulge myself. After it fades I can hear only the crickets. I'd like to stay here with them, but surely my car looks out of place on this street at this hour. I drive around Bristol for a bit, listening to Carter Family songs: "Wildwood Flower" and the lesser-known "One Little Word." Then I peruse my iPod for my favorite — "Meet Me by the Moonlight Alone."

The narrator of this song is about to go to jail on the following day. The lyrics explain that he's had a sad life. But he describes how much, nonetheless, he loves his sweetheart. Like many Carter Family songs, it's a rearrangement (by A. P. Carter) of an older favorite. The song shares the chorus (and some of the lyrics) of the popular "Prisoner's Song," recorded in 1924 by Vernon Dalhart. Variations on the same song have also been titled "Someone to Love Me."

I return to the convenience store to

park and listen some more. I open the window — no crickets here, and no moonlight. Just the bright parking-lot lamps and the rumble of the nearby highway.

> Meet me by the moonlight, love, meet
>   me
> Meet me by the moonlight alone
> For I have a sad story to tell you
> To be told by the moonlight alone

These words have always grabbed me, as they capture a longing I've never known how to express myself. Because deeper than a longing for romance, to me, is the desire to find that one person to whom you can tell your sad story. Once, in the moonlight, before you're ready to go on. It's not an intimacy that lasts forever. That's not the point.

So many of the Carter Family's songs are about that which one cannot have forever. It is a sentiment that their generation surely understood more keenly and experienced more regularly than my own. You can tell from the Carters' voices and their restraint. In the words of the songs A.P. chose, and in the tough, sad beauty of Sara's voice, you can almost always hear a reality that generations after theirs tend not to remember so regularly or so comfortably — the fragility of what we have — or don't have — here.

Their best songs are as beautiful and stark as the rustle of leaves on a cold autumn night. Have you ever heard that sound late at night on your driveway — then shivered, and then hurried inside to avoid the feeling it gives you? Listening to the Carter Family is often like standing firm there in the dark, allowing yourself to be alone in the simple, scary beauty of it.

There's no glitter or sass with the Carter Family. Since their material is primarily Appalachian folk songs, there is naturally a lot of suffering and death. And while many of those songs promise the comfort of a heaven beyond, many simply acknowledge life's difficulties without attempting any reassurances. Life is hard. Marriage is hard ("Single Girl, Married Girl," "Are You Tired of Me, My Darling?"). Love is hard ("I'm Thinking Tonight of My Blue Eyes"). Work is hard ("Coal Miner's Blues"). And death is, of course, merciless ("Sad and Lonesome Day").

And for all the words about heaven, there's a fair amount about what's left behind in death. Where one will be buried, who will remember us, miss us, or care that we were ever here ("Bury Me Under the Weeping Willow," "Will You Miss Me When I'm Gone?," "Lay My Head Beneath the Rose," "See That My Grave Is Kept Green").

While I admire both of the women of the Carter Family, it is A.P.'s story (and his occasional trembling voice in the background of their songs) that haunts me, along with the words of "Meet Me by the Moonlight Alone."

Alvin Pleasant Carter was a peculiar type from boyhood, they say. He was a loner so full of nervous energy that his hands shook — attributed, by his mother, to a lightning bolt that nearly struck her when she was pregnant. Still, he was an accomplished fiddle player and sang as well. He tried several jobs in his youth and apparently wasn't all that good at any one of them. A.P. was working as a fruit salesman, the story goes, when he first heard Sara singing through a window of a house he was approaching in hopes of making a sale. And fell in love.

It wasn't until after over a decade of marriage (and some local performing) that A.P. managed to convince Sara and her talented cousin Maybelle (who was also his sister-in-law) to take a step toward pursuing a real musical career together — something unheard of for people of their background at the time. In 1927, he dragged them down to Bristol, Virginia, to sing for a New York scout from Victor Records. The trip resulted in a recording session, and soon after, the popularity of their music, starting with "Single Girl, Married Girl," their first hit.

While the Carters enjoyed rare success throughout the Depression era, it wasn't all fame and happiness for the family. Sara hated the spotlight, but A.P. drove her and Maybelle to record and perform more. He would also disappear for weeks at a time, searching for songs in the Virginia mountains — leaving Sara alone with their three children and all of the household responsibilities. And when he was home, his moods were unpredictable; he was often brooding, sometimes easily angered. Ever the eccentric, he even had a tendency to wander off during recordings and performances, frustrating Sara and Maybelle.

During his many absences, Sara started a love affair with one of his cousins. That relationship eventually led to their divorce in 1936. Sara continued to record and perform, however — reluctantly, but for the sake of providing for her family. The Carter Family's audience didn't know that she and A.P. had split. That would've significantly damaged their image as a happy, traditional family. They continued to give concerts with bills that proclaimed that "the program is morally good." But in 1943, Sara — by then married to A.P.'s cousin — chose to stop performing with the group.

While Sara lived the rest of her life with her new husband in California, A.P. returned to Virginia and opened a general store. He reportedly spent the rest of his life brokenhearted at his loss of Sara, his loss of the musical life, his forgotten dream. He died in 1960.

He's considered the father of country music, but some aspects of his peculiar personality remain a mystery. Where did his drive to write and discover new songs come from? What was the story he wanted to tell? Was it the story of his people, or something from within that he never found expressed quite right? What was the one little word he never managed to say? Was his love for Sara just about having a personal mouthpiece, or was it simply true and unrequited love?

Perhaps it was enough that her voice inspired him to bring so many songs to so many people. Well, maybe not enough. (Because is there ever really enough for the hungry human soul?) But perhaps a gift like that, however temporary, was more than most of us can reasonably expect to receive.

And again, the point is not — and can never be — to have forever.

The sound of the train and the trucks will fade. Even that of the crickets. The sound of your love's voice fades and the sad story dies with you, or with the one you told it to. Either way, it disappears. A few will wonder what your story was and then no one will at all. There is a certain beauty in that, isn't there — in how it all disappears?

— Tammyland

CHAPTER 60

Sam arrived at the hospital about an hour after they'd set my wrist.

"Jesus Christ, Jamie," he said, when he met me in the empty waiting room. "Does it hurt a lot?"

"Yeah," I answered, showing him my splint.

"What happened?" His tone was more sharp than sympathetic.

"Well, I fell and my fat pregnant ass landed on my own wrist. But I was lucky to fall on that and not on Charlie."

"Very lucky," Sam murmured, without looking at me. "On the phone, you said someone pushed you."

"Yeah," I said. "She's in custody now."

"Like, with the police?"

"Uh-huh."

"Now, how did you end up at her place by yourself?"

"I had a feeling it was her."

"And how did you know they'd come right after you?"

"I didn't," I admitted. "I just got lucky."

"Jesus Christ," he repeated, leaning back into a hospital snack machine. I gestured for him to sit next to me in the ugly green waiting room seats, but he ignored the silent request.

I didn't make him ask anything else. I told him the whole story — starting with Gretchen's final interview with Dr. Skinner and ending with the events in Diane's backyard. When I was finished, he was quiet for a moment.

"What the fuck were you thinking?" he asked.

"I'm fine, thank you very much," I replied.

"I know you're fine. I can see you're fine. In a superficial sense, anyway. So now I'm asking you a deeper question."

"I thought we were gonna try to retire the F-word for the sake of the rugrat."

"Cut the crap, please. He's not here yet. So what the fuck were you thinking?"

I had to stifle a giggle. Sam was finally — and reasonably — angry enough at me to tell me to cut the crap, but had still remembered to say please.

"I was thinking about Gretchen," I said, after thinking about it for a moment.

"Yeah. Someone *killed* Gretchen. You knew that when you left for Emerson on Friday."

"That's true," I said. "But it seemed more important than dangerous. And I didn't want to worry you."

I studied Sam because I couldn't think of a further explanation. His hair was wild, as he'd probably been rubbing his head nervously the whole way up to New Hampshire. His eyes were tired. I wondered if this was how he'd look in the hospital when Charlie Bucket was born. With that thought, a familiar feeling of panic returned to me — one I hadn't felt since Gretchen had died. Perhaps it was being in a hospital that finally brought it back — the sudden, life-stopping, nauseating-exhilarating realization: *One of these days, this kid is actually going to be* born.

"More important than dangerous?" Sam repeated skeptically.

The wind had been knocked out of me, thinking about Charlie's imminent arrival — about Charlie's mere reality. It took me a moment to come back to our conversation.

"Gretchen and I had certain . . . standards for one another," I said, after I'd caught my breath.

"So you're saying she would have expected you to solve this for her."

"No. She wanted to solve it for herself. But she couldn't. Not quite. Someone stopped her before she got to finish. I couldn't stand that."

Sam was silent for a moment, his gaze flickering from me to the magazine table to the window, and then back to me again.

"Of course you couldn't."

"I needed to know that I could fix something. Just one thing. But I'm all right. Charlie is all right."

"I'm still not wild about the name 'Charlie,'" he admitted, finally stepping closer to me. "But I can still think about it."

He sat in the seat next to mine, put his elbows on his knees, and clasped his hands. But said nothing.

"It feels like a hundred years ago," I said. "When Gretchen and I were in college together. When we were so close. And now it feels like a hundred years to go without her."

Sam cast his eyes down. Did he wonder if the comfort of him and Charlie was not enough to endure this vast new life ahead of me, without someone who'd once been so important to me? I didn't ask. Not because I didn't want to reassure both him and myself, but because to do so was impossible. And I didn't want to lie to him.

Sam moved his hand to my splint, and we both stared at it.

After a moment he said, "Tell me a story about Gretchen. About how she was in college."

I was surprised at this request, but happy that he'd made it.

I thought for a minute, and then said, "Well, there was this liquor store about a mile away from campus that would sell weird-flavored schnapps. Disgusting flavors. Blueberry. Grape. But at the time we thought they were yummy. Every couple of weeks, we'd walk there and get a bottle to share. Sometimes late at night, sometimes in the freezing cold. Once or twice in the snow, even.

"And once, when we were walking in the snow, this guy stopped and offered us a ride. This guy was in his late thirties or early forties, I'd have guessed. In some slick black asshole car, though I don't remember the make now. And he just *looked* like a sleaze. Maybe not a psychopath or anything, probably more like someone who'd heard things about Forrester girls and maybe was hoping a ride could lead to a threesome. Something about his eyes and his smell told me that. I could smell his cologne from where I was standing, even though Gretchen was standing much closer.

"And he said, 'You girls want a ride somewhere?'

"And Gretchen stared at him for a second, with this deer-in-headlights way she had about her sometimes. And then she looked at me, and I was wondering if I needed to tell her the answer was no.

"The guy was so startled by Gretchen, by her silence and her weird expression, that it threw him off. He couldn't tell if she was game or just a little crazy.

"Then he said, 'I. . . . uh . . . have heated seats.'

"And then he said again, 'You want a ride?'

"And then Gretchen . . . I'll never forget this. She took the bag with the schnapps in it, took off the cap really slowly, took a little sip, and then said to him, very serenely, 'Not in the least.' "

Sam chuckled a little. I continued.

"He didn't say anything back. He just looked confused for a second and then drove away. We got a good laugh at that, once he'd driven away. And for a couple of years after that, whenever one of us was in some kind of precarious situation or another, the other one would say, 'Well, you know, I have heated seats . . .' "

Sam looked puzzled. "What does that even mean?"

"I don't know. But we thought it was funny at the time. I can just see us like that. Sometimes, when I'm driving somewhere, and I see two girls walking together, talking . . . I think of us then. How we thought we were the most cynical people in the world, with our little paper bag of kiddie liquor. The way we'd make each other laugh. The way we knew how stupid everyone and everything but ourselves was. It was so ridiculous and so perfect. How we understood, finally, what dumb girls we'd been before we knew each other, and what smart women we were going to be."

Sam nodded uncertainly.

"Sometimes," I said, "I think my being sad about her dying is the most selfish thing. I mean, where it comes from. Because it's maybe not just about being sad for her — but being sad for myself, and missing how we were together. Coming back to her was always like being reminded of that part of myself, reminded that it was still there. And without her, how am I going to remember to do that?"

Sam ran a finger up and down my splint,

then cracked a tiny smile.

"I believe you may still be more of that person," he said, "than you think."

"Is that a good thing?" I asked.

Sam thought for a moment before answering.

"Sometimes, Madhat."

I nodded and instinctively began to reach for my stomach, remembering a half second later that my splint would not allow me to. I reached with my left since my right ached.

CHAPTER 61

Diane's theft and attempted destruction of Gretchen's notebooks and files — plus the similarity of her car to one of those described by the librarian — proved enough for investigators to question Diane and take samples of her hair and fingerprints.

When the hairs matched the ones found on Gretchen's coat the night of her fall — and the fingerprints those in Shelly's house the morning of her death — they managed to get a confession out of Diane. When she'd begun to suspect that Gretchen knew about her father, she'd begun to track Gretchen — following her home, and to the library, afraid that Gretchen would report what she knew. She didn't go in for the reading, obviously, but decided to confront her in the parking lot afterward, when she saw that Gretchen was all alone. Diane claimed to have no intention of harming her — just to talk to her, before the information got into the wrong hands. When it became clear that Gretchen not only knew about Diane's father but suspected Diane of involvement in Shelly's death, the conversation became heated. Diane pushed Gretchen. Diane said she didn't mean for her to fall and hurt herself. When she saw how hurt Gretchen was, she panicked and grabbed her purse to make the incident appear like a mugging.

Shelly's death was another story. Diane knew about Shelly and her father as early as high school. It was confirmed when Diane had overheard Shelly threaten to expose her father in 1985 — and her father's futile offers to pay for her silence. On her jog early that morning in 1985, Diane had stopped at Shelly's house, determined to talk some sense into Shelly — with a first payment in hand from her own savings. Despite the early hour, Shelly had welcomed her old friend inside and begun brewing her a pot of coffee. But the conversation had quickly turned bitter. It was clear Shelly had made up her mind. Diane, realizing this, snapped.

When Shelly's back was turned, Diane struck her on the back of the head with an iron that had been sitting on Shelly's kitchen counter. When she realized what she'd done, she hastily removed what evidence she could find. She wiped the handle of the iron clean, washed her hands and face in Shelly's sink, and took one of Shelly's T-shirts so that she wouldn't have to jog the last half block home in a bloody shirt. In the rush to get out quickly, she'd forgotten about the roll of money she'd brought in an attempt to bribe Shelly.

Even before she mentioned seeing Frank's car in Shelly's driveway, people naturally wanted to believe it was him. Diane's father and Judy and Linda were already convinced of Frank's guilt before she ever said a word.

I attended some of Diane's trial, when my mother was able to watch my son, Joe — the spirited baby previously known as Charlie Bucket. He didn't seem like a Charlie Bucket when we met him. Or even a Charlie.

Diane was convicted of murder one for Shelly, involuntary manslaughter for Gretchen. I was there the day they read the verdicts. It was important for me to be there — important for the book I was writing — a combination of Gretchen's words and my own. That was what her family, her publisher, and I came up with. I'd quit my job after Joe was born, anyhow. After my first couple of days with him, I'd felt time would be better spent with him than in front of my old newsroom computer. I had no idea what I was going to do next, and no plans to decide till after he turned one.

When it was all over, someone tapped me on the arm outside of the courthouse.

It took me a moment to recognize Kevin — I hadn't been there the day he testified. But I noted his snug maroon dress shirt and black-checked tie.

"Hey," I said. "I almost didn't recognize you without your stubble."

He smoothed his tie against his chest. "And I almost didn't recognize you without your little belly."

"That's kind of you," I said. "I know it wasn't little."

"How's the baby?"

"Good," I said. "He keeps me pretty busy. He's really into strained peaches at the moment. And flashlights. Those are, like, his two big things right now."

We didn't talk for long. Kevin still missed Gretchen, he said. And he would be sure to pick up a copy of the book when it came out. He wasn't sure he'd want to read it, but he'd want to support Gretchen's family.

"For that scene at Frank Grippo's house, did you write it like I was there, or like I wasn't?" he asked.

"Both ways," I said. "The way she wrote

it and the way you told it."

"You think that's how she'd want it?"

"I can only guess," I admitted. "But I tell myself so. With every page."

We headed away from the courthouse together as we talked.

"Are you going to be around town again?" he asked, when we reached a corner together. "Research for the book?"

"Probably not," I said. "I'm almost done, except for the trial material."

I watched him nod. I thought of telling him I'd dash off an e-mail to him soon, maybe to clarify the paperboy parts of the book. But I knew I had those parts down pretty well. There was no need to talk to him again — as much as I'd have liked to try to keep this person — with a tiny bit of Gretchen in him — close.

"Well," he said. "I'm glad to hear you're almost finished. It must be a hard book to write."

"Hard. Yeah. I'll be sad when it's over, though. It feels kind of like something Gretchen and I are doing together."

"I know what you mean. Hey, where's your car parked?"

"In the garage around the corner."

"You were smarter than me. I did street

parking. I'm probably getting a ticket as we speak."

"I'd better let you go, then."

We said goodbye. I headed quickly to my car so I wouldn't have to watch him walk away.

CHAPTER 62

"I Believe"

Tammy Wynette Highway
Itawamba County, Mississippi

Tammy Wynette never had the money or the mainstream following to build a shrine to herself — a ranch or an amusement park. Dolly's got Dollywood and Loretta's got her lower-key ranch and museum outside of Nashville. (And it's not just a female phenomenon — let's not forget about Conway's Twitty City, may it rest in peace.)

If there was a Tammyland, what would it be? I think Tammy would have liked something with a spa and a botanical garden. Something as classy as she always tried to be.

But I don't think this world was meant to have a Tammyland. A Tammy that could have had the long-term career confidence or financial freedom to set up such a place might have been an entirely different woman.

So Tammyland has to exist only in our minds. It is what we wish for our Tammy. It's a magical place full of song and sequins and self-love, where we can all eat banana pudding and take a bubble bath with Burt Reynolds.

It's a place where the potential measures up to the life that is lived. Where the happiness so desperately sought is finally found. It's not really a place that exists for most of us here on earth. Most of us will not ever have our Dollywood, our Graceland, our Loretta Lynn dude ranch of adoration.

Tammy's life was such a contradiction between success and sadness, and left behind such bittersweet longing. Like most of our lives will. Like most of the lives of the people we've known and lost. There is always so much more that should have been explained, so many longings left unfulfilled.

Tammyland is where we can enjoy her voice without a tear or regret for the tragic parts of her life, or the way it ended too soon — only a feeling of warmth and a simple, loving statement: Yes, that's who she was. Where Tammy might sing her favorite song, "Till I Can Make It on My Own," forever, because she never will, not quite. And where that's actually okay — because it has to be.

— Tammyland

ABOUT THE AUTHOR

Emily Arsenault is also the author of *The Broken Teaglass* and *In Search of the Rose Notes*. She has worked as a lexicographer, an English teacher, and a Peace Corps volunteer in rural South Africa. She now lives in Shelburne Falls, Massachusetts, with her husband.